What
We All Have

RAY DACOLIAS

What We All Have

Copyright © 2015 by Ray Dacolias

ISBN 978-9895646-8-7

Contents

The State of Things

The very moment he entered the house of illusions, he felt a very bright and poisonous yellow aura descend upon him, which proclaimed physical ailments. An imperceptible countenance of scorn drained to the white-tiled floor as he spied other patrons huddled around the shelves of books. "The undead haunting this bottomless ravine of false hope," he thought, stopping in front of a section on the wonder of hormones. "Foolish people, they think the answer to their most passionate prayers lies in books; the gullible fools, the eternal optimists—fools every last one of them." He shook his balding head. "But here I am, again, and the more I know, the less I know I know." He cursed his condition, cursed his life, cursed this waste of time, his endless quest, his sagging, pale, hollowed-out appearance, his folly to believe in what he knew was impossible. "I am lost," he reasoned, reaching now for a book, an act that would commence the interminable cycle again. "I just need to accept it." He closed his tired eyes. "But I cannot…" He opened it up and began to read, sighing all the while as he stood next to fellow lost travelers on the multi-branching, high-peaks-and-deep-valleys road to wellness.

He felt ensnared in a murky labyrinth, occasionally poking pinholes in the fibrous walls to let in shreds of light, luminous projectiles of knowledge that seeped into his benighted mind; but he could not stop, for this would let in the foul stench of encroaching death; life could come only from a relentless searching, from pouring every available moment of his life's electrical energy and vital red juices into looking for the answer that would stem his downward fall into oblivion.

Every day he was not well, he felt that he was losing his youth. "I loathe you," he often repeated to his invisible tormentor, his condition; "I hate you so very, very much."

As it was, he stood, his wisp of a broken-down body parked in front of this section of the health food store. "Not a particularly attractive group," he observed, as three gaunt travelers in his elite circle crept toward where he stood, and then he concentrated once again on the thick text between his thin fingers. "Pseudo-trash," he whispered, and set it back to its proper place.

He had to search, compelled by the memory of what he once was and by his profound yearning to regain his robust health. This philosophy drove him onward. Every day that he sat at home unloved, unmarried, obscured in society by illness, he thought himself without merit. "Lost," he would often say about his fate, "nine years lost."

"Books for fools," he often thought; "they tease and promise like a beckoning, retreating coquette, but right now they are the only way out. Somewhere, someone has written about the disease I have; somewhere, there is a book that is about me, and I will find it or I will die trying."

It was now the second hour of his commiserating with his hard-and soft-cover company, and he thought it best to move on and buy something. He was waiting for the day when an employee might ask him to no longer loiter here. "These are the best salespeople you have," he had always planned to say to them, but he never would have to, for these books—written by quacks and charlatans, health gurus and swindlers, corrupt doctors and greedy scientists who expertly wove product and sales pitches into their twisted narrative, and the few written by medical pioneers who poured their heart and soul and mind into radical ideas—sometimes were the only hope for the chronically ill who had been routinely dismissed by the medical establishment, who would then open their pocketbooks to chase more large white rabbits down more dark holes; and the salespeople understood this, so let the patrons read on.

He walked about the store, down the clean aisles, frowning upon the exorbitant prices of the products. "Now, it's my liver," he bemoaned, picking up a bottle of standardized herbs, "round and round the marble arch, never quite seeing the Golden Fleece, but only a glimmer of its magical power."

He purchased the expensive capsules and lingered for a moment at the book section, looking about. "They always seem to walk in just as I leave," he thought, but then shook his head, and whispered, "What does it matter, anyway?" A beautiful woman walked past him, and he laughed to himself. "It never fails." He proceeded on, thinking of a future where he might go back and talk to her, of a moment where she might not turn away from him in disgust, of a future where she might actually agree to spend time with him.

That night, he ate dinner, and he suffered. It was the way life was for him—impure, painful, untenable—but he had adjusted to it the way a soldier adjusts to a bullet wound during battle. His stomach felt nauseated, he felt the nasty precursors to vomiting rumbling and churning in his twisted gut, but savagely repressed it. A sticky cocoon of exhaustion engulfed him, and so he sat on the small sofa, fighting to stay awake, for to be awake was to live, to stay awake was to be engaged in something meaningful, to be awake meant a momentary disruption in the invading lines of his disease.

Alas, he slowly fell asleep, mumbling, massaging his aching gut. "What a waste, all of it, what a waste, what a fool…"

Mistress

D isease is a merciless taskmaster, whose only mission it is to make its host obedient to it and to it alone. It is in this way that Disease is a jealous mistress, hateful of all other desires of the physical entity it inhabits.

"Spend time with me," Disease whispers sweetly into the bruised ear of its betrothed, "think only of me, worry only of me, speak only of me." For the host to do otherwise only incurs the wrath of sulking Disease; for to be dismissed as typical, as convenient, as of little value compels her to stamp her lithe foot in wrath against being trivialized. "Make love only to me, but with words and deeds, and blood and tears, with your whole being." She deigned to smile sweetly at such times. "Live for me, die for me," she would coo, and her bony, crooked finger would cleave the fractured air as she spoke, her oblong-shaped head tilted sideways, "but only when I say… when! Ha, ha! Hate me, love me, curse me, kiss me, I don't care which, as long as you do it all for me, O Lover!"

And so it was for Tony, that disease had become his companion and nemesis, arbiter and social secretary, wrapping its acrid fragrance around his emaciated body, caressing his thin face, rubbing its slimy form against his wispy, black hair.

"If I play, I die," he often said, when the temptation to engage in activities he considered meaningless raised their collective sinful heads. "Television: what a colossal waste of time; every moment I watch it, I am not researching, and I slip further away from living." He loathed any activity that required long periods of uninterrupted devotion to filling time; thus, he rarely visited relatives or friends or went to places solely for amusement. There was solace in researching his disease, for victory meant family and love. "Then, I will begin to live," he would say.

Whenever his resolve weakened, he would attempt to step back into the constant stream of the living to join society, only to fail. His obsessive mistress was always present to remind him of his unspoken vows to her. It did not matter where he was, or what he was doing: disease would reassert itself. He might be at some event, laughing and smiling and talking, and a pounding surge of nausea or excruciating pain would paralyze his merriment, reminding him of his quest, and in the loud echoes of his mind, he would hear his wicked mistress singing, "To be at home, with me, only; thinking of me, only, that is your life, Lover." And he would leave such social gatherings early, promising himself not to visit such places again until he was well. "How can I enjoy myself when I feel ill?" he would contemplate as he drove home from such episodes. "Every minute I am with healthy people, listening to their happiness, seeing their joy, feeling their love, I am not pursuing my own health; they do not care about my pain, for their joy obscures what their heart should see." Bitterness would sweep away any remaining guilty feelings he had about missing such social events, and Disease would smile wickedly, hug herself, and in so doing, embrace him. "Good boy," she would whisper sweetly to her captive, "they don't understand us; only we understand us; we must associate with our own kind. Yes, my precious, it is you and I against the world; poor, suffering us, no one else cares or understands. We are so very special!"

Thus armed with such a philosophy, that the world did not care for him and that his illness had prevented his inclusion in it, he felt apart from all people, wherever he was. "I am invisible, truly."

Every human being seeks to separate himself from the indistinguishable masses, and for Tony, he had been nominated by cruel Fate to wander away from nearly everyone and into a shadow world where broken-down and discarded people dwell.

Torment

Blood, blood everywhere, blood as he arose in the early morning, red blood in the bed, thick red blood on the sheets and on the blankets, and there, even a dot on his sparse hair, giving him to cursing again. "No way to stop it," he cried, wanting to weep, but refusing to yield to its facile charm. "I hate you," he yelled, not wanting to look at the gory sight, but he was drawn to it, to stare at it and force himself to absorb its filthy presence until he was humiliated and shamed and wanting revenge; and it was here that he threw heavy objects and punched walls, and cursed and shouted and pounded the bed; it was then that he ripped out phone jacks and tore up invitations and letters from friends and refused to answer the door and did not get the mail and talked to no one at work, looked at no one the entire day and avoided mirrors and shook with fury and hated his life and himself, whispering, "Freak, freak, freak…" It was days like this that he pulled even further away from what the greater extent of people were doing and retreated into a darker place where he brooded and thought and thought and waited and studied and waited and researched and blacked out all things not essential for living. "I live for destroying this thing," he would howl at night like a wounded wolf. "I live to crush this vile monster with my own hands, to feel its warm guts run down my face; I dream of devouring you, O Disease." And he did dream of it, he dreamed of meeting his immortal enemy in his own body, sword in his hand, smiting its armies and being covered in their gooey flesh and blood, and meeting the one who sat upon a throne of decay and rust, and fighting her unto death. And these were the days of his waning youth.

Doctor Doctor

He was at the health food store one day, standing limply in front of the book section, his eyes closed, thinking of his fruitless trip to the university library. "How much longer?" he whispered, and he returned his own query with a weighty resolve, "As long as it takes."

"Excuse me?"

He opened his eyes and looked, red-faced, at a young woman to his right. Her face was quizzical.

"Were you talking to me?"

"No," he said, timidly.

She breathed an exasperated vulgarism. "Talking to oneself," she mumbled, and swore once more, frowning in disgust, then shook her head as she walked away, muttering to herself. Her light-golden-brown hair did not even move as she glided down the aisle. He heard a barely audible excerpt from her iron rant, "Loser."

He stood there, incredulous, and thought, "Every man dreams of starting up a conversation with a beautiful woman, but I lose them before we even begin." At this realization, he had to chuckle. "A handsome man would have her phone number after a smile," he reasoned, trying to remember what it had been like to be considered handsome. "Well, I don't remember," he sighed. A deep hurt throttled his being, and he had to turn away to hide his lament. His bony, sinewy body sagged as if punched by an invisible force.

To see him was to see nothing resembling a man as people conceived a real man to be; he had not the physical characteristics to constitute the raw image of a robust man, a virile man, a muscular, confident and thus comely man; and consequently, he was easily dismissed by women, who saw him as infertile, diseased and weak, and men, who saw him as a scrawny, harmless speck in the great galactic swirl of raging manhood, a weak sister at the back of the trailing herd who was no threat to their job, their women, their blessed status; he had the rank and distinction of an incomplete human being who held the lowliest positions in life that allowed those dominant males to view him as drifting flotsam to be eschewed from manly activities. Thus, he was dismissed by the larger part of society as having little or no value, either as man or lover, and so he glided through life, in between the blustery cold spaces discarded by others as they lived all around him. He trailed them, sucking in their sooty exhaust, smelling their foul fumes, living on the very waste products of their vibrant existence, jealous of their lusty parade.

People looked past him, through him and around him, as if he were a common house slave attending to his master's business in town.

And he knew all of this.

"And these are the people I want to rejoin," he pondered, standing at the book section; "thank goodness I have been delivered from their condescending perch, so I may see what is truly important in life."

There were books on real diseases and pseudo-diseases, real cures and pseudo-cures, ones by real medical professionals and pseudo-ones, and there were books by real medical professionals who would gladly fill their volumes with deceit and half-truths and align themselves with vitamin companies, all for the promise of wealth; there were ones by pseudo-medical professionals who really did care about the health of people, and sincerely proffered what they believed was the scientific truth; there were topics such as cancer, diabetes, AIDS, arthritis, parasites, candida, allergies, fasting, digestive woes, heart disease, vitamins and minerals; and books on aerobic exercise, weightlifting, yoga, water cures, herbal cures, homeopathic cures, diets to cure obesity, diets to cure toxicity of the body, and diets to cure all maladies. There was a book for every person, old or young, man or woman; every ailment, authentic or not, misunderstood or misapplied; and all one had to do was to match one's symptoms to one listed therein and adhere to the plan for the all-mighty miraculous cure. He had long ago begun at the beginning, reading everything and believing nothing, testing everything, cross-referencing, researching, but because he had no solid foundation of scientific understanding, the bursts of knowledge about nutrition and exercise had not been digested in a linear fashion, but in frenetic, haphazard leaps, sometimes leading him down, sometimes up, but most often leading him sideways to stick against a stone artifice that was blood-red with the putrid glaze of frustration and stagnation; but slowly, he understood how the world of medicine worked and how it advanced and retreated; so, by now he could pick up a manuscript and gain a sense of value or nonsense from it as it related to the millennia-old, great conversation of medicine.

But right now, he felt an excruciating wave of virulent nausea, spreading out its nasty tentacles into every cell of his body, touching any drops of optimism and affability currently residing in his mind. He felt faint and retreated to the safety of aloneness, the inner sanctum of his mind, a concrete bunker he retreated to in times of overwhelming pain, and here he waited until this high level of insidious noise subsided within him. "Nine years of this is enough," he screamed inside his refuge, the words echoing against the thick walls of his shelter, and he winced as the stench of churning and rumbling in his inflamed gut was joined by piercing agony. Now, he cursed, cursing his pain, his disease, his fate, his cruel solitary existence.

His eyes hurt, a kind of throbbing pins-and-needles hurt from the awful feeling in his bloated stomach; but this flood of physical terror had only to drain down a tiny level in order for him to function, as he had existed so long with it; as it was, he left, for he had lost his enthusiasm to research. He could recycle futility into bile through his bloodstream for only so long, and then, like a stagnant gallbladder, it would turn to stone.

When his research took him down dusty, dark corridors with false exits and icy-cold empty rooms and upside-down signs, he cracked, much like the man who, although he seeks to build a wall on his own, finally admits defeat and enlists the aid of a bricklayer.

The next day he sat in the doctor's office, feeling very much like an infantile child, not because he considered the doctor's knowledge daunting, which he certainly did not, but because his very presence here admitted his failure to rid himself of his own illness.

The slim man in the ubiquitous white coat came in, carrying his wooden clipboard with the patient profile; he introduced himself, and proceeded to allow the patient five minutes of self-babbling; but it was rhetoric devised by the doctor to give the man a chance to disgorge all of his whining, inner alleged atrocities and conspiracies and absurd self-diagnosis. It must be said that the majority of doctors Tony had seen did not believe any of the expert delineation of illness he had given them; but this was so because doctors consider the human body a mystery, a vessel full of unfortunate and unexplainable events that merely occur, and since they find that patients experience a broad range of symptoms, both real and imagined, they consider all of it a game of chance. "For goodness' sake, doctoring is an art," one doctor would say to his spouse while eating at their luxury home; "if we find something, fine; if not, it is probably imaginary," and then, gulp, they would take another swallow of the juicy tenderloin steak the imaginary disease of their patients had bought this white-coated false god. "So, in the end, honey," continued the well-to-do, handsome general practitioner to his beautiful wife, "well, thank goodness for modern medicine; I mean, look, we just slip them a pill to stop or slow down or speed up a normal bodily function, and then, poof! The symptoms are gone, like magic! Oh, darling, these patients are just like children, they just need to see the Band-Aid on the cut," and here he imitated a soothing mother, "all better!" And then said, seriously, "O, if they were to know that vigorous aerobic exercise, and weightlifting, and proper nutrition, adequate sleep, and reducing stress do more than we can ever deliver with our little white pills—well, methinks we would lose our heads on the guillotine."

And his lovely trophy wife—kept for a steady stream of pretty baubles—had rejoined, "Oui, monsieur."

Tony finished his eloquent depiction of his misery, from clear beginning to a clear end, elucidation unlimited.

Indeed, the doctor undeniably nodded, seemingly interested, his countenance screwed up in concern; but shall we be mischievous and invade his mind to see what was developing therein?

"The hour is getting late," he pondered; "Liza is expecting me for dinner; I have four more patients scheduled in the next half-hour; oh, this man just probably needs to consume more calories."

"Well," the physician finally said, seeking authority in his voice to quash what he perceived as weak, jumbled scientific theories strewn past him, "it's been nine years, and you've seen other doctors." He tapped his clean-shaven chin with his finger. "Have you ever seen a nutritionist?"

Tony collapsed inwardly, but managed a cool equanimity on the thin surface. "I am five foot nine, and I weight one hundred and nineteen pounds. I push heavy weights and eat enormous amounts of calories, especially protein. Something is wrong; I know how to train and grow muscle; I used to weigh one hundred and seventy pounds. Something is wrong."

"Hmm," the doctor returned, staring at the patient's chart. He ordered a comprehensive blood panel, and the two men met two weeks later. The blood work had few abnormalities. "Have you ever seen a psychologist?" he said, in their next meeting. "Perhaps for stress?"

Tony sighed as an inner boulder dragged his sagging hope deeper into the disappearing abyss. "But my weight…"

"Well, your weight is normal for your height." The cluttered opening to the mind of the doctor had not yet closed, and a small covert peek inside explained his overt actions on the outside. "Well," he was thinking, "next week, I fly to Hawaii for a two-day seminar sponsored by my favorite drug company, and I get university credits, and my wife accompanies me."

"Here is a referral to a psychologist," he finally stated, deciding that there could be nothing organically wrong with a patient who had reasonable results from blood tests. "Psychosomatic," he thought, and then his thoughts shifted over to the constantly running parallel commentary in his drug-company-sponsored brain, "but next time, Hawaii, maybe without the wife…"

Tony was not incredulous, merely disappointed.

On his trip home, because of the attitude of the physician, he mused upon the way life had become in this world. "People have no time for each other anymore; they pursue, instead, the accumulation of things, other than the accumulation of memories with family and friends, and good deeds done; and consequently, Humanity slips further down an ignominious path." But then he thought of himself, and he was not pleased. "And how am I any different? Because I am ill, I do not have an obligation to help others?" He thought of times he had helped people in need, but he knew this was not enough. "How can I condemn others for not helping me if I do not help others more often? Perhaps, perhaps," and his mind began to examine a new shred of philosophy from various angles, "perhaps, the more I help others, the better off I will be, but how; but why, why, but why must I?" But then he thought of the condescending remark about his weight, and he was too easily shaken from this new breed of reasoning. "If that imbecile weighed that much, he would break the banks of insurance companies to find his problem." He nodded his balding head. "What a fool I was to have believed a doctor would listen to me now—the others did not; fool, you are alone trying to cure this illness," and he cursed, violently, "and I don't want some white-coated hypocrite helping me out, anyway."

He got the flu that night. He was always sick.

The Death of Time

Outside of his abode, it was cold, dark and raining, and inside of his abode, he felt as if it were cold, dark and raining; he experienced this same grim verdict every night as he lay in his bed and cogitated upon the empty and torn annals of his life.

There was famine in his heart and misery in his soul.

The sleep that envelops me, he thought, I am dead in its waxy cocoon, for when I am awake, at least I seek a remedy for what ails me; but sleep, if I was only your master, I would live within your surreal borders and never awaken, for this world I inhabit is an empty grave in which I daily slide down; O sleep, my enemy, yet I pray you were my paramour, that I might never leave your magical kingdom, for this world has abandoned me, and I it; and even if I were well again, I do not know if I would want its offerings, so loathsomely has it treated me and my kind; O, this unjust world, like poison full of its own antidotes, giving elixir to others, and to others, venom." He smiled at such profundities, for his illness had expelled him from the fertile and warm land and into the cold and decaying forest, and therein he dwelled, mad to find an answer to restore his health so he might gain greater knowledge about the world; but he did not care about that now, but only about healing.

He gazed at the keeper of time. Ten o'clock in the p.m. The death of another hour, he thought, as he listened to the lament of Winter's frozen tears upon his roof, another hour gone forever, here and done, and once more I was beside and atop it, under it and at its back and front, begging for entrance, and it did not even acknowledge me, not even once, not even recognizing that I am at least a shadow of a man; another hour forward and I cannot retrieve it, and I die another day, and the loud blare and hot wind that is the waste of life batters against me and causes me to further recede into the blurred and colorless background.

He felt like a young flower that begins to grow toward the sun and unfurls its petals but finds they are wilted, the rich juices of its stem dried up, its roots scrawny and shallow and retreating toward the rocky surface; but he was not another flower, but a man, and he did see the other men around him unfurl their magnificent wings and stout limbs and raise their noble heads and handsome faces toward the golden dawn, and he saw how they flourished and grew up straight and tall and proud and healthy, never once flinching in the midst of a crowd, never once hiding their faces like he did in shame in the company of women, never once having to come out of the slippery abyss from which he pathetically attempted to crawl every morning.

Yes, he thought of those he should have been like, those who had health and wealth and comely looks, and he thought about them the way a man in prison thinks of those in the outside world; he did not understand how they could have such things and not fall upon their knees and weep for joy every hour and for every moment of wonder, weep for their babies born and for joyous weddings and family gatherings and every good and pure thing under the warm, yellow sun;

no, he could not understand why they did not worship such things, such things he worshipped from an impossible impasse that was behind an impossible barrier he felt he could never surmount. Yes, he reflected, as he gazed again at the clock, another hour has come and gone and I am not to be a part of it, having been reduced to a mere reflection in a muddy pool of those who truly live.

Yes, he worshipped what these superhuman creatures had but he did not worship them, he despised them because they were not content with such gifts, for they were continuously pursuing those things that they believed were the essential things in life, and this disturbed him. How can they, he murmured, pursue such vices and risk the loss of such treasures? It was the fact that these creatures, these healthy and happy and wealthy creatures, would set aside their families—the treasure that comes from the gift of health—to pursue physical debauchery and drunkenness and avarice. How could they, he said aloud, how could they forfeit that which yields to Man a paradise on earth, an existence that is exceeded by nothing yet known; O, to have health and wealth and family, that is the prize, that is the aim of Man—it is good for him and the earth—how can they not see that? And so he dwelled upon these themes, and he would not relent.

Eleven o'clock slithered in. He gazed at the clock. Eternity has tucked another hour under her wing, he thought, and I was not a part of it, again, once more away from it, too far away to reach it and grasp it and get inside it and live inside it and become someone; no, I missed it again as I have missed a thousand thousand hours, a fading voice in the harsh wind, an image trodden down upon by the blinding masses as I sink deeper into oblivion.

And he thought about certain elitists—power brokers, politicians, business tycoons and celebrities, heirs to fortunes and superstar athletes—who had attained all of the material goods needed to prod them into the highest echelons by mining all the rich nutrients in the sea with their enormous and spiny tentacles, stuffing every glittering treasure and shiny bauble into their ever-expanding, gaping egos and leaving only those items they deemed flawed or unnecessary—or decided not to murder, so only maimed—to fall to the bottom-dwellers who perpetually lived their boring lives with their mouths up and their hands out; and how these belligerent, bellowing founts of excess and unrestraint had thrown it all away—no, traded it all away for things that did not matter but were simply a lure for those who were weak in spirit and in the end was a safeguard against those who would destroy the equilibrium of Nature; and in the end how they were enslaved by what they could not overcome; and he was amazed at what they had done. How could you, he shouted, how could you have it all and throw it away on things you could not possibly keep? He did not understand such men, nor did he yearn to be like them, but only like a normal man with a normal wife and family and a normal job and living a normal day, like every other man, in every other land, day after day, hour after hour, participating anonymously and serenely in the gentle flow of time. And so he dwelled upon these themes, and he would not relent.

And then frustration set in, bitter frustration that had already bored into his brittle bone and pale marrow and sleeping sinew long ago, a powerful frustration that grew the more he thought about what he did not have, a frustration that was as much a part of him now as contentment is to any other man, and it drove him and teased him and pulled him this way and that but never gave him victory, never allowed him to taste satisfaction, never once allowed him to rest and admire the simple things in life. Frustration was his energy, his private muse, his sharpened and flaming tool he needed to impel himself onward into the impossible storm and past the impossible desert and up the impossible mountain so that one day he might stand on high and see what he was truly meant to be.

He looked at the clock. Twelve midnight, he whispered, another hour spent gazing at the futility of my life; and so he vowed another vow, a vow he had made many times before, that if ever he were to gain health, he would not pursue those things in life that were beyond his grasp, nor would he lose what he had fought so hard to win. I will be just like any other man, and you will never know it, he thought, as if he addressed the humble spirit of Time itself; I will just take my rightful place alongside any ordinary moment, and I will simply be.

He fell asleep, dreaming of times past when he was whole and happy and he had not even known it.

Introductions

Tony Siciliani lived in a small apartment across from a state university, and it suited him just fine, as he was a student there, working on his history degree. On the weekends, after completing his course work, he spent inordinate amounts of time at their library, his second home. He roamed the four-story building with an easy gait, for here he felt a very private solace and joy and friendship; this was his nightclub, his cinema house, his party hall, his gathering of friends and family. "Here," he often thought, admiring the long row of books before him, "I am truly happy." But in order to extract the highest degree of satiety from this peaceful endeavor, he had to adhere to strict protocols; to wit, he had to avoid women at all costs, even abandoning a beloved book he was perusing. He would not, could not, must not look at any woman full in the face, it simply could not be. If he happened to walk down an aisle that already was occupied by any amount of pretty females, he quickly and expertly retreated. To allow a woman to see his shame, his ugly face and scrawny frame, would send him into a deep emotional chasm, and this was absolutely forbidden to happen in the one place that was his sanctuary outside of his home.

As it was, each level of the library had an elegant theater in which there were tall rows of glorious books, comprising long aisles, each containing similar or different subject areas.

He could stand in front of the literary classics for hours, digesting titles and authors, skimming chapters, in awe of the soft texture of these old brown and green, hardbound books, mesmerized by the old drawings, the famous prefaces, the careful detail on the artwork of the covers, the unique writing style of the old masters; and when he held one in his hands, and beheld its humble binding, he felt as if he were peering into the vaults of antiquity. "Herein lie the memories of civilizations buried and yet living," he once murmured, holding *Don Quixote*, the proper title being *The Ingenious Gentleman Don Quixote of La Mancha*, in his left hand, his right hand massaging the cover of the book; he inhaled its pungent aroma as if it were a newly discovered treasure. Here, he forgot about his private rages against selfish people and their electronic toys and their fanatical need for all things not related to literature; here, he did not care that his fellow citizens shunned libraries, loathed sharpening their intellect, and in its stead pursued the false religions of entertainment and recreation. And when he did happen to see another visitor to his sacred chambers, he would smile and think, "Here, I am a freak, proudly," and he would look at the other visitors who too had unattractive trappings that were unacceptable for admission into the palatable bosom of society. "Here, I am at home with my own kind; so be it, let them come and dine with me on this sumptuous meal of knowledge." His love for books prevailed over those who harbored biases against him; here, he forgave them for building a natural wall of conceit around him—a stout, ever-moving-higher and ever-digging-deeper wall that was built every time they ignored him and whispered about him and purposely abused him—for this was his heaven on earth.

There were special times during his trips to the library, august moments, on sun-drenched, golden-beamed rays in clear, azure-sky days, when he felt nearly normal, if only because he was at peace with the world; but he knew these were dangerous times, for his station in life was on the periphery, looking in at all the lost souls scurrying about. He was denied participation in the daily activities of citizens, and to step into their illustrious circle meant embarrassment and shame for him. But, alas, the human mind does not work this way, to wit, to embrace isolation forever, for it continually seeks to return to its celebrated place of birth in the bustle and flow of society.

He had to continually remind himself that his time in this sacred library was not real, and the outside world—his antagonist—still thrived, and waited for his return so it could pummel him down again.

He was standing in front of the card catalogs, looking for a specific book on clinical health and nutrition. A woman with stylish, dark sunglasses was standing to his right and mumbling to herself, and when he happened to see her face, he smiled, which led to his social faux pas, and consequently, allowed him to fall from the fragile tower he had erected every time he hid his face in shame from Woman in this hallowed place.

"Excuse me, were you speaking to me?" He feigned indifference, but he was too aware of his target being the same woman who had recently insulted him at the local health food store. In his old mind, the one that remembered the days before the great dissolution between himself and the world, he could jest easily with women, and they had welcomed his witty conversation.

The woman turned to look at him, scorn written in deep burns across her fragile beauty. "What?" she cried, and upon seeing who accosted her, she let her irritation bloom into seething rage. "You again? Are you following me?" Her voice was loud and piercing, and immediately he produced that cold clammy sweat of the ugly man who has the temerity to flirt in public. "This is harassment; I'm going to tell the librarian that you're bothering me!" Her pale face pumped crimson wrath as she stormed toward the main checkout desk.

He felt ill. "Do I run?" he wondered, watching the outraged woman speaking to the male librarian behind the desk, her face animated, flushed with excitement, her arms flailing and pointing to the spot whereupon he stood like a young buck caught in the headlights of a runaway train. "I'll just stay," he thought, hearing his heart pounding loudly in his skinny chest. "I don't know what she is…" But he let even this thought die as the woman and a disturbed-looking male librarian approached the brown maple wood file cabinets. He showed false interest in the catalog before him, slowly shuffling through the white cards as the woman and the man approached him.

"See," she said, irritated. Tony felt his face flush hot, his skin prickled with anxiety and perspiration. "This drawer is missing." She pointed to an empty slot next to where he stood; indeed, there was a card file box missing. "I really need the 'Rs,'" she said, and laughed. "I know it sounds silly." She even smiled at the librarian. "Maybe if you could do an all-call or something, I would really appreciate it."

Tony was aghast. "Women," he pondered, "mad as hatters…"

After the librarian had walked away, the girl casually said, without even looking at Tony, "Were you worried?"

Tony, vexed now, turned to her, a quizzical look upon his visage. "Excuse me? Are you talking to me?" and when he received no reply, he walked away and thought, "A handsome man would have had a date with her by now," and then cursed, "ugly and diseased men are targets for derision." He felt violated.

He walked up the cement stairs to the fourth floor, and stared out of the window at the high mountains and their thick green and brown foliage they wore, and he contemplated life as an outside observer, forever. "What am I doing here, if I am to be like this, always? Should I not be somewhere helping people in real need? Is it wrong to spend so much time on me?" He then researched for another hour, studying various diseases of the liver and kidneys and adrenals, and then, solemnly, walked down the stairs to the parking lot, feeling guilty about not existing outside of his own selfish orbit.

He sat in his gold Monte Carlo, with its torn black tarp, and he looked about, only to behold a woman standing next to a car with its hood up; immediately, he got out and walked over to offer assistance. It was Winter, and his mistake was acceptable, for the young woman now had her rusty-red fox fur overcoat on, and when he neared her, he shook his head. "Too late," he murmured.

"Say, don't you have eyes—I need assistance over here, for goodness' sake," she said more to herself than to him, and then, looking away, "Where are all the good men when you want them?"

He frowned, smiling inwardly, thinking, "Running from you, if they have any sense," and then outwardly, "Are you harassing me? Here, let me go get the police," and he feigned a steady walk toward the university.

"Oh, you big baby," she said, whipping off her sunglasses and then putting her slender hands on her slender hips, "can't take a woman's verbal teasing."

He stopped, looked back at her, visibly irritated. "Is that an apology?"

"For what? I need help, can't you see?" Her hands gesticulated about. "Do you see anyone else offering assistance?"

Now, he was amused. "Maybe," he said, approaching her with great circumspection, "they have stood next to you somewhere…"

"Oh, please go away if you're going to insult me. I thought you were a gentleman, offering succor to a damsel in distress," she said, her voice profoundly sad. "I'll just call for help," and she went back to the door of her silver Mercedes-Benz midsize luxury sedan, took her Gucci Jackie Soft Python wallet out of her camel-colored Gucci Jackie Soft Leather Top Handle bag, and then removed her cell phone.

"I'll do it," Tony said, walking up to the engine. "Turn on the lights."

She smiled that smile of womanly satisfaction that spoke of subterfuge, and then obeyed.

In a moment, he had diagnosed the problem. "Your battery cells are dry. You need distilled water in them." He looked to the bookstore, and he pointed to it. "It might have some."

The bookstore failed them.

"Well, I'll drive to the store; it won't take me long."

"Let's go, then," she replied, animated.

He frowned. "I think it would be best if I went alone."

She threw her head back in laughter, and said, incredulous, "Afraid of you?" She stared at him, amused. "Look, you're no threat to anybody. Come on, Sir Galahad," and she lit up a cigarette as they walked to his car.

He stopped. "No, I am afraid of you," he said, quite distastefully, and looking at her with disdain, continued, "and no one smokes in my car but my engine."

She knit her brown eyebrows and nearly smiled. "All right," she rejoined, threw down the cigarette onto the black concrete and squished it out with the stiletto heel of her sienna-colored Christian Louboutin Studded Willetta ankle boots. "I was going to quit as it was." And she did quit that day, so great was her iron resolve.

They drove to the store in an uncomfortable silence, the heavy tension laying itself upon them, catching every breath and look and feel to its sticky self; but the drive back meant more time for the possibility of words and conversation, and the idea of a woman in his car emboldened him to speak. He looked at her again. She was a slender beauty, with long, light-golden-brown hair that lay in curls down her back, a face with high cheekbones, generous amounts of expertly applied makeup, thin lips, and layers of expensive clothes. "So, what are you studying, if I may ask?" He glanced at her, and saw her about to speak, her face conducive to geniality; but then, she clutched her side, coughed violently, and pain flushed across her face.

"Look," she said, her voice throttled with agony, "just drive; you're not my type." She grimaced and squeezed her eyes shut.

He chastised himself for trying. Back at the parking lot, he poured the distilled water into the battery cells, started the car, put down the hood, and stood there, brooding.

"Here," she said, handing him a five-dollar bill, "for your services."

He looked at her with contempt. "Give it to the poor." He should have walked away right there and then, but did not.

"Fine," she said, withdrawing it. "I'll just buy another pack of cigarettes."

He put out his hand. "I'll give it to the poor."

She expelled incredulity with a hiss as she gave him the greenback. "I'll bet you will, too, Boy Scout." She lit up a cigarette and abruptly turned away.

The idea of engaging conversation between man and woman perfumed with romance died a little more in his mind. He walked away, wanting to say more, but he was content to let his anger subside; but then his mistress, Disease, arose and flicked one of her wet, black, crooked fingers at him and he was stung with her venom. "Consider me always, darling: all deeds dance for me, all words waltz for me, all thoughts turn for me; won't you, Lover?" she whispered into his outraged, bubbling bloodstream and cells and into the very pale red marrow of his brittle bones. He felt nauseated, nearly faint, as a sharp, dissecting pain in his groin careened up to his screaming eyeballs, and soon, he was speaking without benefit of his mind's natural filter. He had turned toward her, and cried, "You know, people say 'thank you' when someone performs an act of kindness for them, but you don't care about any of that, do you?"

She stood, bemused, leaning against her car, cigarette up to her moist lips, an amused smile accenting her face.

"And I also don't believe in coerced words of gratitude, so save your insincere 'thank yous.'"

She held her hands up as if innocent. "I wasn't going to," she said, frowning.

He cursed, and shook his head.

"People say 'thank you' too often," she said. "Why do we have to say it for every little thing? Don't people know when someone is grateful for a good deed done? I offered you money, after all."

He stood, stone-faced. "You pay a servant for a job, you say 'thank you' to a human being for an act of unselfishness," and he gestured toward her car, "but you wouldn't know about that, now, would you." He turned round and walked away, opened the door of his humble Monte Carlo, got in, sat down on his faded, beige leather seats, and looked at her. She had turned her back and was leaning against her magnificent vehicle, her cigarette handing limply in her hand. "She isn't crying, that's for sure," he said, and watched her for a full minute, noticing that her hands were now on her sides as she bent over. He hesitated to get out and get involved. "She has money, let her doctors figure it out; she isn't my business." He started his car. "I have enough problems without getting mixed up with her kind." He backed it up and drove away slowly, looking at her still leaning against her car.

He could not drive very far. "Are we not here to help each other? Have I not been thinking of helping others more and myself less? Is this not a great secret only the ill understand?" He did not know yet if he believed such a philosophy, but he believed in helping people, and the fact that she had a drowsy kind of comeliness that was coming and going rerouted him back to the parking lot. In one moment, he was there, and in another moment, he was walking up to her, feeling very much the fool, expecting her to scream and kick and yell. "I must be crazy," he reasoned, nearly upon her. He could smell her rare beauty.

"You came back," she whispered, her back still to him as he came up to her; "need another merit badge?"

Equanimity relaxed his body, for he was the man, now. "I'm naturally nosy," he said, firmly, and then, with compassion, "What is it?"

In her mind, in her heated brain, in between the quiet spaces, lay fissures waiting to erupt. Now, she was calm. "It is nothing, really; I'm fine."

He was not totally versed in the mysteries of woman, but he knew that such talk was an automatic response, generally without truth. "Is there anything I can do?"

She felt the gnawing pain grip her and paralyze her body with sweeping torrents of agony, like a new vein of misery leeching into her collapsing body; now, the fissures broke and washed away any sentiment of congeniality. "Please, just go away," she whispered in a guttural tone. She was finished, and she should have been done shutting him down, but the jealous, searing agony ripped a huge hole in her natural defenses, and after screaming in a piercing wail, she turned to face him. "What do you want?" she cried, her pale face twisted in pain. "Do you think you're going to get lucky with me? You, you're pathetic; you're a loser, an ugly, pathetic loser who couldn't even get a date with an ugly, old prostitute." She stood upright. "I go out with real men, handsome men—wealthy and powerful men who are healthy and strong, real men..."

He wanted to walk away, should have walked away, but could not. He stared at her in disbelief and disappointment for a few seconds, then turned, made his way to his faithful car, and drove away.

He retreated even further into his blessed and accursed world and even further from human beings.

Reflections

D ay by day, he labored to reduce his interactions with his own species. "Who am I to them, they who care only for themselves and their own family…" He had come to see the American family as a kind of cruel hatchery, a breeding ground to sow all of one's precious insular life-forces, and he realized they would never recognize him.

In the beginning, when he had plainly lost his health—when he had been transformed in a few short months from a handsome youth with a head full of curly, thick black hair and an athletic, muscular build and a daunting presence in society, to a man trimmed of the power and robust song of health, and who had rapidly lost most of his magnificent mane and fifty pounds of muscle and strength and the very sheen and luster that shines like a newborn star in the young—no one he knew had said a word to him. "Could it be out of respect or shyness, that they do not ask me what is wrong?" He had pondered this at the time, but after a year of ill health he told a few family members and friends about his physical turmoil, and they were shocked. "Could it be that they never knew? Are they so wrapped up in their own affairs and their own family that they care nothing for things outside of their puny sphere of miserable influence?" They, his family and friends, were exceedingly sympathetic as he spoke of his illness, but they never mentioned it again. "Is it possible they viewed it as an acute illness?" he sometimes wondered. "Or is that they truly do not care? Is there too much misery in the world for them to offer succor to anyone other than their own precious family?"

Nine years ago, when it had all begun, he had been sitting on the brown carpeted floor of his apartment, leaning against the blackened wall with his bare back, eating a plain yogurt, when there came upon him a violent need to regurgitate. The great disgorging of his food filled the ceramic sink as he stood retching, his head violently in spasm until, finally, the vile contents of his stomach lay in mushy, pungent heaps. His throat burned with the residue of acid and humiliation.

He had no fever, he did not vomit again that day, but his gut had been altered from that cataclysmic moment.

His brain wanted to feed its body the same nourishment it had always selected, but the body would not hear of it; the old diet was no longer conducive to health for him, and so, he slowly experimented with a menu that eliminated those items that gave him unrest. Within six months he had realized that the only foods he could consume without bodily ache were fruits and vegetables and nuts and seeds. Slowly, then, happiness returned to his life as he doted on this new diet of sweet potatoes and yams and purple russet potatoes and anything vegetable green and all ripe fruits purple and red and yellow and blue, and red and cranberry-colored scrumptious delight. He became a master chef of the new cuisine of mounds of sweet almond butter on hot steaming russet potatoes, topped by fresh, crisp broccoli and adorned with juicy yellow bell peppers and slices of sugary yellow peaches. These foods sang to his stomach, soothed his mind and rested his aching heart; but as fast as he gained on one side, he lost on the other.

The human body needs more than nuts and seeds and fruits and vegetables, but he could master nothing beyond this, for indulging in anything else meant insufferable bellyaches and excruciating screams and innumerable bathroom visitations and restless nights and nausea visiting every pleading cell of his tortured body; so, he happily, willfully, obediently ate his new foods. O, but these were times of great gastronomic joy; there were blissful moments, at the end of a long workday, when he came home from a long day's labor and carefully sat down the icy-cold jar of almond butter and scooped out its rich contents on top of the twenty medjool dates he had already de-pitted; and then, O, and then, he would sweep this delectable cargo into his salivating mouth and hum and rock back and forth like a man sitting at the serene beach soaking in the warm rays of the sun and the fresh breezes of the briny sea culture. He might be denied the ubiquitous foodstuffs accessible to his brothers and sisters of this planet, but he would not be denied indulging his senses in aromatic dishes that soothed his shattered body.

He had gone to a doctor during the first six months of his disease, and the doctor, curiously ignoring his patient, pronounced him "healthy and skinny and normal." Tony could do nothing but watch his precious youth disintegrate before him.

Women now ignored him. People looked past him to fertile young men around him; somehow, he had slid out of sight of the mainstream into a prison space in between the stream of life; he was neither in nor out, living or dead, slave or free, but simply there, on the deadly margin of existence, teetering this way and that, clinging to the altar of survival with his dynamic intellect, living in the callous breezes of the invisible shadows, moving with the forgotten, the oppressed, the walking dead.

He was alone now, scrubbed clean from that stone tablet of society whereupon his name had once resided.

After three years, and two dozen doctors, most of whom pronounced him either neurotic or a liar, he had regained little use of his digestive tract. Then one fine day he discovered another food to safely consume, when he, on a caprice, decided to eat at a restaurant, and he ordered a fillet of salmon, which, to his great surprise, did not give him over to bouts of agony. Thus, fish became his animal protein for the longest time.

But that had all been long ago, and every day he prayed to be normal and forget his inglorious past. He often envisioned himself healthy, saw himself with a woman and married and happy and with children and blissfully happy, happy, happy, eating food and visiting friends and fitting into the proper space allotted to him by natural law; but his clever mistress, Disease, would not hear of it, saying, "Leave me, Darling, are you ridiculous today? We are secret lovers, you and I, the best kind of lovers; we can love each other all day, and no one knows. Darling, you must understand that being with me makes you special, allows you to see that they—yes, darling, the very creatures you emulate—are not who they seem. You want to be like them, but once you know who they truly are, you will be glad you are sucking at my meaty breast; you are mine, mine, mine, Lover, and I will remind you every time you dream of those treacherous, selfish creatures! They don't care about you the way I do—I think about you every moment. Behold!" Every time an attack came he was reminded of who he was: of the futility of seeking to leave his mistress, of the fate of those who have chronic disease, and the reality of the world toward his crippled kind.

One cannot defeat an enemy who is vastly superior in numbers and tactics by sitting and contemplating plans, one must act; and to ensure the possibility of success, one must dedicate oneself to the task at hand. This he did, to the exclusion of all things not necessary for the preservation of life.

He rarely accepted invitations to parties or events or the home of friends, nor went to anything or anywhere that would not further his research into conquering his illness. "How will going to a social event cure my disease?" he would opine. "People there do not care about me, they are not me, I am me, and only me is interested in me. I am alone."

He was alone, yes, but he was also pushed into seclusion by the mighty hand of hypocrisies and prejudices into his small apartment where he sat and sifted through the medical and nutritional books he borrowed and bought and rented; he was always looking and searching for clues, following leads, clinging to any drifting piece of jetsam that might bob up momentarily, chasing any fog of flotsam that appeared, but might sink too quickly beneath the alluring waves of false hope.

There is a dialogue that exists in the fold of scientific research, in medical, and health and nutrition, and exercise journals; to join in this mystical, elusive, at once dying and resuscitative voice, one has to simply wade into its ancient stream and submerge oneself, body and soul, and block out the aimless vibrations and extraneous voices of civilization to hear the melodic hum of pure knowledge rushing past. Such a feat calls for selfless, ruthless dedication to research for the newest human eavesdropper to this great conversation, for to do otherwise, to continue to dress in a traditional intellect, to listen to the influences from the soggy brains of conventional pragmatists would contaminate the voyager and eliminate any chance for success.

His myriad of symptoms caused him to chase phantoms, every genus phantom, every maybe and perhaps and desperate phantom that rose up before him; to wit, because he had problems with nightmarish bouts of incessant urination, he therefore studied the kidneys, the urethra tubes, the prostrate, the bladder, and so these fields of study led him to other phantoms, such as zinc for the prostate, food allergies, infections, bladder crystals, kidney stones, and magnesium deficiencies; and these phantoms sent him hither and thither, so that, in the midst of the befuddled research and in the foggy end, he did not know if his high volume of voiding was a symptom of the disease or the main symptom of the diseased gland or organ.

The phantoms of one theory would soon expire and lead him to follow the vapor trail of another new and potentially exciting discovery; recently, he had decided that the master organ, the liver, was somehow held hostage by diabolical denizens within his person, poisoning it, thickening its gray self with hard, crusty fats.

Thus, he took an herb for the liver, an expensive capsule of the finest quality, hand-harvested organic herb; but he took not just one herb, but many, and not just for a week, but months, with small periods of relief, ad infinitum. And then he treated the theory of the liver in the same fashion he treated all of his potential cures—he attempted to cut it and knead it and shape it and cram it into his own idea of what was wrong with him—and then he would try and match the potential cure with the symptoms and he would ignore the medical research that explicitly stated he was undeniably wrong; and so, when the hope of deliverance from illness by consuming these particular herbs began to crumble and fall, he was skillfully well underway into the next search.

On and on and on it went, one idea melting into another, like multicolored candy on a hot rock, becoming one indistinguishable blob; but, from every false lead, and after every desultory chase after every possible grand unifying theory, he gleaned a tiny, sparkling jewel of fact that would lead him to the next level; and there, the accursed hunt would continue for that long-forgotten, impossible-to-imagine, elusive health.

He couldn't abate the search, for to capitulate meant stagnation, and stagnation meant he was doomed to be palpably unhealthy, despised by society, half not whole, acceding to this villainous illness that had robbed him of his youth; he could not yield now, for his most fervent wish was to climb back to the Fabled Country that was strewn with handsome and healthy mortals and join them as they strolled arm and arm with their sweethearts in the golden sunshine on the road to the Good Life.

First Contact

Each day was like every other day, each week like every other week, each month like every other month, for when one is alone and ill, a second, a minute and an hour have no discernible boundaries as they bleed one dull moment into the next, creating one linear line of vacuous time, without holidays or seasons or birthdays or special occasions; there was nothing to celebrate if celebrations, as he saw it, were for people with family and friends. The properties of time and space had no distinguishing mark from each other, nothing to make each moment unique from each other, no special memory attached to that delightful molecule of memory that could be later recalled in the minds of those who truly lived. For him, New Year's Eve was simply another day on which to pursue ideas related to relieving symptoms or finding cures for his many ailments; it meant nothing else, just as New Year's Day meant nothing else, no clear delineation of one year ending and one year beginning, no joy spread, no resolutions made.

"New Year's resolutions," he often thought when entombed in loneliness in his cluttered place, "are for children; one does not resolve to do something because of some specific date; one resolves to do something based on an event; why, we learn by doing, responding to crises, pain, horror, outrage, not to an artificial timeline." He was becoming so tied to logic and reasoning as his guide to find the answers in the thousands of books and magazines he read that he began to loathe illogic and unreasonable things, even in things that were supposed to be illogical and unreasonable, like love, and parties, and doing things capriciously. "How can people be so absurd?" he would sometimes think, while observing those who were engaged in acts without thorough examination. His mind had become so analytical to separate fact from fiction, and to decide what was good and bad, to follow the correct lead, to question all sources and studies, that he marveled at how people could live their lives without thinking.

But he had accepted this fate to be alone. "So be it," he would say at such thoughts; "I will be alone until I am well; who else will help me?" And thus, nothing but endless passages of time elapsed, whereupon he was involved in the same routine, nothing to look forward to or celebrate or reminisce or anticipate or cherish. His life was a rusty ruin he could not rebuild, an old, sagging building decaying through natural forces he could not possibly keep from collapsing; and yet, he was not alone, for his constant companion, his only companion, the most influential force in his life shaped him and drove him and was always there for him during good times and bad, listening to him and moving him this way or that, his omnipresent companion who knew him better than anybody else, his taskmaster, his impetus, his uninvited body guest: Disease.

One lifeless Autumn day—as interpreted by his purged senses—he once more walked into the health food store to search their library of feints and false hopes. He sighed, thinking of all the years he had wasted searching; but he overcame his weak resolve, and looked once again to the books that mocked him. "Water cures," he whispered, "hokum," and he viewed the other topics: "Balance Your pH," "Yeast Infections," "Parasites, the Real Killer," "Enzyme Therapy," and "Mercury Poisoning." Anything not in mainstream medicine meant a secret hope for all like him, and the books whispered to him, thus, "Doctors won't cure you, they only treat symptoms; they give you drugs, they do not understand; the answer is in Nature's pharmacy, discovered by the ancients, suppressed by drug companies; come, come and partake of our healing wisdom." Yes, he had listened intently to their charming chorus at the beginning of his illness, but now he was able to dismiss unscientific elixirs at a glance; he was proud of himself for this, and it had narrowed his search down to those health practitioners who proffered scientific data.

As it was, he was in the ninth year of his downward spiraling trajectory, and he was beginning to repeat hopeful cures; he had abandoned the liver as culprit, and four months later, after being disappointed by yeast cures, parasite cures and pancreatic and biliary duct cures, he came back to the liver cure. The cycle sometimes veered one way, then another, but always came back to theories he had tried but then had restudied and now decided to approach from another direction. "Well," he would say to himself, "I think it is the liver, but I just did not do it right the last time," was now his sorry refrain for then, but for later, he discovered the fascinating world of food allergies: first, he discovered celiac disease, which he explored with great vigor, as he always did when he convinced himself that "this time, for sure, this time, this must be it, this explains it all, this makes sense, this has to be it." And so he researched this and was led down the paranoid path set down by those who bethought all grains sinister, and should be forsaken; but undaunted, he would attempt to refrain from such grains that had gluten; but as he researched this proposed remedy, he naturally bumped into casein intolerance, a protein found in milk, and so he researched this, and was led down the paranoid path set down by those who bethought all animal milk sinister, and should be forsaken; but undaunted, he would attempt to refrain from all dairy; but as he attempted these two restricted diets, he was exposed to more conspiratorial diets: rotating foods to eliminate allergies diet, the all meat is bad diet, and the all raw food diet; but along this surreptitious path, he did find some absolute truths: to improve his omega three to polyunsaturated fats ratio, to eat smaller meals, and to have adequate proteins and fats with his larger carbohydrate meals, and copious amounts of fruits and vegetables, and nuts and seeds, and legumes; and consume generous amounts of beneficial bacteria, and the substance that fed it, inulin, along with lots of green tea for its epigallocatechin gallate, or EGCG; and fermented soy for its genistein and daidzein, the latter which metabolized into equol, and purple grapes because of their ample resveratrol levels, and flax with its superabundance of lignans; and regarding exercise: to engage in intense aerobic, body-weight, and weight-bearing activities; and yet—and yet as fast as he made gains, he lost them, because he knew he must experiment with one fad-conspiratorial-paranoid-diet-cure at a time; otherwise, if he were to make gains, he would have to begin anew and try one diet at a time—and yet this was killing him, and this was what he had to do, he had to do one thing at a time to eliminate the quack, pseudo-silly theories; and so he did, he threw them all away and began with just one: avoiding all gluten, and taking no herbal pills, no vitamin pills, no other supplements, and then agonizingly waiting for results, all the while looking at the clock and knowing that every day the world was existing just fine without him; and yet, despite this interminable search that proceeded from ruby-colored dawn to the heavy black veil of night, that began and ended, and then was re-ignited with another idea, any lead was still followed through and exhausted, perhaps yielding one more precious clue; and when researched to exhaustion, gave him reference to something else he had read, and so he doubled back, and with more enlightenment, reread the volumes of medicine, and then gleaning from this, he took this invaluable thread and attached it to another loose strand, and pulling on it, waited for something to tighten that would not fray and break apart as everything always did—and despite all of this circuitous looking to and fro, and up and down, and sideways, many times sideways, he somehow managed to break into the secrets of ultimate health: the proper diet, the proper exercise, the proper amount of sleep, the proper attitude, all because he had bumped into them when he was looking for some elusive bit of fluff; so, now he was eating correctly and exercising correctly, but his body could not yet take advantage of all the extraordinary benefits.

He wanted to lie down and rest, to sleep, to dream this old self dead and awake whole, physically whole and alive to rejoin the world and marry and have children and forget this draining, weary disease. "But this is how a child thinks," he would muse, "and I am forced to be a man." He would shake his head. "I am not yet ready."

So, he stood there, reading in the store of illusions, looking for another revelatory fact that he might have overlooked due to insufficient knowledge the last trip out, a fact that would once again start him down the rabbit's hole, when a sweet voice intruded upon his cogitation.

"Excuse me," the woman said, reaching over to a book in front of him. It was she.

His body flushed with nausea, and he quickly replaced the book and walked out of the double glass doors and toward his faithful car.

"Excuse me," the voice said, seeming to trickle weakly along the ground like a bird with a broken wing.

He turned, a victim of social graces, but visibly irritated enough to express unease. He remembered her unkind words from long ago, still stuck in his sensitive mind like sharp thorns from a bramble bush.

She looked more frail than before, thinner, her colorful makeup thicker upon a face wan yet still retaining the spectral images of a superior comeliness. "I need to explain myself to you."

"That isn't necessary, really," he responded, keys in hand, as he thought only of escape. "I am cursed," he thought, "no normal women, only the crazy ones; they must sense something broken in men…"

She stopped too far short of him, indicating her awareness of his sentiment. "I wanted to explain my actions in the parking lot at the university."

"Not necessary, really," he said, nodding his round head; "thank you for offering, though," and he turned to go, frowning all the while.

"You're like me," she said, coughing hoarsely, "you and I are the same; we're both ill."

He turned round, vexed. "And your point?"

"Sometimes people act differently when they are in physical pain," she said, coughing violently.

He stared at her rich apparel: the Stuart Weitzman black suede boots, her silver, diamond-studded Cartier watch, her excellent posture and bearing, her wilting beauty, and said, with confidence, "Sometimes, but it's not always an excuse, is it—so, no, it really doesn't in the long term; illness doesn't change who you are."

"Oh, but it does," she replied, her still-thick eyebrows knit, as she shook her perfectly shaped head. She coughed so badly that he instinctively flinched, for it was his unique quality to live such harsh pronunciations upon a sickly body. Her head was bent down, and she turned away. "Excuse me," she whispered, covering her mouth.

He was glad to see her leave, but his heart reprimanded him. He shut his eyes as he sighed deeply. "I suppose I should go and ask her," he thought; "after all, I want to help people more often and think less of myself." Indeed, he followed her back into the store, waiting outside the restroom she had entered; he grew uneasy at this, and soon retreated to his car, leaning against it until she came out, at which time he approached her. "Is there anything I can do?"

"You can go away," she cried, not looking at him as she clicked the red button on the keychain for her silver Mercedes-Benz compact luxury sedan, and as he walked away, she cursed at herself, and then said, "No, don't, please, no," and then whispered, "not this time." He stopped and turned round. "I didn't mean it; look, I appreciate your offer, but no, you can't help me."

"May I buy you lunch?" He had not planned to say it, absolutely not.

She smiled, amused, taken aback. "Don't men ever stop?"

He smiled. "We'll stop the day women simply tell us what is on their mind."

She laughed. "Fair enough; hmm, but lunch?"

"We'll talk of diseases, and unsympathetic doctors, and private pain." His lament was genuine, as if it had risen from the very blistered, bleeding region of his imprisoned flesh and weak bones to cross over to the perilous boundaries of her hardened heart.

"No, I don't believe so," she said, but then condescension, like wax dripping from a candle once lit that now finally appears, accented her words and revealed the breadth of betrayal, "I have a date with my fiancé." She manufactured a perfect smile of conciliation, a timeless artifice women have developed since time immemorial, a kind of build-in defense system against unwanted predators.

He took out a piece of paper and wrote on it, and stood next to her, gesturing with the white note. "You and I," he said, staring into her now chartreuse-colored eyes—she had a definite hint of jaundice floating like a toxic spill in her sclera—"are always alone, unless we are with our own kind; for only we," he paused, staring unabashedly into her luminous pools from whence her soul hid, "understand the world we inhabit." He handed her the phone number. "If ever you need to talk, call me."

She held the note loosely, as if wanting to disregard it to the hard concrete. "Well, I don't need a friend, really," she replied, indifferent, shaking her head. "I am very busy," and she sought to hand the paper back to him, but he refused it.

"I'm not offering you friendship, I'm offering you wisdom," he said, passionately, and he moved next to her, so she might smell his masculine scent and hot breath. "When you find yourself alone even in the midst of family and friends, because they do not understand you..." And then he turned around and walked away; from his car, he saw that the small paper was now on the black concrete where her car had once rested. He drove by and retrieved the note. "I am alone," he stated, his voice staid, "as it must be, for men such as me. Why, why do I try? Why do I debase myself, even with women unworthy of my slightest glance?"

Grandmother

The pattern and rhythm of the world exist in every part of Nature, its intricate design and properties apparent in the end result, equilibrium; a lush, verdant tree sends its winged seeds to the rich soil to reproduce itself, to boast that it is essential, vital, fertile, an inextricable part of the whole which defines the earth. Every seed-bearing plant, every egg-laying creature, every live-birthing mammal, everything classified as a living thing joins in the exultation that is reproduction. Life eternal demands it, demands the joint venture of male and female to stoke the fiery juices of sexual union to continue the species; life encourages it, celebrates it, begs it, offers it, its throbbing energies shooting golden sparks at the birth of every life-force.

There are members of some species who stand on the outside of this festive celebration, their inert bodies likely to stagnate and die before any opposite sex engages them in this sensual mating ritual.

We speak of those particular human beings who are permeated with stinking disease, who are sickly pale in appearance, their ghastly pheromones encoding the air with the ghastly odors of rotting stench, their listless gobs of doughy and gray flesh repugnant to the vibrant life around them; for these emaciated societal lepers who adorn the barren deserts of streaming life, their only contribution to the eternal fabric of life is faint vestiges, tiny footprints barely indented in the hardened, waxy sediment thrown off by the birth and life and death of living things. These failed creatures, blown to the edge of humanity by their illness, are left sifting through the debris of others' joyous living with their fragile fingers.

Every morsel of life, from the blessed inner sanctum of living they cannot grasp, murders them, microscopically, intellectually, bleeding their natural defenses to a bleak, cold death. This is when they sink below the mire to the stark, dank planet of the underworld, where they tread heavily and exist in isolation with the members of their own lost tribe.

And then there are those who are born into the exclusive inner realm of human perfection: in the beginning, she had always known she was pretty, as surely as a man knows he is male, and a woman, female; the greater majority of humanity lingers in exclusive, horrible doubt about their physical appearance, but if there was one thing she knew, and a fact that was continually confirmed by the world, was her innate, symmetrically perfect, dazzling Beauty.

She was a sparkling, precious white diamond, a prismatic, lush rainbow vision come to life, a heart-shaped, ruby-red, velvety-soft, heavy-scented flower blooming in the yellow bosom of the nourishing sun; she was all these things as people saw her, a girl who set off a cascade of glittering sparks everywhere she went so that her perfectly proportional figure was bathed and highlighted in an incandescent glow; even when she was a child, people recognized her superior position in the hierarchy of splendid looks, her exulted ranking in the elegant pageantry of Nature's bounty; people bowed low before her, and were forced to acknowledge their own dull, lowly flesh as they felt the warm glow from the scintillating aura of her sublime loveliness.

Having thus been christened by sublime Nature and praised by her loyal subjects, she played her part exceedingly well; just as a mother intuitively nurtures her children, she understood the demands of her special kind, and that was to reflect her exquisite light and health and innate loveliness against a sagging, pale lump of ordinary humanity. Just as a person buys perfumed white roses to brighten a room with their innate beauty, she was so much more capable of illuminating even the darkest and dreariest of places with her sentient loveliness.

She was the first silvery droplet of rain unto a dry, cracked desert floor; the blessed first rays of golden shafts of sunlight warming frozen and struggling bodies; she was the eternal flower of Beauty, a constant source of luminous revelation in a world grown over by ugliness and ruin and disease. To see her, to smell her jasmine-scented wind pass by, to touch her smooth, tanned and toned flesh, moved her audience to admiration and awe.

For there to be Light, Darkness must first exist; for Joy to exist, Sorrow must consume the landscape; to have exuberant, irresistible Life, horrible, foul Death must first howl mercilessly across a bleeding, blood-soaked sky; for Health to rise up soulfully and glide gracefully across the burnished floor of white marble—Disease, bloated, cruel, tyrannical Disease— must first soar up here and there, indeed, everywhere, riding like a squealing harpy on the shoulder of mother, father, sister, brother, friend and relative.

To behold Lake Seville was to behold all things that people perceived as electrifyingly alive and singular in creation; she understood she had been blessed with physical and mental attributes mere mortals asked for and intellectuals burned to possess, and it fed her light steps upon the surface of the earth. She heard the murmuring chorus of whispers as she grew up. "Fortunate girl, so lovely and talented and so full of life and radiant health; why, she can be whatever she wants to be, the world is at her delicate feet, there is not a man who will not grovel before her, no woman who will not secretly adore her."

And she did want it all.

People expected her to exhibit her special treasures just as the world expects a rare jewel to yield its spectacular luster and sheen to them.

In the exclusive, private elementary school she attended, she would, on a whim, stand up and gracefully dance across the hard maple wooden floors; the teacher, taken aback, would sigh as the girl's classmates sat in awe, applauding; and yes, the teacher soon found herself vigorously clapping because she too yearned to be like the remarkable little mistress. The girl would recite mature poetry from memory and with passion, whenever asked, and she never displayed an ounce of apprehension or fear in the execution of that or any other task at the school. She was truly a queen among princesses, a princess among duchesses, noblewoman among slaves and servants, yet humble and kind to everyone.

Boys could see a mature beauty in her even when she was still a young teen; an astute observer could imagine how magnificent her physique would be when she reached womanhood, to wit: the rich luster of her thick, long, curly, light-golden-brown hair that hung down her back in lustrous waves—she did not dye or artificially streak her magnificent mane, as she thought this common and vulgar; her translucent, smooth skin; and her eyes were a regaling polychromatic collage—like a brilliant and vivacious desert sunflower bursting with vitality—from the frosty, milky-white sclera pools of opalescence, to an inner-radiating, emerald-green iris outside of a chocolate-colored gleaming pupil—all sang a song of vibrant, robust life; her rosy high cheeks, her thick brown eyelashes, her small nose and strong, ample limbs, all augured fleshly perfection.

As she matured, the prophecies of bodily delight came true, and men trembled before her and willingly played the fool for her slightest glance in their trembling direction.

And Lake knew it, and delighted in it; she bathed in this adulation of her gorgeous, tantalizing flesh that she conditioned with hard exercise, and she understood her mystical power over these seemingly infantile male creatures who would do anything to be in her company.

At eighteen years of age, she dated men who were heirs to financial empires; she attended formal parties on private yachts and at elaborate billionaire-sponsored balls, vacationed on privately owned islands, dated princes and dined with kings and queens, flirted with men who controlled politicians and nation-states; it was her life as she had always known it, as she expected it to be, knew it must be, and began to demand that it must remain, forever.

Her family and their ranking in society had isolated her from the rest of creation.

"I am who I am, others are who they are; I play this role, it is mine to keep," she would sometimes giggle to herself as she gazed at her serene beauty in the full-length mirror. Her comely looks recited their own symphony when she gazed at her astonishing symmetrical perfection: the naturally arched, thick brown eyebrows and her full, luscious cheeks and the delicate cut of her round face. Her legs were supple and strong from exercise and proper nutrition, and her shapely, full-buxom figure benefited, as did the rest of her divine form, from having a singular colony of superior genetics.

As she grew older, any errant message of empathy for the world was immediately intercepted and paralyzed by the pulsing eyes and flashing white smile set in her peaches-and-cream complexion. She often thought, as she gazed into her scintillating lovely face, "Should the rose become a weed out of sadness for it? I should think not! That poor weed needs something to inspire it; it needs a model of Beauty, too! What is wrong with Beauty? Is it a crime? Must we all become loathsome and fat to appease people who are either born plain or live lives full of slothfulness and fast food excuses? I am who I am, and I take my rightful place as heir to a legacy I will toil at to keep." She was forced to giggle at this silly declaration. "If I were ugly, then ugly I would be," but then she smiled, mischievously, "but I am not! So, there you have it...and my burden, as well!"

She attended a prestigious college, which became to her simply another base of operations with which to conduct her global affairs. She could vacation anywhere in the world, attend any prestigious event by private jet and, to her utmost delight, ship her Lamborghini Huracan overseas to Europe, her Ferrari 458 Speciale to South America, and keep her McLaren 650S as her "indigenous ride" in America; and stay in a mansion owned by her family or family's business or friends, or the finest rental homes and hotels: the Soho Townhouse in Manhattan for a mere shrug of one hundred thousand dollars a month, or a sixteen-thousand-foot rental in Holmby Hills in Los Angeles, for a mere trifle of two hundred thousand dollars a month; the Royal Suite at Hotel Plaza Athénée, Paris, for a mere pittance of forty thousand dollars a night; or villas: were she and her little playmates in Italy, then they swooped over to the Castello di Galbino, in Tuscany, a castle that spoke of the Old World mystique of nobility and wealth with its nine bedrooms, maid service, and complete amenities, ensconced in the rich and fertile hills and woods; were they in Spain, then they stopped in for a frantic weekend at the luxury villa in Marbella near pristine beaches and exciting clubs; were they in Greece, then they stopped by for a mad dash at a villa in northern Crete that overlooked the Mediterranean Sea; but where she and her friends were caught up in this dreamlike whirl of opulence and freedom to conquer any geographical region in the grandest style, they sipped the most expensive wines: Domaine de la Romanée-Conti Grand Cru, Côte de Nuits, France; Henri Jayer Cros Parantoux, Vosne-Romanée Premier Cru, France; Le Pin, Pomerol, France; and ingested the finest foods and wore the latest, most lavish styles, and, perhaps, depending upon their whims, forsook the week or month of rent they had paid and departed after a few days in each grandiose palace. Her greatest worries, then, were the choice of vibrant colors and latest styles for her magnificent dresses, an importunate blemish on her flawless face, and the nagging lack of hours in the day to accomplish all the merriment she planned. She slept in between the glorious moments.

And there was always a constant supply of adoring suitors, ready and eager to romance her; upon this weary fact, her grandmother, Lady Camille Seville, sat Lake down one wintry day and divulged those secrets women keep close to their bosom.

"Darling," she began, in her Georgian drawl as she sat on the silken sheets of her granddaughter's bed, "this world is not kind to exceptional creatures, be they handsome or magnificently brilliant." She laid her aged, wrinkled bare hands on her own silken purple pajamas. "Either they are ignored or abused; in the end, my love, it is best to be just either warm or cool—not hot or icy—but, darling, just to be good inside," and she clutched her heart as if she sought to spill out its ancient secrets to her granddaughter.

"Oh, Grandmother," Lake protested, meekly, "how can you say such a thing? Everyone wants to be handsome! Why, everyone says I look just like you when you were young—and you're still so beautiful!"

"Oh, child," she said, gravely, "if only I could allow you to see who I truly was, and what I truly am now! O, Beauty, accursed suitor!"

Lake, her thoughts unassembled by the forlorn inflection in the voice of the woman who had raised her, sat silent, intent on learning.

"Oh, Lake," her grandmother began once more, looking up now, her tired, old eyes wet with regret, "life is for the young and healthy; how strange life is, my darling girl." She was now entranced by an era she desired to retrieve. "It is only with age, miserable, decaying old age, that you know the truth about how you should conduct yourself, and then you can't go back. How cruel! No second chances, even when you sincerely repent; why, to have youth again, how noble I would be, then!" She closed her tired eyes. "The world is so esoteric, impossible to know unless you put quite a bit of intellectual effort into it; it seems so backward, so upside down and all jumbled up and inside out; youth, youth, to go back and be young again, but this time to do what I know is right; but would I fail again, are there no excuses for the elderly who had their chance? Youth, youth, youth," she murmured, swaying to and fro on the crumpled, silken sheets.

The delicate swish, swish of the exorbitant wealth of the Italian handcrafted, chestnut Baldacchino Supreme bed with its ash wood canopy sent sound waves to the ivory statues and

jade washbasin and the original Van Gogh and Picasso paint-
ings and the five-hundred-square-foot closet with two hundred
tailor-made dresses and the eighty pairs of handmade shoes
bought from the finest shops around the globe. An ordinary
thing flung into this room would have suffocated.

"The world is comedy, dear, a tragic comedy because we
allow it to be, thus," she continued, her opal-blue eyes opened
now; "the world is for the young and strong; they live, they love,
they yearn and do not despair and dream of impossible realities;
they move us forward and have families and create a distinct
signature upon their world with their optimism; but then ruin
comes in all its malevolent forms—illness, death, pain, catastro-
phes—the reign of the aging generation is ephemeral, because
new, bright and courageous youth comes up and they fight the
wars and cleanse the land of debris and they build and live and
love and yearn; and the world goes forward, while the old suffer
slowly, the tragic old fools, who struggle to live and regret, and
die for lost days, even those rich old fools who use the young
as fodder to enrich their coffers; what good is money if one is
decaying inside?" She let her head fall back, her eyes closed
again as she swayed back and forth, arms embracing herself, her
voice low and full of a profound melancholy. "If only I could go
back, back, back to the beginning of everything, what I would
do; O, yes, what I would not do, if I were strong enough." She
sat still, her eyes still, her small body rocking slowly back and
forth. "I suppose," she barely whispered, "that is what Heaven is."

The disturbed archaeology of her youth lay discovered,
bare bones bleached from the acid rays of a bitter sun, her
constitution of Being now proven to have been written on the
soft, gray, permeable shores of life.

She opened up eyes that were captured by the baggy folds
of old age, sad eyes sunk into a wrinkled face that yearned for

the freedoms of youth. "Lake, you are so young, how can I tell you what you cannot yet see? I can only tell you of admonitions, signs to see and signs to compel you to hesitate and listen—this is important, Lake—to pause and look about oneself when something feels and looks wrong." Her voice was full of a pleading passion that sought to drive its meaning into the soul of the listener. "Youth latches onto an idea and bleeds it straight ahead, with no concern for what is left or right or up or down, as if glorious youth will bring you to victory and protect you, if only because you're so young and noble and so full of love for life; as if, as if…" She seemed to lose her thoughts, and she frowned as she searched for the answer; and then, she whispered, ardently, "As if your pursuit of what you think is rightfully yours to pursue will protect you from the inevitable." She nodded her head in remembrance. "I was golden Youth, once, Youth without restraint or remorse or pity."

Lake sat dumbfounded, silenced by an organic muzzle that was slowly spun by each lamentation pouring from the lips of a woman who had spent her youth romancing the most powerful men in the country, met privately with presidents and billionaires, married a media mogul, buried him, increased the empire he began, influenced public policy and politicians, watched Lake's mother and father die in an automobile crash, and despite it all, raised Lake as her own daughter; and now, her grandmother proclaimed her debts to society as never before.

"I hate oldness," her Grandmother Camille continued, as if choking on the very black and sordid idea of advancing age; "every day it mercilessly opens you up and lets out sins that you threw onto the rubbish heap." She shook her head, her voice full of sorrow. "There must be some way to bury these sins forever." She gasped and threw out her arms and stretched them upward. "Come back, precious little Camille." She wept now, and looked to her granddaughter and took her trembling hands; when she spoke, her voice was urgent, her face pleading, and when she gazed at Lake, her eyes were isles of desperation. "One day, you will meet a man who might make you happy, but you won't recognize him because you aren't who you should be—you've been corrupted, sweetheart; one day, he'll be there, right in front of you, and you will need to run to him, because he will be good and kind, a real man, a true man; but through your jaundiced eyes, you will dismiss him. O, Lake, to find a man who truly loves you and to have a family and be happy with him, and not care about money or power or meetings or deadlines, but to just be happy and be in love, and see each other every day and see your children grow up, to grow up with them, to grow old as they grow older, and be there whenever they need you; this is what you need, my darling, what we all need; just love and family, and when you have that, you can go anywhere and do anything because you will all have each other; and all you need, my precious child, all you need is love; to love each other is the greatest gift on earth; and not to have it, you are just old and dead inside too early—yes, you just die too early." She grasped both of Lake's hands. "Close your eyes and see him, Lake, see him now, in your mind, this man who can make you truly happy; please, Lake, look at this man who will love you not for your Beauty or wealth, but for simply who you are."

Lake, weeping now, said, "Yes, Grandmother," and she closed her eyes.

A knock came to the wine-colored Honduran mahogany door. "Ten minutes, Mrs. Seville."

"Yes," Camille said, in a voice suddenly full of the power of authority, and then she whispered, "another meeting of the Board with CEO and President Camille Seville." She grew resolute. "I would give it all up, all of it, the power, the glory, the fame, all of it, for the right man; I would wander the earth, for him I would live free and simple; for love, Lake, for real love, I would give up anything because all of it means nothing if you don't know the serenity of God-given, natural, sweet, sweet love; love is all you need, Lake, love is nourishment for the mind and heart and soul; without love, my precious, Lake, all is evanescent, all is lost, all is dead."

She sat up, rigid, fearful, thinking, "I am dead, dead to life, dead, dead, dead to what life should be." But then determination swept over her. "I won't allow that to happen to you anymore, my faithful and beautiful Lake, not you, not again, I should have known better, it's all my fault: I indulged your every whim because you were the only good and decent thing in my life—perhaps I loved you too much, loved in you what I once was and wanted it to flourish; I must be strong," and she held her close as they both wept. "I won't let them seduce you like they did me," and then she said, in a whisper barely audible, "I had my chance at love, and I didn't recognize what it was, how great it was, how rare it was, and now, I feel so hollow inside, and all the money and power in the world…"

Reality for Camille was that she was in control of a corporation that had more than four hundred billion dollars annually in sales, and consequently, her life was dictated by the needs of this avaricious monolith that was growing like a spoiled child, a life severed into tight and tidy segments, fast and concise, no time for excess talk; but now, with her granddaughter, she could be ordinary, the one role she yearned for, that of grandmother to her only grandchild, whom she saw as a blossoming woman capable of surviving in a world of gross temptation and easily accessible sin.

In an hour's time, she was in a private jet flying to another state for the Board meeting, where she wielded power expertly over her obedient adjutants in their dark gray, fourteen-thousand-dollar Brooks Brothers custom suits, their William Fioravanti bespoke twenty-thousand-dollar suits, their Ermenegildo Zegna suits that topped twenty-two thousand dollars; and one man even wore a William Westmancott suit that cost more than seventy thousand dollars. "The fools think clothes make the man, as if the more money spent, the higher the degree of respect," she sometimes scoffed at them in the dark fortress of her sharp mind. "Gerald, that arrogant popinjay, wears a suit that costs nearly as much as a nice little home," and she would wax sentimental, and then think, "Why not a good Armani Collezioni suit I saw on a representative yesterday—he looked handsome and fit in it; why, I would have more respect for these men if they would come in blue jeans and a white t-shirt, if that helped them to be better at what they do." One day, she did come to the Board meeting in her house clothes, a very comfortable and cheap and dull-looking blue-and-white-checkered cotton dress; there was talk of psychological testing for her the next day by two Board members, and when she heard tell of it, she roared.

For three months, she cogitated upon a plan for Lake, and then one fine, clean, brilliant bright blue Summer day, when the mind is free of Winter's pouting reign, she happened upon a story that she had once read to Lake.

The tale was about a puppy that yearns to be a big dog so he can be old enough to fight the other dogs in the neighborhood that were at war with his family; but one day, when the puppy was nearly grown, it was injured when its master accidentally ran over its back hind legs with a car. The puppy, now an adult, grieved that it could not fight, but during its convalescence, it discovered the world about it, and grew to love Nature and People and even honor dogs outside of its family. When the dog could finally walk, it assembled all of the dogs in the neighborhood for a peace treaty, wherein he established his profound ideas into their savage hearts. The dog wars thus ended.

"Lake," Camille whispered to herself, "for you, I will do this marvelous gesture of love."

Four months hence, her plan formulated was then executed.

It was during a skiing trip to the Swiss Alps that Lake first fell ill. The physician at the local hospital thought that perhaps she had suffered from appendicitis, but this proved wrong; back in the States, she saw several specialists, all of whom were baffled by her sudden loss of weight, diarrhea, vomiting, fever and chills. One day, she fainted while driving, and in the ensuing crash, broke two ribs.

"But she lives, she does, she lives still; yes, alive," Camille shouted to herself as she sat in her penthouse suite overlooking the ritzy, glittering guts of New York City. "Endure, baby, endure; you're young and strong; you're on your way, darling, you will adapt, learn to survive, overcome your obstacles," she murmured, imagining, as she did so, her loving words seeping into Lake's heart and soul and mind. But this talk did not soothe her anxiety as she sat drenched in clammy sweat, massaging her dry face. "We overcome those things which fail to destroy us, building our character..." But she sobbed, clutching her chest. "O, child, what have I done? I did it for you, all for you, nothing for me, for I am dead now, and the worms have heard my death knell, and move toward the digging grave..."

Her cell phone rang. "Grandmother, O Grandmother," Lake began, "I am so sick; O Grandmother, I need you so much..."

Camille fell to her knees, covering her mouth to mute her torment, cursing her daughter for marrying so young and dying so recklessly. "But I curse myself," she thought. She hugged herself as she lay on the plush white carpet, her knees drawn up to her chest as she listened to the building terror in the tremulous voice of her beloved granddaughter. "Hold on, child," she whispered, "hold on, you're a Seville…"

The burrowing wound in her soul suffocated her every waking moment, her every thought and word; it hounded her very dreams, in every imaginary scene; and presently, she could neither eat nor drink nor think without the howling specter of remorse and betrayal echoing in her waning mind. Her chest pains began to increase in earnest. "I know Death comes for me, to punish me for my wicked deeds, and I am glad. But it was not wicked! I did it to save a life; I know, I know what it is like to have lived and missed the purpose of life," and she fell to the ground in spasms, "but I won't let it happen to you, Lake! I won't!" She threw a shoe at her cell phone, which had not stopped buzzing. "I will die happy, as no one will make me into a mechanical beast, stitching me together, no sir, no ma'am; when I die, I die wholly human, my flesh and my blood and my bone in me, not dead man's blood…"

She visited her attorney, Matt Gershon, who sat incredulous, unable to speak as he listened to the strict rules of her new will; but he was her faithful servant, and carried out her orders.

Camille drove away from the law office, mumbling to herself. "She won't recognize him if she has money; she won't, so it has to be; she'll miss him, and I can't have that, no." She looked hard at herself in the rearview mirror. "The tragedy of mammon and power stops here and now." She shook her head, as if seeing the future. "I have to do this, for her, my little baby; I ruined her life, and only I can give it back; I must be strong. It is what becomes real in the end that matters." She smiled as her pious tears, trapped in her authentically flabby cheeks, sought downhill progress. "Out of a shapeless form, a distinct form will appear, born from strife." She felt a crushing pain slice her sloughing body in twain. "The sooner I die, the better for her…"

Camille awoke, her silver Jaguar still idling as it sat on the side of the road, and instinctively she looked into the mirror, and gasped, for one side of her face was now frozen in a hideous death mask.

Lo, she had welcomed Death, but now that its frosty grip lay upon her limp body, she feared it as does a child the howling darkness.

But she screwed up her courage. "I won't die among people, God grant me that," she sobbed, feeling the uneasy gait of her injured heart, and drove away.

In four hours' time, in four long hours of swerving across the road and nearly crashing and feeling numbing pain and various spasms of pain in her chest, she moved closer to her goal; despite times of fainting and resting and weeping, she gathered strength for the task at hand.

She finally came upon the big house that sat so serenely in the midst of open fields of tall grass and orange trees; it was her birth home, and she had grown up there among the citrus orchards and open fields and rolling, green hills and the idyllic song of Nature; but when she was twenty, home developers had turned the open spaces into open pots of gold by dropping cookie-cutter homes where once bountiful wildlife had flourished. She had rebelled against this act, protesting at City Hall, vowing to defy the powerful developer and their stooges inside the halls of local government; of course, she had lost, until she acquired vast amounts of wealth, and then had bought all of the shapeless tract houses within a one-mile radius of her birthplace, and immediately had them demolished. She hired a company to tend to the replanted trees and open fields, but had not been back in forty years.

Her home was perfectly preserved, its verdant lawn cut each week by gardeners, its inner environment cleaned of dirt and debris by workers once a month.

One of the most powerful women in America lay against the smooth brown leather interior of her car, exhausted, but her will was stronger than her bodily misery, and she proceeded to open the door, only to fall out onto the soft green grass that divided the clean white driveway from the long rows of red and yellow and white roses. There she lay in a crumpled heap for some time, panting like a dying soldier for hard breath, feeling the heavy weight of a corrupt body plow her to the moist ground. Twilight stitched a feathery black blanket over her tiny form.

After some time, she commenced to crawl, first up to the cement porch, then past the two steps, where she propped herself up and took out her key ring; and on that gold key ring was a key to this house she had not seen since she was thirty-five. Slowly she slipped it into the black hole and lay against the door.

She fell inside, young and innocent again.

Her inglorious past was gone now, wiped clean by her presence in this cherished sanctuary, erased by the fresh, ripe smells of her glorious childhood; and as she breathed in the cherished memories of simpler times, she breathed out the rust and infection of acquired wealth.

With adulthood came freedom, but with freedom had come small forays into darker territories that enlarged once her great power and wealth increased, but occluded the Inviolate

Light that radiated from Love and Goodness from touching her heart; and childhood meant the unknowing of the want of those things destructive to the heart and soul and mind of adults. "All I ever wanted was to be loved," she sobbed, crawling on the glossy hardwood floor as her warm tears streamed freely down her flushed face. "How did I lose my way?"

She navigated along the hallways with her eyes shut, for in her unguarded moments these past years, she had dreamed not of her daily life among the upper tiers in the corporate world, but of times long ago, in this very house, where once she roamed free of worries that plague us all when we grow up.

Now, she was ten years old again, hearing the unrestrained laughter and love of her brother and sister, hearing again the simple joys and easy, honest language of real life; presently, she found her bedroom, and she caressed the white wooden doorframe with her head. She wept regret. "I'm home, baby, I'm home," she murmured, and she continued her straining movements until she reached her childhood bed, and reached up to the same soft, white blanket she had used, and felt the faithful flock of dolls still awaiting the return of their mistress. "Raggedy Ann," she exclaimed, as she caressed its pleasant cloth and yarn form, "you waited for me."

She held the red and white doll as if it were an umbilical cord while she crept under the soothing covers. "I'm home, Mama, Papa, I'm home; your little girl is home; Linda, Jimmy, your little sister has come back," she whispered, curled up now, snug and warm. She could smell the sweet spice of eggnog in the air, the rich aroma of brown rim cookies, the laughter and tears and talk of family love, but then she felt the crushing pain of her pounding chest and paralyzed flesh; her breathing was labored and quicker, as if her body was sputtering on fumes. "Oh, everyone, I feel so warm, I'm not ice anymore." She knew why she had come home, for this was the only time she would come home, when she could come home, without shame, without guilt, without sin in her heart. "How could I have come in here and sullied this holy place with what I have done?" she thought, in the dying embers of her mind. "Could I have not given up all of it before and returned to my home? But I want my little baby to do that; O God, watch over her, watch over her for me," and she imagined a nacreous cloud of love falling over her granddaughter, shielding her from all harm. "O God, what I have done in sin and selfishness, I confess to you, and I tell you that it was all wrong; look into my heart and see if I speak the Truth." The once-mighty Camille Seville shut her eyes. "O God," she thought, "I renounce my kingdom, let me into Yours." Calm smoothed her pained countenance, and then, she peacefully and happily gave up her fleshly life.

Her car was tracked to her ancestral home the next day.

The newspaper reporters were told that she had been visiting her birth home when she had a heart attack. The rich and powerful can bend the light rays of truth so far into themselves that the result is always what they want the world to see.

Lake mourned.

The Will

Weeks passed, and the will of Camille Dolores Seville was read.

"Curiouser and curiouser," Matthew Gershon thought, watching the faces of relatives and friends and associates as the incredible facts were hatched into the stuffy, hot air.

The bulk of Camille's fortune would go to charities, especially those organizations that, in the words of the great lady, "acted as if they were charged by God to give succor to the poor, the infirm, the elderly and the oppressed."

"Lake Claudia Seville," the attorney continued, and all of them, all of the flustered little faces and blanched faces whose gaping mouths had already swallowed bitter gall, turned toward the girl they were most envious of; they had already lost their inheritance, and now they eagerly hoped Lake would lose hers too, or, if not, they had already sworn in the interim between the reading of the will, they would wrest heaps of loot from her.

"As for Lake Seville," the attorney continued, grim-faced, feeling hot inside, his heart racing, his mind squirming from embarrassment and humiliation, "she will receive no monetary compensation, and will have great understanding."

Lake felt her senses drain from her body and flow to the fine brown carpet. "Nothing," echoed loudly in her swirling thoughts, but more importantly, "O Grandmother, I still love you."

Those around her, relieved and smug now, offered false sympathies to her as their wicked schemes left their wicked hearts.

"We will fight it," some said as they stood up, although they knew it would be in vain.

The room presently vomited itself of the money-grabbers as if they were poison to it, until only Lake and the attorney were left. She sat in a red-velvet-cushioned chair, looking somberly at the attorney. "I know my grandmother, Mr. Gershon, and she would have left me something to explain it all," she said, clear-eyed.

"Good girl," Gershon murmured to himself. "As a matter of fact, she did have a letter," he said, and after he handed it to her, he left her alone.

The letter was handwritten in black ink by Camille, and it said, thusly:

"Dearest Lake,

My precious girl, you know how dearly I love you, and I know you love me; and I also know that when love exists between two members of a family, no material objects, no human outsider, no legal arbiter can intercede between them and cause dissension. The faith you have in me, and I in you, will sustain you.

With All My Love,
Grandmother

Lake looked up, frowning. "Where is the rest of it?"

"That is it," Gershon said, upon returning to the room.

She shook his hand, and graciously thanked him for his devotion to her grandmother.

Lake was twenty years old; her father and mother were dead, her grandmother's older brother and sister were dead, and their few children antagonistic toward her, and she was, now, for the first time in her life, responsible for herself. But she refused to cry over the reading of the will, for that would lend itself to a betrayal of her grandmother's sacred image to her; indeed, only time wrapped in bitterness and pain and suffering can efface that which was built by tears and blood and Love. Lake would persevere, she reasoned, and seek to find answers.

A sparkling, crystal-clear stream that abruptly becomes polluted will not die quickly, but seek to purge itself, all the while acting as if it were still pure and healthy.

A month later, Lake sailed on the *Queen Isadora* cruise ship, whose list of passengers for this exclusive journey was politicians and business tycoons and their entourage. Lake came as a guest. She felt at home in the regal cabin and playing her part in the meeting of other travelers—laughing here, smiling when necessary there, talking now, quiet then—all those things she had done for so long that had become innate. She understood her role as well as a daughter at a family reunion, for these people were family—the family who controlled inordinate amounts of wealth and power in the world. She reasoned she was as much one of them as a peasant girl living in a small adobe house is part of her village: the peasant girl belonged there, and Lake here; other people where they understood their role in society, there. To wear diamond necklaces and dance in handmade gowns that, if sold, could feed and clothe, provide shelter and medicine, improve infrastructure and build necessary modern facilities such as schools and hospitals for a poor village in a third-world country for a generation; and talk with men and women who controlled vast business empires and seemingly unlimited power—this was the only world she had known growing up.

She loved to dance, and during the ballroom waltz, she was laughing and smiling and ignoring what was growing inside her; but in a moment, she could no longer ignore this haughty mistress who sought to announce its vile presence to her world. She began to bleed from her nose, very obnoxious and very bright red was the blood that gushed out and onto her white gown, and then she yielded up a fount of noxious vomit. She panicked herself straight into the bathroom.

Her swift escape past the dancers had excited them into speculation and condemnation, but the captain of the ship assured them it was not food poisoning. Rumors of Lake's

prior poor health began to circulate like toxic gas in the grand
hall, and then these wagging tongues began to promote the
royalty of verbal flogging, gossip. "Well," said one cadaver-
ous-looking female glob of doughy white skin, facelifts, and
exotic plumage, "that was unpleasant." And once a malignant
ball is rolled down a crowded hill, it collects more poisonous
dirt. "Certainly," said another old female living-stone statue
whose face was unnaturally smooth as taut silk, but her insides
as rusty and clogged as an abandoned water pipe at the dump,
"she could have the decency to spill her blue blood elsewhere;
why, I pay good money not to see such awful things. This
is the kind of distasteful news that happens to those dreadful poor and uneducated people who have no easy access to
medical care." This squeezed another old woman to spill the
stale contents of her wrinkled mind onto the polished floor:
"Thinning blue blood, I hear; left out of the will, I hear; it's
money that matters at the top, you know, not money once
had." She snorted and held her muddy-brown-colored wig
and round head on high. "Her kind rows the boat, we own
it; well, she never earned her money, and now she'll have to
earn her own." There was hardly disagreement among the
finely painted and perfumed ladies as they commented on the
young woman who had disrupted their pleasant party, and in
their private minds, they knew why—for the greatest fear of
the wealthy and powerful is a fall from grace, and to observe
this in others, at least, is a vicarious pleasure that keeps them
thinking that it is always the other poor fool.

   As it was, Lake spent the remainder of the trip in isolation,
disgraced and feverish while her friends were sympathetic on
their cell phones from their safe, faraway cabins.

   Once the ship docked, Lake never heard from those friends
again, once more proving that they were fair-weather friends,

and slowly, just like a person without a country, she slowly lost her exclusive membership in the highest power tier of America.

In the upper social strata of a society where enormous deposits of fabulous wealth are the marker of success, there is no pity for those members who fall, for their very existence, their very being is for the accumulation of other people's money; it is these fabulous riches that drive their decisions and their fiery thinking, their mating habits, their relationships with family and friends and relations; it is the deep mounds of glittering riches that choke their minds and create a moral philosophy that ultimately exists to defend their empire of divine wealth; for such creatures to exist without wealth would render them cold, naked and lost. It is the long rows of gleaming gold that clothes them, schools them, comforts them, fills their very white spittle and courses through their watery aristocratic blood; it colors their dangling verbs and pungent adjectives, accents their arrogant nouns, creases their punctuation with crackling disdain, it opens and shuts the silver mouthpiece through which they communicate with a world they scorn; it fills their liquid eyes with a shining image of an impregnable fortress on Mount Olympus, wherein they reside with the gods of old and unfurl their corporate souls for all to admire. Wealth becomes their honey-scented nature as they are nourished in the gold-leafed cradle of privilege; and thus, they live in an enchanted forest where they control daily life, for to be without wealth for these lords of power is to be clearly undone, and to be undone is to be unknown, unfulfilled and unloved, and ultimately, unable to simply be.

Lake had been formally banished from the Kingdom of the New Royals, her name expunged from their sacred Book of Riches; and as she no longer drank sweet nectar, the fabled drink of the gods, nor ate ambrosia, the fabled food of the gods, she no longer had a physical address in their affluent society, and now drifted and hung and slipped from one wavering caste to the other. But it is not negotiable for one to leave the diamond-studded halls of power and wealth, and she miserably lifted up her hands in supplication as she fell deeper into the esoteric realm of common society—but they would not reach out to her nor offer her comfort. Poor Lake, her once scintillating armor of appeal engendered by her gorgeous physical beauty gone, wore her illness horribly, her gauntness terrifying now to the opulent rich who stood afar from her and gasped, for her bony mask that proclaimed mortality and malignancy was now making them recede into the comforting shadows that were cast by hordes of diamonds and pearl palaces; poor Lake, who had previously eviscerated the beauty of every woman who stood next to her with a natural beauty: she never wore makeup, never streaked nor colored her hair, for she often had said, "Does the Monarch butterfly need to add streaks to her beautiful wings, or the red ruby change its color? How ridiculous! For when you do such things, you alter who you are and were meant to be, and then live the life of someone else who was born that way; I am me, and that is the only person I will ever be." Poor Lake, with her proud, athletic, erect posture, her translucent, luscious skin, her thick, light-golden-brown, silky smooth hair that she combed slightly to the side at the top, and then combed back so that it fell luxuriously down her lean back, with her gleaming, emerald eyes and effervescent smile, was now a dull, dry, emaciated-looking girl who could not stand in one spot too long without leg cramps or violent muscle spasms or hacking coughs or nosebleeds or abrupt spews of vomit; poor Lake Seville, who once was the subject of jealousy of every woman around her and the desire of every man near her, was now a creature with scaly skin and red blotches on her face and a sickly smell that ripped right through her strong perfume.

But she was holding on to the only life she had known, the only life she thought existed, should exist, the one life she thought she deserved because she was who she was; somehow, she reasoned, everything would be as it once was, if only because she could imagine no other life.

But she became very visual at such spectaculars, and vomiting on her chiffon gown or fainting onto banquet tables or freely bleeding from the nose onto horror-stricken guests garnered her very bad press, and slowly, the fragile, muscular chords that composed her exclusive society frayed until, at last, invitations no longer arrived. Her acquaintances deserted her, her creditors hounded her, her life crumbled into the muddy ash that sat upon her slowly forming grave.

Disease is a selfish mistress.

Lake would travel to the homes of friends whom she had known growing up, expecting the same warm reception she had always received, but even they shunned her, because they intuitively knew where she now stood in the silent rankings in their exclusive community. It was the old memory in their mossy cells that directed them away from her, an old memory that sat in thick layers in their reptilian brains, an old memory that looked down upon the world, a hearty disdain for Mankind once hatched in the tyranny of a primordial soup.

The only friend who would talk to Lake was Lisbeth Hartford. "Lake, you know I love you, as I would a sister, had I one," she said, she who was the daughter of a shipping magnate, and was readying herself for a business trip to Los Angeles. "And like a good sister, I will tell you all." She smiled mischievously, as she was wont to illuminate hypocrisy everywhere. She stood up fully erect as she spoke with a countenance flaming with indignation and a sweet memory. "I slapped Cynthia Wainwright last week when she suggested that you need to be with your own kind, down at the anorexia nervosa convention; and I said to her, after I slapped the slattern with the biscuit face," and she tilted her head, "and I mean it to express my idea of both classical definitions of the unhappy word—I said that she needed to be with her own kind down at the Low-Class Hookers Convention."

Lake laughed. Lisbeth was the only person who had helped her financially and emotionally in the past crucial months.

Lisbeth sat down with her friend and held Lake's hands with her hands. "Little sister, don't you know what you have gone and done? Why, you've done the unspeakable, the most contemptible act imaginable to rich folk: you have presented them with a presentiment of what and probably will befall them, and they desire to set the Furies upon you; why do you think they surround themselves with the finest things, even when they do not desire all of it? Why, my dear, it is to erase a memory of ordinary things, of course! Poverty disgusts us, and you, bad girl, you went and got yourself not only broke, but ill, too; for shame! Fall on your sword, good miss!" She shook her blond head. "You came into their private cocoon reminding them of death, inevitable, terrible death, that they will die, get old and sick; and you, Lake dear, are the official Apocalypse, all four loathsome riders rolled into one mere woman, and then they remember they are not in Heaven, are not angels, nor can they buy their way into God's Kingdom—though the good Lord knows they have tried to buy Heaven itself—and must be amused." She flung her head back. "What a woman to excite such fears in such power brokers; O, how the filthy rich loathe not being able to control all things—and death and illness are their greatest nemesis. Now, Lake, my soul sister, there are exceptions to every rule, and if you are ill but worth a billion or so, they may tolerate you; but, you, girl, you committed a second sin as well, losing your money, which they consider the measure of all things—money, that is—honesty, self-worth, success, every virtue imaginable; to them, now, you're nothing but a helpless beggar; if you came to their home for dinner, they would make you walk past a metal detector on the way out to make sure you hadn't stolen their precious silverware." She smiled. "Why, I am sure they have told their butlers to make sure you don't steal their bathroom towels." But then her lusty glee faded, for Lake was no longer smiling, and so she hugged her childhood friend. "I know it's been hard since your grandmother died, but you know you have friends."

Lake began to weep. "Do I?" and she buried her thin face in her clammy, chalky hands.

Lisbeth picked up her cell phone and instructed her chauffeur to delay her flight departure.

"Oh, no," Lake protested, "please don't let me ruin your…"

"Don't be ridiculous," Lisbeth said, reassuringly, "I would give away my fortune to have the old Lake back, so what is one business trip canceled? And shame on you for continually refusing to join me on these sojourns."

"Well, you know I just didn't want to get sick…"

"How about the last doctor I sent you to?" Lake shook her head forlornly. "That doesn't matter; we will keep trying until we find something." She hugged her friend again. "We will go through this together as family."

The two friends spent the day together, and then Lisbeth journeyed forth on her trip. The next day, Lake received a message that the private jet Lisbeth was on had crashed, a jet that was a replacement for the one that had taken off without her the day before and landed safely.

Lake mourned the death of her last friend and confidante, mourned as she became ill, mourned as she sat in her exquisite apartment in New York City and bemoaned her fate; and in a month, her expenses slowly depleting, she mourned as she moved to California, driving her luxury car across the country and nearly crashing over and over again until she reached her destination. She found a small apartment in the small city of San Bernardino, and having decided to finish her education, enrolled in the university there to study English Literature. It was in the second chapter of her disrupted life that she had met the ill-looking young man at the health food store and the college library, and was repelled by his sickly appearance because he reminded her of her disintegrating health.

Conversations

The inside of his apartment was a world hitherto unknown to the sentient human population of the world; the primary mover of power centered not around specifically defined areas for living, but for the amassing and subsequent stacking of books. He had realized the only way to step back into the rushing stream of civilization was through breaking the esoteric code of medical literature, where he reasoned that a rare species of language resided, and that if he read them long and hard enough, he might discover a cure and then rejoin humanity; of course, reading dry prose often proved monotonous, and for companionship, he read novels, mostly nineteenth century, mostly European, and sometimes he read books on history and science and psychology and philosophy.

He had carefully constructed an entire paper civilization for himself from these books; whatever realms existed in the world—whatever realities, whatever Kingdoms, life-forms, inevitabilities, societies, histories in the world outside of his human touch—he re-created in this small sphere of influence, in this dusty, crowded theater, where he was the supreme ruler. Here, he could indulge in his private fantasies, interpret life his way, live his way, be a man, be a hero, a valued citizen instead of a cold lump of mottled clay that could never be molded into anything attractive to the female of the species.

His friends had married, had children, gained careers, profited from healthy bodies, and had separated themselves from him by virtue of mature lives; he was beginning to understand that a single man, because he had nothing to offer these people, could never have true friends who were married. It would take him many more years to clarify in his mind that married people obsess about their own families, their own children, their in-laws, their relatives, their friends, about trivial and milestone events, about special occasions and any occasion and all occasions if only to celebrate the occasion with family. He understood none of it, now, though bits and pieces of it wafted down to him from the cluttered, buzzing air; later, he would understand that two fathers could stand together and talk of wives and children, burn endless hours in raging debates about intimacy with their women, but a single man must be silent, must be an outside observer who can only imagine, whose remarks are vacuous and off the mark, disjointed, erroneous; if the single man is to join in at all in the life of families, it is for small events that are meaningless to him. The single man is the last phone call late at night when the husband is done with his family, when the husband's children are at peace in bed and his wife is appeased;

the single man receives the late-night phone call on occasion, when the husband has talked with cousins and other friends who have families; the single man is a needless filler to the married person, a meaningless extra topping easily discarded, easily missed, easily replaced by a sports show, a fine alcoholic drink, a car fixed, a movie watched, any trivial event with the blessed and all-encompassing family; to a married couple, the single man has no individual identity, except one that blends in with those cursed to be alone because of poor looks, poor health, or poor choices; and so, this is the fate of the diseased man who lives in the cold comfort of his own lonely shadow, to slowly and agonizingly recede every day deeper and deeper from the world until he is an amount too infinitesimally small to weigh on the scale of life, his number-ranking in society occurring when a digit is added to the biggest known number in existence, until he finally slips through the last outstretched hands of those selfless few who seek to catch the dispossessed, and finally dissolves like foam on the sea, into the tangled labyrinth of the underground home of lost, wandering souls.

Consequently, Tony was alone, except for the company of his antagonizing mistress, Disease, who daily flailed him for his failures to exterminate her. "I will not tolerate infidelity," she cried, rushing him to the bathroom with loathsome bodily ailments. "I am a jealous lover! You will not leave me until I release you, and only then into the fertile boiling tar-pit where you will have fat, yellow worms coming out of your empty, bony eye sockets, and where my ravenous servant, the fiery red ant, will eat the remains of your decaying, viscous brain. Yes, my darling, I will stay with you until the end of your days; and when that delightful day dawns, you will not know, for I will pull you this way and that, proffering false hopes, providing false leads, pulling the golden thread with your blessed salvation heaped upon it right before your sad and pious eyes, its brilliant glare blinding you so that when you finally stumble into the charred pit, you will not know the way back." The impudent maiden of death batted her long, pink eyelashes as she inclined her head. "O, lover, don't you know that a prudent man marks his way along the perilous road?"

He could never abandon hope, lest he abandon himself.

Still, sometimes he was consumed by hopelessness as he researched in his small apartment; here, forlorn, he was dead to the world, and dead to himself; here, nothing mattered to him, not family, not friends, not job, nor the human race—only death, miserable, insufferable, inevitable death, whose increasing weight he felt daily, crushing him more and more, suffocating him, squeezing out his ebullience for life and his exclusive triune wit—charm, intelligence, humor—until he felt as a cold, clammy corpse shuffling along past vibrant, bustling life, who reaches out its skinny hand to touch this streaming life-force but is too frail to absorb its richness, its vitality, its energy and power; but his sickly touch only sent the living, breathing stream recoiling from him, for it intuitively knew the cadaverous face of those who live in the musty house of disease. In the oozing, black palm of Death, he lay nestled in a narcotic haze, embalmed by despair, feeding on the thorny roots of fatalism. "Let me die, let me die," he would whisper, "but I am already dead. This is not living, but death living, death awake, where I inhale its rank odor, where I am smothered by its arrogance." He would lie, melancholy, thus, for hours, already ensured of his morbid solitude by unplugging the irksome phone. He rarely had visitors. "Who will come by, but the undertaker?"

It was during one of these severe bouts of self-flagellation that a knock came to his door, to which he scowled, for he rarely answered it. "For the authorities I answer the knock," he would say, "and for no one else." But he paused. "Well, for my mother, yes." But then he quickly regained his bitterness. "The world has abandoned me, and I, them."

The knock came again, and he ignored it, again, and once more a knock, albeit diffident, resounded through the tiny living room, where he lay like one dead upon the dull, colorless carpet. He heard a female curse. "Gee, no magazine subscriptions today," he whispered, but then decided to see who the offender was, and so arose to see a fleeing image through the glass spy piece in the door.

It was she. His heart leaped. "What?" he whispered, incredulous. "What is that cuckoo bird doing here?" His mind pieced together possible scenarios. "She likes me, she has questions for me—no, you fool, she is harassing me! That's it, she has tracked me down, the emotionally disturbed woman!" He silently cursed. "The average man has a harem of women chasing him, and I have a psychotic female stalking me." He was forced to laugh. "Pathetic! But just what a male human monster like myself deserves—a female human monster," and he slapped his forehead violently with his open palm.

A minute later, the phone rang, at which he nearly leaped clear to the ceiling. "I forgot to unplug the menace," he shouted, upon seeing the importunate plastic jack still stuck in the white stucco wall. Resigned to fate, he answered it.

"Hello, may I speak to Anthony?" the voice asked, politely.

He had options here, of which lying was his most obvious. It was his method of choice, to lie, to deter conversations on the phone; alas, as this voice was female, he softened, and instead chose dubious caution. "May I ask who is calling?"

"Lake Seville." She had never told him her name, but he recognized the voice, for even in these brief words, her good articulation and superior tone heralded the division between aristocrat and commoner.

He closed his eyes and grimaced, knowing that once confronted with a foe who was not truly destructive, he could not be unkind to her in person, at least not initially. "Yes."

"So, you are home," she said, somewhat irritated. "Don't you answer your door?"

He wanted to lie, but then he thought of who she was. "Illness does things to people."

She had to be silent.

"I'm sorry," she said it, nearly without female contriteness, almost as if it were created in a mirror world, devoid of dimension and feeling, as if its utterance is only said to gain something. "I would like to come by," and she paused, "and I am sure you are wondering how I knew where you lived."

"It had crossed my mind."

"Well, I have a ridiculous memory for numbers, and then there are those terribly invasive but handy reverse phone directories; so, Anthony, may I come by?"

He looked about the enormous mess, and then said, hesitantly, "Well, I don't really have many visitors, and normally they don't just drop in..."

"I called last night and this morning, but no one answered."

Ah yes, he thought, I had unplugged the jack properly, then.

"Well, to tell you the truth, the place isn't really that clean, so why don't I meet you..."

"Anthony, I have to get gas, and after that, I'll be by; and Anthony, don't worry about the mess—you are a man, I expect it."

He closed his eyes as he put down the phone, shaking his head all the while, and as he opened them and looked out on the landscape of his place, a creeping, noxious stinging sweat began to cling to his face and balding scalp.

For, indeed, his place was truly an unpleasant oasis of clutter and debris and dust and cobwebs, stained tiles and carpet, black smudged walls, and seemingly uninhabitable and certainly indescribable bathrooms.

"The woman is mad," he cried in a guttural whisper, massaging his face, but unable to knead the terror from his thin, pale flesh; still, he set to work, assiduously attacking the most offensive and palpable sections of the non-symmetrical disaster zone. "The most good in the least amount of time," he cried, laughing, while scrubbing the yellow-stained porcelain kitchen sink in a fury. He glanced to the cheap plastic, cracked clock on the wall every minute, and every minute he seemed to gain more confidence that he could actually, noticeably improve the quality of his unkempt domicile in a few minutes of manic labor.

Five minutes elapsed, and he was already re-stacking books away from the door; then in a short minute, he was catching up thick mounds of dust with a wet rag from the top of the old wooden-framed nineteen-inch black-and-white television.

Ten minutes burned slowly and agonizingly by, and he, the human whirlwind, was now sweeping the kitchen floor of accumulated stale crumbs and discarded, weird-looking dead creatures.

Thirty minutes later, and he hesitated, once more, as he had in the last ten. "She isn't coming, she isn't," he said, breathing hard, but nonetheless, he moved on, cleaning maddeningly.

Two hours hence, and he sat, drenched in sweat, observing a small dent in what was a huge obstruction of freewheeling uncleanliness. "Well, at least I did something," he said to himself; "tricked again by a scheming woman. How many times will I try and kick the foot..." A rhythmic, delicate knocking vibrated against the white door. "Impossible," he declared, and without hesitation, opened the door pathway to his restricted sanctuary.

"Hello," Lake said.

"Got lost?" he replied, visibly irritated.

"No," she returned, smiling, "I decided you were right; I shouldn't have just come by; so, I went and had a coffee and a long read." She looked inside. "Nice."

"What were you reading—*Remembrance of Things Past*?"

She glanced at her silver Bulova watch. "I read that last month," she said, dryly.

"You're a regular comedian."

She smiled that unfortunate female smile that crushes male resistance the world over, a smile of sweetness and promise of pleasantness, to which, in accordance with his genetic code, he yielded the doorway and allowed her entry. Of course, he was a fool for any woman, any woman of any virtue or low caste, even women with unstable mental psychoses, any woman who was decently attired and physically pleasing, because he had never been with Woman, and he would pursue her despite ridicule and poor expectations for success.

Lake sat down on the tired gray sofa and set down her Michael Kors Lana brown and black leather tote, and Anthony stared at this odd circumstance, his perception of this scene coming in from a different angle, and on a different plane, for never had an unrelated woman taken up space on his very private furniture; and now, to think of his small apartment as it had been, all those years—void of a real woman—it seemed empty, lonely, and very wrong. The presence of Lake awakened the idea that there must be a woman at his side, which proffered hope to him.

She did not look about the room as if in judgment; it was not why she had come.

He looked at her more closely, now, desperate not to stare, but curious to dissemble the illusory framework of flesh and color and stylishly cut clothes before him. "There is a woman there, if I can drain away her scented mask, her artificial-rainbow hues—her requisite armor." But he never progressed beyond this pre-analytical stage, as her story now commenced. She was never one to meander around a bush.

"I thought about what you said, in the parking lot," she began, staring straight at him, never once glancing away to refresh her own identity; it was her way, after all, the way of all beautiful women, to take in the gaze of any man and devour it without hesitation or worry, "and I wanted to talk to you." He was about to interrupt, but held himself, knowing that to break her narrative would bring disharmony. "What you said about being alone…" He waited patiently for her to evince gratitude through verbal expression, but he was not rewarded. "I need someone to talk to; I need to talk to my own kind."

His outward expression was absolutely staid, although inside his thoughts were animated with astonishment. "She actually listened to me…" He inhaled the sweet aroma of her perfume and looked at the still-exquisite outline of her face, and he felt somewhat alive.

She let out a low "Hmm," and then smiled briefly. "I have learned that a person can tell you something one day, and you hear it, but it may not mean anything to you until much later."

"A case against nagging," he let slip, and then grimaced inside at his own stupidity.

She tilted her head, her high-collared, cinnamon-colored, imitation-fur coat rustling against her hair. "You don't know much about women, I see."

He could not deny the truth, but her remark leveled his enthusiasm and daring.

She sat upright, head adjusted straight up and down. "How long have you been ill, Anthony?"

He was still embarrassed by his verbal slippage. "Long enough," he answered, coolly.

"Are you going to share the history of your illness with me?"

He frowned, without thinking, without caring, as he so often did alone. "Where am I, in group therapy?" But he cursed himself, for he was acting as he did when alone, for that was when he could be spontaneous, talking to books, talking to himself, talking to the television, talking to anything and anybody inanimate or make-believe, for it was his way when isolated day after day and night after week after month, and, truly, he was still alone, even now, for he was still too much in his own universe, and could only begin to break through and touch hers.

She abruptly stood up, feeling vastly superior to the commoner before her, suddenly feeling foolish in her embarrassment. She was going to express gratitude for his time, but such formalities were for people she would meet and possibly need again; so, thus assured of her noble position and lack of his future company, she turned, walked toward the door, opened it carefully, and exited.

He stood, his head numb. "I am one of those who definitely needs therapy, to let cuckoo birds like that into my private sanctuary," he said, but he stated this in his normal voice, volume not adjusted for recently fleeing female guests, a volume accustomed to its pale, dumb surroundings as its soaring strength sifted through the open windows. He stood up and began to walk toward the kitchen, when the door banged open.

"Who do you think you are, calling me crazy?" Lake demanded, stomping her right foot, which was enclosed in her tan Ann Taylor high heel boot, her figure stopping under the invisible wooden-framed barrier that separated the inside from the outside.

Now, he was on a level playing field, wearing the fiery britches of intolerance. "Because you are," he began, cocksure, looking straight at her; "you're unstable and neurotic; so, please just leave." He stood now, his amused gaze weighed down and stretched to a swelling anger.

His cold words did not deter her from breaking the invisible barrier into his private domain, as if the idea of once asked in meant asked in again. "How dare you judge me without knowing me!"

He was still struck by the thinning remnants of her beauty, small pittance though it was, and this fact allowed her to gain an ounce of staying power; he felt shallow and weak, but secretly he was unrepentant. "She wouldn't be talking to me if she were well; well, ha! She would be spitting on me," he reasoned, observing her wrath, "but now is now." And he inwardly smiled, triumphant and pleased.

"Oh, but I do know you," he said, arrogantly; "you're easily reduced to a mere personality type." He offered her bits and tangled pieces of his growing wisdom of psychology learned, knowing she would be further infuriated, for from her he sought to feel the fresh, ripe tendrils of revenge creeping around him. He watched closely as she pursed her thin lips and pouted. "This is based on two observations: one, that you were once wealthy, and two, that once, and still, you truly are condescending."

Her face became flaccid, like a restorative calm after a violent storm. "You're not worth another…" she said, disgusted, and walked away.

"And I am supposed to feel guilty?" he shouted to her as she quickly vanished down the cement walkway, but he remembered his lowered position in life, and reminded himself that he was condemned to loneliness. "Wait," he cried, and then broke on through to the outside and walked out onto the black concrete of the parking lot. He observed her form not obeying his command as he approached her getaway vehicle. "Look," he said, as he came to rest next to her old and faded white Toyota Corolla, looking at her as she sat sulking inside its comforting womb. She turned the key.

"Look," he began, not wanting to sound as if he were begging, but then paused, looking about, feeling foolish. She wasn't leaving. He stepped closer. "Nine years ago I was just a regular fellow, and then one day I vomited, and I haven't been the same since." He hesitated. "It isn't like I talk to people about it; I know you understand; I know you can appreciate that. You are one of us."

She turned off the motor, and actually turned her mollified gaze toward him. "Thank you for telling me."

"Well, you can say 'thank you,' after all,'" he said, feigning exasperation.

He had smiled sincerely and largely as he said this, and thus, her normally offended nature let the words go unnoticed. She smiled, and then he said, "Say, may I take you to lunch? Maybe we can exchange sob stories," and then he cocked his head as if to impart a secret, and his tone dropped as he said, "my place is a little messy."

She nearly giggled. "Okay," but her voice grew serious, "but this isn't a date."

His inner man fell, but his outer man kept its outer shell of steely resolve. "Thank you for that clear delineation between business and pleasure."

Now, she cocked her head and just stared at him. "You're odd."

He laughed.

And later, they ate lunch, and talked of things that once were, of a world that had slowly and agonizingly evaporated before their imploring eyes, and the new one that changed every day and separated them from their ubiquitous yet distant brethren.

Camouflage

"I grew up swaddled in wealth," Lake began, inspecting her chicken salad and picking out these items she knew would offend her delicate digestive tract. Her demeanor reflected the tempest in her heart—her face changed from melancholy to weariness to mangled hope to a cursory joy, and then back again, as if a poisonous wet fog drifted past her thin face, descending to bring pain, ascending to bring pleasure. "To me, it was normal to have the finest of things." She paused, her arched, light-brown eyebrows knit in dismay. "I can see by your perplexed countenance that you do not approve of those who are surrounded by mammon, even if we inevitably acknowledge it." She wanted to say more, but she let him say something.

"Talking isn't doing," he said, nonchalantly, carefully inspecting the steaming hot, plain russet potato that was smothered in plump, ripe raisins, nonpareil almonds, and extra virgin olive oil.

"You fault me for enjoying money to begin life."

"Gosh, yes," he said with his sincerest derision, taking a scoop of the white-hot flesh of the brown tuber to his mouth.

"Well, do you feel guilty living like a prince compared with the rest of the world? Oh, no, not you," and she sat back and smiled; "for every wagging finger, there is another one wagging at your back."

And then she promptly vomited all over the crisp and chunky chicken salad, bits of her green bile and acid secretion and clumps of gooey, gray, chalky food landing on his plate. She arose, and dashed to the bathroom.

His instinct was to follow, to offer succor, but he trailed a bit, not sure of his role in her private struggle.

He stood at his post, faithful to the chivalrous creed, awaiting news of his distressed damsel. He heard faint echoes of terrible retches and gasps that wilted his posture. "And I thought I was unwell," he pondered.

A female patron would enter the forbidden, ceramic chambers, and he would anxiously await her exit to quiz her on the physical state of Lake; but no woman he asked could satisfactorily answer his questions, compelling him to curse in muted howls. He thought of men of valor, men of supreme confidence, intrepid men who simply acted, and these stalwart images inspired him to move out of the comfort of his own recognizable actions; thus resolved, he walked straight away into a scented room that led to the glitzy theater of the unknown.

In her swirling mind, her very soul was being flushed down the filthy toilet, not just her pernicious, brown vomit; and so when Anthony walked into the bathroom stall and proffered assistance, she was incensed. He had seen her as she should never have been, and by a man she never should have known, a man naturally eclipsed from the regal world into which she had been graciously born.

"Get out," she shouted at him, turning to see his sickly figure staring at her with his countenance of concern. "I don't need your kind; get out!" But then the rest of her tortured body waged war against her, and her nauseated lower intestines began to flow, and she flushed humiliation. She lost all semblance of sanity, and screamed hysteria.

He departed, quickly, grateful to reach his car without incident from the restaurant employees. "Oh, I forgot to pay," he shouted, pounding the black steering wheel of his trusted car. He was resigned to reenter the eatery and surreptitiously slide up to the counter and pay the bill; this he did, quietly, unobtrusively, and arrived once more in the safe, warm confines of his getaway vehicle. A sense of relief fell upon him. "But I do feel sorry for her," he thought, "but I cannot help her, she isn't my problem. After all," he said aloud, to comfort himself, "you can't force someone to accept help." And armed with such rationale, he drove away, confident that he had done all he could do, all he was expected to do. "My conscience is clear," he thought. And then he cursed, and pulled the car abruptly to the side of the dirt road, cursing his incessant analyzing of situations and his inherent weakness to care when he should not. "Why must I help someone who does not care about me, who doesn't want my help? It isn't my business," he shouted, thinking still of the idea of his unreasonable selflessness while another soul is indeed needful. "Well, leave me out, that isn't me, I'm not that strong, all I can do is think about myself; no one else worries about me, why should I worry about them?" And though he did not believe any of it, still he sped off down the road once more, away from the restaurant.

He had to continue his tirade against her lest guilt devour him. "She doesn't need me nor want me nor care about me," he thought, "she is self-absorbed and rude," but for every foolish argument against her, he found one for her. "So, I should help only those who are good and kind," and he cursed so loudly that the passengers in the car next to him glanced his way. He knew what he had to do, he had to turn around and go back to the restaurant and lay down his cloak for her. He hoped she was gone.

Her car passed him going the other way. He cursed once more and spun the car around and chased her. "If she sees me, then I am dead," he thought, as he carefully stayed just far enough behind the white sedan so as not to be detected.

When she began to weave across lanes, he felt vindicated, and when she slowly pulled over to the dirt side of the road, he too pulled over, but too far back for her to see him. "Why, she must be too ill to know I am here," he said to himself, looking about for the authorities. He sat, baking in delicious sweat, waiting for movement in her car. He thought no longer of fleeing like a trailing dumb animal who comes whenever its master turns upon it. "Now, I am in control," he reminded himself, sitting up erect, and when she opened the passenger side door of her car and let her head fall toward the ground as her mouth sprayed ghastly red vomit, he bolted out of his car and ran up to the fallen damsel.

"Come on," he said, helping her off the hot dirt, her body limp as a boneless chicken.

"No," she protested, meekly, wiping the hideous concoction of gooey, the-color-of-dirt-from-a fresh-cut-grave vomit from her face, "leave me alone."

"No," he commanded, "you're coming with me." He lifted her up into his skinny arms.

"But, but, but…" she said, choking on her remaining bile and phlegm, "I don't want to go with…" and as she vomited once more, she was sure to direct her shame to fall to his side.

Even in her death throes and painful delusions, she afforded her intended rescuers her best manners.

"Tough," he said, looking at her eroding beauty, and he marched her to his car, carefully sat her down in the back seat, secured her and himself, and drove away, utterly in harmony with his blossoming male powers.

War of Attrition

L ake dreamed a dream of rosy borders and idyllic pastures, of silver springs and fertile fields of golden poppies and yellow and white lilies, and populated by those whom she loved but who were no longer on earth; her loveliness shimmered in an effulgent flood of nascent light, pouring over the rainbow-drenched land; and her health, her inner might, her great energy radiated about her like an incandescent halo. This was her sincerest desire, to recover what once was and to live that life, forever. Here, she knew inner harmony and tranquility.

At the vanishing point in the far, crimson, silky horizon that dripped pearl-shaped drops of golden rain, a pale figure approached, unappetizing in her emaciated, sallow flesh, creeping closer to her field of Desert Poppies; finally, the silent figure, dressed in a coarse robe of purple sackcloth, and wearing black ash and olive oil rubbed upon her high protruding forehead, came upon her; and consequently, the field of lovely flowers began to wilt.

"You are thus ill," the tormented creature began in an eerie yet soothing tone, "I shall never let you forget that; O, fair lady, others might bribe you with soft lies and strong kisses, but I, married to abstinence, will devour your dead mistress, beauty and mammon, and tell you not what you were or might be, but what you are and will be."

She spat upon her. "You loathsome creature, disease is beneath me; you people belong in a filthy cave, far away from healthy, handsome, happy people such as myself."

"Join me then," she returned, unperturbed by her frantic exclamations, "for you too are one of the Blighted Underground." She held out her thin, bony hand to her, and behold, her skin became white as snow with leprosy.

She screamed in horror, cursing her. "But I am not like you," she cried, and beat her savagely about her body.

"No, but you are exactly like me," she said, softly, unflinching; "disease frees all men from their earthly desires, and consigns us to the forgotten, hollow spaces in between the stream of life, where life truly begins."

"No," she cried.

And she awoke, crying out, "No," and seeing her dreamy tormentor before her, she lashed out against him, buffeting his body with her weak, wet fists.

Unschooled in the art of applying a soothing balm to a woman's entangling fears, he practiced the only art he knew, that of male egotism.

"It's me, Lake; it's me, Tony."

She abruptly abated her flailing hands, stared at him, and said, gritting her teeth, "I know," and continued her timid pounding. When she became acutely aware of her surroundings, she grew panicked, and demanded, "Where am I?"

"You didn't want to go to the hospital; you were very adamant, in fact," he said, stepping away from her, "so, I took you to my…"

But her lethal screams and shrieks lifted the last words from his lips as easily as a sweeping eagle harpoons an unsuspecting mouse on a bare hill. "You kidnapped me!"

He cursed inside himself, cursed like a commander in battle facing mutiny from his troops and then an assault from the enemy. "Nightmare," echoed within his mind, banging between foul stinking invectives and bloody adjectives that bespoke his unfortunate condition. He stared at her moist, clammy skin, her disheveled hair, her decaying, sinewy beauty, and thought, "Why can't I leave the strays to die in their own blood and confusion…"

He reached over, grabbed the plastic phone and thrust the receiver into her hands. "Dial the authorities," he said, and he suddenly stood up. "I'm done with you, you crazy, arrogant woman." His analytical mind raged against proffering encouragement to a woman in a hyper-intensive state of panic and disorientation, but his emotions blared louder in blinding flashes of red and regret.

She began to actually dial the troublesome three digits that would bring unwanted anguish into his already anguished life, and he quickly bent over and snatched the phone from her hands. "You are an ungrateful brat," he shouted.

"Give me that phone," she cried, sitting up from the bed in which she lay; but he merely stood back at a safe distance and stared, scornfully, at her meager form.

Then, she caught sight of her surroundings again, and she sat, stunned as memory rushed back into her still-foggy brain.

"The little fool is remembering," he thought to himself.

Lake turned her head this way and that, her mind inhaling the fine remnants of memory. "The restaurant," she said, only to herself, "and then I was driving home." She looked, absent-mindedly, to her rescuer, as if he were a mere attendant, a page, an indentured servant. "You were there." She released the scrunched-up blankets from her body. "You took me to your home." Her tone was one of revelation, not acceptance, not kindness or gratitude. "And why not the hospital?"

He wanted to run her to her bare feet and throw her far out onto the lumpy, black pavement and watch with satisfaction as her irritating self tumbled toward oblivion. But instead, he said, coolly, "You have an aversion to those places; something, I believe, to do with unflattering photographs."

She sat, dumbfounded. "Of course," she nodded, "you can read."

"It didn't take long to find out about the once future heiress to a Fortune 500 company who has virtually disappeared from the society page."

She focused her tired eyes once more and surveyed the room. "And look at me now, living in this lousy rathole; why, my dog lived better than this." Her head hung low as she wept. "And to be with the likes of you…"

Now, he was amused, because he had a sparring partner. "I am flattered, believe me—but firstly, you aren't living here; and secondly, this place is too good for your kind because you don't deserve shelter with humans."

She laughed, albeit weakly, but still she was forced to hold her head, grimacing through her wide, mocking grin. "And who are you?" she finally expelled, pulling her matted brown hair tight to her aching scalp. She looked at her clothes, and she laughed louder, uncontrollably, wildly. "I'll bet," she said, nearly weeping with gaiety, "you had your sister put these awful pajamas on me."

He stood, stone-faced, immobile, a faint smear of disdain raised at his lips. "Actually, it was my mother."

"Oh, how perfectly honorable and rural of you." But her pleasure quickly slipped behind a creeping, cold shadow cast by a malicious idea. "But I'll bet you thought about little ol' me lying helpless when your kindhearted mother…"

"My mother," he said, quickly and forcefully cutting into her slander, "stayed here for two days and nights with you; she left only an hour ago. I didn't think it would be right for you to be here alone without…" And he paused for a moment to exhale timidity and inhale wrath. "And how dare you…"

She held up only the index finger and middle finger of her right hand. "Scout's honor?" she said, gushing giggles.

"You give yourself too much credit; you're not my type."

She feigned a frown. "Really? I would think, for a handsome man like you, any woman who acquiesces to your sordid request is your type—oh, and conscious or not, of course."

"Yes," he said, incredulous, letting his arms fall at his sides, "you definitely need to go." He tossed the phone to the bed. "Call someone, call anyone, but just call, and do it now, and then go now, right now…"

Once again, she feigned an emotional mask, this time for sympathy. "Gosh, did I hurt your sensitive feelings?"

"Obviously, the type of man you're used to—one without honor—is the kind of man you need now." He looked to the phone. "Call quickly," he finished, coldly, and exited the room.

He paced his small living room, disgusted now at the piles of books. "What good are you," he whispered to them, "you're not practical."

In ten minutes' time, when she had regained some strength, she came out. "Where is my car?" She was dressed in the clothes she had worn to the restaurant, clothes washed and ironed by him.

"Here," he said, barely looking at her.

"Look," she began, and it sounded like the surface of explication for her harsh words, and so he impeded her progress with his upturned, raised hand.

"Don't bother; just go," he said, handing her the keys.

"How did the car get here?"

"I had it towed."

She stood, silent, unmoved, and then walked past him.

"Don't forget the rape kit; I am sure the local drugstore has them." He squeezed his eyes shut in shame.

She turned, shaking her head. "And just when I thought you might be a decent man."

"Go away," he said, irritated, "and torment your aristocratic brothers and sisters." He walked toward her. "Yes, enchant them with stories about how the lowlifes of the world live." He loathed her right now as much for what she was as for what she was not. And then he thought, watching her face blanch with shame, "Now I know how men can hate women so much; women whom I want to love so much."

But then she doubled over and dropped to her knees, tumbling helplessly to the faded carpet, and his hate, tethered to loose soil, lost its anchor and tore upward, scattering the seeds of compassion.

From hate conquered comes unconquered love.

He picked her up and brought her back to his bed; but he hesitated, holding her next to his slender body, staring at the skeletal remains of her exquisite loveliness, imagining the genetic superhuman marvel of physical greatness she had once been. "What men must have wanted in you," he whispered, and he stared deeply into her still-dazzling emerald eyes, "to kiss a creature with such immortal Beauty." And he lowered her gently to the comforting, warm sheets.

It rained softly that cold November night, a watery veil for the misty, starry, silvery moon.

Becoming Acclimated

The young woman dined at the sumptuous banquet of her ruddy hostess, Fever, whose sole purpose it was to dig her host's body out of the hot trenches of acute illness. "Dine with me," Fever said, yellow flame licking her white-waxen lips, and she held up a ruby-encrusted, golden goblet from which she poured a smoldering, crimson sauce. "Purge yourself of me, and see who still binds thee to the jagged mountain, where your raw, screaming flesh is picked clean by day and regrown by night; is it not that zealous scholar, Disease, who guides thee? Is it not that unctuous villain, who practices the art of deception on those he loves most? So, I say unto thee, seek his marble palace and storm his stony gargoyles; I do but your bidding to arouse your pithy troops." But the woman could not speak, for her face, pinched by internal wreckage, was a frozen, ashen mask. " I see your face," the temptress Fever spake, "full of abscess and scars, birthmarks of Disease; but I bring you the cool breezes of relief, yet he brings you the boiling sores of pain; love me, loathe him; honor me, dishonor him, but do not fear him." The woman put down the fuming goblet, and leaned closer to the scorching plumes of pale red vapors that was Fever, and listened intently. "Remember, what he hath done to you can be undone. See yonder the red marrow of the towering theater with its high-arching glass ceilings and garnet and onyx columns, wherein sorrow dwells;

it is there he has set inside your heart and mind for you to gaze upon, these glories you once had; to live, you must unbuild it, you must be unborn and begin anew, and only then will you become stronger, when you realize you no longer yearn for the lusts of the flesh. Remember," Fever whispered urgently as her voice trailed away, "remember the ugly oyster—at peace, a common peasant, but once in the throes of agony, a creator of rarefied Beauty."

Lake awoke, her mind sleepy with delusion, her weak body nestled on the sodden sheets. "Where am I?" she whispered, her voice hoarse from inflammation, her eyes focusing on the image above her bed as she felt the uncomfortable plastic sheets beneath her limp body.

He wanted to say nothing, but he feared silence would seed more of her anxiety, and so he said, softly, assuredly, "You're still with me." He had decided, at least, not to say his name, instead waiting for her to assemble her scattered bits of memory into clarity.

"Oh," she said, dejected, and then, weakly, "I feel so tired."

"Your fever broke."

Her voice was drained of life-force. "I feel," she closed her eyes, "so very tired, like I want to sleep; sleep is good, so very, very good," and her voice drifted away, but her eyes abruptly opened. "That is what It wants me to say; but no, sleep now is bad, if I want sleep, I am ill." She looked up at him. "Am I ill?"

"She is calmer now," he thought; "how long before she resumes her unbridled angst against me?"

"Yes, you were ill; a high fever, but you're better now."

She felt the crumpled sheets as a frown arose like a disturbed shadow across her wet face. "What are these? Am I in a hospital?"

"No," he said, cautiously, "Lake, you're with me, in my home." He wondered if this memory lapse of hers was chronic.

She screwed up her eyes and knit her arched, thick eyebrows. "Yes, yes, I remember, now," she said, massaging her flushed face, "your mother was here."

"She was, and she came back, but she had to go back to the hospital. She's a nurse."

"But the plastic, I don't understand…"

He had to tell her. "You were very ill, Lake; I had to take you back and forth to the bathroom when my mother was here, and even when she was not…" He felt, looking at her accusatory face, like a convicted rapist. He needed to say it all, but he could not.

Her countenance soured at this harsh reality, but then she mused upon it and placed this event in the proper context of the long history of her disease, and she knew he was telling the truth. "Yes, of course," she whispered, and then did a remarkable thing—she turned her head aside to deflect his gaze. She was ashamed.

For a moment, he nearly felt compassion for her, but quickly regained his apathy and mistrust against her. "Then comes the insensible screaming," he reasoned, scrutinizing her ruddy face, and he heard what appeared to be a light sob. "Impossible," he thought, "does a cold slab of stone weep?"

"I am so ashamed," she said, softly, her hands curiously at her sides, her face unshielded from his gaze.

He focused his incredulity upon her pained countenance. "I don't trust you," he thought. "I will hold to logic, and refuse any sympathy—even empathy for you—because I cannot believe you, because I don't believe in you."

She was openly weeping now, her warm tears flowing freely down her cool cheeks. "What has become of me," she sobbed, her head still turned away from him into the dark plastic covers, "nursed as if I were an invalid?"

"Fascinating," he thought, "she has risen to a stage of self-awareness, attacking her mired state, and, for the moment, ignoring me; but how long, how long until she..."

"You have seen my shame, my naked, ugly, shameful body," she said, choking now on her sobs, and then screaming, as she looked at him, "Did you clean me up as if I were an old woman who has lost control of herself?" He would not speak. "Did you?" His silence was her answer. "I am humiliated," she cried, her face contorted in agony. "Why, why, O God, why, why me?" but then her voice strained with an authentic, primal pathos that bled frustration and horror. "O, why, God? I used to be so healthy and beautiful," she moaned deeply, painfully, her anguish rising with the realization of her full misery. "What happened to me? O God, what have I become?" And then said, as if all of her recent life had been scooped up and distilled into one maddening quest, "Why can't I just be well again?"

He looked at her, judgment swallowing his staid gaze. "She's out of her head; she doesn't mean it," he reasoned, watching her from a comfortable distance within his mind as she writhed and turned in her mental pain. "She's a trapped animal—a wolf with its foot caught in a steel trap—who puts on a docile face for rescue, but then to open the trap: ah, then she will devour you." He laughed inside of his amused thoughts, and then thought, "Who, the wolf or her?" He looked again at her subdued body. "The body is the master of the mind at such times."

Indeed, she now became like the mighty leviathan that is trapped in the tangled net, rising in its death throes above the foamy water and crying in terror, only to sink beneath the turbulent waves, raging against the world.

"How dare you," she shouted, turning her mean gaze at him, "you had no right to clean me up like I was an old drunkard! How dare you put your diseased hands on my nakedness!"

"Ah, that's my girl," he thought, staring in fascination at her flashing evolution into hysteria. This time he suffered no personal discomfort from her terrible verbal abuse. He then thought, "Be who you are; at least I know what to expect."

She spat at him, and her weak, white foamy spittle landed easily upon his white shirt. "You're pathetic! You couldn't wait to get your filthy hands on the little rich girl gone bad and rape her. Did you debase me enough? Did you take pictures of me naked? Have you sold them to the papers?" She fumed electric hate, sizzling, steaming, nauseating hatred, her face burning bright from cancerous wrath. "That's the only way you can have a woman, isn't it?" She demanded his response, yet he stood, immobile, a testimony to the imbedded scars of his youth. "Silence is guilt!"

He turned round and walked out of the room. "You cannot stand the sight of your accuser, you pig!" she shouted, sobbing again, pounding the sodden sheets with her fists, sheets she now began to pummel and pull and toss to the thin, brown carpet below. "I hate you, too," she screamed at the heap of mess about her.

Tony walked in with three white plastic hangers upon which hung three complete outfits. "My mother bought these for you," he said, hanging them up upon the doorway overhang. "She took your other clothes home to wash."

She sat there, teeth clenched, eyes wide, her pale face scowling, breathing heavily, staring at him; she sought to speak, but found herself mute, and bewilderment leaked its sticky sap upon her burning scalp. Her eyes screwed up in amazement at the clothes, and once more she sought to condemn him, but found her malignant self slain by a singular kindness she did not recognize. "Why did she buy those for me?" she finally asked, suspicious still, inclining her head.

He stood, affixed to the floor, staring blankly at her, and then walked up to the bed and sat beside her. His voice was smeared with a quiescent harvest of gentleness and humility. "After my mother left, I hired a health care advocate to come here, but you would not have it, and threw a fit, saying you mustn't go to the hospital, and emphatically stated you must not be alone, since these episodes had begun of late, and you were frightened, because the last time it happened, you thought you were going to die; well, what was I to do then, throw you out into the street like a wounded dog, or dismiss your wishes? So, me—myself, by myself, I bathed you and fed you and cleaned you, and it was frightening at first and I wanted to just throw you out because I kept thinking about what you might do; but then I realized that you can't always have things the way you want them, and sometimes things just happen and you are in a situation that is not of your will; but it is the moment, and you have to make a decision either to walk away from it or just do it because it is the right thing to do and you can't worry about what may come tomorrow, that somehow what you are doing now, right now, is good and noble, and that is your shield—and so, I just did it; but then it just became natural, to offer succor to someone who was helpless and absolutely needs you, and I felt like I was—necessary," but then his words were hard and mean and angry, "and never once did I take advantage of you." His brown eyes were a translucent storm of guileless radiance. "And don't ever," he continued, but now in a guttural storm, "expect me to explain myself again when I am innocent."

Her weeping was stilled, her mouth agape at his candid declaration. She stared unafraid into the deep aura of his innocent gaze, and she blanched shock, now, from horrible shame. "I shouldn't have accused," she murmured, searching his face for forgiveness, "I shouldn't have accused…"

"No," he said, putting his hand to her lips, "it doesn't exist anymore; it lies in the sea of forgetfulness."

She sat, stunned, and then, slowly, she began to weep as she closed her eyes and then murmured, "I am so ashamed," and she turned her head from him as she spoke in a deep and passionate hurt, "If only you had seen me as I once was…"

He gazed into her flushed face, which was wet with her soul's repentant tears. "I have," he said, gently, "I have seen you." He was no longer analyzing every nuance of their encounter; he allowed his instinctual heart to guide him. "Fools see only flesh, but people like you and I see with our hearts."

She opened her teary eyes. "Who could ever love me? I can't be loved."

There was a ripe blossoming of innocence melting the cold, hard field of bitterness that was between them, and he sensed it, embraced it, tasted its sweetness and felt his passions flow. "You can be loved, if only," his voice was adjusted appropriately to maintain the clarity of purpose established in his mind, "someone would love who you are."

"What! Are you drunk? I don't want your pity," she cried. His delightful crop of melodic virtues was quieted, his countenance fell, his bitterness regaining strength. "I want my beauty back! I deserve my beauty back! I haven't done anything to deserve this cruelty! Love! Ha! Love from whom, some degenerate pig who can't get a real woman?" But she didn't regard him as the heir to this old, bitter accusation. She closed her eyes tight, and pounded her fists harder. "I'm sorry; I am really sorry," she whispered, clutching tightly her head. "I didn't mean you. It's just that…this thing…it drives daggers into my mind when I hurt the worst."

He was who he was again, and now he could think, once more; being in a bold new world, albeit ephemeral, had engaged his compass to falter. "Now," he thought, secretly relieved, "she might be a friend."

That long, hard night, he stayed with her as she recovered from her desolation of mind and body and soul.

The Battle Wages On

I t was as if he had swallowed hunks and bits of shattered glass that slowly and meticulously plowed their way through his stomach and beyond. The pain traveled from the right side of his stomach to its center, then radiated up through his chest and up his eyes and to his scrawny back. He leaped up and ran to the bathroom and turned on the light and then looked into the mirror and cursed as he beheld the yellow poison of disease spilling into his white sclera. He ran to his cabinet and took out two capsules of herbs renowned for their effect on the liver, and he swallowed them. He fell among his books and researched the master gland and the pancreas and the bile duct and everything and anything connected to the biliary tree, convincing himself that this indeed was his focal point of disease. Time swept past him, and then it was time to go to work, and he went to work, thinking all the day of his rejuvenation and how he would begin to live again; he would check his eyes in the mirror every chance he could, expecting to see the attack of jaundice dwindling, staring again and again until he would see less and less of the yellow liquid permeating his eyes; but it did not go away, and he tried not to look directly at people for fear of them seeing his condition and hearing their stupid questions he would never answer.

He got home and spent a good hour looking into the mirror and examining his eyes and looking for the dissipation of yellow pus, but the breadth and width of the toxic pool was the same, and he pounded his fist upon the ceramic top. He decided he had to fast and that fasting would do something, because what he was doing was doing nothing, and if he was like everyone else who was ill and did nothing, he knew he might as well be dead. So, he fasted, and for three days he drank only water, and as his hunger increased, so did his irritation at the steadfast yellow sea inviting itself like an irksome guest into the milky-white land of its gracious host. He knew what to do. He had always known what to do—even though he was so mixed up in the head with good and bad medicine, with alternative therapies and accepted therapies—or at least he thought he knew what to do. So, he did it anyway. He went to bed that night, but before he did so, he took special herbs that stimulate the flow of bile from the gallbladder, and mixed them with the juice of five freshly squeezed lemons. He awoke in the morning and ran to the mirror and shouted in triumph at the draining of the yellow fiend from his eyes. He railed against the scientists who said such dangerous practices were part of the hokum and snake oil of the alternative therapy quacks. But he did not care, and maybe it had been a coincidence, but all of it was gone now, and he expected to get better, and so he waited for his health to return.

But his health did not return, and soon he knew that this had been merely another symptom, so once again he sunk into oblivion. A week later he was investigating the kidney and its hundreds of renal filters, and it all looked so promising because there were so many symptoms that pointed to the bean-shaped glands that sometimes ached in his emaciated body.

The kidney idea fell apart and the rest of his ideas fell apart and he fell apart, too; it seemed that there was nothing left to do but die, but he couldn't kill himself because that would mean he had capitulated to that assassin, Disease, and he would never let that happen. No. He would never retreat, but he had to admit he felt as if he were dying in small, bitter pieces every day, small pieces that were scattered and sometimes could he retrieved and put back together again so that he might find some clarity; but lately, yes, lately the pieces were floating away further and further from his reach and he was beginning to realize he might never be able to put the pieces back together again.

And then he was sick; he was always sick, there was always something he was coming down with or catching, always the flu or the cold atop the chronic monster that lay upon his courage and drained it to puffs of white salt. It was when he was really sick and the old monsters were flailing him with their barbed whips that he felt the blackness descend upon him; it was then that he would not talk to anyone, be they friend or relative, acquaintance or otherwise; it was then that he would not answer the phone or the door or letters or go anywhere or have any fun, for this was the time of his retreat against the unnatural forces of disease that mercilessly pounded against his hearty resolve as if they were the churning sea and he the high rock cliff. They would turn him to little bits of sand over time, he knew, and he could not stop them, and felt helpless and forlorn in the wake of this slow disintegration, and he lamented his presaged early death at the hands of his tormentors. Just let me know who and what they are, he would lament, and I will destroy them. But this is the lament of the dying man.

Being alive isn't living if you're dying in pieces every day.

The acute illness would clear up and he would continue his research. He could never stop looking for a cure, for to stop meant to capitulate, and this meant he would never have the chance to truly live. He must live, he must know what it was like to be normal, to be like people he knew who went to their homes and hugged and kissed their family and lived; sometimes, at night, he would close his eyes while his ethereal music was playing and pretend that he was coming home to his family and his beloved children would run up to him and hug him and say, "Hi Daddy," and he would kiss them and hug them, and everything was all right again; sometimes, in these grand visions, he would sit there on the sofa in the warmth of his family and simply glow in love at the splendor of it all, and then he would ask his daughter how her day was, and she would sit on his knee, and tell him about her wonderful adventures in kindergarten, and he would listen attentively, feeling her warmth and her love in his heart, and he would feel the tears of joy spreading inside his soul; and then he would have his little boy, whom he would have on his other knee, tell him about his wonderful adventures in second grade, and he would feel the warm flow of love inside, and he would feel the warm tears of joy spreading in his soul; and then his wife would say, Honey, are you and the kids ready for dinner? And he would race his kids to the dinner table and kiss his wife and help his children to their places and they would all sit down and smell the gorgeous scents of the splendid home-cooked meal and they would smile at the thought of it all, and when bliss had been achieved and love radiating from his family had woven a protective web around them as they sat and talked and ate and laughed together, he would awaken from his warm vision.

So, you see, he could not yield to disease, for to do so would forever banish him from a chance at paradise, and he could not let that happen. At such times, he might even pray, even though he had not decided about God, yet; he would say little prayers about how he would promise to be a good husband and good father and not do the awful things healthy people do to their families; he vowed this with such passion that he knew it was a vow he would keep, for it was one of those special vows men make when they are dying and reach out to the light and the light demands their pledge to be more virtuous. Men always assent to such requests if only their wishes are granted.

But, as it was, he was still not making progress, and he was dying in bigger pieces now, and the world around him was not concerned or helping him, because they were living and worried about their own insular universe. He was just drifting space debris to them, and they were entire planets, self-subsisting, self-motivated, self-reliant; they did not need him, they needed only Love.

It was at such times that he thought more and more of helping others instead of thinking of himself, troubled times when he was at the deepest depth of his black despair and he could not see the light shining down from above, times when his thoughts turned to others sicker than himself, and he felt noble.

Limits

Frustration rips tiny tears in the sinewy fabric of man's essence, so when the infinitesimally small silken threads of repair stitch the bald wound, a man must retire to heal. Nearly every nuanced affair of his being was conducted in his home, the place Tony found solace and joy and grief and amusement. Home was his spiritual palace, his sovereign nation, which he ruled absolutely and tolerated no rude behavior; alas, it was also his pit of sulfur and fire, into which he sunk daily toward the sharp talons of death.

Yet, there were times he needed to vacate this structure that had become all inclusive except for the one essential ingredient it could not provide, and that was social interaction.

No matter how hard he pressed the issue of self-imposed exile from human contact, no matter how many times he vowed to free himself from the need to speak to his fellow humans, no matter how ill he was when he cursed the rest of humanity for abandoning him, he was still a prisoner of his weak human genes. Thus, he frequented the local shops when his anxieties grew and his desire for human dialogue flooded his mind with urgency. "Human beings, I so desperately want not to need them," he often repeated to himself.

And along the road teeming with people he considered the walking unconscious, he was very careful not to look handsome women full in the face, nor walk toward them, nor talk to them; while in his car, at stop signs, he would sit in his car, his profile covered by his hand for fear of being abused by women next to him.

There were a few select individuals he had engaged in casual conversation throughout the year, people he sensed shared a commonality with him; these he visited with fervent joy, those chosen few who inhabited a local farmer's market, a small health food store, the white-haired woman who sat behind the reference desk at the local library; at other businesses, he was simply another bodiless echo coming down the ceramic-tiled aisle.

He interpreted the mall as a refuge from the masses of lazybones who came in from the harsh weather to allow their soft brains and balloon-like bodies to coagulate. "What do they do with their time?" he wondered as he strolled past the faceless drones and worker bees who walked up and down the noisy walkways while they stuffed their gaping mouths with greasy fat and sugary pap. "O, how I do loathe waste." He felt a deep injustice when he observed healthy people assiduously destroying their outraged flesh and ravaged internal organs. As he saw it, here he was, dying for health, longing to be normal and to be free to pursue family and lofty goals, but he was on the outside, looking in at their idyllic lives. "But lives they willfully throw away; why do they throw away what I cannot have? They mock me, and I can do nothing but die in pieces."

He was walking to the bookstore when a most singular voice split the air, one distinguished by its wormy tone and spineless heritage, shooting its tiny, poisoned quills into his unguarded mind.

"Freak, freak," the voice squealed, like the awful caw of that shameless black-feathered villain, the crow, who taunts the wounded cat below it. "Hey, freak," split the air again, as the male voice crashed into the reddening face and tingling scalp of his prey. The girls next to the brave youth laughed uproariously, emboldening the youth to further his malicious attacks. "Hey, pal," now the voice was not strangled by the false high-pitched twang of lampooning, "for goodness' sake, go eat a sandwich or something, before the wind blows you away," and as he gestured with his hand to his mouth, laughter from these mannequin-like beings rained down like incendiary ashes upon their target.

Tony did care—despite the most ardent protestations of his intellectual mind—not what they thought of him, but that they could overtly ridicule him without fear of physical reprisal. He preferred the personal Justice of the Old West and honor of the Ancient Greeks in such situations. "Give us weapons, and we shall see then, you vermin," he thought, as he passed by his antagonist and his requisite attendants, the loyal gang of females, the kind who debased themselves so they could be seen in the company of handsome and dangerous men.

Tony was nearly past the mongrel invaders when the most singular of events occurred, to wit: the black-cloaked, black-spiked-haired, skinny utensil of a monster stood up to proffer a physical, if only feigned demonstration of his displeasure with his human target. The voice of the mongrel was rife with the black pitch and dry spittle of fuming rage against all things it considered beneath itself. "Hey, freak," he shouted, standing up, scrawny chest thrust forward, "I'm talking to you; are you deaf, too, you pathetic-looking thing!" And his slender face scrunched up in utter disgust as he thrust out his black-gloved hand toward his target. "Go eat some food; you disgust me; what do you have, AIDS, you ugly queer!" But then as quickly as the mongrel had assumed the air of fury and fire, he fell back upon laughter and smiles as he sat next to his two twin vessels of whoredom. He thought his performance was over, and so he began to eye the crowd for his next victim.

"He's dead," Tony thought, slowing his gait, thinking of confrontation now, but allowing his great capacity for reason and patience to drive him further away from his established enemy. "He doesn't know he is dead, but he is, a walking dead man." If he had had a gun, he surely would have used it. "I don't bother people; I don't know this piece of residual trash from the dung heap of filth at the bottom of the world, and yet he attacks me. But he needs to die." He needed a victory somewhere in his misbegotten life, and he would gain satisfaction through the infliction of pain onto those who willfully persecuted him.

Violent men sustain hot wrath against a foe as easily as a man fuels passion for a fresh paramour; ordinary men seek to hold onto anger, but it drains away, leaving the man limp and humiliated.

Tony bled combustion with every stride toward his car, madness reaching deep into the recesses of his stagnant, muddy pools wherein lay the hollow reflection of his former self. Unearthly fires began to burn in his inner, renewed chaos, and screeching and howling trampled this barren plain and pitted, weird landscape, and gory vengeance rose out of the bubbling mire, seeking fame and glory.

He was savage now, as savage as any man protecting his home and family against barbaric invaders. He would take life as easily as planting seeds; he had to do this, he had to defend his right to privacy as he dwindled physically to a hideous skeleton. Consequences meant nothing now as he was driven to keep his crumbling tower of pride intact.

He would not think of anything now but a plan for revenge based on intellectual cunning; he rushed home in the fine sooty sphere of darkness, retrieved his black cotton pullover mask, changed into throwaway clothes, and hurried back to the parking lot of the mall. "I will teach this peon," he screamed in the midst of his car, "to mock the ill."

Casually, he sat in the dark shadows of his car, his heart pumping potent blood, his mind spilling over with power. "Come on, you cockroach," he raged, "how dare you make fun of someone who appears weak," he cried, scanning the parking lot for the importunate security cars that patrolled the aisles. "How many others have you insulted, how many?" he shouted, nodding his head. In his civilized and virtuous mind, he desired that the greasy rodent had vacated the premises, but his brutish mind cared nothing for these feeble ramblings, and grabbed these soft ideas with its yellow fangs and tore them into distant memories. His mind was void of moral structure, snarling at universal laws.

"Come to me, you filthy germ." The hunter had now reduced his game to the stature of a meaningless microbe in order to continue channeling funds to the guerrilla insurgents who had set up camp in his raging mind. Then, to his insatiable delight, the aforementioned cockroach appeared, igniting the seething pleasure of the hunter. "Now you will die, and no one will miss you," he whispered, in a voice strong with the echoes of utter savagery. Finally, there was a physical foe, and he would not lose the opportunity to smash it to bits, smash it to tiny atoms, if only to imagine this enemy his real enemy.

He gripped the thick wooden branch and took the black mask off his lap. "Maybe I should wait and follow him home; yes, that's it; then they won't be able to trace it to me." He repressed the idea that he was backpedaling like a frightened wimp, returning to his own putrid boasts of vomit. He started the engine. "There," he cursed, madly, loudly, "now, we will see who…"

A tap upon his window blew out his concentration, and he nearly jumped out of his sodden skin. He looked up; his face blanched with shock. He cursed. "Lake," he muttered incredulously.

She was motioning for him to roll down the window, a look of impatience upon her pale, ravaged face. "What on earth," she cried, frowning as he obeyed her order, "are you doing?"

He looked up at her, and then down at his vigilante gear, then up to her.

"Right," she said, nodding, "it's a man-code-of-silence-thing."

He stared at her, unblinking, taking in the slowly disintegrating attractiveness of her face, assembling the intricately soft features of her face, slowly remembering all she was to him, and only then did he release his grip on the hard wood. He glanced over at his fleeing prey, his pulsing mind playing a quiet refrain in the charred remains of his manhood, "Good, good, gone, I live another day, but I would have…"

He looked up at her, his stern expression cleansed by her gentle smile. "Hi."

She laughed, and rubbed his balding head. "I don't want to know," she said, giggling and shaking her head.

It had not occurred to him that she was in a rare mood of good humor, nor that he had not seen her in a few weeks, even though they had talked on the phone and become what she called "phone acquaintances," and realized they had more in common than they would have imagined, and during this time he had lost three more precious pounds. "Can anyone tell the difference?" he often wondered. "Do they see a bony skeleton, or a bony skeleton with a thin layer of thinning meat underneath called flesh?" He wasn't sure he was glad to see her, for she represented an unknown element in his life he could not control.

All of those things that caused him grief he excised cleanly and forever from his misbegotten life.

"Well," he said, the purple smoke of wrath clearing from his mind, "are you stalking me?"

She laughed, again. "I'll bet you say that to all the women you've helped to urinate."

He nearly smiled. "What is it with her?" he wondered. He did not yet understand that what was with her was with all women.

She leaned her head in, smiling boldly. "You know, you're the only man who has ever seen me naked without wanting something sexual from me."

"An honor I will cherish forever," he replied, half-smiling, bowing his head.

"Say, Tony, let's go to dinner; I want to tell you some good news." She paused and frowned. "Remember, you called me?"

"She called me 'Tony,'" he thought, as he watched her walk away to her paint-fading, blue Toyota Camry, "and not just on the phone, hmm."

In the restaurant with her, he had forgotten about the proposed demolition of his intended target; he no longer cared, for the frenzied, bubbling morass of madness had settled to the smooth bottom of his sagging muscle of memory.

"I think I am well since going off all that medication with those nasty side effects," she declared, effervescent, setting down her beige Simply Vera Vera Wang tote; "really, Tony, I feel so good; oh, occasionally," the mere mention of a blemish in the delicate tissues of her carefully constructed idea of victory tore her down, "I feel a tug, but not often."

"Remission," he thought to himself, "false hope caused by a brief remission." He had experienced such a phenomenon countless times, where twenty-four hours, even forty-eight hours without illness might occur, and he would begin to think like a normal human male; but then a legion of virulent assassins that were merely recuperating in between operations from inside his blinded borders would arise from their slumber and teach him a valuable lesson in disease diplomacy. His omnipresent disease had flung its bristled gauzy wings over his stupid smug smile so many times that eventually he capitulated and finally understood that when authentic health finally came, he would know it.

He listened to her conversation, her words containing a universal pattern from the same rock of illusions that all chronically ill people experience for the sake of self-survival; she spoke of great exit plans once she was free from the deformed grip of disease, and he heard the tiny tinkling of crystal bells chiming rhythmically in her sweet voice, the sound of rapture born from the perception of rejuvenation of mind and body and spirit. But how could he tell her she was doomed?

"If not now, tonight; if not then, tomorrow, if not the next day, soon, soon, poor Lake, poor unconventional fool," he thought as he looked at the delicate curves of her sensuously crafted lips. "Even black disease cannot diminish all Beauty." His gaze drifted over the doughy canvas of skin that lay upon her so brittle and dry. "She dies from within, like me; and like me, she is driven to seek Restoration. Is this not the way of all who live in between the precious moments?"

"I feel so wonderful, just like a Yellow Tulip blooming in the desert for the first time," she gushed, and as she threw open her toothpick-like arms, she accompanied this wide gesture with a quick burst of unexpected vomit, which came to lay its green, sickly bile self upon her fresh fruit salad.

"You have been emancipated from the hideous grief of false hope," he lamented to himself, but he did not know how sad his face had become, as if it reflected another part of himself that had believed in her.

Her paralyzed face hung in the hungry breezes of the restaurant, until, at last, she coerced herself to see a rainbow horizon no one else could see. "Maybe," she said, breathing finally, and wiping her mouth, "it was just a momentary relapse," her face frozen in a dreaded anticipation, sitting motionless, as if waiting for the rest of the vomit to announce its selfish presence.

Nothing came.

"That's it," she said, nearly weeping, shaking slightly, "I've read that sometimes, as the body heals, you get worse…" But then she truncated her words, just like a woman who, standing at the edge of a cliff, freezes as she feels rumbling underneath her bare feet; and then it came, the greater mass of bubbling, searing vomit pouring out of her mouth. She gulped and gasped as she attempted to curse, but in its stead, she gulped and gasped rancid air and humiliation.

Tony interceded in between the unfortunate act and any further embarrassment by quickly pulling her to the women's bathroom and then standing guard for her.

The waiters and waitresses issued him furtive glances and whispered fast words under their sweet and sour breaths to passing compatriots; eventually, the manager approached the human sentry, at which time Tony proffered payment, with tip, in full; but, graciously, the manager declined the money as he waxed anxiety about the loathsome possibility of food poisoning even being discussed in his fine establishment. The manager then smiled warmly and exited slowly, as if to exhibit no fear of legal reprisals.

The minutes crawled by, accompanied by the calamitous sound of resurgent illness. Lake finally appeared, limp, dejected, a sweaty figure of throttled flesh, her face drooping, shuffling her feet apathetically.

He took her home, as would be the custom, and nursed her back to the subnormal limits to which she had begrudgingly become accustomed. Her recovery was quicker this time, but she lingered longer in his care, for she had grown fond of his gentle ways.

The refractory disease had been most deadly, for it had sabotaged her weak immune system. She lay on her bed like a helpless, limp rag doll, soaked in toxic perspiration, staring up at her caretaker.

"We are the same," she said, watching him come back from the laundry room, "two peas in a diseased pod."

He smiled, unable to suppress it.

"Well, the iceberg melts into a smile! Imagine that!"

He smiled again.

She whistled. "Twice! You'll be human, yet!"

He sat down next to her on the small twin-sized bed. His voice was playful. "Don't push it, Goldilocks."

She did laugh, then, and said, wistfully, "I'll have you know this is my natural hair color; and I hate your bed, by the way."

He wiped her forehead with a beige cotton towel and gave her a glass of cool spring water.

She held up a mirror to see herself. "Did you comb my hair?" She smiled, and her contemplation sank into her happiness. "Tony, do you think I am beautiful—I mean, do you think men still desire me?"

His lack of an immediate answer tore a small circle of apprehension into her weak psyche; she watched his brown eyes stare silently at her, his face expressionless as it was ferried across this uneasy query.

He had learned that it was best sometimes to answer a question with a question. But this was not the time. "What do you think?"

She cursed. "I didn't ask you to ask me; I asked you," she cried, irritated.

"Fine." His voice was colorless. "No."

"Good," she said, sitting up, "if I have to get mad at you for you to tell me the truth, then for goodness' sake, I'll do it; but do I have to? You are trying to spare my feelings because you are sensitive to that pain." She lay down again, turning her head. "That's a female trait, and not very becoming of a man." She looked at him, and her hard countenance softened as she whispered, "I am sorry, that is not true," and then she performed an act hitherto unknown between them: she physically touched him. "You're being sensitive to my feelings, and that isn't being a wimp. That is being a real man."

Her touch on his bare flesh had enthralled him. "Gosh, thanks," he replied, as if to hide his ecstasy.

"I know I'm not attractive to men, anymore," she said, dejectedly, and then let out a small "hmm," while not looking at him again. "Me, who used to have men lined up for breakfast, lunch and dinner," she nearly whispered, and then looking at him, continued, "and the finest men, too; rich men, powerful men, good men, all of them…." Her words sank to a fervent whisper as she remembered her past glory.

He arose, abruptly, walked out of the room, opened the door, stuck his head outside, shut it slowly, came back inside her room, sat upon the bed, and said, innocently, "I don't see them."

Of course, she cursed him. "You're cruel."

"You wanted truth; and besides, one thing you cannot do, when you accept your illness, is deceive yourself; you die every day when you make yourself believe what you know is a lie, because if you believe it, you'll expect it to happen; and when it doesn't, you die, again, and again, and again…"

"And give up hope? Never!"

"Why, it's your disease talking; shame."

"No, it's pragmatism talking; but don't get me wrong, I have hope, but I am practical about it." Her face screwed up courage. "I wake up every day expecting to get well." She stared at him, and revelation chewed up one mood and set it ablaze with wrath. "And what about that unkind remark about my men? Are you implying that I am so vulgar ugly that they don't want to see me?"

"No," he replied, unflinching now, stolid in his criticism, unbound now to export to her a stark candor. "They never loved you," he pointed to her head, and slowly touched her thick hair, and then pointed to her heart, and touched her there. "They never loved you; they loved a living, breathing, dazzling jewel. They loved an illusion, the paradigm of Beauty, they loved you because they saw themselves in you; they loved an eternal Beauty they saw in you; all men pursue it. We can't help it, it is who we are." He paused, and then added reverently, "They loved the idea of you."

She looked at him for the longest time, silent, her countenance washing over with a new breed of emotion. "You never quit, do you?"

"Why should I? I can't stand a lie, and healthy people live with a lie; in a way, I have benefited from being ill, because I don't live the lie, anymore. Disease makes you honest, it forces you to listen to your body and mind and understand where you have been and where you are going and how you will get to where you need to be. Healthy people just go forward and do whatever comes to mind, never thinking about the consequences of their idiotic actions; but we, well, if we lie to ourselves and try to be like everyone else, we stumble and fall on our emaciated faces. We are the ones who cleanse our bodies of guile, by scrutinizing our every deed and thought, and so healthy people do not understand us." He paused, looking at her intense scrutiny of him, and then continued with philosophy he had gained over the seeming millennia of illness. "In many ways, I am a superior man. But this is not so in society, is it? They, our inquisitors, judge us by our physical body, and not by what is unseen. This is why I told you long ago that we need to be with our own kind, for only we understand one another. We are unique in the world, and our struggle is our own."

She had followed the trajectory of his philosophical flight to its logical destination; her voice was melancholy, born from lamentation and loss. "But I still see the world through my old eyes—eyes new and young and strong and beautiful—it is still who I am; I have not accepted what has happened." Her mind drifted now into another hemisphere of reality. "Sometimes, if I don't look straight at myself in the mirror and see all of my face, I think I am really beautiful again, and I cannot understand why young men aren't simply falling over themselves to get to me." She sighed, her voice full of longing. "Sometimes, well, sometimes I will believe it for what seems like the longest time, and I wait for the phone to ring or a knock at the door, and I sit there looking at the silent phone, and looking at the silent door, and I wait, and I wait, and…" and then she began to weep, so great was her grief. And then she remembered her beloved grandmother and Lisbeth, of whom she often thought, and her suffering increased, and she whispered, "I am all alone in this miserable world."

"No," he returned, adamant, leaning closer to her, and pointing to the outside, "you are alone in their world," and then he pointed his outstretched, chalky hand to her and himself, "but not in ours."

There is a universal signal activated when two people cross the hard border of passion together; the old world slips away, a new world is created, and life seems to begin again.

Tony leaned down, and meeting no resistance, kissed Lake slowly and gently upon her soft, slender, provocative lips. She smelled of jasmine and decaying flowers.

Everything had changed because he had kissed her; no, everything was changed now because she had allowed him to kiss her, and now she realized how much she not only wanted love, but how much she yearned for love from him. She had once resisted her inner female voice that yearned for his touch, because she did not want to ever be with a man who was not extraordinary: extraordinarily handsome, extraordinarily rich, and extraordinarily powerful. Soon, she had convinced herself, I will be well, and I will not have to accept a lesser man. But now was now, and her resolve to wait for the impossible had diminished, and somewhere, deep within her confusion, there was the transforming idea that the man in front of her was as good as she would ever find.

He lifted his head on high, the two lovers staring at each other with rapture flooding over their tingling, warm bodies. He smiled. "Slow and steady wins the race," he thought, smiling on the inside.

Brief Encounter

Nothing that had transpired between them mattered, for what mattered now was this new feeling of sensuous desire in their dried, brittle and formerly dead human roots. Vital juices began to flow into their stagnant veins, and this great awakening compelled them to drink voraciously of this fragrant nectar during these many months. And they realized how close they were in temperament and passion, in politics and religion, in intellect and interests; they loved the theater, they truly did—she: Euripides' plays: *Electra, Orestes, and The Trojan Women;* and Shakespeare's plays: *Romeo and Juliet, The Taming of the Shrew,* and *Antony and Cleopatra;* he: Aeschylus' plays: *Agamemnon, The Libation Bearers, and Eumenides;* and Shakespeare's plays: *Hamlet, Prince of Denmark, Macbeth,* and *Julius Caesar*—and attended plays as long as they could last there; they loved the symphony orchestra, they truly did—she: Mozart, Bach, and Rachmaninoff, and he: Beethoven, Tchaikovsky, and Schubert—and attended performances as long as they could last there; they loved the cinema—especially classic movies and the charismatic stars that created and inhabited them; of the ladies: Lombard, Loy, and Monroe, of the gentlemen: Olivier, Tracy, and Garfield, she influenced him to watch; of the gentlemen: Gable, Lancaster, and Stewart; of the ladies: Davis, Sydney, and O'Sullivan, he influenced her to watch — as long as they could last there; and as long as they could last there, they traveled to those places young lovers explore together: amusement parks, idyllic pastoral reserves, county fairs, museums, and quiet beaches; and it was literature they truly loved, sharing books they had read, the authors they admired, the poets they revered—of the ladies: Austen, Bronte, and Dickinson, of the gentlemen: Byron, Keats, and Shelly, she influenced him to read; of the gentlemen: Tolstoy, Dickens, and Hugo; of the ladies: Stowe, Mitchell, and Buck, he influenced her to read—and of these things they read so happily and contentedly, it was a consequence of their illness: burrowing into the insular world of make-believe where the lives of others were so carefully scripted and happy endings could occur despite the recalcitrant objections of a cold, unfeeling, outside reality.

And so, if the soul be composed of fine, sinewy cords, these two lovers, as they realized how much closer they were to each other than apart, felt their own souls become slowly entwined, cord by cord; and with every laugh together, and cry together, and smile together, and mourning together, they were inextricably bound, not in toto, but in sufficient ways, that they had forfeited forever their individual identities; and were no longer complete without the presence of the other, that any absence between them suffered their souls most grievously, for what once was bound in love yearns to grow freely and completely, and this without prejudice.

Every sensual kiss erased a memory of suffering, every long, joyful kiss transported them to the exquisite land of the living, where they knew their blistered feet could not yet touch this hallowed ground; but every moment the lovers were apart, they were rudely brought back to their exile, conferring to them a special revelation that they had indeed left their own private prison, and thus were nearly inseparable, as if neither could properly live without the presence of the other.

A simple walk for the lovers in the cool shade of Spruce trees, which lined the park paths, was dependent upon one crucial factor: their health.

"I am like a prisoner who gets to stretch his legs once a day," Lake said, as she walked with her new beau, holding his hand, watching the Blue Jays squawking and hopping from tree to tree. "In a prison I live, a prison cell with the comforts of home, but it is an absence of freedom."

In the beginning of her illness, she had felt an explicit urgency to divulge her private pain to those she was intimate with, and had spoken of her private sorrow to male lovers, none of whom were willing to listen, for her role in their lives was as a physical marvel of Beauty that brought them intense pleasure and notoriety, simply a narcotic to numb the self-induced woes in their harried lives. Her female friends listened as long as it took them to apply their multicolored makeup to their featureless faces, and her only true friend who had listened, Lisbeth, had died. Her beloved grandmother was dead.

"At least we are on the same floor," he said.

"Cell block D," she added, laughing, and rubbing her sore larynx.

"Prison break," he suddenly shouted, and began to run wildly with her toward a cluster of small, fluffy brown rabbits.

Joy flew in like a winged white dove, alighting upon their slight shoulders, carrying them like wandering, carefree children to clusters of scarlet California Fuchsia, blue-violet Globe Gilias and pale-pink Seaside Daisies. All about the lovers was robust health bursting in vibrant colors and intoxicating aroma. Dancing and frolicking among such raw, flaming youth injected them with the idea that they too truly lived, that here they could live inside a plush, honey-scented garden of illusions.

A cough, now, a single, explosive hacking cough would signal the commencement of decay for their idyllic fare, and it occurred; but a cough again, a harsh, deep, bloody cough could be the death knell for their fragile business, and it transpired. Paradise lost.

She bled bitterness. "Can we go nowhere and hide from this torment?" she wept, as they walked back to his car. She coughed violently again. "I hate this misery."

He held her firmly, as was his duty, and he keep silent, as was dictated to him by wisdom gained; but he too was not spared the rod of disease, and he calmly dismissed himself to the nearest restroom, and returned quickly.

She bled internally, bright red blood staining the residue of her violent attack. "I hate you," she cried, staring at the traitorous drops of her precious carrier system upon the dirt, "you're supposed to stay inside me, you idiot!" And looking to her lover, she said, shaking her head, "Whoever heard of blood outside of the body? Do I look wounded?" She fell to her knees, weeping, her hands held out to her sides, as if to accept succor from above. "Is there no Justice? Is there no God? I want life," she pleaded, in profound sorrow, as she let her head fall backward, her eyes gazing up at the clear blue sky; "must I enjoy nothing but pain?

How have I offended You? Speak to me! Am I so rotten that I warrant a slow execution? For that is what You are doing to me," she cried, her eyes shut now, "executing me as if I were a wretched dog, a disgusting criminal; O God, help me, help me, help me to understand what I need to do to be free." She then disgorged a gruesome scream born blind from the ripped and torn and shredded, burnt pastures of her suffering, an unnatural blast of her primal trumpet that seemed to drain her body of its waning powers. She then fell over upon the verdant grass, as if one dead.

Tony, unsure of his role when she had shouted from the inner depths of her poisoned well spring, now took her in his arms and held her, stroking her wet hair and warm forehead.

He took her to her home, and there she lay in bed for a day, and though she recovered quickly from this acute illness, she had not the will to arise. "Why should I get up?" she would shout, as he sat next to her, "For what reason? Do I look stupid? To get up only to be sabotaged by this murderous thing?" and she grabbed her weak flesh. "Tell me!" She shut her eyes. "O Tony, it isn't you, it's this disease; I cannot," and she hesitated, and then said in a voice forlorn and free of hope, "I cannot be with you like this."

A cold chill stiffened him. "What does she mean," he thought, "now, or forever?"

"I cannot," she continued, holding her head, "be with you as long as I am ill; it isn't fair to you or me."

"Lake," he replied, ardently, "don't let it destroy the one good thing in your life."

"But don't you see," she returned, nearly sobbing, "it's spoiling the one good thing in my life," and she rose up and kissed him, and held him tight, and said, passionately and defiantly, "and I won't let it."

There was nothing more to be said. She departed.

Agonizingly, tormenting and desperate months went by, and she became a mere memory to him.

Advice

He had waited his entire life for a woman who would love him unconditionally, and whom he would love, and now that woman was hidden behind the same veil of tears to which he banished other misfortunes. "Healthy or ill, no woman could want me," he said, staring into his dusty mirror, "not as long as the monster within lives." He closed his eyes. "Did she exist?" He looked awry at the fleeting answer in his mind. "No," he said, softly, knowing that in order for him to survive he must efface the very idea of her. "But how can I?" he cried, sitting now at his wooden desk, whereupon in heaps, like sandy pebbles on the shore, sat his blessed books. "I must drive out her image with another woman, but I cannot have another, unless she is mad, corrupt, or diseased." But he pounded the desk so hard that his hand became bruised as he cried out, "How can I give up that which I waited for my entire life?"

Before him lay a spreading web of medical texts. "Therein lies my salvation," he was fond of saying as he beheld their dull glory.

This day was like any other day. "Today, I investigate the pancreas," he announced to the undulating hills of checked-out, bought-cheap, and borrowed books. "Sure," he followed, smiling, for he knew that analysis of the pancreas inevitably led to study of the liver, gallbladder and adrenal glands.

Morning commenced when he opened the current edition of the *Textbook of Internal Medicine*.

Three hours hence, and he was still in the warm embrace of scholarly research, one of the few pursuits where he found solace. "Is it the disease that wreaks havoc on my pancreas, or the pancreas itself?" he wondered aloud.

Every day he traveled a foggy path, blindly groping for evidence that would render a distinct road to follow; and every day he stumbled and fell to bruising and cuts and scrapes, and shame; but every day, he lifted himself up and renewed his adventure.

He was at the library on a sultry Spring day, sitting next to a mound of medical literature, lost in the great knowledge of these mystical scrolls.

"Son."

He looked up to see an elderly man sitting next to him.

"Hello," the man said; his old man's voice was rich with the nobility of kindness.

"Hello," Tony returned, smiling, and shook the man's outstretched hand.

The man smiled, looking at the books, and he put his large, wrinkled hands upon them, caressing them as does a hunter who strokes the furry head of his faithful hound dog. He closed his big eyes, nodding his head. "Hmm," he murmured, "books, I do remember you." He spoke as do old people who have truly lived, who live without fear, without worry of condemnation, who speak without appealing to their listeners for approval. He opened his soft, brown eyes. "Son, I am you."

"Sir?"

"I am you, young man; it was so long ago, I sometimes forget I lived like this; but praise God I followed the road least likely traveled."

Tony said, politely, "Well, nice meeting you, but I have to go now," letting loose the typical exit line found in the uncommon shopper's guide to avoiding such unwanted company.

The ordinary, elderly-looking man merely smiled, and reached out to touch the target of his speech, to which Tony instinctively pulled away, his body still rising up.

"Son, you're ill—physically ill, like I was." The man frowned desperately. "Don't go, son, I am not mad, as classically defined by behavior pseudo-scientists," and he smiled, "just lived in."

Tony hesitated, and cursed himself for lacking the gene of cruelty that enabled the mind to ignore people who walked outside the crowded geography of mainstream society.

The old man pursed his thick lips and nodded his white-haired head. "Sit down, youngster, and listen to the story you're living, and how it will all turn out." He laughed. "You're hesitant, boy, because of my cryptic words," and he laughed again, a laugh wrapped in a wonderful secret. "Look deep into my ancient eyes, son, and see who you were, and what you might become."

Tony, inexplicably, sat back down, but on the ready to flee. "Go on," he said, circumspectly.

"Good, good," the old gentleman continued, "I am so glad you have decided to stay; but I must convince you I am you, or you will not, eh? Fair enough." He leaned back in the rigid, black vinyl chair. "When you lose your health, you become a member of a privileged race that previously you saw, but," and he raised his hand, index finger up, "did not see! They are your own kind, son, all around you, but your eyes see only yourself." He nodded and hummed a sad note, and his visage grew grim. "Disease carves out a fearful vision, boy, and only those afflicted can see others enchained to its terrible oars as it pulls us slowly to the shore, into its fiery Lake of Death."

He nodded, as if he were the carrier of such esoteric wisdom. "Look around you, and tell me what you see; do you see another like you?" The two men casually gazed about.

Tony looked but did not see what the man wanted him to see, for his eyes focused on the deception created by the movements and dress and speech of the people in the library, and so he peered deeper beneath the supremely crafted veneer of health to find the truth.

It wasn't very long until he noticed a man who was sitting alone at a table, the world bustling about him, children laughing and mothers searching and young people being led by their exuberant curiosity to explore the magic of the place; but the man, in the midst of this vibrant color and joy and energy, sat dull and lifeless, a fading patch of burned, musty grass in a lovely flower garden of brilliant hues and powerful scents. The compassion he felt for the man gave him over to pity for himself, and he shook his head. "There," he whispered, somberly, "the man next to the newspapers."

"Why him?" the old man said, his voice rich with passion. "Why not," the old man pointed to a young woman near them, "her?"

"Well, she is merely skinny, but the man," he continued, looking again at the weathered soul at the other table, "is not that old," he paused, searching for the proper word, "but he is decaying before his time."

"Yes," the old man with the large hands said fervently, "it is as you say; we know each other, as surely as a dog knows its own domesticated kind from his cousin, the wolf."

"The point," Tony rejoined, beginning to feel uncomfortable about this eerie business.

The old man, his face feverish with want, spoke. "Every day you are faced with two paths to travel: the first one involves self, leading to destruction; while the second one, denying one-self and helping others, leads to liberation; follow your flawed human instincts and you'll find yourself walking up and down the hill with our old friend Sisyphus. Life is a puzzle, son, and as long as you're a willing piece of it, you will never understand why," and he gestured mightily, as if recalling past glories. "You need to break free," he stated, firmly, and he simulated the act of breaking chains with his wrinkled hands, "and look around at the world and see the unnatural divisions; illness does that for you, son, so does poverty and persecution, but you cannot let it destroy you. You must use its oppression for good, to free your inner mind from its petty attacks so you can see the world taking shape about you; ah," but he gestured with both hands now, "do what seems counterintuitive—that which seems to deny reason and logic, and let your heart and soul guide you, and you will live." He abruptly stood up and extended his hand, which Tony shook.

Tony watched the old man begin to leave, but he said quickly, "Sir," and he watched the old man turn round. "If there was a woman," he hesitated, "a woman, like me, who could not be with me because it brought her pain not to be who she wanted to be…" He wanted to say more, but he wasn't sure why he had said anything at all.

"How long?"

"Months—and I haven't heard from her."

The old man smiled gently, and bending down next to him, his large, strong hands upon the youth's shoulders, spoke each word distinctively and with great force. "You are the man—you lead." He shook the youth's hand once more, and promptly disappeared into the velvet stillness of the book palace.

When a human being suffers from a long illness, they will accept charity from whoever has the noble heart to offer it.

Tony cogitated upon the old man's remarks, and then thought of Lake. "Have I been a fool? If she wants to talk to me, why doesn't she just call?"

The next day, at work, Tony sat next to a colleague, Blair, who said, with a sly grin, after hearing the former's lament concerning his ladylove, "You are so naive about women, my brother; women don't pursue, they sit on their lofty perch like a rainbow-colored bird and wait while the stupid males fight it out for the right to mate with them." Blair laughed, he who had persuaded hundreds of women to forsake their vows of chastity for him, a man who was master of the female psyche of desire and fulfillment, a man who had read no book or seen no instructional show on how to seduce the enigmatic female of the species, but who had been invited by his lovers to peer into the exclusive, fragile chamber of their female heart, and therein had gathered untold treasures.

It was a lunch break. "Sit down, Tony, my man," he continued, feeling every bit the mentor, "and let me tell you about our mutual friend, Woman," and he accentuated the last word with finesse. He put his hands up to his own fiery, ultramarine eyes. "You cannot see her through your rigid male mind; the trick is you have to get inside her mind and see through her strange and yet fantastically complicated psyche." He leaned back in the chair, raised his muscular arms, laced his hands behind his blond head, and then said with a laugh, "Good luck with that!"

"You mean," Tony queried with furrowed brow, "that when a woman doesn't want you to call her, you do call her?" Such questions professed his prevailing ignorance of the delicate balance reached between pursuer and pursued in the fiery game of love.

"Tony, Tony, Tony," Blair responded, feigning shame, his head low, "every woman wants to be chased and caught and swept off her dainty little feet; now," he raised his hand, as if to ward off direct objections, "I can't be there for you and tell you not to pursue women who really don't like you and don't want to be bothered; that being said, all other women are fair game. Women," he paused, his thick brows knit, "just aren't wired to lie down and say 'yes': it takes away their power over us." He leaned closer and whispered, "And run far and fast from those women who circumvent that genetic command, if you get my drift." He leaned back and clasped his hands again behind his handsome head, and watching a few female employees lumber past, he smiled at them, and received a smile in return. "Those chicks, those women who don't listen to their mother's rules about men, once they're with us, it's all over for them—it's like they've been contaminated by radiation: no one will get near them for a thousand years; so, you see what happens is that the smart women keep up the power game in the beginning, because it is the only time, my brother, that they are going to have a disproportionate piece of the power pie." Both men instinctively raised right hands and mightily slapped them together. Blair leaned in again and whispered, "Now, that isn't to say some men don't have issues with other women," and here his dark countenance took on an ominous grimace. "Listen, there are no equal rights in marriage; that's just another one of those silly urban legends." He leaned back again. "You can't have two chiefs under the same tent, understand? One chief would have to fold up his tepee every day and be content with weaving rugs." His hands crossed over themselves. "One chief, one Indian; a man or woman, I don't care which," and then his voice took on the tone of absolute, undeniable authority, "there can only be just one." He leaned forward and said in a definitive, defiant tone, "And I'll tell you one thing right now, Kemosabe, the day a woman is wearing the white feathered headdress in my house is the day this brave goes on the warpath."

These words seemed powerful and true to the fledgling man of romance, and Tony embraced their lusty spirit.

Three months hence, and the word on the fermented skins of the grapevine had it that Blair was finally in the deep entanglements of True Love, and that, according to the most reliable of sources, his woman had her young brave happily turning cartwheels and somersaults through a flaming hoop.

Love is.

Conscience, Conscience

L ake was walking along the sidewalk one cold and Winter morning, on a hazy, black, bad-storm-approaching day, a humorless, lackluster day when the world seems to thrust its sharpest daggers into the softest and most vulnerable part of the human heart; she was walking along doing nothing but listening to her own wheezing and hacking coughing, and feeling her inflamed esophagus, hearing her measured breathing and her weak steps and imagining how she must look to passersby; she was lost and lonely and had no one to turn to and no one who cared for her, and it was all too much and too soon for her. "Not now," she grieved, "in seventy years, but not now; but no, not even then." She felt like a young sapling uprooted by the wind and lying on its side while its exposed roots burned and desperately sought to find rich soil and precious water and nourishment; she felt trapped and forgotten and pointless, aimless, abandoned. "What is to become of me," she wondered, "I, who was once so young and beautiful, how can I make anyone understand what I once was," and then pleaded in a maddened tone, "and what I still should be, what I deserve to be."

But there she was, walking along the cracked white sidewalk and minding her own business and stepping in the leaking gore of her disease, when a man leaped out of a black sedan and pulled up a camera and took her picture. She hung in mid-step, her ashen face frozen in shock, her skinny body trembling like a deer in the icy shadows of the black panther. His face met hers and her emerald-colored eyes cracked the thick armor of callousness in his tiny heart; he stood, motionless, studying her frail body and her tainted beauty, and his mouth hung open and his countenance dropped and he turned his head slightly as if he did not believe when he beheld.

She was standing there, a captured soldier, a prisoner of war in this hollow and macabre game, and she bore to him, with great facileness, her gaunt face with its horrible, scaly patches of eczema and doughy skin and her reddened, enlarged throat and her dull, frizzled hair; his head shook in horror and he felt his body rocking to and fro and his mind sought to latch together every bit of her loose and dying form, to stitch it up into what he knew she once was and imagine what she had become and how far she had fallen and whether or not he cared about it all or if he even had a practicing conscience about it. No, he decided, one could not have a conscience about such things, it was simply business, and there was no conscience in business, only capital value and sellers and buyers and everyone in between. It was just business, he decided, but then she knelt down and vomited and his flimsy compassion reared up, but he beat it down and tried to remember that it was just business, business as usual; and then he thought, one cannot have a heart about such things if one wants to make a living. She vomited and he stared at her bony spine as she bent down in front of him, as she vomited decently on the dirt path, as she vomited blood and bile and agony—as he stood, his slick veneer evaporating into the grim ether.

Then he felt like the intruder and had to decide to flee or stay because to stay any longer meant poor manners and ambiguity; he watched in horror as she clutched her stomach and her entire body shuddered and sank like a sick animal and he suddenly found himself kneeling next to her and holding her and stroking her back and head and whispering to her that everything would be all right. He would not think about it, anymore.

Right now he was doing what was instinctual regarding what the good things of the world had taught him, and that was to be human no matter what your job taught you or demanded of you or what you thought you had to do for a living; and right now he was being a man, listening to the noble pulse of chivalry and kindness as it laid its shimmering cloak of love over her. He didn't care anymore about his job or his deadlines but only about helping her, a human being, a woman, an innocent damsel in distress he could offer succor, someone he could help, someone he could protect; he was human, now, and nothing on earth could stop him.

He had not been human for so long.

In the end, he helped her up and took her home and opened the car door for her and helped her to her door and stood there standing erect even though inside he was trying to bury his past crawling cowardice; he was standing there, and there were no words between them, and then he reached out his weapon, his deadly, life-threatening weapon to her, nodding his head that it was okay; and he watched her take it, turn with a small smile of gratitude on her pale face, and then go inside her modest dwelling; and then he turned and went back to his car and sat for a while, not wanting to think about anything or say anything, until finally he decided to drive away, knowing only one thing, that he was through with this job and this sordid lifestyle and the thrill of the chase, and whatever he would do now, he would make sure it was good and clean and decent so it would help others and thereby help him to truly live again.

In Praise of Folly

L ake was disintegrating like a mountain of loose pebbles, a small avalanche each day that shed more of her resilience, wounding her deeper, frustrating her, breaking down her will to live; but worst of all, what terrorized her dreams and rent her spirit asunder was the aloneness, the very idea that she was without fellowship with others of her kind, and the villainous idea that she had no man to love her; yes, she had a few female friends, but they were healthy, and married now, and Lake had no role in their lives except as an incidental decorative ornament fading sadly into the tangled background at birthdays and holidays and get-togethers. The proper sequence of life events for her had been interrupted by her illness; she floundered aimlessly, flitting here and there, paralyzed often with depression, a dark, encumbering desolation where she felt violently shaken and then pressed down, down, down into the inky, murky depths of a bottomless well.

And Tony did not call. She hated him for that. "Why won't you call," she often cried aloud, "don't you know the proper etiquette of such things? Boy meets girl, girl pulls away, boy pursues! O, foolish, noble Tony! Don't listen to us at such times—you know there are rules of engagement I simply cannot breach." She would sigh, then, and say, sadly, "I must be silent in this game."

One breezy Autumn day, when the leaves on the trees are beginning to lose their cranberry-colored charm and their soft and pliable nature, when an occasional waterfall of breeze descends upon the people, bringing with it ripples of cold currents, Lake was returning from another visit to yet another doctor who told her that her illness was psychosomatic; she walked into her small apartment, bitter and sobbing. "Surrounded by fools! And how dare they accuse me of feigning disease? Mad as a March Hare!" and she looked at the yellow plastic bottle of pills in her hand and she flung it against the wall. "Always treating the symptoms with more poisonous drugs, and never the problem! It's so much cheaper and easier, isn't it!" Her eyes narrowed and her face grew crimson with wrath. "O, how I pray that they assume my disease; how I would love to walk past them and point to my head," which she did, "and say, 'cuckoo, cuckoo'!"

The phone rang.

"Hello," she answered.

"Hi, Lake. How have you been?"

Exhilaration riding a lightning bolt of energy pulsated throughout her excited body; but she caught herself, and in a flash, her once-ecstatic tone turned icy cold. "Tony."

He felt the chilly blast from her frosty reception, thus dismantling all of his carefully constructed dialogues, impelling him to offer her a muddled and weak, "Well, how are you?"

to which, it must be told, he cringed and knelt down in profound embarrassment.

"Why do you care?" Her heart had turned to stone at the memory of his too-long absence.

Now, he did not care, at least, not in this boiling moment, and his male pride would not allow him to go begging for precious conversation with her. "Well, I just thought I would call and say hello. Goodbye." He hesitated, and then put down the phone.

She said, in a lost panic, "Tony?" But he had already hung up. She slammed down the receiver, felt ill, and spent the rest of the raggedy night and the following formless day in bed, crying, screaming, despondent.

The next week she was terminated from her job due to excessive absences. The world seemed a foreign host to her, which she had chosen to never understand. "I have forgotten you," she was fond of saying about the world as she spiraled down into dark despair. "Get away from me, I never knew you; you were a false lover, a mere coquette, but really never loving me; better to be alone than with a cruel lover."

Winter crept slowly over the land, its tiny soldiers of ice spreading frost with their tiny, cold kisses.

Glaciers of freezing weather outside of manmade structures seep into the very blood and bone and sinew of the ill, freezing them from within, giving them no chance to escape to solace; woe to those ill who live in blustery Winter without indoor heat, woe to them and praise to those good citizens who help them.

She hated the Winter season now, where before, as a youth, it had brought a sense of excitement and wonder as she and her wealthy playmates jetted across the world in search of the finest snow to ski and the best resorts with the richest and handsomest men. "Those times were not real," she thought now, "not real, not true." She began to think that perhaps a life of endless, trivial pursuits was a life not worth examining; she was certain, at least, that she now loathed people who lived such a lifestyle. "I am not sure if it is my petty jealousy," she would wonder, "or if people like that are just wax caricatures of reality." Occasionally a laugh would come at such musings as she lay in the soft comfort of her bed. It was a good and safe and warm bed, a delicious warmth and tight environment controlled by her very will. "No one goes in or out without my explicit approval," she would giggle, looking about the bedroom of her humble apartment. But these were momentary refrains from the onslaught of her miserable disease, and it was at such times that she lived passionately and happily.

And then the monster within would return from its brief slumber and bring chaos upon her tranquil world.

"It is as if it is alive," she would shriek, as her symptoms would once more penetrate her consciousness.

And so it was, a virulent cycle where she was slowly massacred from within every bloody, vomiting day, and every feverish, vomiting night, only to be reborn by the first shreds of a glorious dawn inclined to a spectacular curtain of vermillion that was fringed with streaks and swirls of burnished gold; remission brought bountiful peace and blessed hope, and relapse brought her mentally and physically further into a deeper and darker schism where she was beginning to lose her way.

She took down every mirror in the apartment; and as she no longer wished to see her face in its entirety, she now owned only a small compact mirror.

Her phone did not ring for days, sometimes weeks; she called no one, visited no one, went nowhere, accomplished nothing in her secluded sanitarium.

Every morning that she awoke she was disappointed to be alive, but she had not the courage to terminate her own life; secretly, perhaps, she still had hope that one fine day, for some reason presently unknown to her, she would awaken cured—and it was this fantasy that stayed her hand from accepting the executioner's sharp razor to her thin wrists.

She took to unplugging the phone jack; her cell phone she had destroyed with a hammer long ago; her mail she refused to open unless it was a bill; her door she would not answer unless it was the authorities.

She was becoming what she had always hated in others when she was healthy. "I am a reclusive old spinster," she would say, and upon uttering these words, she would burst into hot tears. "O, how horrible I have become; I am no doubt worth more dead than alive."

Using a pseudonym, she found employment as a maid at Motel Excelsior, a job she took only because she needed to be near bathrooms.

Then there came on a sweet Spring night, when the freshly rained-upon flowers exuded their fragrance incense into the rarefied air, that Lake decided to actually listen to her phone messages. There was no real reason for such a radical departure from her now-established quarantine on contacts with the human race, except that sometimes Nature had the power to lift her sagging spirits off the funeral pyre.

"Hey, Lake, it's Carl van Buren."

She nearly lost her stale, rotting breath.

"Say, Lake, we're having a little get-together at…"

She heard no more, and saw only the flashing neon sign in her mind's eye that proclaimed ebullient youth rejoined, and cried, enthralled, "And tomorrow night; tomorrow tonight, and I have nothing to wear!" There was a dull pounding of a loud drum in her heart that promoted Health and Restoration, as if intermingling with her former class and celestial lifestyle would somehow bring her back from the dead; as if this elitist gathering would impart magical properties to her and with a special authority repudiate her illness and lift her back onto the pedestal of luxurious health and romance. "After all, we are special," she sang that starry, joyous morning.

The gala affair was at the newly built and grand Rothschild Room at the Ritz-Carlton Ballroom in New York City, in Central Park, located near Tiffany's, a place she had once frequented like an ordinary woman frequents the discount diamond shop in the town mall; and near Carnegie Hall, a place she had once frequented like an ordinary woman frequents the local cinema house for the early matinee. She borrowed on her credit card to fly to the glittering Big Apple the next day.

When she arrived at the spectacular palace, it was full of the old and new nobility, replete with celebrities, and dyads of politicians, triads of captains of industry, quartets of billionaires, princes, princesses, dukes, and duchesses—luminaries all, all providing ample resplendent light to dazzle and blind an ordinary human being; ah, but it was not so with Lake, for she had grown up around them, and her eyes—just like the eyes of a man condemned to the coal mines adjusts to the dark—had adjusted to the blaring glare by growing an invisible sheath that filtered out the images of one world and let in the images of another. "I'm home, I'm home," she murmured to herself, feeling very much the fairy princess finding her charming prince, "here I am somebody, with my own kind, as if I had never left, with people who understand me—with friends." She had not been sick on the flight here, nor did she feel sick now. "The fountain of youth, you foolish girl, is always right in front of you," she decided, and with that charming thought, she smoothed her amber-colored gown and walked in, her head held high.

A man and woman, their hands holding the ubiquitous alcoholic beverage that fuels their moral judgment, observed the new arrival.

"Egad, is that the late, great Lake Seville?" the thin man exclaimed in an explosive whisper to his amused partner. "She looks like a male concentration camp survivor in drag."

"Oh, the poor thing," the woman said, attempting to lose her smile as he playfully nudged her; but upon further examination of the target, she remarked, feeling very much the superior woman, "So, the stories are true."

The smirking man adjusted his security blanket—his six-carat emerald-diamond cluster that was embedded in his platinum ring—and screwed up his amused face as he observed the young woman walk about; he felt his pulse increase and his excitement flash onto his oily skin, for it was reasons such as this walking tragedy that he came to such events. "I do say, but, be honest, Margo, does she look more like a female walking skeleton or a male walking skeleton in a dress? I mean, well, you know I do not want to be insincere, but, egad, look at the atrocity," he exclaimed, as the woman neared his vicinity; "she has on so much powder and paint that she looks like a very sad clown on her way to join the circus." He giggled. "Yes, a circus of the dead." He was very proud of his sharp tongue and extraordinary ability to make people laugh, even when they thought best not to—but great wealth and power can subdue morality and subvert morality.

"Oh, Wilson, stop it, now," she said, weakly rebuking him, but her smile never dissipated as the woman neared them.

Lake acknowledged them with a gentle touch as she walked by, her eyes still searching for the gracious host.

"Egad," the thin man whispered, dangerously close in the wake of Lake's walk past them, "she smells like formaldehyde." He chuckled, wanting very much to pass along his fabulous witticisms.

Margo slapped his face. "Now, you are not amusing…"

As Lake walked past the clearly defined cliques of power, it was as if she were a social lightning rod that compelled the excessively groomed heads to turn toward her, with their stretched and pampered and powdered faces now turning sour, and their red, wicked tongues inside their masks to start wagging; this current phenomenon was unknown to her as she gently approached her lifeline, Carl van Buren, a young man heir to a textile empire.

Carl was able to suppress the aghast look upon his face before she could properly decode it. "Lake," he cried, as if to announce he was unashamed of her coming to him. He embraced her like an old friend, which is the formal greeting of all people empowered by wealth.

"Lake," he said, again, subdued this time, as if an exclamation would have seemed too false, "glad you could come."

She embraced him like a girl rescued at sea by a handsome captain. "Oh, Carl," she said, wistfully, and she pulled back to look at him, "it is so good to see you again!"

The superficial fortress he had staged around himself collapsed early in the conversation as he craftily brought up the exclusive impetus for her inclusion in this annual gala event. "So, Lake, congratulations are in order on your inheritance."

She had been laughing too eagerly and extending herself too much to recognize his memorized witty banter, so his intrusive remark fell short of her attention. "What now?" she said, talking a sip of her bubbly champagne.

He let all remaining pretense devour its gutter-bred self; the rich do not feel they ever have to put up a veil of kindness to anyone; instead they dig their rapacious fangs into their bloody victims when announcing their intentions. "I heard your late grandmother —and a very wonderful woman, may I add—left you a handsome sum of money," he felt thirsty and gulped his pink brew, "after all." He smiled, shaking his head in anticipation. "Well?"

Everything around her had receded as she fell three body-lengths deeper into her humid, dark, private well. She shook her numb head. "Inheritance?" she replied, without hearing her own words.

She wondered why she had not thought of Tony before, now that suddenly she thought of him. "What is he to me?" she wondered, but then she heard his penetrating words, "You must be with your own kind," and what he had also told her, later, "but you can never be with those whom you knew before; you are forever rudely marked."

"Yes, word around the sauna is that you are wealthy again; welcome back, young lady!"

She scrutinized his vacuous face, and then looked around at the elite populace, who had been stealing furtive glances at her. "Could it be possible I have been so foolish not to know what is happening around me?" She looked again to her host as she felt a cold shiver snake over her trembling body. "There must be some mistake," she said, her head still spinning from shame. "I have no inheritance."

He sought to argue the point, but he saw her genuine denial, and his voice became thin and not too terribly gracious in masking disappointment. "Well, rumors, rumors..." and he carved out a coerced smile as he began to look elsewhere for rescue; now, let it be said that the truly wealthy barons of the world do not allow a furrowed brow to wrinkle their face for too long—and even if it did occur, they would simply have it unwrinkled—nor do they believe that tact is a virtue they need address when talking to people they consider of inferior social status. "Well, I am the host," he said, looking about, and touching her bare shoulder, he said, "Mingle," and then deliberately walked away into the swirling nebulous of the Gold Queens and Kings, and the Silver Queens and Kings, and the Diamond Kings and Queens…

She could no longer feel her sagging body, for it had been slain by the icy breath of her host's treacherous words; yet, she still looked around, knowing the inner dynamics of these affairs. She was like a foreign fish, detestable in odor and appearance in a small, shallow pond where her every movement was keenly tracked by those aquatic eavesdroppers around her, her every movement sending ripples to be felt by those bubbling gossips. "I have shamed myself," throbbed in her befuddled mind. She did not remember walking past the gawking judges and jury, but she soon found herself in a yellow cab, then in her hotel room, then in the bathroom, vomiting.

She awoke the next day, sober to the fantasy. "I have to leave—and the cost," she mumbled.

During the flight home, a lingering vapor from her brutal embarrassment hung about her. "The inheritance," she whispered, shaking herself from her self-imposed languor, "is it possible?"

Once she was home, she dialed, with trembling hands, the number of her grandmother's lawyer, Matthew Gershon.

"Matt," she began, nearly faint with anticipation; she did not need to say her name.

"Lake! How nice to hear from you! I have called you often over the years, and written letters; so, how are you? Are you well?"

"Is it true?" she wondered, beginning to imagine her old lifestyle again. "Thank you for your concern, Matt, but I am fine, really; but the reason I am calling, well, I heard something about my inheritance…" She could say no more.

Dead silence, abrupt silence came, as if the connection had been severed. "Lake," he responded, gravely, "you know there was no inheritance."

She felt a whirling sensation in her brain as her body rocked to and fro; she vaguely remembered thanking him for his time, and again, thanking him for his solicitude regarding her health; she hung up and crawled wearily under her warm bed covers, and sobbed uncontrollably.

"Now," she thought, and quoted the narcotic formed from the bursting boils of depression that sat in the dark pools of her exposed brain, "would be a good time to die." But, alas, she was a coward, still, and still, secretly hoping and praying for a miracle she felt she deserved.

She mourned the passing of possible wealth. "C'est la vie," she moaned, hiding her head under her pink pillows; but then the thought of her unfortunate attendance at the grand ball made her nauseated. "I know they are talking about it," she whispered, now staring up at the ceiling in her darkened room; "I once did the same; it was my culture, the culture of the almighty powerful elitists, preying upon those unlike us from whom we derived our daily sustenance." She knew what she had done so many times in the past, as part of the natural consequence of brimming health, youth, and exceeding wealth; she and her smug friends had made no little amusement of people in their inner circle who had fallen from the high echelons of power and privilege; and hadn't her grandmother chastised her and her friends for such rude behavior? She thought of him. "O, Lake, you fool, he was right all along; O, Tony, Tony…" She cried more pious tears.

She felt herself shrinking. "I am alone in the world; unloved, unknown, unremembered; people look past me, people look around me, people..." But then her wounded spirit sunk and disappeared within her, and thus she could not finish her soliloquy of self-pity.

Twilight had descended, and she felt her thoughts were more honest and private now; she felt more solace when the darkness cuddled her in its smoky bosom. "Where have I been," she wondered aloud, "to be like this? How unprepared I am for the real world; is not the life of the wealthy adequate to prepare them for such grievous hardships?" She reflected for days, alternated between sleeping, lying in bed, drinking warm, honey-flavored tea, and listening to a species of symphony orchestra music she deemed capable of arousing human passions.

She lost her job at the Excelsior, a hotel that her grandmother's corporation still owned.

"How can I yet deliver myself from this tide of blood?" she wondered on the fifth day of her delicate despair, but she meant not liberty from illness, but freedom from mental anguish. "Can I live with it in grace? Are others able to be embalmed in physical mayhem and yet be happy? Is it possible?" She frowned, staring into the quieting black pitch of her room, and thought of whom she had once been and how strong she had been physically and mentally. "No! Never! It wants me to say that! I demand complete restoration! I demand satisfaction! I must not let it conquer me; I must conquer it!"

It was then, during this bald revelation, that the landline phone rang. "Oh," she cried, reaching for the plastic phone, "I forgot to unplug that worthless phone, again; if I had more resolve, I would disconnect that irksome... Hello."

"I want to see you."

She felt a cold shudder flow throughout her limp body, and she lay, stunned; several vowels and consonants formed upon her exquisitely designed, thin lips, but they all died an empty death; in her thoughts, she thought of many responses, and then selected one, and then she shouted in the comfort of her brain, "Fine," and then irritatingly thought "Fine," and then aloud, she said, curtly, "Fine." She was pleased with this choice of responses, for it sounded so much more hard and unyielding to her, precisely the reason she had plucked it from a long cascading line of ready responses such as "All right" and "well" and "okay."

It was raining, gently raining, sometimes a silver veil of misty, pearly drops christening the land, sometimes a steady drizzle, and occasionally a direct current of steady, soft showers, rain like soft velvet kisses that never seem to soak the body, rain made luminous by the sunlight breaking through the gray clouds; it was Winter, pulling back her white veil to let in a stream of warmth to bring relief to the land.

He would meet her in the neighborhood park under the towering Elm tree; she did not understand the merit of such a meeting place, but she had acquiesced easily. So, she stood, navy-blue umbrella in her pale white hand, looking very color-coordinated in her sienna-colored cowl neck sweater and khaki pants and worn, brown leather boots, anxiously awaiting the man she had not seen in nearly one year. "I have so much to tell you, Tony," she thought, but she shook her head, looking up at the wisps of falling raindrops, "but we have wasted so much time, you and I."

A man approached, not from any discernible car, and his appearance was familiar yet unknown to her; still, he was coming at her, slowly, without an umbrella; she reached into her brown purse for an object to dissuade the intruder, muttering for rescue from Tony. She hesitated, studying the walk and body language of the man.

"Tony has a brother?" she wondered, staring at the man as he drew nearer. "He looks so very much like him." She gasped. "Perhaps Tony is hurt, and he has come in his stead to tell me, perhaps," but the figure, who had been in the stream of shadow and fog, had just come into the clearing of resplendent white light. Her mind quit; her entire body was lifted up by an electric shudder that swelled the chamber of her heart with rapture, and dropping her umbrella, instinctively ran toward him, unable to speak, so full of Love and Joy was she.

He ran toward her, too.

"Tony," she said, weeping now as they embraced.

"Lake, my darling Lake."

She realized now how much she needed him because of who he had been to her; he had opened her whole world to what was and must be and could be, and he had done it with Truth and Honesty and Love.

"Tony," she said, sobbing, as she hugged him tightly, her eyes closed, "you're well." Yes, the impossible had been made possible. He was completely healed.

Revelations

They kissed and cried and kissed, laughed, kissed again, and then he held her out from him. "I've missed you so much, Lake Seville."

She smiled, and said, "Tony, I'm so happy for you," and her unselfish joy for him compelled her to embrace him once more. She laughed as she stroked the glorious, thick, curly black mane that was combed nearly straight back. "Your beautiful hair," she exclaimed, laughing through her warm tears. "O, Tony, how wonderful for you! I'll bet you're just fighting off the girls!"

His smile yielded to solicitude. "Lake," he began, ardently, staring passionately into her still lovely and luminous eyes, the color of springtime grass, "you're the only woman I want to fight off."

She abruptly pulled away from him. "No," she stammered, looking fully at his rejuvenated self for the first time.

He stood, bewildered. "Lake," he began, but could say no more.

"You're not like me, anymore," she said, shaking her head; and her soul spoke, dejected unto death. "I no longer know you."

"Lake," he whispered, pleading, "it doesn't make a difference."

"Tell me," she replied, feigning a smile and sobbing, "what was it? Which theory was correct? Pancreatitis? Adrenal exhaustion? Celiac disease?"

He embraced her, once more. "Lake, stop it; we celebrate my victory by combining our energies to solve your illness."

"No," she said, casting her glance downward, "I am finished."

He lifted up her chin with his hand. "Where is the indomitable spirit I knew so well?"

She smiled, but it was an ephemeral smile, wiped clean by an aged cynicism. "A pragmatist." She pulled away from him.

He was forced to look away, albeit briefly. "That part of me is dead and buried."

"Well, that part of me is alive and well," she said, scornfully, and then added, chillingly, "you taught me so well," and grabbing her heart, finished, "it is the larger part of me." She closed her eyes. "Tony, it is me, and you've left me alone," she whispered, and fell into his waiting arms.

"No," he protested, lovingly, holding her, stroking her moist, round head. "We can never be alone because we know each other as people should, without pretension."

She pulled away from him, again, stepping back several steps this time, her right hand to her feverish forehead. "Oh, please stop, Tony; you're killing me with your Moral Love." Her voice fell into an acrid vat of despair. "It cannot work." And as she stepped back further away from him, she felt their special bond disintegrating. "It's hopeless." Her face was frozen numb with a new horror. "It's over."

"No," he moved toward her, but her outstretched hand stopped him.

"We can't be together because we are two different people."

"No," he nearly shouted, his face aflame with wild desperation.

"Yes," she said, shaking her head, a smile fading into a frown as she stopped weeping, "it's ironic, isn't it?"

The raindrops fluttered and danced about them, sprinkling the two people with loving touches. No other sounds could be heard; no other movement in the park could be detected.

He sought to talk but his past philosophy betrayed him.

"Everything you said about eternal divisions between the classes of healthy people and those disenfranchised by disease was correct; O, Tony," she said, sorrowfully, shaking her head as if to impede her tears, "you lived it and you know it's true." He started to speak. "Yes, you know it," her voice was rent by deep pathos, "you know it; you're one of them, now, and I've fallen into the mud pit, forgotten; you live, and I slowly die." She wept now. "Tony, I am so happy for you, you don't know, can't know how I rejoice for you in my heart," and she clutched her breasts, "but you belong to the living now, and need a woman who is alive, not dead." She fell to her knees, and he ran and embraced her. "Tony, hold me, hold me one last time, so I might remember…"

He was on his knees and was holding her head close to his brawny chest. "Lake, my beautiful darling," he murmured.

"No, Tony, no," she began, as if breaking away from a loving dream that would soon become a nightmare, and she thought of the future, and was driven upward, freeing herself from him. "No," she cried, staggering backward, almost in fear, "you need to go; now, go," and she moved back again as he advanced toward her with supplicating hands. "This is my punishment for what I once was." She was staring at him now, seeing him from a different angle, engaging all of his wondrous new flesh and bone and marvelous luster of health. Her heart felt the warm droplets of solace seep into its sinewy fiber. "This is my burden and I alone have to struggle with it; no joy, no rest, no love until I understand it. Isn't that what you always said; isn't that what guided you to victory?"

He had stopped his forward motion now. His tone was devotion and loyalty. "I will not abandon you." He wanted to say he loved her, but his internal sense of timing and necessity begged him off. "Not now, you fool," he thought, "she won't hear it now; she'll be driven further back; wait, wait, wait!"

She tried in vain to smile, but managed only sorrow. "Go live, Tony." She talked as if she desperately sought to plant her loving desires for him into his heart. "Have a wonderful life."

She turned and walked away.

Hard rain poured upon the park now, an unrelenting, pounding, cold rain, a new species of rain as if to announce a change of seasons. The empty blackness, the harsh beauty of icy Winter resumed; and that which had once seemed attainable now seemed dead, ideas that could only be awakened in the long-forgotten, golden rays of Spring.

Love Settles In

I t is a curious thing to observe how a man who has been lost at sea reacts to his rescuers; if the man has been lost but for a brief time, his chief sentiment is one of profound relief, born from the implied dangers of the possibilities of utter abandonment; if, conversely, the man has been lost a longer time, and had his inner mettle tested to the utmost, he will respond to his rescuers with profound joy, and will extend this joy for many weeks and perhaps months thereafter.

There is, however, a more curious phenomenon while observing the man who has been lost at sea for a very long duration; if the man has adjusted to his dire conditions, and has become accustomed to the severe isolation of the environment, then when he is finally rescued, he feels a deep, private joy, ineffable to his rescuers except as physical and spiritual gestures. His rejoicing is muted as he once more adjusts to life on land and the memory of the lost voyage fades away. If, conversely, the man is lost at sea for an even longer period, to the point he has given up all hope of rescue, and has seen numerous ships pass him by that are seemingly cognizant of his unfortunate circumstances and are purposely avoiding him, his existence at sea is now most singular as he adapts to a new testament for survival. He now knows it is his own resolve that will propel him toward rescue; thus, once this man is rescued, either by providence or his own reckoning, his celebrations are ephemeral, and he simply continues to live, now on land, but often as if he is still lost on the vast blue skin of the listless sea.

Tony had been too long ill to dwell upon his rejuvenation; thus, he simply came back, by way of seamlessly slipping into the bubbling, frothy brook of mainstream society.

Now that he was back, he wondered why it had all been so important. "Of course, I am pleased to be healthy again," he thought, sitting at his oak desk, *The Odyssey* in hand, staring at the silver mirror, which evinced a handsome youth. "I am still not one of them, because I have been there and back again." Melancholy brooded in him, nesting comfortably in his past reflections. "How can I let go of who I was? A soldier changes who he is to survive in combat; he becomes a warrior, responding to every nuance of perceived peril in battle; he must become that which he had been capable of, and do what he must, to survive; home from war, can he easily slip off this new man and become the old he once was? I think not; I am now who I have become; why, going back is impossible." He put the epic poem down, and cursed. "I don't want to go back," and he cursed again. "I won't go anywhere without you, Lake, my love." He stood up, standing next to the mirror. "I will not, I cannot, for we are the same…"

Men are fools for love, gladly, madly, desperate fools who will sweep the height and depth and breadth of the known universe for the one woman they will love and who will love them. To love and be loved is a great gift: honorable, free and good; and once a man allows Love to envelop him completely, once he tastes its savory, fragrant juices assiduously pumping through his hot blood, he cannot rightly live without it.

For Love, men will forsake mother and father, sister and brother, friends, job, wealth, opportunity, country, all things not absolutely necessary for the survival of that inviolate Love, a Love through which he draws piety, strength, peace; once this Love transforms him, the prudent man nurtures it and guards it from all foreign influences; to lose Love, then, is to lose part of self; therefore, Man will kill for Love, search the great expanse of land and sea and sky, conquer, sacrifice, metamorphose; Love must abide in him, or he grows ice crystals in his paralyzed heart. Death loves the shriveled heart.

Without Love, Man is a pillar of salt, its amber grains slowly blown away by the relentless grinding of wind and rain and sleet and snow.

Persistence

Tony pursued Lake to give life to two people.

He would call and she would not answer her phone; he would send her letters, and she would keep them, unopened; he would come by her small apartment, but she would not answer the door.

"My tactics are sloppy, too regional," he mused, devising plans at his home on how to gain access to her ear. "I must think outside of my small influences." And so he thought and thought and thought, about strategies that in no way resembled any previously recognized stratagems, thinking this way and that, analyzing every detail, scrutinizing every subtlety, examining every tiny particle of fiber covering his ideas, but he found only frustration.

"But I cannot let another year go by, not again; why, if I can regain health after so long dead, even proving those nasty gainsaying creatures, those iconic doctors, absolutely wrong, why can't I regain a woman whom I love and who loves me? Ha!"

Desperate men do desperate things, and desperate men in love have no known geographical or metaphysical boundaries.

He came upon a gray calico cat who was engaged in a worthy field of investigation; to wit, the female feline was sitting on its furry haunches, head down, jade-colored eyes staring into the dark hole of its potential dinner companion, the common gopher rat.

Epiphany crackled in the rarefied air above his head, showering him with its shafts of luminous light. "So help me, I'll do it," he whispered in a great shout, so as not to disturb the patient hunter.

He meditated upon his new revelation for a day. "I know the danger of this," he decided; "the longer I think about it, the greater chance I will forsake it; so, just do it, you fool," he shouted, as if truly he were talking to a part of himself he could motivate.

But he could not do it; the pull of comfort and safety that a common life promised, menial and repetitive though it was, was preferable to the unknown. Lo, even when he capitulated and began to dream of a normal life, he never once thought of pursuing a "normal" woman, for he had seen them now as they really were, as their physical equal—that is to say, they saw him, too—since he was healthy again, and what he saw did not please him. "They do not understand life," he sadly observed, whenever he chanced to talk to them; "what can they offer me but the rants of a spoiled child?"

He paced his apartment, in spirals and circles and curlicues and up and down and all around, thinking and planning, evaluating his options. "But I must quit my job," he repeated to himself again; "I must be a man, a man would do this: give it all up for the woman he loves; nothing else matters if I don't have her; what good is playing it safe when my whole world is at risk? Did I play it safe all these lost years? No, may it never be said!" He stood fully erect as he faced the mirror that had captured his trials and tribulations, and he sought to speak to a part of himself that had lain hidden for too long, dead in some men from disuse, corrupted in other men from sin. "Be a man," he began, looking at his fine physique, "do what must be done; extraordinary circumstances call for extraordinary actions, and extraordinary men," he shouted. Alas, his courage was false, without foundation, without fortifications, without fortitude; such courage as he needed must not stand alone, but must be an amalgam of courage and strength, but also infused with Love and Hope and Sacrifice. He had been entrenched in the fantasy of the linear events of life too long, he knew no other: it was birth to school to job, then marriage and home and security; to veer from the carefully chosen path heaped upon him by the dictates of a safe, trusted history placed him into the unknown, which was peril.

Cruel weeks passed, cruel, then more long, angry weeks crawled up one side of his body and down the other, infecting him with their slimy trial of shame and bitterness; his egregious mistress, Disease, had been uncreated, and now in her place was humiliation, utter humiliation derived from the inability to go forward based on superior knowledge of the right thing to do at the right time; but in the wake of what was clearly known as right stood that oblique marble statue, fear, utter fear of the unknown, which disrupts what has been attained after a life's hard labor.

What kind of man will forfeit his hard-won career and station in society to win the love of a woman?

Shame wore its wicked bald "S" proudly upon his chest, mocking him, draining his inner power, devouring his manhood, vanquishing his ego, stripping his confidence, eroding, crushing and pilfering his reason for existence. His body was flaccid, his posture low, his demeanor sunken; he could not extract himself from this rotten gloom because victory could come only from an action he would not execute.

When he was ill, he had been fond of saying, "I don't understand people who have physical health, and yet let emotional debris poison their well; oh, if only I had health again, I would forswear any petty emotional arrow that would bring me down."

Pity the ramblings of the theoretical boaster and philosopher.

He was being bored from within by self-flagellation, his very psyche shelled by the heavy armament of self-debasement, self-hatred, and self-persecution.

Then came justification as it had to for rescue, for without even a shadow of relief, his inner man would have died; but the act of allowing in justification set him further away from his goal.

"It wouldn't work, anyway," he began to say, his mind desperate to find shreds of precious light to free itself from its dark prison; "she is ill; I am not ill, anymore; she isn't my kind; we have grown apart." He cursed. "Why doesn't she call?" He began to lift himself from the sinking mire he was in with this disingenuous flak; but it was all subterfuge, for in reality, he was not extracting himself toward the light falling from the high azure vault of Heaven but toward the unholy flickering light emanating from the red flames of self-destruction below. He soon realized his folly, repented of his sins, and lamented his fate.

The mind, at once a prisoner of depression, tries desperately to free itself of this fierce enemy; to wrestle with the mighty talons and sharp fangs of black depression is futile, so the mind will devise a plan to draw sustenance from another source to empower itself. As it is consumed by that heartless fiend, depression, the mind will adjust its psychological compass and find true North; once this is done, it will find a single point of light and focus upon it; but if there is no light, it must go searching for it.

Since he could not solve his dilemma, his mind signaled him one message again and again, and knew that he must flee his abode; he must put one heavy foot in front of the other and walk away from his comfortable surroundings and not look back; so, he ventured forth, walking some days, driving others, looking, searching the landscape for answers.

He drove aimlessly for hours on some days, looking at every fragment of humanity and extrapolating it into its greater role. He found nothing.

"I have decided," he reasoned, a week hence, "that if a man is to find answers, he must go looking for them." He laughed. "Well, of course." But upon further reflection he decided this was indeed profound. He would now tour his city on foot. "From the vantage point of a car, the city is a distant, impersonal, moving picture," he thought to himself as he began his fateful journey. "I don't know what I am looking for," he whispered, walking into a neighborhood a mile from his home, "but I'll know it when I see it."

For a week, he traversed the local terrain, observing the citizens in various stages of life—recreation, work, rest, communication—and he was unable, initially, to make sense of it all. "How do I know what a family is? Oh, this is all a waste of time! What am I looking for?" Depression began to descend once more upon him, sealing the entry points of light to his aching mind.

He checked the messages on his phone: nothing; he ran to his gray metal mailbox, and although with every letter turned upside down, he decided, there was the possibility of it being from her, with every letter turned right side up issued darts of gloom to him.

The stark words of the man at the library came to him as he sat dejected in his apartment. "You are the man—you lead."

"But I cannot," he cried, pounding his fist into the faded white walls of his home, "but I must!"

A cowardly man must die a thousand humiliating deaths before he can raise himself to the level of true Courage.

After every mortal death and rejuvenation, a man is rebuilt outside, from strong feet to proud head, and inside, from rich red blood and strong, white bone to tough sinew, every molecule seasoned with a new variety of fortitude; the next obstacle must be overcome, or what was once constructed under stress and storm will wither and die; it is like climbing a tall, rugged mountain: the climber suffers for every misstep, and for every misstep he takes, he may lose not just one step but slide three steps backward, or even further, to the rocky flat below.

Each obstacle before a man seems insurmountable, but after the man has prevailed against it, the once-formidable obstacle seems insignificant; this, then, is the secret of a man's journey to the mountaintop: with every step and every obstacle conquered, he gains not only Courage but a superior knowledge based on strategies and attitudes in attacking any object, inanimate or animate, that is placed in his way, either by himself or by others.

It was an exceptionally hot June night, a sultry, humid, ethereal night when the human body is wrapped in a fine, gauzy, silken sweat, where the exhausting heat seems to permeate the air and boil a human body on the inside, when he approached her small condominium. He smiled at her dying arrogance. "She still wants to live as a blue blood."

He stared hard at the impenetrable white stucco domicile. "Therein lies salvation or condemnation." He expelled hot breath with a short "Hmm," and looked about himself—at all points of the compass, and then upward. "Of all the things on earth, it comes down to one." He cogitated upon the wisdom of such a possibility. "Somehow, it all seems too exclusive; but I am a wretched human being, and a prisoner of my dreams."

On the thinnest of whims, he decided to sit down upon a small mound of verdant grass that was part of her homeland security network, in the hopes of yielding up some noble idea concerning his current dilemma. "Is there nothing more," he wondered; "have I allowed my passions to smother all reason?" He grimaced. "But if I walked away now, and I lost my love for her, it would mean that all of it was foolish, or that passion dies." He shook his head, and grieved, "I would know the answers to such questions if I had been a real man all of these years; why, I'm flying blind." He buried his head in his hands, and murmured, "And I once cursed the healthy for their lack of willpower," and he opened his eyes, and whispered, solemnly, "With health comes a world of responsibility and woe; the pain is of the same nature, without reason or clearly delineated paths to follow. This world I have encountered, others have lived and conquered." He stared, transfixed, at her home. "Born free, yet enchained." He pounded the soft, moist soil. "O Man, fated to taste misery forever, a prisoner of his lusts." He threw up his arms, supplicating the Heavens. "What good is intellect and reason when all is lost by the lusts of the flesh?" He tore at his new layers of gorgeous, well-muscled body. "Cast off this old man and create a new man." He looked about. "But how? Think! Think, you fool!"

His mind entered a dark terrain wherein dwelled vast deserts and the scorching heat of ignorance. "Here I sit," he thought, "until I create that which was previously unknown, and give it life; I must think unlike myself, feel unlike myself, act unlike myself; I must put away this old flesh and see the world as does a newborn babe." He fell as if unto a deep trance, shutting off all extraneous clutter, humor and otherwise.

On that moist mound of sumptuous fescue and Kentucky grass, he sat, then lay, staring deep into the black void of icy space, thinking thoughts he never had, discovering a person born from the persecution of disease.

On that warm Summer night, in the sweet caress of the gentle breezes, he blew his mind up with a dream.

And in his dream, he was sitting, naked upon a mountain of translucent ice, sparkling, pure, unyielding blue ice; he was staring out upon the hordes of people who were scurrying about. "What are they to me?" he asked, in earnest. "They are not part of me." But then he listened to their lamentations and wailing cries, and discerned that there was a famine in the land. "No water," he said to himself, looking down at the glassy surface upon which his feet rested, "but this is my mountain I have labored hard for, earned and deserve; this is my mountain, of whom I dearly love," and he felt a soothing warmth swaddling his skin, and he was pleased.

And though he heard their desperate cries, still he did nothing, for their pleas meant nothing to him. "They are not me, and I am not them; they have their problems, and me, mine; it is the way of the world; no one worried about me when I was alone and my body full of disease; likewise, they too must be alone, and deal with their problems, if only to make them stronger; yes, it is good," he decided, and he smiled.

One day, a white dove descended from the foggy sky, and began to fly in a tight orbit about his bare head. "Ridiculous bird," he whined, "get thee gone, scoundrel," and he attempted to motivate the bird to leave by wild hand gestures, but the bird was unrelenting in his harpy-like attitude upon its seated prey.

He cursed at the bird, and presently found himself standing to better fight this winged adversary; affixed solidly in this stance, he found the creature hovering in midair before him, its small white head moving from side to side, its luminous black eyes staring with a strange tranquility into his mind; nevertheless, he smote the dove, knocking it to the side of the mountain, whereupon it immediately froze.

Standing now, he found himself quite stark naked. "What is this," he exclaimed, scrutinizing his own bare flesh, "and not only naked," and he beheld the people below, "but blue with freezing." He was drawn to the pink, happy faces of the people below. "How is it that they smile with such a skin, while I, with so much wealth, am a bluer shade of the ocean sky?" And then the most extraordinary event occurred; to wit, he commenced to shaking. "How can this be? I sit upon an ice mountain with no sense of cold, and now that I stand, I shiver like a newborn babe in a snow blizzard?"

And he looked and looked upon the scorched land, searching for answers; and what did he see? "Why," he announced to himself, he being the only sentient creature about the iceberg monument, "the people are in dumb ecstasies! What can be the cause? Who—whoa!" he shouted, watching drops of the blessed, chilled water sliding off his private sanctuary. "What fiend steals my inner guarded treasures?"

The pearl-shaped droplets wept down the mountainside, moistening the parched tongues of the people, softening the dry, cracked earth, and forming puddles, which soon gave way to small tributary streams, then ponds, and lakes, then mighty rivers; all this he watched in amazement, and in amazement, he watched his body slowly shed its blue hue and animate to pink, a glowing, robust, hot-pink-flavored, smooth skin. His shivering ceased as the ice mountain dwindled to the size of a small hill.

The white dove, freed from its frozen prison, came upon him with other doves of silver and gold, which carried freshly made trousers and shirt and shoes, and they dropped the garments at his feet. He presently wore the new clothes, and gazed in wonder at the white dove, and smiled at it as it alighted upon his shoulder; he kissed its soft, furry forehead, and watched it fly away into a sizzling cerulean patch of sky.

"Once," he murmured to himself, now standing upon the ground, and watching a town spread out before himself, "I thought I was alive; but I now know I was not alive, only alive to myself, which is not a life at all; but now, I truly live because I am alive among people. Hmm." He smiled. "We are responsible for each other because none of us are above anyone; we are the same, searching creatures; and when we are alone, we are lost for certain."

He awoke, outstretched on the dewy grass, his gaze into the black pitch of night interrupted by the face of a man in adorned in black.

"Son," the officer said, standing, and waiting amusedly as Tony carefully sat up, "had a good dream, did you?"

"Well, sir," he responded, lucid, as he was one to clear his mind quickly after a sleep, "yes."

The big man in the smart uniform of power bent down next to him; his voice was seeded with kindness. "I received a phone call about a man camped out on this lawn." He nodded his big head, and tilted back his hat. "I'm a civil servant, son, and I'm bound by the narrowest of laws to respond faithfully to the public's anxious fears, realized or not, and calm such citizens' minds." He let slip a knowing "Hmm," and nodded toward the condominium in question.

Tony felt nauseated, as if betrayal devoured his naked heart.

"I talked to the little lady in there, and it wasn't her doing." He smiled reassuringly. Tony's soul lived once more. "She said you could stay; it is, after all, her patch of land." He passed two bottles of spring drinking water to the youth. "She wants you to have these."

The officer stood up, as if suddenly he was aware of a transgression of the boundary between the public and officers of the law. His voice was harder now. "Do you love her?"

Tony stood up. "Yes, sir, I do."

The elderly gentleman with the shiny silver badge looked about, nodded his head, and then looked directly into Tony's eyes, his words passionate and pious as he considered his own past. "Men never really know much about the mind and heart of a woman, but this thing they do know, son: women are to be won." He stood up fully erect. "No good woman wants some fool to take her easily; she wants to feel as if there is some man who is willing to—well, someone who is willing to give up more than a meal and a show for her; a man who will forsake mother and father and job, and anything else…" He nodded his head and looked beyond himself. "This is her golden moment, son, to know that there is a man out there," he pointed into the dark horizon, "who considers her more important than anything else on this God's good green earth; for goodness' sake, this could be her only time, and she has to be certain if she is going to promise you her future…" He smiled, nodded his head, and evened out his black-rimmed cap.

"Sometimes," he stated, and with such utter sorrow that Tony wanted to weep, "a man gets only one chance." He slapped the youth on his shoulder, and faded away into the swirling tide of anonymity.

Tony looked up at her home, and whispered, "And here I will stay, until my love leads me away," and he sat down, cross-legged, and drank the cool, refreshing water; and as the balmy night air encircled him, he thought of the officer, and felt deep sorrow for him.

The Road Home

She watched him through the small slit in the eggshell-colored blinds, clutching her weak chest. "O God, how he must love me so," she said, and fell upon her knees, coughing in horrific spasms, "but I cannot trust him! How can I?" She cursed loudly as she observed the red blood drain out with her phlegm. "It's pity; not love, it cannot be; I won't stand for pity, I won't," she shouted, and she crashed a book against the wall. "I hate him for this," and she fell prostrate, weeping, "but I love him! O, how I hate myself!" She could smell the acrid odor of disease fouling her lungs. "It's a wonder I don't drink or smoke," but she laughed at this, "but I would be dead, for sure; and no, this little termite of an illness would be my maker, then." She felt the urgency to stand, in defiance of her lethargy, and once standing, spied he whom she loved. "This is why I cannot be with you, my beloved; because I will be well, one day, and one day, I will be with my own kind, again, as I must be; O Tony, I love you, but you are not my own kind, only someone once like me; strangers—and both of us healthy—I never would have known you, even if you had been with me." A deep melancholy fell over her, and she stumbled to her tomb, her bed, and murmured, "Is that it, are we destined to be strangers?" and she wept because she feared she was right, and she wept, because she feared she was wrong.

But she wept because the intricately woven fabric that is life had become inaccessible to her, barring her entrance into its silky bosom. "I cannot get back," she sobbed into her white pillow; "once you are removed, the world dismisses you. No one cares." Intellectually, she acknowledged his love, but she dismissed it to reinforce her brooding bitterness. "I am alone," she shouted, "and unloved, and that is the way it should be." She nearly looked into the mirror. "Who would love me anyway, but a fool or a madman?" She massaged her moist, pale face. "Oh, I need to be alone to figure all this out," and she said with profound disgust, "or crawl into the woods and expire like a dying, mad dog." She wanted to die like a forgotten, beaten, bloodied wild beast, kicked out of civilization by even the lowest of Man's vessels, debased and humiliated and spat upon. "I don't deserve life," she murmured, thinking of what she considered now her most ignominious past, for it was her past that ensnared her conscience and beat her as if she was the lowest form of slave.

If she could not have it all, then she wanted nothing at all.

"My past has buried my future," she said, feeling an icy chill stream over her languid body. "I am filth, wretched, undesirable," she choked on this last self-debasement, for her sublime beauty had been the flawless engine that had driven her entire existence before her disease.

Her past, her wicked past, her deceitful, self-absorbed and arrogant past had been like powerful waves crashing against a mighty rock cliff, eroding her weighty resolve to ignore her sins; but now the mighty dam within her mind had become porous and decayed, and bits had fallen off into the foaming, turbulent sea, leaving her exposed to unknown philosophies and truths, exposing her to ideas hitherto unknown: Beauty, Love and Justice.

She wept sin, she bled it, she oozed it out of her every pore and it engulfed her with its galling spittle, but it did not free her from it; indeed, the more sin that piled upon her mottled, cold flesh, the worse her soul grieved.

She inhaled it, expelling this acrimonious stench of death from her weak lungs, but it lingered, this hard sin, like a thick, heavy fog, and she breathed it in, gagging on its slick consciousness, its lumpy tumors, sucking its vile vapors into her hot nostrils. She felt as if she dwelled within its being, trapped like an irksome fly on a sticky spider web.

And from within the belly of the beast, she beheld shapeless oblivion.

This was her day, a day for the dying.

Now, for the living, a day is like every other day, indistinguishable from one moment to the next; but still, their day is buoyant, dynamic and flowing, not in the brilliant context of superior events, but in the tiniest details, the indescribable nuances, the imperceptible changes. In the world of the family living, life moves inexorably forward despite the best intentions of outside forces or sometimes even the family; a man and woman wed, jobs are secured, a baby is born, the father and woman dote upon the baby, the baby grows up, another baby is born; there is illness, perhaps death, a grandfather dies, an aunt is stricken ill, another baby is born, the mother and father dote upon the baby, the family grows; parties are given, anniversaries and weddings celebrated; there is divorce, and separation, perhaps, even death, but the woman remains, a baby is born, grandparents dote upon the baby; there is school and church and birthdays and holidays, and cars bought and arguments about friends and acquaintances and lovers, but life goes forward, perhaps not all at once, but in the accumulated actions of everyday living. The baby crawls, the baby walks, a house is bought, there are arguments and reconciliation and trips and reunions and joy and pain and sorrow, and good love and bad love and betrayal and forgiveness, good times and bad, defeats and triumphs, money made, money spent, fortunes squandered, fortunes gained, graduations, tears, laughter, funerals, and in the end, in the last detail of the final finish, there is completion, an utter satisfaction and feeling of a special accomplishment, born from all of the seen and unseen events that might have taken the family sideways or backward or into the cold ground, but in the very last detail, to a consummate victory. The family does as Nature compels them: to go forth and populate the planet, and in doing so, contribute to its core inner workings, making them no less important than any other organism, an intricate part of the greater network that makes up humanity.

But for those chronically ill who are alone, a day is like every other day, indistinguishable from the next, and for these tortured souls, there is no life forward, no loving satisfaction of good deeds done at the final finish; no, for those dispossessed from society, life, daily, exists in agonizingly endless tyranny, which merely heaps up more misery and more pain and more bitterness upon their crushed heads; and every day that ends in nothing gained but emotional horror, and physical torment bewails a haunting tune to their decaying hearts. Comes then a spiny-covered shaft with finely honed grooves built from the bemoaning and lamentations of the afflicted, and when it is whistling through the air in the house of the dead, the stale air feeds into the sharp-edged grooves and plays a mournful song, "Loss, loss, another day without Love, without Family, without Joy, another day gone forever; you are alone, abandoned by the world, alone, forever alone, you have been fated to die a pitiful death, alone, alone in life, alone in death. Die."

Lake felt the horrible scream of painful absence bang inside her mind. "I am forgotten," she sobbed.

Her privileged past was an aversion to her, now; she retched at the repulsive thought of how she had once viewed society. "When all is said and done," she whispered, lifting her head from the tear-stained pillow, "I will die a human being."

The emotional and financial carnage wrought by existence with her former people had slowly been grafted upon her soul the past year. "One cannot see that one exists in excrement unless one steps away from it," she whispered to herself, "but one has to want to; when I was one of them," she would not use the word "rich" now, "I inhaled excrement and ate it so often and so long that I grew used to its pungent taste; in fact, I grew to think it was the elixir of life; but now..." She suppressed the idea that she still longed for wealth and fine clothes and fine food, and experiencing the finest countries and the finest men; these were the ideas that her weak flesh burned for, these were still prevalent lustful memories that lingered in her like the remains of an infestation.

The flesh, it must be stated, has memory, much like the brain, and what was sensuous to it once, it still aches for: the supple touch of a lover's intoxicating skin, the silky smooth surface of exquisitely handcrafted clothes, a sumptuous meal served from a golden tray atop a high mountaintop in the French Alps, the exhilaration of silvery moonlight in Rome at night as you walk hand in hand with your lover, the splendor of a rosy dawn in the vineyard fields of France as you ride with the son who is heir to a wine fortune; this, then, is the charred memory of the flesh, which smolders upon the injured mind, tilting it, until the jelly-like brain slips down the ribbed, slimy sides of the gutter and into perdition.

She stared into a black pitch where not even her out-stretched hand could be seen. "This is the life of the rich," she whispered; "they think this is the light; to think," and she laughed, "to think I felt I deserved my elitist position because I was born into it. O Grandmother," she averted her head, as if to avert sorrow, "I miss your wisdom. You tried to tell me about such things, but I could not see beyond wealth and entitlement. I thought I was happy, but now I know I was not even alive…"

Lake had the unique ability to see and feel and become her surroundings, be it near her, seen from afar, read by her, or viewed on the magic screen; her illness did not allow her to sleep easily or long: and so, she often watched late-night television shows that were produced by reputable charitable organizations, focusing on their efforts to help the impover-ished, the helpless, the diseased around the world; and also, she read books about the lives of the poor, the downtrodden, the ill around the world; and so, it was her habit these past many months to lie in bed and listen to a particular radio show that explored the human condition through the eyes of people who were not born into the good graces of health and wealth and endless opportunities, who were representative of the half of the world that lives on one to two dollars a day.

Every night, the host, suffused with passion and solici-tude, took the listener to places the Modern Era had not yet touched with its magic healing wand, and painted a harsh real-ity with his own imploring heart, and the authentic words of the afflicted: in the southernmost part of Asia, where barefoot children play in dirty streets, happy children who live with their mothers in brothels, happy, but if female, will follow the heavy footsteps of their mother into this unseen purgatory; in Africa, young girls, refused an education by society, work as maids and laundresses in the homes of the unsympathetic wealthy, and may be paid barely two dollars a day for their sixteen hours of labor—but they are better off than those kidnapped and sold into servitude for the wealthy, where they are paid nothing and are beaten for any transgression and sexually assaulted for any carnal whim of their masters; in south Asia, young girls are captured, sold into prostitution, sometimes sold by their desperate parents, to live a life so unreal and unknown to shielded and privileged minds, that to hear the horror of it was unattainable and unrecognizable to the lazy, comforted mind of the contented and free person; in the Middle East, families live in makeshift refugee camps, exposed to the harsh environs in small tents, in need of medicine, and adequate food and shelter, at the mercy of rebels and a weak government; and in South America, the translator began as the young woman spoke: "I worked at the clothes factory with thirty-three other women; I felt like I was rich; I made ten dollars a day for fourteen hours of work—the work was hard, but I had three children at home; and then one day a man from an American company came, and demanded that our employer make the shirts cheaper, so they could sell it to their customers for only eight dollars, and so we had our pay cut to seven dollars and fifty cents a day; and then we had to buy our own uniforms, and use outside facilities to wash; and then when we were late, even a minute, we lost half a day's wages, but we did not complain, you see; and then many of us were laid off, including me; so, I began to wash clothes and scrub floors in the neighborhood, and the women were surprised to see me, but I think they understood that a mother will do what she needs to do for her children; but even then I received about two dollars a day for this kind of hard work, but what could I do, it was all I could find—I have no education; but this was not enough money, so I began to beg on the streets and search for jobs, but it was so crowded with women like me; even the government would not help me; so, how was I to raise three children on these paltry wages? I will tell you, sir, I did what I must—my babies began to work in factories and not go to school, and this broke my heart, for I did not want them to ever live my life, so, to my shame, I became a streetwalker; many of the neighborhood ladies saw me and shook their heads, but I did what I had to, being with twenty to thirty men a day, and maybe I earned ten dollars a day; and you know, sometimes I got beat up, but my children must go to school, they must escape this poverty, they must know there are other worlds out there than this terrible prison we are in." She paused. "How can life be so horrible; if I had never been born, it would be better for everyone, even for my babies—no matter how much I love them—I did this to them; but then again, I love them, and maybe, somehow, we will survive all of this—God willing."

In Africa, there were refugee families who made a hut out of sticks and discarded bits of cloth and pieces of bags in the scorching desert; women who scooped water from a hole near a river into a plastic jug, and then walked home for several hours with the eighty-pound container atop their ninety-pound frame; children stolen by rebels and coerced to be soldiers; poor children leaving their homes to go find work in the city, only to find work with wealthy families who treated them like indentured servants; in Eastern Europe, girls who quit school to go to work, and then quit work after being promised a better job by smiling entrepreneurs, and became slaves in the world of prostitution.

The abject horrors of the world never ceased to float by in this macabre parade, and thus, she felt the agony, saw the pain, heard the plaintive cries, smelled the fear of the Innocents, and touched the suffering of the oppressed.

And then she dreamed a dream of past deeds, as she had dreamed before, and she dreamed of things she should have done, and of things that were nevermore; but these dreams she had already dreamed, and many like it too; and it was these dreams, and others like it, that had begun to wash away her old self and make this present self brand new.

And here was her first dream: she was standing upon a high citadel in front of a Pilgrim whose face was covered by a hood and who wore a purple robe of fine linen, who presently pointed to the valley below her, and spoke, in grave tones, "Behold, on your left hand liveth the children of privilege, where the cradle of power and mammon breeds like flowers in Spring, where no voice cries out in want of food or clothes or shelter; and on thy right hand liveth the children of poverty, and the cradle of pain and suffering breeds like maggots in heat, where the suffering cry of the starving child never ceases, and the violence of desperation never stays silent; now, choose thy life."

And she smiled easily, and whispered, pointing to the left, "There, where there is unceasing joy and light."

"Yea, first we shall see what grows in the land of sorrows, that thou mayest know for certain of thy choice," she said, solemnly, and with the wave of her long, robed hand, she took her there; but she saw the people not in their flesh covering, but in the bared covering of their immortal soul; and she saw and felt some who were good and noble, who sought to live righteous and true, and some succeeded, and others failed; and she saw some who were bad and ignoble, who sought to live like animals while attacking those weaker and exploiting their environs with violence and pestilence of moral filth; and misery and chaos abounded, and there seemed no beginning nor end of it; and the Pilgrim pressed her face down into the swirling river of pollution that poverty creates, and she beheld the foul stench, and it was more than she could bear, and the Pilgrim said, "Behold, the stench of destitution and disease, remember its coarse nature and aroma; does thou seek this place to live?"

And she pleaded fervently, "No, no, not here; take me to the choice of my generation, of my societal class, of the vaunted life I deserve."

"So be it," the Pilgrim returned, and with a wave of her robed hand, she took Lake there, but when she stood in the midst of this fabled land, she saw the people not in their flesh covering, but in the covering of their bared immortal souls, and behold: she smelled the foul disregard of fellow Man that stems from their rotting, black hearts, and the cruel machinations of their minds as they sought to subjugate the masses for their own favor, and the singular want to lie and cheat and steal for the sake of mammon and power; and there were a few who attempted to do good; and yea, the Pilgrim laid hold upon her head and pressed her face down into the stinking fumes of unbridled avarice and power, and the stink was more than she could bear, and the Pilgrim said, "Behold, the stench of wealth and power, remember its coarse nature and aroma."

And lo, they were presently atop the high citadel once more, and the Pilgrim asked her, "What didst thou learn?"

"The stench of both worlds is unpleasant; but where can I yet live?"

And her countenance grew pale, and a great sadness overtook her. "Thou are not ready for the remission of thy sins; thou are not ready to live, yet, in either world, and must create thy own."

And that was the end of her first dream, and here was her second dream:

She was standing in the midst of a long stretch of barren desert, and the ground was dry and hard, pockmarked by the memories of war; there were tufts of yellow sand, and hills of yellow sand, and when the hot wind blew, the tiny pebbles from the mounds revealed to her the remains of a civilization.

And she looked about herself, and behold, she saw human misery in every form—emaciated children with sallow skin and bloated bellies lay scattered in their death throes; men, with their bony limbs and sunken cheeks and skinny bodies covered by legions of big, black flies, lay in heaps and despair; and women, their heads adorned by white cotton coverings, their arms around their starving babies, were looking about, their hands supplicating to the Heavens for succor.

And then one of the women, her black skin rubbed and chewed to a leathery texture by the tortuous sun, and her face covered in pustules and boils as she waved flies off her newborn, held out her left arm—an arm with more bone than flesh—and then she whispered in a voice born of pain and sorrow, "Please, please, a drop of water…"

Now, this woman she spoke to was of surpassing Beauty and Elegance, her body youthful and bursting with great energy, and she was dressed in raiment of finely spun gold, and upon her feet were silver slippers, and upon her head was a crown of precious stones; and lo, she responded, as if the voice of the dying woman was a faceless voice that came from the hot winds, "But I must not tarry, for I am late for the ball, and I must buy a dress that befits a princess such as I." And lo, the sand beneath her feet became as a mire, and she sank a little into it.

And Lake was watching this scene near them, and now recognizing the fair-haired woman as herself of long ago, she cried out, "Fool! What is a dress to you, if you do an act of charity instead!" But the young Lake frowned when she heard this, and ignored her.

Again, the dying woman held out her hands in a supplicating gesture, and said in a feeble voice, "A bowl of rice for my baby…"

And the woman before her, the young and voluptuous and healthy Lake said, "But I have to ready myself for the ball, and my attendants all await me." And lo, she sank a little more into the muck beneath her.

Now, Lake felt a mirror pressed into her hand, and she brought it up to her face, and she was astonished to see that she was still beautiful, but that now a few patches of blistering eczema were forming on her face. "Fool," she cried out to the younger Lake, "what is a moment to you, when in its stead you might help those less fortunate!" But the younger Lake ignored her.

And again, the dying woman held out her hands in a supplicating gesture, and said, in a voice gentle and loving, "May God bless you for all of your remaining days; please, kind lady, my breasts are dry, so, a cup of milk for my baby…"

And the young and handsome Lake said, "But I must have my nails done—they are so atrocious these days—anything less would be a scandal!" And lo, her body sank even further, even up to her knees, into the bubbling morass below.

"Fool!" Lake cried, seeing blistering boils and pustules forming all about her now worn and abused body. "What are trivial and narcissistic things when the value of human life is compared!"

And the younger Lake ignored her.

And again the dying woman held out her withered hands in a supplicating gesture, and said, in a voice barely alive, "God bless you all the rest of your days; but please find a deep grave to bury my precious child," for her baby had just died.

"But I must not dirty my hands, it will diminish my beauty," the young and comely Lake said, and lo, she sank up to her shoulders into the soft gush of sand, and only her arms were still free.

"Fool," Lake cried, feeling her life-force ebb, and she saw herself as she was now, "you cannot give one ounce of gold, one moment of your time to feed and comfort the poor?"

But the rich and younger Lake ignored her.

And then all of the people who were strewn across the vast, scorched horizon, those who lay dying and diseased, put out their arms in a supplicating gesture, and said, with one agonizing, imploring voice, "Please, save us, save us, only you can, only you, no one else, no one else…"

And behold, a jewel-encrusted bidet of solid gold appeared in the hands of the young Lake, and she grasped it, and admired its ostentatious, glittering opulence; but as she embraced it, it slowly pulled her down into the soft, molten earth.

"Fool!" Lake cried. "What is that stupid, vile thing compared with saving a generation of human beings? It is unnecessary for life, it is excess, it is coveting that which takes food and water and medicine from those who need it to live! Yield it up, for the sake of humanity and to save yourself, yield it up and allow the sick and the poor to gain some measure of comfort from something that should never have been!"

But the young Lake merely looked at her, and said, as if she were riding now in her shiny black limousine to the grand ball, "But it was you who had it ordered, it was you; it was you who had it designed, it was you; it was you who delighted in showing it off to friends and who never once cared where it came from or how it was made or whether or not you should have it, it was you; and so it is me who deserves it, it is me; it is me who needs it, it is me; it is me who cannot imagine life without it, for life without it is life without the private jets and the four-hundred-foot yachts and the luxury villas," and she began to sink further down, "and the rich and powerful men and the fabulous dresses," and she sank up to her neck, "and the private parties atop skyscrapers, and trips to palaces and the diamond rings and the notoriety and the …" but then her mouth was covered by the gritty sand and slowly, slowly, her blinking, blinking, still-blinking, unknowing, but still-seeing eyes fell below the surface and finally her lustrous brown hair disappeared and then she was completely gone.

And as Lake was standing there and grieving over the wickedness of her past, she felt a change come upon her, and lo, she held up the golden mirror and found herself young and beautiful again, and dressed in the finest raiment and with a crown of glittering jewels upon her head; and she heard the collective cries of the suffering souls around her, but as she reached out her hands to them, she began to admire the quality and sheen of her garments and the precious stones upon her; and presently, she forgot about those who were hungry and thirsty and diseased, and remembered about pouring more of herself into her overflowing silver chalice of avarice and vanity; and lo, she began to sank into the flaming earth, and she did not feel it, so absorbed was she with the divine image she beheld in the mirror before her.

And then she awoke, sobbing quietly, sobbing in shame, sobbing in reflection of her own foibles.

But her heart was beating in a disturbingly loud, quick rhythm, and this presently drove away the thoughts of the past. "Always back to you," she cried, tearing at her fraying, stringy hair; "you just can't leave me alone for a moment." She screamed the last word so loud that she hurt her reddened, swollen throat. Sometimes her flailing heart would accelerate for a maddening pace for hours, and she would be paralyzed with cold, sweaty fear. "I can't let go," she sobbed, "I can't let go of you, you ghastly fiend, you won't give me rest until you have ripped out every desire I have for the past—you monster, you devious monster; yes, yes, I repent, I hate what I was, I hate everything I once was, that I despised the poor and ignored the sickly and the infirm; I didn't understand what it was like, I was imprisoned, imprisoned by a wall I built every day by my own selfishness and greed while I did not see the world before me; every day I did not ask why, why me, why not them—why, why, why, O God, why some and not others; why are some born into misery and others into pain, and some born luxury and others born into poverty; why, why, O God, why are some born healthy and others born ill, and why are some born handsome and others ugly still; it isn't fair, it isn't the way it should be, we should all start out fair..." She felt Truth swirling inside her beleaguered mind, and it unleashed undefined bits of ideas to float above her, and now she was trying to understand them, piecing them together, splicing some that didn't belong, forcing others into a pattern that would dissolve in days. "I know now, but it's too late, too late for me..." She felt revelation and frustration, and her mind was a blistering tempest; soon, though, happily, though, slumber took pity upon her and took her to the misty clouds of dreamland.

So, a day passed, like every other day for her, but unlike any other day for the living.

Decisions

He was there, seemingly to her, in perpetuity, faithful among the faithless, true man among a mass of faceless men; he was blessing and curse to her, a soothing balm for her pain, but pain for her love for him. She called out in muted cries for him, cursed him into her wet pillow, loathed him for his ridiculous pursuit of her, adored him for his obstinacy to leave. Her pure, unrefined love for him hurt her weary heart, hurt her confused mind, bore her soul unto the clear, starry skies; she rejoiced at his noble purpose, shouted at his stupidity not to come in; she gazed at him for hours, entranced by his resiliency and courage, and cursed him for what she knew was his most serious folly. "A tragic miscalculation," she would shout at him as she turned away from the window, bent over in pain. "A fool's dream," she sighed, crawling back to her soft bed on her sore hands and knees. She smiled secretly at the thought of a healthy man wanting her for who she was, now.

Another day passed.

She awoke in the warm embrace of a sunny morning. She nearly leaped out of bed, ran to the window, breathless, closed her eyes, opened them slowly and beheld his silent, granite-like sitting form still on her small green lawn. "My hero," she said, smiling brightly, as she sat down on the cool tiles of her kitchen, her knees drawn up to her chest. She smiled warily.

"He is like a lion, stalking me," she said, giggling; "I never would have guessed him to be so zealous." She giggled again. "I think I like it, though." She felt good at the thought of a man so devoted to her that he would risk more than comfortable losses; but such unbound devotion frightened her, and she crept away to the safety of her dark bedroom, sitting against her flesh-colored bed, knees drawn into her trembling stomach, her body shaking, her mind tormented by doubt. Here, she dwelled, all day, rising only to take care of necessary functions of the body; and here, in her special place, she drank much water, and thought and thought and thought about he who apparently loved her more than his own life; and here, in this room of solitude, she convinced herself that he must not devote himself to her. "He would leave me," she whispered; "no normal human being could long stay with me; he has to be with his own kind." And she rose up, late in the afternoon, and violated her own vow and looked in the mirror at the gaunt, pale mass of skeletal flesh and bone; she cursed herself with all of her waning strength, and as she spoke, there was not one dead word in her callused voice. "You monster, you ugly monster, how dare you expect love; how dare you take the love of anyone, after all you have done, after the way you lived, after the way you have treated people," she pointed at the mirror. "They walked right past you and you didn't even look at them, you looked right through them as if they weren't real or necessary; how could you not recognize them; why, why did I, why couldn't I just see what was around me; did I have to become like them to see who I once was? Yes," she screamed, "I'm glad I did, I deserve this," and she placed her hands over her throbbing heart, "I deserve this fate." Disgust ravaged her face. "You're fit only for the cold grave," she murmured, and sobbed, falling sideways onto her bed, her head buried in her outstretched arms. "I must leave; I must do what is right." She sat up and felt nobility swelling inside her. "I must free him of me; yes, that is what I must do, and I must do it now, do what is right, now, because there won't be many chances left for me to do the right thing."

She made the proper arrangements.

Dancing in the Moonlight

He knew what he had to do. "But she has to want me," Tony thought, sitting on the lawn as dusk was close to breaking upon the land, watching the wispy cumulus clouds sweep past the silvery moon like white wheels in a translucent sea.

A door opened.

Lake came out, two light-brown suitcases in her hands.

He stood up, stunned. "Lake," he said, unsure of himself, and then turning to look at the dark street, again saw the yellow taxicab that had been there for several minutes. She walked right past him, her face buried in anguish, her eyes averted.

"Lake, don't go." He wanted to touch her, but relented, and instead followed her. "Where are you going?" She was without voice. "Lake, stop," he commanded. He was still in the throes of incertitude, and all of his grand speeches he had carefully crafted upon her reunion with him dissipated. She was still in full loco-motion toward the cab, which was parked on the other side of this small cul-de-sac. His past, present and future were crumbling before him; his logical mind had failed to impede her progress; thus, it was now the era of his heart and its arrows of love

"I love you."

She halted.

"I love you, and I want to be with you."

She stood, staring at the glittering night sky. Her voice was melancholy. "You can't be with me."

"It doesn't matter, Lake; all I know is that I love you, and you love me."

She moved on.

"Lake," he nearly shouted, his words lassoing her, "we really love each other."

She felt the joy of ecstasy radiate within her diseased body; for a moment, she felt alive, but then bitterness crept in. "Don't," she said, "don't pity me…"

"Lake, it's not pity, I love you," and then he repeated it again as if it were the first time, so passionate and true were his words, "Lake, I really love you."

Her head fell backward, her eyes closed, tears forming. "O Tony, do you think Love will conquer everything?"

"Yes, yes, my love, my darling, I do, and I know that I love you."

She finally turned around, her countenance in torment. "Don't you understand," she cried, "it wouldn't work! We're different people!" Her voice dropped to the dust. "I no longer belong to the living," and she shook her head; "you taught me that."

"No," he protested, "then I was wrong."

"Yes," she said, her head nodding with authority. She shook her head, frowning. "It's the way things are, Tony; you've changed because you're well, now, and you can't see me anymore; I'm gone from you, Tony, you must accept that. O, Tony, it's your emotions talking, not your head; love with your mind as well as your heart."

He walked toward her. "I love you with all of my heart and soul and mind."

"Stop," she cried, "you would leave me, like everybody else; yes, it's true, it has to be true, must be true." She looked to the getaway car. "And I have to go." Her shaking head cut short his advance. "Have a good life," she whispered, in agony, and turned to leave.

His courage blossomed. "Lake," he said, watching her walk away, and then he said, simply, but ardently and tenderly, "Marry me."

She dropped the suitcases upon the graveled street, but then regained them, entered the silent cab, and he watched as the car drove off and she faded away into the sooty cloak of darkness; but he was unmoved, thinking that his love could rein her in against any formidable obstacle and at any distance. He watched as the last glimpse of the chromium bumper turned the corner; he looked to the left, to where the car must pass an open street to gain the intersection, anticipation throttling him. "She will come back to me, she must," he whispered. The image of the speeding yellow cab would have been like cement in his veins. A car rushed past, and time hit a high bump on the road to forward motion. "No," he said, breathing again, "not her; if not her, then where is she?" Then the taxicab came into view and rolled slowly past the narrow street and out of view. "No," he said, incredulous, "no," he restated with such fervor, it was as if his steely resoluteness could itself alter what had been. "No," he said once more, with utter confidence. "No," he shouted, observing still the empty pocket of a hazy street. "She will come, she must come, she…"

And there she was, standing at the end of the street, in the middle of the street, suitcases in hand, standing still, staring straight ahead at him.

Presently, this was the greatest moment of his misbegotten life.

His spirit leaped at the sight of her coming back to him.

She came on slowly, slowly, her eyes keeping their course upon him, her frail body silhouetted in the silvery moonlight.

"You quit your job for me," she said, softly, sensing this great upheaval of economic security within him, and now stopping across from him on the sidewalk.

"Yes, I suppose so," he replied, joy bursting about him like a cascading shower of glittering sparks.

Her countenance was quizzical. She walked across the street, but stopped halfway as she tilted her head and said, "Why?"

"I love you, Lake." No human being would be able to hear this dialogue and doubt the sincerity of his words, so fiercely passionate was his tone, so dedicated, so unselfish and loving and kind. Her heart listened, and would not be deceived.

"But your job…"

"You're my life, Lake," he said, wanting to run to her, but he held his ground; "to be without you is to be dead; to be anywhere with you is life."

Warm tears formed luminous pools of piety in her eyes. "I want to believe you, I really do." She shook her head. "But Tony, how can I? Everyone who has ever loved me is dead, or was false to me…"

"There is nothing else I can say to you except that I love you and I want to be with you, and I'll never abandon you." Her soul heard this last declaration, and flushed radiant joy. "Lake, I don't make promises lightly, but I vow to you now, no matter what happens, no matter what you do, no matter what happens to us, I will be with you as long as you will have me; this is me," he gestured with arms outstretched, "all or nothing. I love you, and this is all I know. I have nothing to offer you except myself, and all I have is my love for you."

"If you left me, if I let you in," she began to sob, "if I let you in, and you left me…" but so great and deep was her pathos that she could no longer speak.

"O Lake," he said, his eyes full of tears, "I could never leave you; I love you so much; I've never loved anyone or anything so deeply or understood love as much as I understand my love for you; because of you, I know what Love is; my love, my darling Lake, all the world's treasures are in you, how can I care about anything else? O, Lake, my love, my health did not make me a complete man; it is my love for you…"

She ran to him and fell into his strong, waiting arms.

"Tony, you mustn't leave me, promise me," she sobbed, "I love you…"

He held her, as it was the only thing and the right thing to do now, and not speak now was what his instincts told him. "Tony, I love you so much—to be without you," but she could not speak anymore, and held him tighter. When he felt her grip lessen, he then held her out from himself. "What will we do now?" she looked up at him as no woman ever had, yes, as no human being ever had; to wit, she looked to him as if without his guidance she was forsaken.

He was finally needed by a human being, and there was nothing he would not do for her.

"I have it all figured out," he said, smiling with a sense of a rising manliness.

She smiled, too. "Tony, always thinking…"

"But first," he murmured, and he reached into his pants pocket and took out a small, velvet, black case, opened it, took out the diamond ring and looked into her misty green eyes.

"Marry me, Lake Seville, marry me, and make me happier than I ever deserve to be."

She wept for joy. "Tony," she said, as he placed the glittering ring upon her finger, and she wanted to verbally post an admonition about her ill health to him, but she let it die like the whining rabid dog it was. "Yes, my love, I will."

They embraced; and after they had embraced for the longest time, they danced, right there, on the gray cement, waltzing in the pale moonlight to an idyllic tune that only they could hear; and after they danced so serenely and beautifully, they went and got married, simply, bravely, happily.

Hope

He knew the way out, as all men do who empty their heart of fleshly lusts and prejudices and arrogance, and he would show her the way. "It is my right," he reasoned, "as a man, to take the lead." He smiled at the recollection this thought awakened.

They were married now, but as the both of them were without employment, immediate action had to be taken. "Right action must follow each other," he decided, "and then things become clearer."

Once a muddy dog has ruined a clean floor, his filthy friends come over with dirty feet just to make more modern art.

"Well, I'm broken already," she said to herself, staring into the vanity mirror, having now completely abandoned her vow concerning the gazing at her reflection, for his love had made her feel acceptable, "what is one more ailment?" She smiled.

"But I know he loves me and will take care of me." This was her solace now, his love; her burden was softer now, not gone; she would never be alone, again.

She brushed her thinning brown hair, fancying herself still young and strong; she could smell her past beauty, her fragrant, soft hair, and she could still see her face, an array of radiant hues, of sultry pink and deep rose red, high cheekbones atop a smooth, creamy, cocoa complexion, boasting a robust, fertile health and vitality. Men had instinctively acknowledged her superior genetic pool and groveled to mate with her; she had always been in complete control of men because no man could risk losing so great a physically perfect woman as she was; she gazed deeper into her reflection and saw a face drained of color and life, strained by diseases, scrubbed clean to the very marrow of plainness and homeliness. "But he loves me," she whispered, "he loves me, and everything will be all right. He has plans for us," she smiled, anxiously.

Though her physical body was pulverized daily into pulp, she now dismissed the mental carnage of this torment, resting all of her hopes upon him.

They were married now, and he was certain to put all of his energies into saving her. "She must understand," he considered, walking up the five stone steps to their small condominium. He smiled when he nearly knocked upon the pale green door. He hesitated before entering, because on this fine Summer day, he would tell her how she must live in order to save herself from destruction.

But there is a great chasm between what we know emotionally and what we theorize intellectually, and because of his love for her and his profound love for Love, he had supposed that Love, being a supernatural force, could enjoin these two regions of the brain for important matters.

When he opened the door, smoky twilight seeped in, just as bits of snow drift in during a snowstorm; when he sat down with her in the quaint den with the small beige sofa and the cheap pictures on the faded wall, he sat down with utter confidence; but when he opened his loving mouth to divulge the secrets of the world to her, which he said would save her, he was suddenly alone.

"How dare you," did not merely blow out of her mouth with great scorn, but the sharp edge of these words cleaved the air and turned it to hot embers and black ash.

Tony sat as if a heap of burning coals had been heaped upon his head.

"How dare you," these metallic-tasting words, bleeding wrath, sprang from her deepest pain and bored tiny holes into his shrinking heart, "suggest such a horrible thing." She felt the undeniable and familiar urge to vomit, and desperately wanted to strike him full on his face; but it was not she who sought to hit him, it was the enemy, Disease, provoking her fancy to strike out at those whom she loved most, because she blamed them for being healthy and not being able to heal her.

She had fully intended to vomit her base emotions and profound nausea upon his shocked person, but she turned aside and at the last moment ran to the bathroom to discharge her physical noxious cargo. She would come out, cursing him and his folly, only to be yanked back by that invisible chain, illness, to once more deposit her foul spew inside the bathroom.

She flushed the toilet and watched her corrosive stomach shake disappear into oblivion, and then she began the horrible cursing; she cursed, cursed, cursed him as she felt the sinister stench of disease coating her reddened throat; she cursed, cursed, cursed him as she bathed her throat in cool water; she cursed, cursed, cursed his insulting plan to the vast regions of desolation; and then came a very enlightening pause, when she felt her stomach was quiet, and guilt became her new vomit.

But then she felt the sickening urge to discharge her food contents through her remaining orifice, and her humiliation and outrage at this, in light of his seemingly pompous proposal, ripped the last piece of civility from her waning heart.

"I can't believe I married you," she cried, her voice echoing from within the small wallpapered chamber of horrors, "you're a dreamer and a coward! O, my grandmother was right about men, 'Cowards use darkness to veil their cowardliness!' Oh, it's so funny! Be with my own kind, ha! Well, here is a news flash, lover: fabulously wealthy men know how to treat a woman right—they are my own kind!" Loathing vibrated in her voice like rocks in a steel barrel rolling down a bumpy hill; reason had no chance in such sessions of her magnified mental anguish. Horribly, she was about to shout divorce, to seed the air with its venomous presence, to drive it under his skin and watch it until it maddened him; but something in her, which is in all of us, impeded her; formless, within our consciousness, rests a furtive domain that exists as the last barrier against madness, when the rest of the mind and body has lost its normal checks and balances.

But she did hate him now, despise him, now, and sought to punish him for being healthy and leaving her behind; yet, she also knew, in this sacred domain, that she would not hate him long, that truly he had not done wrong to her; she knew this but would not verbalize it in her own mind, yet she recognized it in this most secret of faraway places, and so relented from thrusting the final mortal wound to her dying vision.

Truly, he lived or died on her praise or condemnation.

And truly, he had torn out the last remaining vestiges of those bitter days when he brooded alone in the icy darkness, condemning the world for abandoning him, cursing women for loathing him, threatening his removal from society to a faraway, secluded land; life was anew now, his station affixed to a virgin compass that never failed to point in the right direction, as it was a very special compass built from the trials and tribulations of their lives. This blind compass, this compass of burnished gold and a sparkling white diamond needle, pointed only to Love.

He would not yield easily to the temptation of hate. He believed that hate had been bred out of him because he had come back from societal banishment for a noble purpose. "I have come back from the dead not to change her, but to be with her," he had decided the day of their wedding.

But now was now, and here she was, clutching her weak chest and nearly fainting upon the tiled floor, and there he was, rescuing her and bringing her to their bed, to nurse her not even to adequate health, but to the low state of well-being she had become accustomed to; for two days and nights he nursed her, bathed her, cleaned her, read to her, stroked her fair brow, kissed her clammy forehead and calmed her deliriums.

She awoke in a delicious lather of cool, refreshing exultation, for the fever had broken. "A burning coal dipped in a river of frost," she said, opening her blurry eyes.

"A poet to the last," he murmured, holding her hand as he kissed her awake.

She looked up at him with admiration, stroking his hand. "Why don't you hate me?"

He kissed her hands. "I love you," he said, accenting the last word.

She understood.

Life slowly drained back into her, just as a dry riverbed fills up again with fresh water from a melting snow after a long Summer drought.

As it was, he had to get food and supplies. "I shall not be too long, my darling," he said, and vanished into the grasp of night.

There was a soft, purring wind swirling around his humble home as he came round the corner and up to the five stone steps. A caravan of blue and green and orange leaves danced around his feet as he ascended the concrete barriers.

He went in.

A dead quiet draped the dark rooms, as if no conscious being could exist in such a place and be so unnaturally still; he flipped on the cream-colored plastic light switch, put away the groceries, and walked quietly to the white fold-out double doors that contained his precious wife.

She loved to listen to music that seemed to set her emotional colors; the sweet melody of the *Mother Goose* ballet diffused across the dim room as he walked in.

She lay as if one far removed from the world in which she lived, a cold lump of flesh fused to the white cotton sheets, a crab within its encrusted home, a tortoise in its bony shell; here, in this small room, Lake found solace and safety within the home that was now her natural habitat.

She had found her niche.

He walked over to her, adorned by light musical notes that fell like soft rose petals around his feet. He gazed down at her limp form, which was soaked in perspiration, and he nearly wept. "Lake," he murmured, his words caressing her pain.

She awoke, and turning her head toward him, smiled weakly.

Amazed, he gently sat down beside her and held her warm hands and kissed them. "Good morning—I mean, good dawn, my beloved."

She let out a small laugh. "My entertainer," but her voice was barely audible.

"How do you feel?"

"Hmm," fell on her dry lips. Her voice was soaked in dejection and weariness. "Far away." She looked up at him. "I dreamed that I woke up and I couldn't even see your face," and she let out a soft cry, "even though you were right there in front of me." She closed her eyes. "I might as well be dead."

"Don't talk like that," he said, with urgency.

"I have to talk like that, my darling; I have to be honest with myself; didn't you teach me that? 'To find health,' you said, 'don't lie about the illness you have.' Well, Tony, I won't lie, and you won't either. I'm dying."

"No," he rejoined, piety radiating from his handsome visage.

"I was healthy once, so my body has not broken down completely, yet…"

"You mustn't talk like this…"

"Mustn't I? You did for yourself."

"Lake, I have learned that there is always something to find, some road not yet traveled; the body wants to be healed…"

"No," she took his hand, "no, it's over for me." She was nearly weeping, now. "O Tony, I'm so tired of fighting this thing, this terrible thing that makes me do things I hate," and she closed her eyes tight; "I want rest, I want eternal rest; I want death, sweet, calming death…"

"No, Lake, no, you mustn't talk of dying." He moved closer to her sorrowful face. "Lake, there is always something, something new, some idea to research; I have researched your illness for so long, and I feel as if I am getting so close to an answer." He kissed her warm, moist head. "There is always hope."

The fairy music ascended to the mystical realms and paused for attention.

"Hope?" she whispered, slowly, and then she repeated it, in even more despair, "Hope?" she asked, incredulous, frowning, her light-brown eyebrows knit as she opened her eyes. "No, Tony, all of my hope is gone; my body yearns for peace now, and so do I."

He leaned even nearer to her thin face, and whispered in hushed, passionate tones. "I can prove it to you, Lake, my love; I can show you that there is hope." He had already slipped his powerful hands underneath her fragile body. "Come with me, now, my darling," he whispered, and he lifted her up close to him, and kissed her gently on her full lips, "and close your eyes."

The music was swirling and flooding the air with a rising storm of tempo.

Lake was obediently silent as he walked over to the wooden folding doors, which he pulled back; he then opened the sliding glass door, carried her to the small balcony, and set her upon a plastic white chair. He looked to the tall mountains and then back to her, and smiled. He bent down in front of his wife, and whispered, lovingly, passionately, adoringly, "Now, my darling, my love, when I tell you to open your eyes, tell me what you see," and he stood up, backing away to the side to not obstruct her view.

She could feel the cool shadow of early morning flutter over her eyes, but then, slowly, sheepishly, a warm sensation crept over her face, and then her husband said to her, as if his hushed voice was coming from a special time and place and dimension, "Now, Lake, open your eyes."

The music was ethereal and starry as she opened her eyes and beheld the wide world before her, the serenity of the bold flower of dawn blossoming into blessed morning and the red flames of the sun fanning up behind the horizon; but she saw this vision separately, and thus she shook her head, bewildered, desperately seeking what he had proposed.

But when the arc of the resplendent sun rose above the tops of the majestic mountains and ringed them in a shimmering halo, sublime revelation came unto her as she beheld the essence of the natural event. The music reached its crescendo in a sensuous burst of heavenly tonality; the enchanting chords and strings fell upon the listeners like little silken snowflakes; the perfumed soul of the melody laid to dust any sorrow, any gloom, any dread. Tears filled her eyes. "I see it," she murmured, deep in ecstasy. "O, Tony, I see it, I see," but so great was her awe that she lost her voice for a moment; and then she whispered, "the rising of the sun," as tears formed in her eyes, and she then gushed with exceeding joy, "I see the hope of a new day," and then leaped into his waiting arms, weeping, "O Tony."

The two lovers stood in the grand sweep of a red-flamed dawn blooming across the land, the signal from the celestial heavens that previous miseries might dissolve like foam on the misty shores of the sea of forgetfulness.

Open Doors

The next day, she cogitated upon his plan that had seemed so senseless; a plan that now somehow seemed plausible. "To empty oneself of oneself, and then to serve others," he had said. She had protested violently against the implications of this philosophy, but he had pressed on. "To concentrate solely on oneself in good times and bad is folly; to look after others, there we will find resolution and absolution." She had deemed him mad because of this, for he wanted to leave everything and devote their energies to bringing solace to the poor and diseased.

"And what am I?" she had shouted.

"Privileged."

"Maybe you are," she had returned, pouting, "but I am still ill."

He had merely gazed intensely at her, then. "Help others, and your needs will be met."

She had fumed. "You mean God? Now, you conjure up God to cure my ailments? You're as bad as those idiot witch doctors who change course more often than a tornado." She stood, fuming, her mind erecting the walls of conspiracy. "And by the way, where was He yesterday?"

He had not meant that God was part of the intricate equation, but now he would not disclaim it. "I don't know about any of it, yet; but I do know this, that thinking of self every moment is wrong; salvation," he had pointed in the direction of the nearest ghettos, "lies therein."

Now, she mused upon this bold idea of heaving away the congested, mean image of self and aiding those truly in need; she mixed the history of her past life as an esteemed aristocrat and the idea of self-denial. She retched. "Who of that ilk could conceive of such a thing?" She was shocked that she had spoken of the rich as an entity separate from her identity, for secretly she had always considered herself one of them, even now, as much as she loathed them, regardless of her wealth or societal position. She purposely kept the two opposing images in her mind, and then fused them into one, each bleeding into the other, until the amalgam dripped into her mouth, and she tasted the bitter gall of this tempting fruit. "I do not understand it fully," she said to him late one night, "but I am beginning to see that there are more worlds than the one you are born into."

Soon, they would enter a world hitherto unknown to them.

Exploring

There is an undiscovered region of poverty in every town, and every member of that town who has plenty either chooses to offer help or pretend it does not exist. Sometimes poverty is a two-footed messenger of filth and insensible acts strolling up and down the faded sidewalks, such as the lost soul who rides the rusty old bike with the high handlebars, which carries bags of cans and plastic bottles; but more often it is not the kind of trash that seeps into the porous ground like a cool rain in Summer, it is the species of blight that stays atop the hardened soil as it casts carelessly about with no rhyme or reason or order to its structures, such as the single dwelling consumed by rot and despair; poverty is sometimes like this, strewn in bits and pieces, and thus, those who have plenty may not see beyond one dead home, as they see no inherent pattern in this bloodless carnage; it is only when poverty, as if crushed together by the force of gravity and pooled into a deliberate large swath of land, that outsiders may begin to acknowledge it.

Those who have plenty do not mind taking out the smelly trash to the curb, for they know it will soon be gone;

and they have the same mind about poverty: they do not mind driving past it as long as it exists outside of their full range of vision.

Who happily exposes trash outside of his home, the rich man asks; does one not seek to bury it? Is the city dump in the heart of the city or located on the periphery of town?

Tony, alone, journeyed to this city within a city, this culture within a culture, wherein dwelled the poorest people, the dirtiest streets, the worst crime, the direst need for love and peace and joy. "Here," he had said, standing at the tip of an embedded pulse under the thick skin of his town, "will I find Truth," and he walked in like a man adorned with the armor of righteousness.

He walked along urine-stained, beer-soaked sidewalks of a place that seemed to sweep objects toward it, just as a giant object in space traps objects in its powerful gravitational pull; but the objects in this ghetto were tainted and broken, lost and abandoned.

"Does poverty have an aroma?" he wondered aloud, mocking those who would call him foolhardy. He hesitated to approach the residents. "What would I say to them?" He halted, hesitating as he smelled the scant residue to flee the premises. "And why shouldn't I just leave? Have I obligation here? I see no chains upon their wrists, no fetters on their feet, why don't they simply leave?" He sighed. "Yes, but I do have an obligation," he whispered, "because I am a human being, and no, it doesn't matter if they leave, for they will merely take it with them. They cannot see it, but perhaps if I can help them see..." and he walked on, knowing that his daily presence here would attract attention.

He walked through two decaying neighborhoods, digesting the ruins therein; everywhere there was a clear break in the laws of uniformity of cleanliness and order. Depressed, he retired to his home, where he tended to his sickly wife.

That night, he came upon a plan, and the next day, he executed it.

He rode his bicycle through the impoverished field of uncovered, living graves, looking for good deeds to be done; and so, day after day, he rode on, begging for action. The first week he weaved through this maelstrom's harvest, hiding deep within his impenetrable shell. "Coward," he cursed himself.

The first day of the second week, he was riding down Pavilion Street, when he heard a distressed mother crying out for her own. "My children," she cried, "my children are gone." Her accent was thick with the flavor and history of the country to the south; the neighborhood was aroused, and residents exited their safe houses, wearing expressions of concern.

Tony felt the chilly sweat of paranoia lay atop his warm skin. "They'll accuse me," he thought, "the foreigner in the nest." He feigned a look of innocence and ignorance as he rode past.

"You," a fat neighbor screamed at him. Tony nearly fell off his bike. "Have you seen two little Mexican kids wandering down the street?"

"No," he returned, concerned, "but I'll look." His heart pounded loudly in his chest. He had quite forgotten he was well, that he had been accepted back into mainstream society, that he was the freak no more, no longer the suspicious, ugly villain by virtue of his diseased looks.

He wasn't sure to pedal fast or slow. "If I pedal slower, will it show that I have something to hide? But if I pedal faster, will this show I am fleeing?" The memory of the ugly man in the presence of Innocents and being accused of untoward crimes stuck in him like a bloody knife, a well-worn knife already cut through the throat of another victim of blind justice.

He accelerated at a steady rate that he reasoned was inconspicuous until he successfully reached the end of the street and turned the corner; he was relieved, yet he was now determined to search the area for the two missing children.

Rescue

There is an engineer sitting in the locomotive of a long train, his sharp gaze straight ahead. He knows that the tremendous power and bulk of the iron horse can be a weapon against anything happening to stray upon the railroad tracks; he has heard the unsettling stories about what happens when man and thousands of tons of roaring steel meet, and he prays daily to run his black beauty clean from station to station.

The big man with the pink cranium and drooping brown mustache is looking hard ahead when he sees two seemingly insignificant figures in the distance, but significant enough to prompt him to reach for his binoculars and take them to his eyes.

His entire life-force drains out of him, leaving a hollow white shell as he beholds two tiny human beings playing on the exact curves of the track; he pulls the dangling brake cord hard and blows the loud siren of the iron locomotive.

He understands the folly of screaming at the two distant figures, but the humanity in him commands that he create as much of a disturbance as possible to avoid disaster.

Closer and closer the screeching hulk of hot metal nears its young targets, and the man aboard is frantic with desire to make his will known to them; he checks the speed, and he knows that at fifty-five miles per hour now, he will be at forty miles per hour then, too fast for him to jump off and beat his ride to sweep up the two figures; he now knows, even above the clamorous din, that disaster will not be averted. But he still prays for rescue.

Panic seizes him like a jagged harpoon, and he waves his arms and screams and shouts and thrusts his entire soul into his energies to thwart what he knows is inevitable; he does not care about his job now, nor his career, and as for the press, the condemnation and sympathy—all of those incendiary ingredients to come—he cares only for the lives of the Innocents just ahead.

It is almost done. He checks the speed. The speedometer reads forty-three miles per hour. He wants to do something, but he knows the physics of the situation and he knows all is futile. He will force himself to watch the human carnage to punish himself for his sins once committed, if only to punish himself for his failure as watcher and keeper of the rails. He is the last hope of all trespassers on his domain, and now, he is about to allow the most grievous sin of all to occur; today, while he is at the helm, while he is master of the tracks, his powerful engines will mercilessly crush two small infants, and he must remain absolutely helpless.

He weeps, numb, dead, wishing himself unborn, if only to save them.

But then, it happens, the impossible miracle all pray for but secretly know will not occur because no one really believes in miracles anymore unless one is desperate—and even then, is it only the faithful who believe and receive miracles? Yet he believes now as he watches a golden-winged vision delivered at the end of the iridescent rainbow; he sees a fiery youth swooping down, a delightful, wild-eyed madman on a blue mountain bike speeding faster than any human being has the right to do, coming directly toward the giggling infants as they joyfully pick up small, shiny pebbles in the middle of the wooden planks of the tracks. The body of the conductor leaps in ecstasy, and his face, flushed with fresh red blood, radiates hope and joy as he cries victory for the rushing youth, the furiously pedaling youth who moves like Mercury unbound and is streaming gloriously and smoothly across the loosely packed gravel path leading to the crouching girls.

The ancient locomotive is still wailing, smoking brakes proclaiming its foreboding song as it creeps closer to the white-diapered toddler and her silly older sister.

And then the cyclist comes, turning his bike expertly at the exact right time and jumping off it and dashing adroitly to the two girls and scooping them up just as if it were all carefully planned—seamlessly, effortlessly, magnificently; and then, he hauls them over the last rusted rail and past the path of destruction, just as the slugging train with the sobbing, wildly cheering engineer rips by.

It is over now. The crest of this wave of hysteria has begun to subside, giving way to sobs of relief and joy for the lone observer to it all; first comes the engineer who enthusiastically embraces the savior on the bike and hugs the crying children; now come the people from the neighborhood and the distraught mother, all who hear the story from the engineer about the heroism of the man on the bicycle; then come hugs and kisses for all concerned, and many tears of happiness, and speaking of gratitude for deeds done.

Even the chubby engineer is embraced as if he too were a hero. He blushes pink embarrassment.

The neighborhood celebrates the return of two children once lost and now found.

Tony finds a way in.

Sylve

The time frame for the hero as a character who can do no wrong is transitory and possessing the same nature as a warm Summer thunderstorm; when the storm hits, all bow to it, believing it all powerful, yielding to its every whim; but when it leaves, one wonders why anyone bowed to it at all. And life goes on.

When Tony came to his adopted neighborhood with his new bride, she too was accepted as family. Everyone wanted to know their opinion on matters, and whatever they said seemed so lucid and wise, yet so simple and commonsensical, that the people were amazed they had never thought of it before.

Slowly, the two foreigners were christened into the slum neighborhood by being allowed into the homes of the residents.

Tony and Lake came to the house of Maria, the woman who had allowed her two babies to wander away from her care because she had been so high up in the crowded clouds of hallucinatory drugs that she had had no idea of her immediate surroundings.

Today it was a Tuesday, in the a.m., and there was a misty gray fog draping the town. "So, you know," Maria said, to her visitors, bending down to pick up soiled baby clothes that cluttered the small home, "I got to live, you know? I tried to do the secretary thing, but those people," and her tongue erupted curse words like a maddened volcano, "they no like Mexicans, you know? So, you know, I try other things; but, you know, I got no skills, and my old man, oh," and then her emotionally damaged heart and mind manufactured chilled, barbed words that seemed to coat the walls with her purple venom. The four-year-old child looked up at her mother and frowned. "That's your father, the lowlife," she said to her baby, evincing the idea that could she interject an occasional non-slang, non-obscenity to honor her guests. "So, I trick sometimes, you know? Hey, it's a living, what can I say? A girl got to work, got to feed the babies, you know?" The phone rang; it was her man, from whom she had recently separated, and for whom she instantly provided a fresh hash of wicked language barbecued on the open pit of enmity. Tony and Lake slowly drifted out of the door in due time and to the next house of humiliation and shame.

Then came Vince October, a renowned drunk and woman beater; he did not answer the door because he was drunk and about to beat a woman after having had relations with her; she lay sucking on a bottle of gin, and he stood, huffing and puffing, holding a bottle of rye in one hand and a black leather whip in the other.

Three doors down, it was the Woolridge family; the mother weighed three hundred and fifty pounds and complained about her constant illnesses, and the man, he weighed one hundred and thirty pounds, and whined about his bad luck in the whole wide world of finance, which is to say, he was speaking of the small, narrow world of horse racing and casino gambling. The three children were filthy, simpleminded creatures who seemed lost whenever the two visitors spoke to them. On this day, Lake left them each a storybook and a bottle of chocolate vitamin pills.

In one dwelling there existed one human atrocity, in another dwelling, one more, and in another, two atrocities, and in one next to that, the atrocities changed daily or were added to until there were so many vile sins that it seemed the very wooden and concrete structure itself would burst from the horror of it all. Tony and Lake soon realized they could not help these people because these people did not seek any kind of spiritual or intellectual awakening. These people, Tony said, were like the drug addict who lives in a rusted and gutted-out, old, gray, faded Chevy, and who then wins the lottery; in a month, Tony reasoned, the addict would now live in several gutted-out, old, gray, faded Chevy cars; but no, Lake protested, they would be living in one very expensive, and very soon gutted-out, old, red, faded car.

"We offer them heart and mind, and instead they choose the flesh," Tony said, dismayed at the impenetrable chaos of these people.

"Money," Lake had said, depressed. "It burns in you when you have too much, and burns in you when you have too little."

Every day the two practitioners of altruism ventured to the emotionally disjointed carcass of this small hump in Nature called slum, and every day they found base reality, degradation, unspeakable physical mayhem and mind horrors. "Every day I walk onto the battlefield and I find more wounded, too many who have wounded themselves and cannot see it," Tony said in a somber tone to his wife as they neared the invisible barrier that poverty had erected; he felt an uncomfortable chill rippling down his spine as he espied the first mangled heaps of this discolored, discarded, disorganized culture. He felt like his former self, sloughing off to reveal a man who had imbibed an immature cynicism. The day was charred in psychological turmoil and physical abomination.

"Maybe it's us," he said to her that night as they lay in bed together; "maybe we don't know how to reach them because we don't understand them."

She only squeezed his hand, and kissed him. For the three weeks while she had journeyed to the land of the impoverished people, she had carefully monitored her health, and it hadn't worsened. She marveled at this.

"It's as if they can't see who they are or who we are; maybe that's why they are who they are; they're fated to be there because they are born into it and will never fit in mainstream society," he said.

"Like us?" Lake whispered, staring up at the flitting shadows dancing upon the darkened ceiling.

He smiled, emitting a small "Hmm—thou art my conscience."

"Well, there is always hope for the children," Lake said, "if they can be rescued first."

Day after day they visited the human blight of the city, a blight like a human oil spill that never quite dissolved into the hard, unyielding ground.

Three months later, they were beginning to think that the inhabitants of the ghetto were merely the progeny of those who had come before them, a generation gone who had passed down an immortal gene that bred insanity and confusion and hysteria and a propensity for the recipient to turn from the light and reach for the swirling bright specks in the bloody darkness.

"In every ray of sun a little rain must fall," he stated, as they were walking toward the inner core of the city on a fine Summer day.

"But sometimes, the rain does not penetrate the earth," she said, referring to one of the people whom they had found to be true.

"Sylve," they said together.

Sylve indeed lived in the battleground known as slum field, and indeed she was an inheritor of poverty and family dysfunction, but she was a crude white diamond covered in new soot that was sitting at the bottom of a cesspool of misery and madness.

She was unlike the rest of the world, for at a very early age, she had decided that her station in life could be affected by her own will; she had extracted herself from the perverted vision that had engulfed her family and had set a course to evolve beyond the grasp of the familiar, fat, greasy fingers of mental ambiguity.

Tony and Lake had met Sylve late in their campaign to save these dwellers from self-destruction; but upon further introspection they now realized that the tumult therein — that is, the emotional windstorm stirred up by each of the participants in the projects — was mostly self-generated, and mostly refueled by self-pity, self-loathing, and pure stupidity and unethical behavior. They then decided to save those whom they deemed were capable of erecting their own sail to move out of these stagnant waters, giving vitamin and mineral supplements and books to the children, and oftentimes tutoring them. Their first candidate, and transparently so, was Sylve, a young woman, who was likened to a pincushion for so many wounds there were about her strong body—but yea, she had resolved to live.

As she sat there on the chocolate-brown sofa, she related to them the disturbing events of her misbegotten life. Her hard voice belched the purple smoke and yellow flame of the soldier who has inhaled too long the scars of interminable battle. She lit a cigarette and inhaled deeply, her gentian-colored eyes radiating coldness, harshness, an intensity magnified by her vibrant, cruel, yet sensuous voice.

She spoke like a character evicted from a horror story who was still covered in the hot blood and guts of her attacker.

"My father raped me when I was thirteen," she began, nodding her head as if she had acknowledged it for the first time. She crossed her strong, supple, bronzed legs. "I gave birth to Charlotte nine months later; my mother raised the child as her own. I was hooking by fourteen, addicted to heroin by fifteen." She let out an ironic "Hmm," and shook her blond head. "I'm twenty-two, and I feel fifty-two, like I just skipped being a kid and a young adult and woke up…" She frowned, expelling a long breath as she took in a long inhale of cigarette smoke. "My father, the pimp."

Lake squeezed her husband's hand.

Sylve, grim-faced, continued on. "I ran away at seventeen with a boy named Kidro." She smiled, remembering something innocent. "He was just a boy, a decent, nice boy…" The smile faded like water in the desert heat. "My father caught us and beat him until he nearly died. I didn't run away again for nearly two years." Her countenance became severe, as if an inviolate memory had awakened awe in her. She extinguished the cigarette, as if its acrid odor would foul her reverie. "Then—I believe it was an Autumn night," and she closed her violet eyes, "it was warm to the flesh," and she opened them, "as I was whoring downtown, I approached a man and offered my flesh to him." There was an imperceptible smile hidden behind the etchings of pain. "And he said to me, 'My dear, I am a child of God, as you are, and you are more precious to God than you know; let me help you.'" Pious tears welled up in her dazzling eyes. "I thought it was a come-on, you know, a kinky kind of foreplay—that's how perverted I was; I couldn't even recognize a decent man—but it wasn't, and he wasn't a minister, either, just a man." The thought of her human savior whipped the levees apart in her eyes and let the warm tears trail down her swarthy cheeks. "Here was a man who cared for me for no reason other than I was lost; well, he took me into his home, with his family, and protected me against my father. He was the only man in my life who didn't lay a hand on me for my flesh." She was weeping now, but her voice was a solid stream of unbroken clarity. "I lived with his family for six months, and it was then I realized who I was, and who my father and mother were. Yes, I did not know." She smiled in reflection of the irony. "How can a dog know it lives in its own waste until it is removed from it?"

She never wiped away her tears.

"I left when my father found out where I was and shot bullets into this good man's home; I left and never returned. Oh," she looked past her guests and through the open window, "there is Charlotte."

The special yellow bus opened its doors, and out ran the eight-year-old daughter of Sylve; she came into the house and into the waiting arms of her mother. "My treasure," Sylve said, pulling back the child's black hair. Shortly, the precious girl ran to her room to do her homework. "God has saved me, I know that, in here," she touched her heart. "I know that in His love I am pure again. I have been chaste for so long now…" She wept again, but her body was stone still. "I have a burden, you know—I don't feel emotions; tears, yes, but nothing inside; inside I am dead, like a burned-out, hollowed-out fallen tree, and I hate my father for that. He took away the part of me that makes life worth living." She shut tight her eyes. "I know that hatred is wrong, but it focuses me, like a shot arrow on a wide and faraway target." She let out a small sigh. "But it isn't even real hatred, just a burning inside that eats my gut."

"Hmm," she hummed, eyes still closed, "hmm," she continued, as if her mind was re-engaging itself. "People I know die, and I don't cry; people I love die, and I don't cry; I worry about that." She opened her eyes. "I want to be fully human again, Lake and Tony, I really do; but I don't know how; I never had the chance, and I'm scared that I never will be—human." She sniffed, and finally wiped away some of the salty droplets upon her rosy cheeks. "I know a way, God forgive me, now; I know how, God forgive me, then, too."

Charlotte ran into the room, "Mommy, Mommy, I'm done," she cried, carrying a single sheet of basic mathematics problems. "Teacher said I was good today; a star, Mommy, a star for Charlotte."

Sylve hugged her as only a mother who loved a child more than her own life could; mother and daughter embraced each other as if it were their last; presently, the little bouncing sweetheart, after giving great big hugs to the two guests, retired to her room.

Sylve Sylvestre, her eyes shut again, inhaled the deeply perfumed scent of life's invincible forces that radiated about her like a golden aura. "But in the end," she continued, her tone breathing hope and glory, "it surely doesn't matter who you are or where you've been, or who you've been with or the sins you've committed; you know, you can be covered with greasy filth, living in the disgusting gutter, full of wrong ideas, lost, confused, abandoned, alone; and in the end, in the final end," and she smiled, weeping now, as she thought of her own misbegotten life; "it really doesn't matter where you are or who you're with or if you're covered in terrible sin, because your heart," and she choked on her next thoughts as she clutched her heart, "because if you believe in your heart—God—He exists; if you truly believe—God—if you pray, you can find

Him, no matter where you are or what you have done or who you are with, because God wants you to love Him." She shook her head. "God has to be, because He has to be there for people like me," she nearly stopped altogether from grief, "who have been murdered by life." She gestured pleadingly to the Heavens. "It has to be, it must be, for without God, there is no reason to be. Life would just be a slow, torturous, insane death."

On the way home, the two young lovers walked hand in hand, reflecting on the stories they had heard.

"Of course," Lake said, after some time in silence, "I am glad Sylve has faith, however primitive, to hold on to." He was without comment on the subject, his eyes straight ahead. She pressed on. "It is perfectly natural for people in pain to invent a supernatural entity to soothe their sorrow; every culture has done it, so why not ours? We have just attached ourselves to one particular faith; another culture, another faith; one is as good as another as long as it doesn't hurt anybody." Still, he said nothing. She stopped walking. "You agree with me?"

He looked to her, silent and deep in reverie.

"Oh, you're not serious," she said, stopping, frowning and shaking her head. He stood, encased in obstinacy. "But we've talked about this," she demanded. "God is for peasants, a silly superstition from antiquity, as real as fairies and leprechauns, like throwing salt over your shoulder," and she was still shaking her head in disbelief, "make-believe for children and the ignorant masses, foolish people who believe in witches and everything superstitious that takes the place of their tiny brain." She expelled a breath of frustration, looking this way and that at the passing cars. "Look around us," she gestured, waving to the human carnage that would never feel the sting of her accusing fingers. "What divine being allows this—all this pain and suffering? Deformed babies, mangled bodies, disease—O, how I hate disease." She nearly wept at the thought of how destructive her illness had become, and how wonderful the world would be without it. "Who, Tony, who would allow so much unfairness? What is the point of allowing a child to be born without a chance to have a good life?"

He stared at her with wonder in his eyes. "You give me all of the reasons for God not to exist," and he looked upward at the cerulean blue sky and billowy white clouds, "but what about all of the reasons for Him to exist?" He smiled as he held her shoulders. "Look at us." He stroked her smooth forehead. "We are a miracle happening every day," and he kissed her hand.

She frowned. "You've been healthy too long," she said, disappointment dripping from her mouth like juice from a bitter lemon. She looked away from him. "When you're in love, the whole world is in love; when you're in pain, the whole world is in pain." She turned toward him as they continued walking. "You're in love with life again, and you want to see the world through rose-colored glasses, optimism behind every dying bush, but I just cannot, I won't." Her hand dropped from his as she walked on ahead.

"I believe in us, Lake," he said, "that's all I know; I want to believe in God, but I don't want to believe in Him only when I am healthy." He admired her defiance, her resoluteness, her steadfastness.

She was sick that night, delirious the next day. He stayed beside her, ever faithful, ever true to her, unwavering in his devotion to easing her physical and emotional pain. "If there are answers out there," he thought, swabbing her hot forehead with a damp cloth, "I will lead by example." He thought of the old man at the library, and he smiled. "If there is a path to God, our Love will find it."

Lake was bound to him through such tribulations, a bond few forces on earth could destroy, a bond held together by their sacred Love for each other.

As Lake recovered, even as Tony sat by her bedside, Sylve Sylvestre was trailing her father, who had recently kidnapped Charlotte; she was searching for him in the high San Gabriel Hills, and she did find him there, found him standing like a howling wolf over the dead, raped body of her daughter. It was then that Sylve put a .38 Special bullet into his gapping, saliva-covered mouth.

She wept blood over the body of her precious child.

Story Time

Tony and Lake went every day to the trial of Sylve Sylvestre; the latter was found innocent and, shortly thereafter, vanished from town.

The two young lovers sat in their condominium, pondering the complexities of life, and how to pay rent with no money.

Lake lamented over the fate of Sylve.

"We found one alive in a graveyard of human tragedies," she said, watching her husband looking over the unpaid bills. "Was it worth it to waste all of our time and effort to find one lost soul?"

His voice was full of passion as he looked up at her. "It was to her."

"Oh, I know that," she protested, meekly, "but look at the rest of her degenerate neighbors—drunkards, drug addicts, criminals; are we supposed to waste our time with these virulent germs, hoping they might reform? Oh, for good-ness' sake, it's like trying to fill a bottomless cup; no, that isn't mean enough, what I meant to say was that these peo-ple are simply this way and that is why they live there and there will always be people like that and they will always be living together; and you can't eradicate this kind of behavior any more than you can eradicate bad weather. These people just are, and I am sick of seeing them. They are who they are because they want to be, and we are who we are because we want to be, so let each group live alone." She stared at him, waiting for a reply.

"You don't see me arguing with you…"

"Tony, we need money right now or we're going to be the ones some stupid do-gooder finds living in a soggy cardboard box on a greasy sidewalk on Skid Row." He stroked her hair and let her head fall gently onto the table beside her husband. "I don't mind being poor, I really don't, as long as I am with you." They held hands. "Misery loves company, darling." He smiled. She held her head up high. "And I don't want to sound ungrateful for what I have, but I know that talking about this is just being human, that they are not all so bad, because in the end we both know we're not going to give up on them…"

He leaned over and kissed her.

She smiled, cuddled in the warm bliss of his love. Her body felt relaxed as she felt his strong hands moving slowly over her cool neck and shoulders. She was lulled into a momen-tary peace, where she imagined disease at once removed and far away, where she felt normal, healthy, alive again; and then she felt the tingling urge of nausea bore up in her and swell upward like a tidal wave and pound through her stomach and rush like a raging river up her esophagus and splash out of her mouth and spread its noxious self over the kitchen glass table. He cleaned up while she allowed her body to discharge itself in the bathroom.

Upon returning to the family room, she sat hard upon the old brown sofa, her head down in her thin, pale hands; she coughed in a raspy, hoarse voice. "I die, yet I die unvanquished…" He sat next to her and held her, saying nothing.

Every good husband must know the delicate rhythms and winding roads upon which his wife navigates with her innermost feminine voice, so that he might properly love her.

"I don't want to die a miserable wretch," she whispered, lying now in his arms, her head resting upon his lap, "a terrible wretch who lived for nothing, died for nothing." She sat up and put her arms around him. "O Tony, I don't want to have lived on earth and have done no good thing; O Tony, Tony, my beautiful Tony, how could I have lived so long and not seen what an empty vessel I was?"

"But you have done a good thing," he said, tenderly, kissing her warm tears; "you've loved this miserable wretch whom you call your husband."

She drew her head back, smiling through her tears. "I love you," she murmured, and she kissed him with great passion; she laid her head upon his strong shoulders. "Sometimes I dream that you leave me," she continued, her arms close against the warm flesh of his side and back, "because you have found a beautiful woman," but her soaring emotions smothered her speech.

"O, my love, I have found the most beautiful woman in the world," he said, caressing her wet hair, kissing her moist forehead, holding her warm body close to his.

She created a weak smile through the very tangled and sharp fabric of her internal physical torment.

"When I was young," she sorrowed, "I dreamed a world whose birth entitled you to privilege or poverty." She winced at the very thought of this aberration. "If one is born in the sea, how can one conceive of dry land?"

He listened to her lament, patiently waiting to respond, and then said, "If one is born in tyranny, how can one dream of freedom?"

She lifted her head up to him. "That's why I love you so, you're never shy about speaking what you think is the truth; yes, my kind—no, those whom I used to adore but now disown—they are tyrants, and have no right not to think of the world about them." She let her head rest upon his shoulders. "How I do miss Grandmother and Lisbeth, they understood, but I did not listen." She paused in reflection, then said, "How did they know?"

The lovers felt their bodies, acting as if joined by a common impulse, fall gently to the soft cushions of the sofa; they lay together, undisturbed in their physical union, hearing each other's measured breath, feeling each other's rhythmic heartbeat, smelling each other's radiant fragrance of love; he sensed the tiniest movement in her frail body and was able to interpret its provocative meaning; for the moment, a slight hum from her, short and two-toned, meant words, but not an ordinary production of words; these were special times for her, rare times when her accursed disease hid in its watery shed and plotted future vicious attacks against her; so, at such tranquil moments, when her heart did not race and pound nor her chest ache, and when her bodily sores were healing, when her head did not throb, nor her kidneys hurt or her liver pain her nor her stomach ache or her throat feel like the crusty grave of a charcoal pit, she was clearly, madly, joyfully as human as she could possibly be.

Her voice was soft and melodious, like the light and lyrical whisper of the wind through a field of yellow corn. "When I was a little girl, my grandmother used to come home after those awful Board meetings, tired and irritable, and she would come up to my room and tell me bedtime stories." She was smiling at the treasure this sumptuous memory lit in her heart; as she told it, she was a little girl again, healthy again, part of the functioning and industrious world again. Her luminous green eyes were liquid pools of pure love. "Grandmother would sit down on my pink bed sheets, she who was one of the most powerful women in America would sit down and talk to me, and only then did she say her life had meaning; the rest of it—the fame and wealth and power—meant nothing to her."

"Well, daughter," Lady Seville once said to her eleven-year-old grandchild, stroking her lustrous hair, "what knowledge did you gain about the grand wide world today?" She always wanted to know what Lake had learned, eager to guide her in the ways of the world.

"Well, Grandmom," she replied, "Mr. Kierkegaard explained to us that there aren't really many oceans, but one; and that there really aren't many nations, but one, because people are divided by artificial borders."

She smiled. "Your Mr. Kierkegaard is a radical." She smiled at her own amusement. She seemed to stare past the original Matisse painting that hung on the east wall. "People change once you divide them up; they take sides, even when they don't have to." She frowned, musing upon her own affairs. "Well, one day the lion will lie down with the lamb. Hmm." She looked back to her precious darling. "Story time."

Lake instantly sat up in bed, placing her silken pink pillow against the redwood headboard, her countenance radiating anticipation of a fancy fairy tale as she clicked the dim button for the lights.

Grandmother clapped both of her brown hands into her lap, and thus, the story began. "There once upon a time lived a people who were made entirely of ice." The rich, deep verdant luster of Lake's eyes glowed anticipation. "They lived on ice, on an ice mountain, on ice lakes—anywhere there was ice, there they were; oh, but they had to be careful not to touch anything warm, lest it melt them instantly into a puddle of water." She smiled outwardly, and inwardly, she smiled cunningly, as she mused upon the absent audience she sought to satirize. "Now, child, it must be told that once, long ago, the Ice People were of flesh and blood, just like you and I, but something very strange happened to them," she leaned closer to Lake, and whispered mysteriously, "they were all once, each one of them, fabulously wealthy, and had decided that human contact was a waste of their precious time; money, only money, they had decided, money all the time was the only thing worth working for and think about and desiring, and every movement had to be a movement for the sake of making money—loving a person doesn't make you money and it gets in the way, they decided, so love was forgotten." She leaned back, magnifying her elaborate pause. "Hmm," she hummed, "they knew what was happening to them but the fever of riches blinded their minds to the Truth, until, sadly, they had no humanity at all, just ice; dumb, translucent, dead ice for a heart and a clump of gauzy ice for a head and a chunk of chiseled dirty ice for a body; but oh, did I tell you that they were still fabulously rich?"

Lake smiled, but knit her brows when she thought the story was over, then smiled joyously when her grandmother readied to speak again.

The dark room was scented with the rich nectar of imagination, icy shadows flitting about, faint chimes of a whirling carousel falling like soft raindrops, other worlds creeping here, other worlds speaking there, chorusing, "Listen, listen, listen!"

"Ice," Grandmother continued, her southern accent speckled with a light, magical tinkling, "becomes you, it became them, fashioning itself perfectly after their very form and frown; it soothed them, just like a good mother does as a newborn baby clings to her warm bosom; oh, how they did shrink from fleshly things, just like a spider flees from the roaring fire. Hmm." She paused, satisfied. "But they weren't alone, not at all, they still had their treasures stored up in hidden ice caverns, treasures no good to them, anymore. Dogs on hay, says the oxen," and she nodded her head as she watched the message of a once-read Aesop's fable reveal itself upon Lake's face.

"Well, my little sweetheart, one fine Winter day, when the icy air crackled from the fierce frost, a daring young ice girl appeared at the edge of the frozen world and by chance beheld a handsome boy of flesh and blood, and immediately they fell in love with each other; but danger lurked, for when she took one step too close to him, she felt his natural heat furnace seeping into her crystal skin, impelling her backward; but she did not flee, but stared at the boy, entranced.

"So, night after night, the two secret lovers met at the division of their two worlds, unmoving and silent, stricken with a passionate romance reserved for the young."

This was the time when the omnipotent teller of tales lifted up her tired old feet and laid them outstretched upon the bed, her head propped against the silk pillow, her purple-robed arm around her precious listener.

"O child, True Love has no reins, no physical borders; its magical power spans time and space! Our lovers could not be separated even by the threat of death; every night they appeared at the same time, without a single word ever being spoken between them—it must have been two hearts speaking to each other as One; the magical language of amore! On the seventh night of their stealthy affair, without so much as a single word or gesture, they moved toward each other and finally met in an ardent embrace. Ah," she sang, smiling slyly, "and do you know what happened next, best beloved?" The master storyteller paused, her hands held out before her, palms up in a supplicating plea. "Yes, our heroine melted, but as her translucent skin of ice melted, it revealed her human flesh, and the lovers rejoiced at this marvelous sight; and immediately they ran away and were married, and lived happily ever after!" She hesitated, gazing down at her enraptured audience. "But do you know that the rest of the Ice People did not follow her when they heard what had happened? They had long since decided that it was their very ice nature that had secured their wealth, and they refused to yield up their treasures for the true treasure of Love and Humanity." She laughed. "And that is the way it was, and is, for all stories—done, done, done."

Lake clapped heartily.

The storyteller smiled, and thought to herself, "They call me the Ice Queen," but then she looked at Lake. "Yet I am human now, for my precious little girl." She felt deep sorrow in her maternal breast. "O Lake, you must never lose sight of your humanity as I once did; I will simply not allow it; I will do whatever is in my power to stop it." She embraced her granddaughter, and the two of them held each other fast. "No, you must never become as ice, lest you lose your soul; I will gladly lose all to gain your soul for you, my precious, my darling, my innocent Lake."

This memory fell away as the sable night rose up.

Lake fell asleep in the strong arms of her husband as the evening waxed on in strength and purpose, a heavy black veil subduing the land, pressing the people into the relaxing servitude of sleep within whose dreamy universe good things may yet come, and where bad things are made good again.

So, the two lovers slept, wrapped in a gauzy love cocoon, love pouring its spicy perfumed essence over them, bathing them, sweeping its silvery mist over their gentle figures, humming a sweet lullaby in their ears.

"Innocent as white-fleeced lambs ye lie down with golden lions; the world loves you."

Love

The next morning blossomed sunny and rose red, and life began anew, but disease was still hollowing Lake out as if she were a statue of sand, and soon, it began to assume her shape. Every day she wanted to live and be happy and free, but every day she woke up and realized that she was falling deeper and deeper into a place she felt no one could possibly rescue her from.

The two lovers began to quarrel, as lovers sometimes do, but their quarreling came from the poisonous fumes of the bitter past; they argued sometimes early and sometimes late, and sometimes they argued from ugly night until ugly dawn, allowing their virulent emotions to continue into the silvery light of day. They were exploring each other and listening to each other and deciding on each other, but still they could not refrain from starting at opposite ends of the cramped and silent room and then running at high speeds and ramming each other into their fragile hearts.

"We've no food left," Lake said, many weeks later, standing barefoot one day in her white nightgown as she peered into the empty refrigerator; she turned round, and sent a volley of loud words into the bedroom, "but, O, we have each other." She fell to the hard floor, bemused, slapping the cool white tiles, and then said, while holding herself and holding her head slightly tilted in a mock affection, "Love just fills my tummy; say, is that flapjacks and maple syrup I feel?"

Tony stood over her, arms folded, weary of her last month of tantrums.

"If only they could see me now, those silly people I grew up with who own the whole world—would they be proud of me?" she cried, and then laughed as she squirmed about the floor.

"They wouldn't recognize who you are, either."

"Oh, please," she shouted, frowning terribly, "spare me your philosophical-pop- psychoanalytical babble, it's beginning to bore me." She looked away from his intense stare, ashamed of her unprovoked attack. She felt the stale, waxy offense of yesterday's pain swelling inside her, and the very fact that it had not departed forever vexed her. "There's always some pearl of wisdom hanging over my head, for goodness' sake," but she whispered this, for she was embarrassed, now. "Why can't I shut up?" she queried herself. "Do I want to drive him away? Why, why, why would I want that! What is wrong with me?"

He was made of living flesh and bone and blood and sinew, not of inanimate stone, and every verbal dart that stuck into his mortal frame anesthetized him to holding on to her and loving her, driving him closer to his breaking point. "Fine," he said, turning away, "you live alone." He turned round, found the bathroom, showered, all the while stoking the fire of wrath within, smothering the small voice of compassion that said Lake was simply who he had once been and doing what he used to do all the time, and that he should be the better man and the better human being for it, and should have understood it better than anyone. No, he would have none of it; he wanted her in as much pain as he felt; so, presently, he left the place.

He came home late, and did not speak to her; he woke up the next day, showered, and left, once more without speaking to her, punishing her for her transgressions. He would be relentless and unforgiving now, hardening his heart against her; he returned again that night, again silent toward her, again ignoring her contrite body posture, her sad refrain, her subtle motions to him; the next day was the same, and the next, and the next, until she too came to resent her lover, and she too grew silent and brooding. This then was an inflexible brooding stitched together by bitter bits of thorny thread, a blanket of brooding resentment that was not easily usurped; it grew like a malignant tumor that had its origins from the day they had met; and it grew on residual crumbs of old that should have been purged from their relationship the moment they were united in holy matrimony.

O, the wicked past, how its hateful self stuck in each of the lovers and rotted in their flesh because they would not obliterate it, would not concentrate on the joy and love and wonder of the now; to bury the past would allow them to truly live, and both of them so desperately wanted to live and be happy and to celebrate life with someone they dearly loved. He had dreamed of happiness his entire existence, and she had come to realize she had been dead until he came to her; but still, they would not forgive and forget transgressions against each other, and in doing so, the cold anchor round their neck grew heavier and heavier and slowly pulled them deeper and deeper into the murky depths of bitterness.

One day, one fine, cool, crisp day when the body aches for the solace of hearth and home, he came back, late at night, still besieged by this mad urge to ignore her, still fearing that his breaking of this long silence would define him as weak. "I will show her just how much I don't need her," he thought as he walked past his wife.

Lake had been sitting upon a barstool of wood, anxiously awaiting the arrival of her husband; before that she had been lying on the old sofa, weeping, and before that, in bed, weeping, weeping for what might have been, weeping for what was, weeping for what she imagined life should be.

For two weeks, she had lived in a black void, a perilous darkness apart from his love, abandoned by her protector, and she desperately sought to appease him, but she could not allow her pride to suffer the blow of admitting she needed any living thing.

"I will break you," he thought, walking past her slumping form, "you will learn to respect me, or go away forever." He neither looked at her nor spoke to her, for she was invisible to his senses, as he had banished her to a parallel universe where she was unable to break on through to the other side.

She died every day for his manly warmth, for his strong touch, his smooth voice, his earnest praise and reassurance; but every day she grew colder toward him as she shrank from his presence. "He has abandoned me, as I knew he would," she thought, watching him walk away, and then she said, quite suddenly, "I want a divorce."

He turned round, incredulous, staring at her with contempt.

She realized she had spoken what she did not truly mean, but now had to act on her own words or lose her strength with him. Her voice came from the grave of sorrow. "You heard me; I can't live like this, I hate you for what you are doing to me; I hate you because you left me just when I needed you most, when I was at my darkest hour, when I reached out and you weren't there; you betrayed me; I can't live like this with someone I cannot depend on; you were supposed to be there for me forever," and she clutched her bosom as she nearly wept; "you promised me you would be there always; I can't do this, I can't, I want to but I can't—for me, for self-preservation, I want a divorce, I need a divorce." And the more she spoke of this forbidden fruit, the more she believed in the powerful force of its malignant heresy, and she began to weep, but bitterness dried her first tear. "You leave me all day, you don't talk to me; our marriage is over." Her spoken words were a catalyst to cause the greatest emotional harm possible upon his vulnerable heart.

He had thus far adorned himself in a splendid robe of tissued black that dripped bitter-tasting gall, an eerie, dark brooding feverish charm bleeding into his thick skin; he had felt comfort in its sharp wit, for even sharp objects can subdue the greatest of philosophers if they slowly and easily slip into their victim.

This black, seething, murderous spring welled up in him and fed his willing brain. "I will have her hate me," he had reasoned, "I will push her away; I will see if our Love is True," he had thought, and had thought often while observing her from the safety of his faraway place high above her station, but had not expected her demand for a dissolution of their union. His linear train of thinking was hauled off its smooth, well-oiled tracks, and he felt like something filthy, like something dead inside and filthy and rotten, like someone who steps on poor, innocent creatures and watches them squirm for life. He wanted to say something, to say he hadn't really meant any of it, that he was just hurt and wanted her to know it, but instead he stood, silent and hard.

But this affront mauled his mistress of chaos. To speak against her wishes meant her appeasement, to remain silent meant affirmation. His stark, barren countenance now was a wasteland to her heart, a dying heart that now huddled in its cavern of ice and darkness, and the season of warmth was not yet upon it.

He crucified her remaining vestiges of hope when he turned away and walked out of the house, without even a look back, without words, without acknowledgment of her terrible proclamation.

That night, she was sick, sicker than she had been for weeks, and she dreamed of him coming back to her, but he did not come; no, he did not come home till the early sprays of dawn sprinkled their magenta haze, and when he did come in, he ignored her, walking right past her sickbed to gather a few things and then he went right out of the house. "He has another lover—a woman healthy and strong, as I once was; he has finally abandoned me, as I always knew he would; he lied," she began to sob, "he lied as I always knew he would; all men are liars, they just want to use women for physical pleasures; they can't love, and women who want their love are just fools."

She was ill that day, very ill, coughing up bright red blood, feeling her weak heart pounding and hurting inside her sore, skinny chest; her kidneys burned and ached, her green eyes were a liquid, bloodshot red; large cramps strangled her calves and hamstrings; hard, bumpy cramps felled her to the ground in agony, and she cried out to the only person alive who still cared for her. "Tony, Tony, where are you?" and even then she would have gladly forgiven him, for in her deep love she yearned for him, still; but he did not come, and her heart grew more bitter and cold, until it seemed a lump of dry, misshapen ice. Yet, it was the ice of a wrathful lover seeking vengeance for perceived wrongs and willing to shed its outer husk in return for pure love, rarefied love, inviolate love.

Night squeezed day out of its vaulted throne and cooled the collective heels of the inhabitants of this city. People were forced to be together in the shelter of their homes, forced to talk, forced to communicate, and thus, epic battles began that would end only in emotional death, battles that should never have begun, battles conceived in the misunderstanding of communication.

He came home that gloomy, dark night, bringing in the black funeral procession of dying unions with him. He stood before her bed, wrapped in an eerie fog of the death of dis-solution. "I found a lawyer," his words seemed to originate from the rotting underbelly of sin, his tone scripted from fire and smoke. "He will work with us to dissolve this marriage, posthaste; in the meantime, I am moving out." He was killing her with his righteous decree, terrorizing her heart and mind. He waited, as if to taste her loathing foment.

"I hate you," she cried in a hoarse voice, lying on their bed. "You lied to me! You abandoned me just when I needed you most; you never really wanted me, only what I once was. You raped my image, you raped a dead woman. You're disgusting!" She coughed violently and vomited on the brown sheets, then rolled out of bed, and crawled on the plastic covering toward the bathroom like a dying animal. Waste was dribbling from her diseased body as she moaned in agony. "I hate you, I hate you," she murmured, "I'll never love you again. You betrayed me," she shouted, her head hanging down as she entered the bathroom. "Traitor! Traitor! Traitor!" But only her vomiting abated her piercing words.

He wanted to say he did not mean it, that he did not know how it had all come to this, but he could not say anything as he stood there lacerated by the caustic Truth of her dying words; he desperately wanted to tell her he loved her and that he would care for her always, but it all seemed so wrong to say it now. "Too late, too late," echoed in his raging mind. He felt himself fading away into a hollow oblivion.

"I would be weak to help her now; she would never respect me; it's her own fault, after all." He did not believe any of this, but he had to heal the giant cracks in his weak logic for punishing her, and to ameliorate his own guilt and strengthen his resolve. "It's for the best; we're two different people."

Yet, as he spoke, words shifted from a far different geographical region of his brain and came to the forefront of his innocent thoughts and slithered out of his dumb mouth. "Never believe people when they speak in the fits of passion." He heard her violent bodily explosions in the bathroom. "You can't believe people when they are in love or hate," he shouted; "passion is a poor arbiter of reason." He paused, irritated that she had not hit back his hard volley. "Did you hear me, Lake?" He had not said her name in what seemed an eternity, and its blissful sound penetrated straight into his deaf heart. He crossed from flitting shadows into the dim light of the bathroom, and saw her huddled form around the white porcelain toilet. He felt a vast emptiness engulf him, and shame and humiliation swallowed him whole as his entire body shuddered. "I should have been there for her," he thought, but he fought this natural urge to comfort his wife. "I must do what seems unnatural if I want this to end once and for all, not like other people who linger in pain for years; this, then, is the secret, no mercy." But her bodily purging strangled his illogical, mad ramblings.

He felt himself dying with her.

"She is me," he thought, and experienced, not merely as words, but as a whole mind-body soul refrain, where he felt the chill and embarrassment and humiliation for being so wrong, so petty, so vindictive for absolutely nothing worth this much pain or any pain at all, especially not involving someone like himself, who had been there all before and should have known better; and he knew now that he had lost his will to steel himself against compassion; now, he knew, he must somehow climb out of the abyss he had constructed, an abyss he knew from the beginning he could never sustain, nor truly even wanted.

She would hate him, he knew this, as he watched her tormented body writhing on the wet bathroom floor; he would be attempting to tame a wild animal he deliberately had made wild. He marveled at his abrupt reversal of emotions toward her; but he had known all along that he had wanted her and would never leave her, and as much as he drove himself to alienate her, he knew he could not do it forever.

"But I mustn't crawl," he decided, daring now to open his mouth before his slain queen. He felt the beauty and innocence of pure love bore up in him, and he was unbound.

She smelled him as he stood in the doorway, smelling his perfumed arrogance, smelled him awash in condemnation.

"Get out," she cried, "go watch another freak show somewhere else!"

He knew anything he would say would elicit her wrath; he had been the relentless, merciless enemy, and now he had to convince her he had capitulated and pledged loyalty to her once more.

He slowly bent down to help her up.

"Don't touch me, you swine," she screamed, her voice strained to hoarseness, her emaciated face trembling, a burning red. She looked up at him with a hitherto unknown mask of enmity. "I don't need you, anymore." She cursed him into submission; she inhaled his contrition into her flaring nostrils, but she would grind down his proffer of love and chew it and mix it up with her bile and saliva and spit it into his face; she wanted to knock him down and humiliate him and make him cry for what he had done to her. She had been unjustly crushed by him, and she would justly crush him; her voice was death to his love, stone cold, barren, sterile death to him, her countenance singing an arcane song of promise to despise, to scorn, to shun. Her face shook a righteous fury. "I don't love you anymore." She would not say his name as she screamed her dying heart. "I don't love you, I don't love you," and she clutched her stomach as if she were in great physical anguish. "I can't love you anymore, not anymore, no, never again." Salted silver droplets of tiny crystalline tears were burning down her ruddy cheeks. "I can't take that chance, again, that you'll leave me, again." She bent over in pain. "I have to know if you'll be there; I can't live not knowing." She then looked up at him as if she were having a violent abortion. Her voice resonated with exceptional clarity and a vicious animus. "You lost me." She hung her head low as if she had just witnessed the execution of a loved one.

He could have left, which was certainly the facile strategy of the coward. He could easily have sliced coldly through the sinewy heartstrings that bound them and tied them into a Gordian knot, divorcing her as does a man who lets loose a drunkard, a prostitute, a drug-addicted wife; but, lo, in light of her own sins, he saw his own, and he was shamed into submission by Virtue. "I will suffer to amend my ways," he contemplated, staring at her slumped figure.

Her powder-blue nightgown was soaked with toxic perspiration that covered her drawn-in knees and thin legs, and her scraggly brown hair was draped over her bare shoulders. The thin gown covered her body like a death wreath. It was this fragile wisp of a creature that he had trampled with his verbal stampede and iron resolution of ignoring her, and yet he had been so proud of his industrious labor to disinherit himself from her.

"How could I destroy the thing I love most," he lamented, staring at her bony neck and shoulders; "how could I put so much energy and passion into one moment of hurting her while at that same moment I could have eased her pain?"

His panoramic view of the world, with all of its lessons learned from horrible suffering, widened at this realization; for at that moment where two disparate worlds collide, one full of a nucleus that begged to feed itself, and another nucleus that yearned to feed others, he saw what was universally imprinted on the soul of wicked Man but hidden from the heart by the accumulation and pursuance of ignoble purpose.

"Why," he pondered, "I understand, now," and his burning brown eyes narrowed as he stared at her bowed head, which was drenched in the heavy perspiration of foul disease; and it was a revelation he and other men of equal philosophical fervor have at times of volcanic insight into the nature of Man—beast and saint.

"Lake," he pronounced, carefully, and gently, "I love you." He had no idea what words would drop from her frozen tongue, but he had to talk to her.

Her head rose up as if these words had yanked it on high. She wore a pale visage of disgust and contempt and then flung up her arms as she said, "And that is how you solve all of it, all of this?" She began to vomit, but nothing came out. "Maybe in your fantasy world, that works, but not in mine."

He resolved to withstand the hatred exploding from her damaged heart, but he had to believe it was hatred floating in a windswept sea and not anchored to the rocky bottom. "I love you, Lake, I do; I will always…"

"Oh, stop," she screamed, exasperated, "stop with your embarrassing, romantic blithering; people can't say they'll love someone forever; just look at those who say that in marriage, look at how they end up, things happen…" She shook her head. "You're so immature where women and reality are concerned."

"Maybe I am," he returned, careful not to become entangled in her accusations, "but I love you, still."

"Oh, good," she said, frowning, "and that takes away all of the pain of the past? And what about tomorrow, what happens if tomorrow your love takes a holiday? What then, big man…" She abruptly stuck out her hand at him as he began to speak. "And don't give me those weak promises about what will or will not happen; men are so fond of promising anything when they want something."

"I'm sorry."

A spontaneous laugh poured out of her. "Oh, that's good, you're sorry, now." Her entire body was still slumped forward while thick, beaded sweat poured off her trembling body, as if truly she was chained to the white tiled floor and every one of his words felt like the lash of the leather whip across her naked back. "The murderer is sorry as he stands over the corpse, that's precious." But then she looked up at him, her feigned mirth scattered, and her voice was like the wind blowing through burned ashes. "Never believe anyone when they're in the fit of passion, isn't that right, Mr. Walking Gainsayer," and when she slung a vulgar mud ball to dirty his name, she was full of enmity again. "You change your song and dance whenever it best suits you; you make me sick, the healthy and beautiful people subverting those ill and ugly." She vomited into the toilet. "Get out," she cried, nearly losing her voice, her strained words echoing wildly in this enclosed ceramic tomb. "Oh, please, just get out and leave me alone, please," she moaned, and collapsed to the cold tiles, "let me die in peace."

He refused to analyze any of it. He bent down next to her, his voice low and passionate. "You must believe me when I say I love you, and how sorry I am."

She refused to look up at him from her bent-over, tucked-in position. She held her stomach fast as agonizing contractions wracked her body. "Oh, I believe you believe it, but I don't believe you."

"I love you and I want to take care of you." He tried to put his hand upon her trembling, bare shoulders, but she pushed it away. "I can't go back and forth anymore, Lake, I have to go forward with you, now; forgive me, now, and we can start again."

Her words were barely perceptible, falling like tiny pieces of broken glass to the cool floor below. "I can't."

"And I can't walk away again, not again." He leaned his body closer to hers. "I can't abandon you again, not again." His hot breath and sweet words caressed her aching body. "There is no life apart from you, from you I draw purpose." His promise of devotion was like a warm salve on her fresh wounds. "Lake, apart, we are dead; together, we are alive." His soft, soothing tone enveloped her hurt in a soothing aura.

"Go away," she shouted, turning suddenly to meet his face, which was slowly creeping forward. "I can't take your love anymore."

He would take every kind of abuse from her, and like it, because he had been the villain, because he had been the deserter, because he had been the murderer of their sacred bond of holy matrimony. "I was wrong, Lake, I was wrong to treat you this way," and even as he said this, he knew this sounded hollow, mere words to gain something, to amend something.

"Deeds, not words," he thought, and then he whispered, as if he had never said it before and meant it, "I love you," and then let his right hand gently rest upon her hunched shoulders. She did not shrug his touch away, compelling him to proceed with the circumspection of a land-mine walker.

He grimaced in grief as he felt a body that was even more consumed with disease than the last time he had touched her; she felt lifeless, a flaccid form of icy, cold flesh and brittle bone; she was a heap of dust and anguish sewn together with shredded sinew and thinning cartilage. And it was she, this disinherited, sagging creature, that he had emotionally mauled. He felt a profound sense of penance pouring into his grieving heart.

"I must deliver us from this life," he decided, placing the side of his head against her moist face. She did not move away. He kissed her tangled brown curls. "I will save us from destruction; we must leave this place or die." He had known this long ago but could not intellectually grasp it as he could now, and now, he lived it. "I see the consequences of self, and the past," he thought, and looked far beyond the horizon of his own country; "the future is where we have never been nor could ever imagine going to; this, then, is salvation, where we are born again, apart from the rotting sludge of civilization that has buried us, the sludge that comes from the pursuance of self; why, we gain on one side, and lose on another..." But he chastised himself for philosophizing, and turned his attention to the delicate task at hand.

He reasoned he had come home again, retraced his steps, conquered the unconquerable with unconditional and pure love; he was proud as he embraced her, stroked her sore body, whispered dreamy recitations of affection into her ears. "I am home," he whispered.

"Get away from me," she screamed, and so abruptly and with such primordial force that he fairly leaped off of her. "You don't have the right to touch me ever again." She had not yet raised her head. Her words were mired in agony. "You forfeited that right."

He was on his knees now, hands on hips, feeling very much the naïve fool.

When she raised her head, she raised a specter of a terrifying hollowness clinging to the pasty complexion of her face. "You lost me, you're finished here; how can I make you understand that? I can't trust you ever again. My love for you died," and she clutched her sore breasts, "it died within me, like a dying baby; I felt it wail and scream and beg for life and I had to carry it with me every day, listening to it cry for love; I had to listen to its last gasps, begging for precious life." She was weeping now as she looked up at him. "You hurt me, you, of all the people who knew how much I had been through, and how much I trusted you and needed you, you hurt me so much, more than anyone else ever has." Her head fell as her voice broke from the strain of her raw hurt. "I opened myself up to you, I gave myself to you, completely, as a good wife should give herself to her husband—who is supposed to protect her from the world—and you betrayed me, you, from within my heart, you knew just how to bring me down, and you did, how could you…" But she could no longer speak as she sat, slumped over, hugging herself for solace.

He stood up, vanquished, numb, embarrassed. "If I leave now and come back, maybe she'll forgive me," he thought, but his instincts to stay prevailed.

He stood up, aware of only his mind.

"I did what I did," his voice was drained of enthusiasm for reconciliation, "because you hurt me; and please don't play the victim with me, Lake." His words were an icy wind draping her limp figure. "You're not beyond reproach; don't talk about only your pain; I'm human, too; I hurt you, yes, I confess, but you drove me there; and now I apologize, and you turn to stone. People who live together and love each other don't quit because they hurt each other; they learn from it, and grow together." She wasn't moving. "I can't force you to forgive me; I forgive you; you think about yourself, Lake, you think about your sins, not just mine. I know my sins, and I'm sorry for them. Ours," he pleaded, his hands wide apart, "is a difficult Love, but we can make it if we learn to forgive as easily as we condemn."

She was silent in the heavy, acrid air, and he enjoyed it; he wanted her to eat his spicy, meaty words and suffer enough to see who he was, to free her from her vehement loathing of him. He loved her and wanted her and respected her but he would not bow to her and scrape the ground without her conceding guilt.

"It takes two people to hate each other, and two to love each other." His tone was softer now, sprinkled with affection. "When two people of great passion, such as we, are together…" But his words failed him, and he mused upon it, and decided to remain silent. He was suddenly tired of talking, and embarrassed that his declaration of devotion and love for her had fallen into the swelling chasm between them.

She still lay crumpled upon the floor, a weak mass of sodden flesh and fragile bone. She barely moved, saying nothing, refusing his presence; she had entered into her own safe universe for survival.

He would leave now. "I can't crawl to you, Lake, you know it's not me," he said, leaving the hot fumes of the bathroom. "I can't make you accept me back, and I can't wait forever, either;

we know each other better than anyone else ever could, that's why we're married. We're no good for anyone else." He issued a soft laugh and shook his head. "No one else would understand us; we are unique in all the world." Each word had to be exquisitely drawn and put into honey-scented sentences, filling up her mind with a final image of their eternal love and its inherent, inviolate right to live. "You need to think of the future, see it now, live it now, hmm," and he paused, thinking of her ways; "you've always been good at being practical. It's what sets you apart from the rest of the impractical world." He smiled, wishing she could see his genuine admiration. "I've lost her," he whispered to himself, "it's my own fault." He turned and walked slowly to retrieve his white satchel. His senses were deadened by acceptance of the dissolution of their marriage. "It has been better to serve as one part of an unhappy whole in this paradise than to be half, not part of anyone, in purgatory." He was an unthinking automaton now, stuffing the cloth bag with things necessary for his survival elsewhere, walking about, head held low, every movement of his hands taking him closer to a task that once done, would remove him forever from his beloved. He stood in the small family room, looking at her sprawled, silent form, and then he spoke, in a low voice, unsure if he wanted her to hear his final words. "Don't you understand that people aren't perfect, that they do foolish things, that they even hurt the ones they love—it happens; we're not saints, not angels, were flawed people, and we do things we cannot explain; and when it does happen, we need forgiveness when we ask for it; I'm not saying anyone deserves to come back, some people do go too far, and aren't really sorry, they just miss hurting their Love; but you know me, darling, you know I only hurt you because I love you so much..." but he could speak no longer, so full of pathos was he.

He turned, his legs heavy, his posture weak, as he walked toward the door.

She was standing in the bathroom doorway now, silhouetted against the bright light, arisen from her diseased slumber, her face radiant with hope. He turned around and stood as erect as a marble statue.

"Do you love me?" she said, in earnest, her blue gown glowing at her sides. "Do you really love me, Tony?"

He was breathless, intoxicated with passion, revived by love as he heard his name mentioned by she whom he adored above all others. "Among the faithless, faithful only she," he said, ardently, his skin alive with the tingling of anticipation.

Her face shone with adoration. "I love you, my darling husband, I do," she said as she closed her eyes and brought her bent arms to her chest.

"I love you, Lake, I love you, my precious love," he said, nearly weeping from exhilaration, "without you I am nothing again; without you, my wife, my love, I might as well be who I once was; through you I have life, my darling, my beautiful Lake."

He moved ever so slowly toward her, and when he was nearly upon her, he stopped, his hands near her bare brown arms; it was as if he were about to touch her for the first time.

"Love me, Tony," she whispered, weeping pious tears, "love me forever."

"Yes," he whispered, and touched her skin, gorgeous and soft to him, and he looked into her radiant eyes. "I will." He kissed her, and their warm tears flowed as one.

Love had conquered once again that which seemed unconquerable.

Plans

Morning came, light and airy, and a raspberry sky came, draping the bedded young lovers in a resplendent robe.

Apart, their hearts beat to a different rhythm; together, their hearts beat as one; separated again, their agitated hearts tormented their masters until the blissful union was once more achieved; heart and mind and body enjoined, and their souls were at peace with themselves and the world.

Tony spoke, his voice full of reverence, as if he spoke to a basic element in Nature, as if he were speaking to a doleful doe, a fertile flower, a deep cerulean sky filled with geysers of billowing white clouds, "I know now how to live," he began, gazing lovingly into her adoring eyes, stroking her pale body. "We have to leave this place, this valley, this state, this country." He peered deeper into her still sparkling eyes, looking for a response. "People who have plenty are corrupt, we know that; people who have less, like those we tried to help, too often do not appreciate what is offered to them because they see plenty about them. They cannot see what is good enough for them."

"Mmm," she purred, and closed her eyes as she snuggled closer to his warm body.

He smiled.

The bed was deliciously warm and cozy as they lay next to each other; the cream-colored sheets were strewn about them, the cinnamon-colored covers lay in crumpled heaps next to their lazy bodies; this, then, was their solace, their insular paradise.

"So, you think we should leave all of this?" she said, raising her head and then gesturing about the bare room. She giggled.

"Yes."

She grew somber. "I know what you mean." She lay still for a moment, pondering the new path he led her on. "From the stories you told me of the people you have been helping these past weeks, I believe I know." She grew anxious. "It's hard to please people who have things, but not everything; they don't appreciate what you are doing for them." She knit her brows. "We should help those who have no food—they won't turn us away; we should help those with no shelter— they will appreciate us." She propped up her head upon her dry and cracked, peeling right elbow, proud revelation written upon her face. "A starving man won't turn down a cup of rice."

"No, he won't."

"Hmm," she let out, again, with an exclamation of surprise, "so, we must find people who don't have even the most fundamental necessities in life to survive, or maybe are just struggling to survive."

"Say, know any around here?"

She looked at him. "I know someone who thinks he's so clever," she whispered, and she reached over and kissed his smug smile. "When do we leave? Where do we go?"

He reached down, picked up a world atlas book, and placed it beside her. "Your choice," he said. He watched her pour over the colorful pictures. "You look like you're shopping," he said, amused.

"Uh huh," she purred.

He watched her for a few minutes, and could no longer remain silent. "But I am serious about all of this, honey."

She looked up, frowning, and stated, matter-of-factly, "But so am I."

"Oh."

"You aren't the only one who is tired of this life."

"Hmm."

She touched his face. "Together."

He kissed her rough, dry hand.

"Now, I haven't told you how we're going to get there."

She smiled, and said melodramatically, while looking upward with arms spreading out in a wide gesture, "On the wings of True Love."

"No," he said, curiously, "on the donations of a Christian church."

She sat up and weakly threw the book across the room.

"Missionaries!"

He had only the courage to nod his head.

"I can't believe you would talk to church people about us becoming missionaries without consulting me."

He paused for a valuable second. "How did you think we were going to get there? You don't just show up in a third-world country and say, 'Hello, I am a do-gooder from America— anybody need help?'"

She tried to suppress an amused smile. "Still, you should have told me."

"And how do you think," he continued, reasoning that this bit of information should somewhat appease her, "I have been able to feed us and pay the bills this last month? When I was volunteering for the church, working in their food pantry, visiting the elderly and the sickly with their minister, I met a few people who had private businesses, and managed to get some part-time employment; I did not intend to get work this way, but people offered me jobs." He terminated this narrative as he watched her outrage grow like a mushroom cloud after a rock thrown into a crater of dust.

"Without me? You did all of this without me? How could you?"

"We weren't exactly best friends during that time, Lake, my love, and I know how you feel about churches." He bit his lip, realizing his words had just dug up the fresh soil upon the warm corpse of their recently painful past. "Sorry."

She baked in the hot fumes of her anger, then shook her head, and kissed him. "So, who is this minister of God?"

He was astonished, and pleased. He was flushed with excitement when he divulged the extent of the plan to her eager ears.

"But we shall not be converts," she declared, emphatically.

"Of course, not," he said, "the church is just a vehicle for us."

"And we'll drive it across the Seven Seas," she laughed, but then said, with gravity, "but won't they mind that we are not believers?"

"They will take whom they can, and I have not explicitly told them we are not believers; but I must admit I do like the church and the people there, and the minister in his sermons has such wisdom."

She nodded in agreement.

Equilibrium had been achieved once again.

They visited the church, the minister and the congregation; Tony took Lake to the people he visited and who appreciated him—the sickly, the elderly, the dying, those with no hope, no joy, no future, those given up by loved ones, by friends, by society; the minister inspired them to take a pilgrimage to the farmlands to bring workers food and clothing and Bibles, and see how those truly humble in spirit live, to see how poor workers live while they pick grapes and dates and onions and strawberries and lettuce for the rich American farmer; Lake and

Tony labored alongside the workers and listened to their stories;
they ate with them in their makeshift tents, in their cars, in
dilapidated mobile homes, and shared rented rooms; they heard
their woeful stories and listened as the workers spoke of their
own lives sacrificed for a better life for their sons and daughters,
their mothers and fathers, for their brothers and sisters; nearly
all of them were of Mexican descent, and all of them considered themselves privileged to be in America. Tony and Lake
marveled at the resilience of these people, who, despite every
imaginable obstacle in their way, moved forward; the workers
arose every morning and moved their tattered and beaten and
battered and callused bodies up and out the door and into the
early morning sweet harvest of Nature's bounty to pick and
pull and separate and stack and pile and haul the produce for
their masters; every day they did this, despite finishing the
night exhausted and hearing the internal rhythm of their bodies slowing down and skipping beats and being entirely thrown
off sequence; and despite it all, they told Tony and Lake, all of
them told them that they—the pickers—were the lucky ones,
that they were at least here, in the United States of America, in
the land of plenty, that they had made it, were with loved ones,
relying on each other, comforting one each other, a family united,
a family loyal to another; and that the unlucky ones were still
back in Mexico, whom they still sent money to, living the life
of authentic pain and struggle and heartache. "Go to Mexico,"
one of the old men said, who had picked grapes in this valley
for forty years, "go to Mexico if you want to really help people
who need you." He stood before them as he told them this, with
a deeply furrowed forehead and his brown, wrinkled face that
was like leather, his gnarled and arthritic hands proclaiming
the unvarnished Truth, as if he sought to paint its magnificence
before them, as if he truly wanted them to go right there and

then and help those he had left behind. He had smiled then, and his kindly face reflected the honesty of his words; and then with his hands palm up in an imploring gesture, he said, quietly, sincerely, lovingly, "They will not turn you away, for they who have very little appreciate any little thing that is given to them from the heart."

It was through such acts that Lake began to understand what Tony had often said: "We are on earth to help each other; be selfless in your dedication to bring succor to your fellow Man, and your needs will be taken care of."

Thus, it was decided by these two lovers to forgo all of the pleasures of civilized society and sell all that they owned, and leave to a faraway country where human beings exist in a world hitherto unknown to them.

The night before their departure, she had become ill again, and slept soundly in her bed, while he sat anxiously outside in the den.

The Letter

A man came to their door, dressed in fine attire, and he stood for the longest time, pondering his deliberate actions. "Fate," he whispered, "merciless and unrelenting." He inhaled deeply, so that his smart navy-blue pinstriped suit rose like an iceberg in a swell. He knocked upon the door of white-painted wood. His tone was steady and cool when the man opened it.

"Mr. Siciliani? Yes, my name is Matthew Gershon. I am the attorney for Camille Seville, Lake's grandmother." He handed

Tony a business card. The two men shook hands. Mr. Gershon entered the house, and the men sat down on separate sofas.

Every word he spoke now was tortured. "Mr. Siciliani, where is Lake?"

"Tony," he replied, easily, "and Lake is resting right now."

"Tony," he declared, as if it calmed him to pause during the inevitable deed. "I am an attorney in good standing with the state of California, having practiced my trade for thirty-five years without complaint against me; and yet, here I am before you, delivering what must be deemed the most unusual of services to a client." He sat forward into the light, and his age became apparent; indeed, he was old—the deep creases, the pronounced wrinkles, the tired gray eyes, the sad frown all portrayed a weary man, a lonely man consumed by the haunting bloodstains of acts necessary for survival. "Camille Seville left a will, as I am sure you know, that left Lake nothing in terms of monetary value; but I am here to tell you," he seemed to rush his words for fear that they would not come out otherwise, "that is not the whole truth." He sought to convey reassurance, but his countenance merely paled.

"Why tell me?"

Matthew Gershon reached into his brown leather briefcase, and took out a letter, a carefully folded letter he massaged nervously between his fingers. He wanted to preface the transference of the document to Tony with a brace, a cushion of words, a suitable landing field, but he could not, and so he simply handed the one-page, handwritten letter to him.

Tony commenced to read the narrative in a low hush. "My Dearest Lake," it began, "you must know I have always loved you more than any other; you know in your heart I have always wanted the best for you, and would never allow any harm to come to you.

"My darling girl, as you read this, you are, prayerfully, a transformed human being; your life has been hard, you have little money, your health has been shattered, but you have prevailed, and now are readied to be restored to a robust health and a life you will understand.

"It was I who caused your illness; I purposely made you ill to save you from a life that destroyed your mother and father and grandfather and me.

"Lake, you will me hate for some time, but you will not hate me forever.

"Six years ago, I placed a parasite into your bodily systems that is extremely difficult to detect. It wreaks havoc upon your health, but it does not kill you. I have enclosed the name of the parasite and of several scientific labs, and the description of accompanying cures, to rid your body of this plague.

"Do not think of how bad your life has been, but how your life would have turned out had you been free to pursue it, unrestrained, and how wonderful your life will be.

"As you are now a nobler, humbler creature, you will be better equipped to handle the money I have left you.

"Remember always that I loved you, Lake; think of our love for each other, and all will be well. You will have what I always dreamed of but could never achieve—true happiness, not because of money or health, but because of who you are and how you are able to see the world for what it is and to help it grow toward the light.

"With all my love,

"Camille Seville"

Matt scrutinized the pain emanating from the face of the reader of the letter, knowing Tony lived every piercing word. He was waiting for the test.

Tony, his face blanched from horror, looked at the attorney. "I understand."

"But the money," he said, handing Tony the amount on a piece of paper.

"I don't care about that," his voice was soaked in the venom of scorn and righteousness.

"But the amount…"

His voice was hard as war. "I don't care about the money—a hundred million dollars is meaningless to someone who has lost their health; I would trade it all for one day of health for Lake."

"Good boy," thought the attorney, feeling as if his soul had been crushed by giant stones for the longest time, and was now free.

"And what if we can't kill the parasite? What if the damage is too much for her system?"

"Her grandmother was rather certain this particular parasite did not kill the host and could be destroyed. She spent a great deal of time researching it." He handed Tony a thick document concerning the name of the parasite, which had been prepared by Camille and also included an addendum by himself.

"The risk," he returned, "to risk so much…"

"To gain so much, great risks are necessary." He took the letter back. "Listen, Tony, I have always tried to monitor Lake's activities—as her grandmother wished—always watching out for her." Tony merely stared. "Everything is going to be all right."

"Is it? If you know so much, then you know we're going away." His tone rose, but it dropped as he looked back to the white bedroom doors. He walked over, opened them a bit, peered in to check on his beloved and, satisfied, returned to the sofa. "She can't know about this letter, not now."

"Lake turned twenty-six last week," the gray-haired attorney said, "that is the chronological age at which she was to have the letter and the money."

His voice pleaded mercy. "But not now," he began, "not now," he set his clenched teeth and flaring nostrils in a fit of passion, "we have to get out of this place; we have to lose ourselves, forget ourselves, or die here." His countenance was terrifying in his fervor to deliver his sacred script. "Staying here, we'll never know who we are or what we we're supposed to be; we'll never know what it means to simply live in harmony with those things in the world intended for those who seek them." His eyebrows arched as his head swayed side to side. "We'll never know each other, never, because there is too much here that gets in the way. Can you understand that?" He looked back to the white doors that shielded his beloved, then back again to his lone audience, and his voice was melancholy. "There are things in this world we don't even recognize because everything gets in the way—everything; we begin as innocent children, and then we're devoured by greed and the pursuit of things—ridiculous accumulation of things—we do not need; and in the end, what do we have? Who are we? We have things—tangible things—but we're not happy because we become defined by these things; we don't really know each other because there is no time, no time for friendship, no time for love, no time just for living and trying to find out if there is more to life than just…things." He swept his strong hands through his thick, black, wavy hair. "This is why we need to leave—to live, because staying here will kill us both; we would be alive, but dead, because now we know better, and once you know what you have to do and don't do it, then you die, slowly, and we will not have that, not for any amount of money."

This boy knows, Matt thought, and then said, "And what of the inheritance?"

Tony smiled, ironically. "What good is it to gain the whole world and lose your soul?"

"So, what about the money?" he restated, firmly. "It is Lake's inheritance."

Tony stared at the slender attorney for a searing moment of intensity. "We will delay our trip to investigate this parasite," he stated, with considerable vehemence against the bug, "and as for the money..."

They spoke in such hushed whispers that even if the walls had ears to hear, they would have strained to hear anything at all.

There came a noise, briefly, in the stolen hush of a blink of the eye, so subtle even the most sensitive radar ear might not have gathered in its delicate whisper: a body sliding into a soft spread of cloth, followed by a diminutive, stifled cry, and then, an abrupt silence.

Tony, attuned to his wife's internal rhythms and rhymes, lifted his head from the close conference with the attorney, turned his attention to the bedroom, whereupon he swept effortlessly across the carpet, opened the doors, and observed the restless form of his wife.

He sat down again, and once more laid his head with his fellow into a tight male circle of supreme secrecy.

An inaudible song of sorrow slid under the hearing range of the two men.

Tony turned his head again and looked at the bedroom doors.

Another Chance

He must convince her to delay the voyage for a brief period of time, he knew, but he must not arouse suspicion in her suspicious mind.

"Delay?" she cried, frowning the next morning as she sat at the breakfast table. "Like ordinary folk?"

"How did you sleep last night, dear?" he asked, innocently.

She knit her arched eyebrows, pursed her thin lips, and said, after raising the right portion of her lips, "Fine, I suppose," and then shaking her head and stroking her cheeks, "I dreamed of Grandmother." That special smile of a special history people wish they could live again appeared upon her face. "I woke up crying." She tilted her head, a quizzical look upon her face. "I don't know why."

Tony flushed relief. "Well, I've done some more research on a particular parasite…"

"Oh, Tony, not the 'parasite conspiracy' again," she moaned, sipping her morning cup of green and chamomile tea.

"Well, it's different this time." He was careful to seclude his great hope of finding a cure for her in his voice. "It won't take past a month."

Despite her greatest protestations, he convinced her to take the tests.

There were tests performed on human waste, done with special fluorescent equipment, some with special stains, others with conventional chemical agents.

"It is all too easy," he thought, pacing back and forth the day the test results were to be read and sent to their doctor. "She has suffered long and hard, and she deserves recovery; but somehow, it seems all too easy to blame it all on one tiny microorganism and then flush it from her system with a simple pill."

Six labs were involved in taking samples and conducting tests on her body and its related waste products.

It was a Tuesday, a cold, gray, foggy, drenched day, where the sun was drained of its power, its heat, its very wealth of yellow flame and golden rays; and ill tidings swirled in the blustery air, blowing icy blades at any rising current of hope. The phone rang.

"Hello," he said. It was the results from the first lab. The nurse for their doctor disseminated the information as if she were reading an advertisement. He put down the phone, his arm seemingly detached from him. "Negative," his words were drained of energy.

"Well," she said, undisturbed, "what of it? It's just another idiot theory."

He suppressed the natural urge to shame the words down her reddened throat. "But it isn't," he wanted to cry; "your grandmother poisoned you with a parasite so you could live! O, you stupid girl, what she did was wrong, but without what she did, you would be lost, and I would be alone."

"Well," he did say aloud, dispassionately, "five more."

Five more phone calls came and went during the next two days, and five more times he lost hope, and with the last monotone pronouncement of "Negative" from the final nurse, he mind began to follow a paradigm long ago established during his own illness.

"But we must order more tests," he anxiously said to her; "too many laboratories make mistakes."

"Oh, stop it," she said, frowning. "You're becoming unhinged on some ridiculous freak; why is this idea different from any other inane one?"

He sought not to be evasive, but his packaging of words danced a familiar pattern around the truth she normally received. "It seemed to make sense at the time," his voice hid a profound disappointment. "But it can't be still in her," he reasoned, "so then we must assess damage done."

"Well?" she queried, adamantly.

"Just a few more tests to check on internal..."

His sentence formed a fragile dome between the two histories of each other's personalities, and she smashed it to feathery snowdrops as she hurled a book on internal medicine near him; she cursed fuming blue walls into their midst, her ruddy face now fuming scarlet rage. "No more tests, Tony!" She sat down abruptly and let her face fall into her hands. "I can't take it anymore," she said, in a barely audible, beaten-down voice, and then looked up at him, her wet eyes pleading mercy. "Can't we just leave? I thought the whole idea behind leaving was to forget..."

This was no time for him to drive home his fierce logic and sit upon her burning anger until it mercifully died; no, it was the time for holding her and loving her and soothing her pain; it was the time for sharing a passionate bond that exists only between husband and wife, time to penetrate a universe where two people are as one, where they rise and fall together, live and die together, laugh and cry together, wail and grieve, rage and forgive together, unite as one to exist in the world, and to exist without the world. Together they were a newborn culture, a complete culture, a defined personality; apart, they were destined to spin in the same grooved circles, fated to dip deeper in the same path, unaware that they were purposeless, aimless, and devouring their own debris.

Precious hours elapsed, hours spent dwelling in a timeless, spaceless dimension of patient love.

She would agree to one last battery of tests, but she adamantly declared that she did not wish to know the results.

A comprehensive MRI scan, a CAT scan, and blood work and biopsies were done on her; they had to sell their car to pay the expense.

A week later, Tony walked the few miles to the doctor's office. He heard the results but was not satisfied, and so he saw another doctor, but was not satisfied, either, and so sought out another, and then another, and still another, and then one more highly qualified specialist in the field of parasitology.

The woman in the white coat stared at the husband of the patient, and then reached for the manila folder that was filled with the results, but then dropped it onto her desk.

"Your wife is seriously ill," she began, "she has an enlarged heart and diseased liver; she has polyps in her esophagus; her kidneys are inflamed; her spleen is enlarged, and she has several blockages in her main arteries. She has two small cancers growing, one in her left breast, the other in her ovaries." She breathed in a deep sigh bound with the rusty ointment of impending death. "She could die at any time."

Tony, undaunted, explained the theory of the worm king and its intercession into the body of his wife.

The doctor screwed up her large eyes, and pondered for a moment. "Yes, gone undetected for that length of time, it is possible it could cause such destruction."

"How long have we known how destructive this parasite is?"

"Oh, about the last five years; before that, we assumed it was not so invasive, a minor player in disease, and very hard to detect; but now we know that it uses one very virulent parasite to hitch a ride into a human host."

"Yes," Tony said, numbly, thinking of Camille, "but what is there to be done, even if we had all the money in the world?"

The doctor with the long black hair and kind eyes hesitated, and then echoed what all the other specialists had gravely declared in no uncertain terms, "We can lessen her pain before she dies."

Tony expressed gratitude for the knowledge of the doctor, and then walked home.

Lake was asleep when arrived. "Now we go," he whispered toward her, closing the white shuttered doors, "and start anew."

A week later and they were gone.

Mexico

Human misery flourishes in the barren lands of Mexico like golden wheat grows in the fertile fields of Kansas, and Justice therein lays trampled; equality is buried in a pit of bleached bones and broken promises and dead revolutions, and the open sores of grief paint the citizens with blood and betrayal.

Mexico stretched out its crippled Beauty to the small plane that landed on its parched earth. The two Americans came quietly down the steel steps, the man helping the woman to the runway, and then again helping her to the waiting driver, who took them to his car and then out to the distant countryside.

It was a desert sun that branded its sizzling scorch marks upon their weary bodies. The dirt roads that stretched before them were dusty and bumpy. The Summer air was a burning fever that crawled into every pore and hatched pools of thick, beaded sweat.

The old, dark blue sedan with the rusted chrome rims passed through small towns where the nuances of civilization lay scattered about the small shops and dirt streets. There were rest stops in these isles of antiquity, and the people were kind and courteous and without pretensions.

But none of it made sense to these two Americans, for the vanguard of their receding society was missing; small but intricate pieces were absent, and therefore, the entire picture collapsed, for here, Nature ran the store, and the laws of sanitation and modernity were intruding vagabonds.

Insects pranced about the towns like marching bands, unrestrained, dancing with their sinister partner, disease; the both of them waltzed lazily alongside skinny dogs and fat cows and scampering goats and pecking white chickens.

Lake was sick during the ride, vomiting and expelling waste on numerous occasions as the car and driver drove deeper into the heartland of Mexico.

They drove through many cities and towns and states on this long voyage, experiencing the disparate socioeconomic levels that paraded past them like scenes from a kaleidoscope; it was always time to drink and eat, and the driver knew just the right places.

There was a small roadside stand owned by a pleasant-looking man who was dressed in white clothes and wearing a large straw hat and black leather sandals. He stood up when he saw the blue sedan coming toward him.

"Buenos tardes," he said, greeting his customers with a genuine smile.

The driver knew the language, and he ordered three cool lemonades and three warm taquitos. The man obliged him, and soon the order was filled; but even as he prepared the meal, he could not take his kindly brown eyes off the ailing woman.

"Sir," he said to Tony, at once understanding that the one he addressed was the husband, "your wife is sick." His English was broken, but honest.

"Yes," Tony responded.

The owner of the stand spoke to the driver, who then turned to Tony. "He says he is saddened by her misery, and begs you tell him her ailment, for he has many fine herbs."

"No," Lake shouted from inside the swelter of the black car, "no witch doctor's medicine! Is there no compassion anywhere?" She lay back on the white vinyl seats, delirious.

Tony motioned to his stomach and mouth, and then nodded to the man.

The uneducated man with the large, yellow sombrero walked over on the granite pebbles and looked into the car, staring intensely for a few moments at the face and curled-up body of the woman who was massaging her knotted stomach and aching head; upon rubbing his whiskered chin and narrowing his small eyes, he then turned around and walked back to his wooden counter, bent down and retrieved several packages of finally chopped herbs and put them into an iron pot of water. "Por favor, to wait," he said, politely, with outstretched hands.

Tony looked back toward the car. "I'm sorry, but," and then his wife produced more noxious waste upon the desert baked yellow ground, and after attending to her, he came back to the man who had never read even a single book on internal medicine.

"Aquí, for you," the man said, gesturing to the boiling water, "wait, wait," and in ten minutes' time, he had poured the tea and walked over to Tony and handed him the white Styrofoam cup. "No charge," he said, smiling. When Tony protested and offered payment, the man waved him away and spoke assuredly to the driver.

"He says," the driver repeated, "he would never charge for a very sick woman; it is not Christian to do such things."

The owner of the food stand crossed himself and folded his hands, while looking upward through the brilliant cerulean sky.

Tony looked quizzically at the driver, a man who was a native to Mexico.

"These people know things," the driver said.

Tony motioned the driver to a safe distance from the owner, to the other side of the faded Pontiac. "What about contaminants?" he whispered.

The driver smiled and frowned simultaneously. "American cynicism." He nodded his head. "You're going to be living down here."

Tony walked over to Lake and gave her the hot cup of honey-flavored herbal tea.

"Sweet," she murmured, sipping the green brew, drinking it until her lips met the tender, dark herbal leaves that had sunk to the bottom of the cup. "Mmm," she sighed, and lay down.

Tony convulsed anxiety as he watched her lie in torment. "What have I done?"

But in a few minutes she was resting peacefully. The peasant came up to the husband and put his strong hand upon his shoulders. "She will be good," he said, nodding his head.

He wanted to believe. "Yes," he returned, graciously, and vigorously shook the strong hand of the man; he asked the man for the name of the herbs, and after receiving them, said, "Gracias, muchas gracias."

"You're welcome."

After the driver again reassured Tony that he must not even attempt to pay the owner for the tea, the two men entered the car and drove away.

Tony sat in the back seat, the head of his beloved resting upon his lap. He wrote down the site of the food stand, and looked at the tranquil face of his wife as he stroked her wet hair and face. "We're home, darling," he whispered to her tortured soul, and he looked up at the passing scenery. "Is it possible," he wondered, "that all this time, we have been away from the world, and that now it unveils itself to us?" No, he decided, it was too early for such exhilaration; he had learned this much from his illness. "I mustn't let one event...no, I won't think of it, now," and he looked at her beautiful face. "I will think of you only, my beloved."

He awoke when the car entered an uneven, bumpy, winding road that ascended a small mountain pass, and he looked to his wife, who still slept soundly. "Where are we now?" he asked the driver.

"About an hour from the Village de Francisco."

Dust swirled around the car as it scaled narrow roads that wound steeply up and then steeply down and sharply around and over and along rolling hills and thick green foliage.

Tony could see no familiar markers of civilization as he watched the terrain assume the tilt toward a land less traveled; every minute the car sped toward the village, he felt that they were receding from the present. But Lake and he had asked for a remote place where the people were without any modern infrastructure. He looked at her, and let out a small laugh. "Look how far you have come, my ladylove." He looked at the raw sensuality of the eternal forests around him, and he inhaled its succulent aromas, which anointed his rigid, linear, city-built image of the world with a fresh notion of vital life. He sensed that he had entered a new-fashioned era. "Now, life begins," he murmured, kissing his wife upon her fair brow, and stared out through the vacant window and into the multicolored vegetation and the indigenous wildlife, out to the humble family, dressed in white clothes, who walked along the dusty roads to market, and his soul rose in rapture. "Life," he whispered, "is for living."

Village de Francisco

There are villages populating this country, lying like scattered pebbles about the hard land near small towns, upon which they draw sustenance. In these communal, small villages, the people live a life prescribed by their ancestors, doomed to invisible boundaries built by the past, living with little government assistance, subsisting on their own crops, their own ingenuity, their own iron will to live.

In Mexico, it may be said that it is the land of opportunity, but it is the opportunity for most to live in deep-rooted poverty, and also an opportunity for a few to escape to the cities to chase and grab the elusive, rising upper middle class and ride this wave to prosperity.

The blue sedan passed tiny villages and people walking to market and peasants working the land, and then it traveled for more miles into denser mountains, climbing up through narrow passages and over steep hills, until, finally, in the near horizon, a clear picture of more villages appeared.

It was an early morning when the automobile pulled up into the Village de Francisco. The red swath of a hot dawn had already summoned the people to labor, and when the car came rolling in, these people cast furtive glances at it until their suspicions were allayed.

Lake lifted her sleepy eyes to the world around her, and wonder filled her mind. There were brown and white adobe houses with flat roofs, square houses with hard dirt floors, and there were chickens and goats and dogs loitering about; and the people, wearing their white clothes, the men in their cloth pants and shirts and yellow sombreros, and the women in their white cloth pants and yellow sombreros were busy at work. She smelled the air, with its heavy scent of fresh fertilizer and the strong, pungent odor of native plants, and she inhaled the saturating molecules of food that was cooking on black steel stoves, and she sat, her face awash in disbelief. She was motionless for a time past rudeness, and then she buried her head in her hands and slumped to the seat and wept like a spoiled child who has lost her very own dollhouse.

"Come with me," Tony said, softly, stroking her head, ignoring the stares of the people around them.

"Get away from me," she cried, and then looked up at him, "none of this is real," and she pointed to the homes near them, "Look at this!" and she molested the ripe air with her vulgar tongue. "What century is this?" she frowned, incredulous to the very marrow of her chagrined being. "How can we manage savages? We're not miracle workers," and she abruptly shouted, "Take me home, take me out of here!" And she collapsed onto the seat once more. "Please, Tony, get me to civilization! I want a manicure, I want to shop at Tiffany's, I want, I want..." She moaned and wailed and groaned about like a wounded animal, thick sweat pouring off her burning forehead as she writhed in agony.

"It is the fever," the driver said, looking quietly at Tony.

A woman, upon hearing the words of the driver, approached the men.

"She is ill," she stated, politely, in her best, broken English.

"Yes, Teresa," the driver returned.

The woman proceeded to lay her dark hands upon the prostrate figure. "Yes, sick," she said, and turning to Tony, she asked, "Are you her man?"

"Yes."

They exchanged polite greetings.

"We will take her inside," she said, motioning to two other women who had obediently waited some proper distance away.

"Yes," he said, with great intensity.

"Eduardo," she continued, addressing the driver now, "show Mr. Siciliani his house."

"Of course she knows," Tony thought, walking away with Eduardo, glancing back at the woman in the white dress and with the long black hair, and then he looked about at the people, who issued him surreptitious looks. "They all know about the newcomers; why, they live here."

He walked into the small adobe building and was surprised at the coolness of the rooms. "I have to check on Lake," he murmured to himself, putting down his suitcases, and he walked back outside, only to see two women escorting Lake to a nearby house. "The conquering Americans," he sighed.

He sat anxiously in his new home, walking about the village with Eduardo, meeting the villagers. When the humid night and startling clear black sky crept over the village, he visited Lake again, who was sleeping peacefully. He slept at her side.

The next morning, Eduardo made an announcement while he and Tony ate breakfast.

"I have some disturbing news," he said to Tony as the men ate their tortillas, rice and beans. "The missionary couple assigned to be here has quit."

"Well," Tony said, frowning, "I suppose so."

"It happens; you must know how hard this life can be for these people; as hard as their life will be, yours will be, too."

"What? No motel with a five-star rating?"

He smiled, only. "You can always be reassigned." He sipped the hot, steaming black coffee.

"No," he said, with certitude, "we're here. We'll figure it out."

Eduardo munched the aromatic food with quiet joy. "I must inquire, Tony, I must ask you: do you believe in the Christian faith?"

Tony also luxuriated in the delicious banquet of home-grown food. "I believe," he responded, and he hesitated, looking at his inquisitor, "I believe in the work of the Church."

"I see," Eduardo replied, and slowly chewed his yellow tortilla, and then continued, "God has purpose for everyone; for you and Lake, for me," he nearly laughed, but his hard demeanor stepped back from accepting it. He then took Tony out to the blue sedan, and shook his hand. "In the beginning of every hard task, everything is always good, and we have hope and optimism; it is only after some time that our true mettle is tested, when we look around and everything and everyone is crumbling." He looked at the homes near him. "God speaks to all of us, Tony," he said, and pointed to his own head, as if the lesson were for himself; "you just have to want to hear it. Don't let being human get in the way. Aspire to better than ordinary." He heard his past speeches echoed in these words, and he winced inside.

Tony barely nodded his head, if only to evince acknowledgment. "Thank you."

Eduardo entered the car. "I'll be back when I can." He started the engine and drove slowly away, waving his hand outside of the open window.

Lake came outside then, and upon seeing the car receding down the hilly, dirt path, began to run after it. The car stopped, and backed up toward her. Tony let the affair unfurl as it should, free from his will. He watched as Lake came up to Eduardo, who was now standing on the dirt road, and she embraced him. They talked for a full minute, embraced once more, and then Eduardo entered his car and drove away. Tony watched her walk slowly backward, waving to the man who was still waving outside of the window of the slowly moving car. Once it disappeared from view, she turned round, and smiled a special smile meant only for her husband, a smile only he would recognize because it came from her healing soul.

She ran up to him, clasped her weak arms round his waist, and said, her flushed face smiling brightly, "Darling, we're home!"

Maria

A man lives at the bottom of a cold, dark well; he mines for his food, and wants for nothing, having his basic needs satisfied; how, then, to convince this man that the whole world is not a muddy, moss-covered bottom of a circular, brick prison? Lead this man up the nasty, slimy walls of his home and the first soft, white sunbeams of light will drown his senses and catapult him right back down into the ignorant solace of his compact universe.

Tony and Lake knew they must hold the hand of the villagers and lead them up the monolithic wall so these people might see that new creation called the dawning of the twenty-first century. Tony and Lake also knew that with the absence of the missionaries, who were to set up a school in the village and help the people manage their lives, their influence with the people would be negligible for some time.

"But how can we show them the light if they are blinded by it?" Lake said, walking arm in arm with her husband, and watching the people toiling at their daily chores.

He said nothing for a short while, and then spoke, watching a child helping its mother knead bread dough. "By teaching them to understand the light, photon by photon."

"I suppose a prudent man would simply tell us to leave, that our mission was over before it began, that we cannot possible succeed by ourselves. We have nothing to offer these people, do we? I mean, we were supposed to work with these missionaries, they were supposed to teach us; what do we know about leading these people to where they need to go?" She was simply telling him about her doubts and fears so he would soothe her.

He was silent for the longest time, and then stopped, looking at her, while nodding his head. "A prudent man wouldn't come here."

They decided to do what they had set out to do, and that was to bring an education to the villagers. There had been supplies ordered for the making of a school, and so, a little schoolhouse was set up, the first such structure in this village or any other village near them; and they sought to talk to the people about the schoolhouse, but the people merely stood with their arms folded and a bewildered look upon their swarthy faces—these men who shook the hands of the newcomers with great caution, and these women, who slowly put out their callused hands as if they too were unsure of the latest incarnation of saviors from the North. Conversations regarding the schoolhouse between the foreigners and the villagers were curt; nonetheless, Tony and Lake decorated the small adobe structure as if they were still in America. They went to each home in the village to announce the opening of the school; the people graciously acknowledged the invitation, but made no commitment to come.

Saturday night, at dusk, and Tony and Lake stood, dressed in their finest clothes, in front of the door with the sign "Escuela" above it. By eight o'clock in the p.m., no one had come, and by eight-thirty, no one had walked by, but by nine o'clock, an elderly man stopped to inquire about the place, but soon turned round, and wandered away, mumbling to himself.

Eduardo walked in at nine-fifteen in the p.m., trying to appear somber.

"Our first customer," Lake said, feigning a smile. "Well, sir, do you know your ABCs?"

He raised his right hand freely, three fingers up. "At age three!"

"Head of the class," Tony said, slumping on his yellow wooden chair.

He did sit down, and at the front of the rows of wooden chairs that the church had sent up months ago. "Well, tell me," he said, looking to both of them, "tell me what you're thinking."

"I'm devastated," Lake said, head in chin, "but I guess I should have known."

Eduardo looked to Tony, who said, "They don't understand what they're missing," but his voice dropped away. "I suppose the children will just keep being taught by Juan and Teresa, who are good people, but there is so much more we can offer them; I don't know…"

"Tell us, tell, Eduardo, about the other villages…"

"The Wileys, the couple who were supposed to have been here with you, failed in four other villages over a two-year time to get a school going."

"Two years," Tony anguished, pushing his hands through his black, curly hair. "Didn't they accomplish anything?"

"Well, yes, they did help the villagers to get medical supplies and taught them about carpentry and farming innovations and gave them Bibles in Spanish; look, the couples who have succeeded with the villagers teach them practical skills—the latest techniques in farming, like crop rotation, or basic carpentry skills, new equipment—practicality, all of it; hands-on, all of it, no books, no pencil, no paper." He reached out both of his hands, and turned them over. "There, this is what these people know and rely upon; it is their only memory of salvation, through hard work and broken backs and sweat and blood. Remember, most of them live like your American farmers did in the nineteenth century—if a man could put two Xs on the paper he was asked to sign, well, then, he was proud as ever. Books meant nothing to him because the society he lived in didn't demand it of him, yet; you didn't have to know how to read a book to plow a field and plant seed and milk the cow and hunt for wild game. It was a different world, just like the one you are in now. Welcome to my world, señor and señorita."

"So, why are we here, then?"

"You volunteered."

Lake interjected, "We need ideas, we need help."

Eduardo frowned. "I can't babysit you all day; I have twelve other villages I have to manage. You college-educated folks from the land of plenty should have come prepared with a failsafe plan. This country does not look kindly on rich Americans who come here on a caprice."

Tony silently cursed. "We might as well go back home."

"No," Lake cried, "we're not leaving; this is home, now."
She did not believe it, but saying it soothed her apprehension.

"And exactly how much Spanish do you know— and I am
talking about the specific dialect of these indigenous people;
and their history, too—well?"

"There is nothing like learning on the job," Tony rejoined,
glibly.

He frowned, as if all of it meant nothing to him. "Well,
what are your plans, then? We're not paying you to teach,"
and he gestured about the empty room, "nothing." He pointed
behind himself to the far horizon of the North. "Head to the
border to the land of wealth, it's what we poor, helpless peons
do when this life here is just too much…"

"No," Tony said, his voice hard, "we're here to stay…"

"All right, so you're here to stay; but we want success, not
the both of you merely occupying space. We are sending you
food and supplies for a reason." He stood up abruptly, and
said, sharply, "Get on it," and then departed.

Lake, incredulous, stared at the open doorway, and then,
only then, once she was truly livid, did she curse. "Mr. Cheery,"
she whispered, shaking her head, "we don't need him." Her
thin lips curled up in defiance. "We don't need anybody." But
she thought of the failure of the missionaries before them, and
this silenced her; she mused upon the misery and humiliation
of their defeat, and shortly, her eyebrows still knit, she said,
"I haven't felt ill all day."

He was fuming gall and bitterness at failure, and he wanted
to soak in its hard cradle as it rocked him roughly back and
forth. But even though his wife's announcement heartened
him, he still ached to be draped in dark, brooding thoughts.
"That's good, honey," he barely whispered.

"Tony, I have an idea," she said, abruptly standing up. "We need to travel to the other villages and see why the missionaries failed."

Once again, he was prompted to celebrate her, and slowly, as his foul mood dissipated, he wanted to love her; he walked over to her, kissed her, and embraced her. "I knew there was a reason I married you," he said, smiling, watching her smile appear, "and when I think of it, I'll tell you." Her laughter blunted the fine edge of his brooding that was slowly receding, and then her passionate kiss sent it shattering to the ground.

They would walk the land, as there was no car available; they would walk the hilly trails and dusty roads as the peasants walked them, their journey to start the next morning. As they prepared to leave the village with their small provisions and proper clothing to shield the effects of the sun, no one in the village seemed interested in their departure.

Lake could walk for only a few minutes until she had to rest. Three miles from the village, she became ill. Tony sat down and comforted her, instinctively looking about for an automobile. "Something tells me we're not in California anymore, Toto," he said, smiling as he stroked her hot, moist forehead.

"Always joking," she whispered, her head in anguish, her body writhing in his strong arms.

The oppressive heat ate into their muscle, bones and tissue.

"We need shade, darling," he said, spying a clump of tall mahogany trees in the near distance, and he lifted up her scrawny body and starting walking. Two minutes later, an old, rickety, rusty, faded Ford truck came rambling by. He cursed the ill-fated luck as he looked back. "But I can't leave her in either place," he reasoned, laying her softly in the soft cushion of the green grass that grew splendidly under the protection of the thick boughs above. Still, he kept a keen eye on the road, and for two hours, not a single vehicle came by, increasing his anxiety that he had erred.

Another steamy hour elapsed, during which he soothed her and condemned himself for this walk. He heard a voice echoing in the distance, and he stood up, looking about, yet saw nothing. He climbed a Spruce tree, and lo, he saw it. "A river," he said, ebullient.

"Bueno," a small wistful voice drifted up to him.

He spied a young boy and girl, standing in the tall grass, staring curiously up at him.

"Hola," he returned, using one of the few Spanish words he knew.

Tony leaped off the big limbs of the tree. "Ayuda mujer," he said, pointing to Lake, who still lay uneasily.

The children crept closer, unafraid; upon seeing the woman, the little girl said, in Spanish, "Your woman is ill?"

"Si," he answered, and then pointing to himself and his wife, "we are from the Village de Francisco."

"Si."

The children suddenly turned round and ran back to the stream that flowed along the shallow banks of the forest. Five women were standing in the cool water, laundering clothes.

A few minutes later, the women came up the path with an old black burro behind them. The long dresses of the women were adorned with shawls and blankets of red and yellow and white.

"Your woman is sick?" the lead woman addressed Tony. Her English was fluent and nearly devoid of any accent.

"Yes, my wife," he replied, inclined to proffer the least amount of information to strangers, as was the practice in the States; but he threw off this heavy-laden standard when he thought of Lake. "She is ill; we just arrived in the Village de Francisco last week."

"Missionaries?" the young woman queried, crouching next to Lake.

"Yes." He stated it as if it meant something above and beyond who and what she was, and this subtle intonation landed upon her colorful plaid dress with haughty bits of residual mud and spittle, and then was shamed.

However, she ignored it. "My village is two miles north of here; we can take her there. Do you have access to a car?"

"No."

Lake was lifted up onto the burro, and the group walked back to the stream where the women and children were finishing the daily washing; presently, they departed, and Tony noticed that the two women who had come to his assistance were carrying more clothes in their yellow straw baskets than the other women. "The burro," he reasoned, looking at Lake, and he walked up to the women. "Let me help you with that," he said, and motioned to their freshly laundered clothes.

"Very heavy," the older woman said to him, lifting the yellow basket up and down.

Tony lifted up the straw, handwoven basket and was astonished at the heaviness of it; he watched as the two other women placed their baskets upon their sturdy heads.

The women laughed, and the children danced and ran along the steep path, picking brightly colored flowers and giggling and putting the flowers into the hair of their mothers.

He wanted to ask the young woman many questions about her village, but he refrained. He moved closer to her. "You speak good English."

She smiled. "Gracias."

He extended his right hand, quickly, to shake hers. "Tony Siciliani."

"Maria Vargas."

He pondered the proper questions to ask so as not to offend her. He wanted to say, "I admire your people for their hard work," but he thought it too patronizing, or, "I don't see how your women carry these baskets up this hill," which seemed, to him, reaching for a compliment, and damaging to his image, especially in this culture of machismo; so, in the end, he said, simply, "I want to thank you for helping me with my wife; I'll try to get back to Francisco tonight."

"Oh, no," she exclaimed, and then spoke in Spanish to the women about her, who also exclaimed their hearty disapproval with a vigorous shake of their heads. "She will stay with us until she is well; we will send word to the Village de Francisco."

An offer of kindness must never be refused, he knew. "Thank you," he said, graciously.

"This mule stinks," said the sleepy rider.

Tony looked toward Lake, then to Maria, who smiled and nodded her head to assure him she understood.

Lake, loosely astride the creature, and supported by two women who walked on either side of her, had raised her head. "Pony ride," she sighed.

Maria laughed, and spoke in her native tongue to her two women friends, who laughed, too.

"They know it is the fever," she said, and then, of sober face, "we have heard of you, the two Americans who came to Village de Francisco, and one who is sick." She paused, not to seem too intrusive. "Has she been ill long? Here, in Mexico, we have many wonderful herbs that modern medicine will not acknowledge."

He smiled inside his mind. "Yes, I have heard of your herbs, and thank you; later, I may ask you about them."

But Lake began to tremble, and carefully placing the straw basket down on the dirty path, he hurried to her side. "The fever is worse," he lamented. He watched as one of the women, who was balancing a basket of laundry atop her head, picked up his basket. "No," he emphatically stated, and walking up to the woman, retrieved the basket. "The fever isn't going to go away with me next to her."

Conversation died.

Once inside the Village de Zapata, Lake was taken to a home, one made of white adobe.

A woman was preparing a meal of chalupas; she carefully placed the brown tender beans and the sliced, juicy tomatoes, red chilies and white meat into the corn tortilla, and then placed them in a yellow ceramic bowl. Coffee simmered in the old, iron pot on the ancient black stovetop, but it would not be drunk until the main meal had been consumed. A thick soup of beans and onion and tomatoes and spices and chilies simmered on the hot plate.

"La comida," said Maria, quietly to Tony, as she offered him a chair. "It is our big meal of the day."

He said nothing, watching as the two women administered warm herbal teas to Lake. He watched as the women expertly prepared the noonday meal and attended to Lake and then instructed their children, folded and put away the freshly laundered clothes, and then greeted their men who had just come in from the cornfields. The men warmly greeted him with a handshake, and inquired about the health of his wife, and then sat down to la comida. He sat next to Lake, helping her drink her tea from her white clay cup.

The two families spoke quietly in Spanish, and then one man reached over and turned on the old, brown wooden radio box with the yellow plastic knobs. Maria had positioned herself near to Tony so as to provide necessary commentary. "Mexican soap operas," she whispered, smiling; "they are just like yours—drama, drama," and she pointed to her head, "but ours is all up here."

The meal eaten, the soap opera over, the black, hot coffee sipped, the families went to siesta, resting peacefully on cots on the dirt floor, all except Maria, who sat next to Lake, tending to her.

"We'll leave as soon as possible," Tony said, still held captive by his native country's uptight and insular culture, "hopefully by tonight."

She shook her head, so that her beautiful, long, black hair swayed over her bare, brown shoulders. "You can stay as long as you like; this isn't America, Tony; we don't have somewhere urgent to go, nor do we resent foreigners." She smiled to heal any mischief caused by her words. "A visitor becomes like our family; it is our culture; we don't have time to put on airs."

"Thank you, again," he said, sipping more of the herbal tea. "Tell me, Maria, where did you get your education?"

"It shows?" she said, laughing. "Mexico City, and then I lived in the States for a while." She sighed, wistfully. "But I had to come back to help my people—there is plenty of time for me; I am only twenty-two."

She seemed to him the antithesis of what he had expected here. He then told her a cursory, footnoted story of his life with Lake, including only those things she needed to know if he needed her as ally. "So, Maria, you can see why your presence here is a surprise."

She frowned. "Antonio, do you think Mexico is one big prison, which every Mexican citizen seeks to escape? Why shouldn't we stay here and improve the quality of life in mi tierra, especially for the Indians: the Nahua, Mixtec, the Zapotec, the Wixaritari, and even for the Mestizos, who are the majority—even though many people do not use that word anymore—many of them still struggle; it's the Creoles that own the wealth, not the indigenous people; we are proud of our heritage: we are Maya first, then Indian, and Mexican; and even though we still have the caste system, Mexico is changing, people are having fewer babies, the middle class is growing; we are growing up." Passion amplified her iridescent beauty.

"Viva la revolución," he said, a half-smile bathed in shadow and spicy fragrances, "spoken just like a sixties radical in America."

"Don't make fun, Antonio," she said, her black brows knit, her full red lips pouting.

"I'm not," he returned, with a full smile to evince his sincerity. "I am all for change. I didn't come here to prop up the aristocracy; the caste system here is just wrong. Your country is going through growing pains, just like mine did, once. It is the same everywhere."

This remark bent her thoughts back to kinship with him. She smiled.

He did not want to commit a social faux pas in this country, especially not now, with people who were treating him and Lake with such solicitude. He decided that sharing more information would prove his sincerity to her. He then told her of the failure of the schoolhouse. She was about to elucidate his errors, but Lake awakened, received a warm greeting from Maria, and then quietly rested.

"Imagine if people came to your neighborhood," Maria then began, "saying they were to save you from ignorance, and improve your life; what would you say? I'm afraid you would be as untrusting as the people of Francisco."

"This is true," he thought, as he remembered how he had gained the trust of the people in the impoverished neighborhood back in the States.

They talked, of many things, of many times, exchanging ideas and intimate stories; it was the way of things in this hard land to divulge the affairs of one's heart to friends, for hard labor and a hard life without all the conveniences of the Modern Era tends to relax the rigid borders of secrecy and compel people to share their minds and intimate thoughts with each other.

In the morning, the three friends walked up to the Village de Francisco. The people there greeted Maria heartily.

"They thought you had left for good," she said, translating and looking at the two Americans. "You didn't even say where you were going—bad manners here." But this was a gentle chastisement.

She walked them to their house and there they drank more honey-flavored tea; and as she prepared to leave, she stood with them, her face hopeful. "God has plans for you, Antonio and Lake Siciliani; that is why he sent both of you to me." But she saw the muted responses in their smooth faces. "Oh," she said, frowning, "you don't believe in God?" She laughed, a knowing laugh born from a mature wisdom gained early in life. "Missionaries who do not believe in God; well," and she put her hands on their shoulders, "don't tell the people here, they would not understand. It would be like a priest who does not believe. Perhaps it is as they say, that a good life takes God out of life." She nodded her head to reassure them. "You must forgive me for being candid—it is the way of my world; we have no time for masquerades. But I honor your choice; you have good hearts to come here." But she gave them a furtive wink and a warm smile. "Well, you will believe, one day; so, you must come to our church, it is in the next village; our local villagers go there; I am inviting you, so, you are committed," she said, smiling, her soft voice like a soft Summer breeze, her countenance illuminated by a greater power. She departed from them then, walking back to her village, clothed in traditional dress, her mind cloaked in love.

Lake hugged her husband. "We start anew."

"Hmm," he replied, waving to the esoteric figure receding down the steep dusty trail.

Assimilation

It is true that intellect weaves a better path in life for the liberated man, but for the man enslaved to hard toil, it can be a burden, an importunate mistress who presses him to seek idyllic pastures.

Tony and Lake slowly assimilated into the indigenous culture of the village: working in the cornfields, eating spicy peasant foods, learning about special herbs and plants that kept the people healthy and strong, listening to peasant music, celebrating peasant customs, learning the language, attending church with them, and becoming friends with the people they lived among.

Weeks passed, and they would discuss old ways and distant lands, but still, Tony and Lake knew who they were, and celebrated their proud heritage.

Lake bonded with the women as they taught her to weave and sew and bake and cook and clean and harvest a good nature in the wake of hardship. She learned at their side the same way any young girl learned at her mother's side. They taught her about important herbs for particular ailments, and they were often asking her specific questions about her illness, and preparing for her local herbs they had picked and dried.

Months passed, and Lake and Tony fondly remembered who they were, and who they had been, but still, they knew who they always would be.

Tony bonded with the men as he worked by their sides, as they tilled the soil with the oxen, and engaged in milpa agriculture, where many crops were grown here at once: maize and squash, and beans and tomatoes, amaranth and sweet potato; and listened to their talk of family and friends and relations, and God and Country and the importance of loyalty.

The two lovers took longer walks and had tranquil picnics in the hills; they committed many social infractions here, but it was fine—fine with the villagers because the Americans were genuine and humble; and Tony and Lake, beyond simple social interaction, slowly learned their special dialect of Spanish and how to talk to the people by playing with them and dining with them and laboring with them and laughing with them and crying with them. It is the way of all such worlds.

A mountain is not formed in a day—its slow progress over the eons is imperceptible to a passerby; it is the same way for any culture, where customs are formed over long periods of time; but just as a man climbing a mountain does not see its brown flesh cover him, nor does the man who goes to live in another culture see how it is affecting him.

One year hence, Tony and Lake still had not begun the educational classes for the villagers.

Maria came by for a visit one day, as she had many times before. "Hola," she said, waving to them as she approached their small house. "Lake, I love your dress. It's so colorful."

"Hola, Maria," Lake exclaimed, standing up now outside the house, "do you really like it?" She turned toward the open window, and said, "Don't let the beans burn, darling." She turned back toward Maria, smiling sheepishly. "He'll learn how to cook, yet."

"Another plate," he yelled from within.

"Si," Maria called, cupping her hands with her mouth as she neared Lake, whom she embraced. "How go the tortillas?"

Lake had been sitting outside on a gray stone bench, placing corncobs that she had picked, soaked and hulled on a stone metate, and then grinding them with the stone metlapil.

"Muscles," Maria said, touching Lake's biceps.

"Hmm," she replied, staring at her brown arms, as if for the first time in years. "Well, yes," she nodded, and then looked at her friend, "muscles." She smiled.

Maria directed her melodious voice inside the clay dwelling. "Ready for the wedding?"

A man from Village de Francisco and a woman from Village de Zapata were to be married on the morrow.

"Ask El Jefe," he answered, nodding in the direction of his wife.

Maria looked to Lake. "Yes," Lake said, tossing her head. "We'll be ready." She smiled, one born of pride, and she looked down at the finely ground corn, and then up to Maria. "I sewed the dress for the wedding myself; it is inside."

"Lake," Maria exclaimed, hugging her, "I am so proud of you."

Tony came outside. "The beans are done; here, I'll finish." He continued the grinding of the corn as the two women went inside to inspect the ceremonial dress.

"Oh, Lake," Maria gushed genuine enthusiasm, beholding the exquisitely crafted, multicolored garment, "beautiful!" She held it in her hands as if it were a newly woven robe of finespun gold for the coronation of a king.

Lake blushed with pride, for she had never sewn any kind of garment in her life, never once stitching anything, nor even observing such an act before she had come here.

At the wedding in Village de Francisco, there were long wooden tables covered by yellow and red cotton cloth, and upon these lay yellow and red and brown wooden bowls and plates brimming with warm tacos, spicy chalupas, tangy chiles rellenos, grilled tortillas, hot café con leche, warm and thick champurrado, and fine alcoholic beverages, pulque, mescal and tequila. Everywhere there were people with animated faces, dancing without care in their brightly colored clothes as they listened to the mariachi band; the musicians, playing their guitarron and vihuela and trumpet and violin, were handsome in their black pants, which had rows of silver buttons up and down the length of the outside, and long, black coats decorated with more silver buttons, and big, black, wide-brimmed sombreros and big, black, silver-stitched, decorated leather cowboy boots.

Labor in the fields, discrimination from the city folk, illness without adequate medical care, the strive and frustration of poverty—all of it was conducted into small cracks and crags in the fertile ground with every musical blow of the trumpet and drum and violin, while every authentic laugh, kiss, and hug, and every free-flowing silver tear streaming down a radiant face, fell into these small fissures and stitched sorrow shut until the hot sun rose again and the hard life rose with it.

The high mountain community had joined together to celebrate the blessed union of their own; the people here were family, all of them, despite distance, relations, and nationality. Everyone was accepted, and every bad thing forgotten.

Lake had selected a love verse to speak in Spanish before the two young people who were to be betrothed; she had practiced for two months, reciting Robert Burns' poem and injecting the proper native accents and color into every syllable and consonant. Finally, she stood up, her courage frail and thin as she looked out among the crowd who anxiously awaited her contribution.

She stood before them, the great celestial pageantry of bright white stars floating in the deep black open sky behind her. She smiled, her bronze skin flush with pleasure as she briefly explained the poem, and then commenced.

"Oh, my Love is like a red, red rose,

that's newly sprung in June;

O, my love is like the melodie,

That's sweetly played in tune."

Her rich voice resonated like the delicate tinkling of crystal bells fluttering in a sensual dance about the eager ears of the audience; her Spanish was like a clean, sparkling river that bubbled with the simplicity of life. She looked to her beloved.

"As fair art thou, my bonnie lass

so deep in love am I,

and I will love thee still, my dear

till a' the seas gone dry."

Her enunciation and precise delivery of the stanzas and capturing of the proper rhythm and meter of the poem was a sweet melody.

"Till a' the seas gone dry, my Dear

And the rocks melt wi' the sun—"

But then, independent of her excitement to perform, she oozed nausea in her stomach, and she felt the thorny vine of illness sprout up through her to sabotage any budding joy in her life; she burned feverish rage inside, and closed her emerald-colored eyes, as if to see inside her pain, to confront her old, battered mistress, Disease. "Go away, you old whore! You're not wanted, not necessary anymore," she thought, but did not verbalize it, lest she ruin her own recital.

Tony scrutinized the subtle fluxes of anguish upon her countenance, and felt the terror of panic freeze his senses; she wavered, just for an imperceptible moment, like a brief wind that flickers the steady yellow candle flame; but, then, in the next stanza, seemingly unbroken, she continued the steady stream of lovely verse, which she accented at the proper time, and slowed with great emotion at the proper word, playing out the meaning of each lovely image.

"And I will love thee still, my Dear,
while the sands o' life shall run."

Her voice glided through the ephemeral air on feathery wings of exalted Love; she exhaled such intense emotion that it seemed to her beloved that it was her soul which spoke to him. She looked now to the engaged couple, who were smiling radiantly.

"And fare thee well, my only love!
And fare thee well, a while!
And I will come again, my Love,
Tho' it were ten thousand mile!"

The crowd, largely uneducated peasants, was conducted into an awed state of being at the personal beauty and passion of the poem, and when Lake had finished the sublime recital, they applauded with wild abandon.

Tony embraced his triumphant wife; she had lived a cycle of birth to existence to a crawling, tormented, agonizing death to a renewed, vigorous life, and she was here, now, full of love for these people and this gorgeous land, full of hope because of the simplest things.

She left the stage and embraced him. "I love you," she whispered to him, and so full of love for him that she wept; to her, this was life, this was joy, this was love, this was happiness, this was fulfillment, this was reality; her past life was a macabre illusion that had blinded her to what life truly is.

She felt the mellow waves of a good life break over her, covering her in their golden foam, and her soul was exalted into the inviolate chambers of Love. "O Grandmother, thank you," she whispered to herself, "I love you."

Realization

The next day, Lake was going down to the river to wash laundry when several young women approached her.

"Lake," they cried from behind, smiling and waving their hands in the warm plumes of the sun.

She smiled, and waved back, her hand brushing against the gentian sage with its deep blue petals bobbing gently in the liquid, steaming, warm air.

It was Lupe, Grezelda, and Consuelo, beautiful, enchanting youth, unbounded, enthusiastic fresh youth, flush with the noble belief that all was possible in the world if one had only a good heart and a determined mind.

"We want to know about the poem you read last night at the wedding—it was so beautiful," Grezelda cried, her face so effusive with simple joy and comely looks that she seemed a dazzling part of Nature about her.

Lake welled up with great emotion, for these women, these handsome women, reminded herself of her untarnished youth. "Of course," she said, as they all began to walk toward the clear, silver stream below.

Lupe, with her long hair flowing in the warm breezes, skipped ahead of them, and commenced to walking backward. "We want to know everything about it—simply everything! Don't leave anything out, not even if it seems boring!" She was not yet eighteen, and the hot sun and heavy burden of hard labor had not broken her innate spirit to want to know more about the world than mere survival.

"We want to know who wrote it, when, and why," Consuelo said, bubbly and bright, like a chirping robin; "was it because of a girl?" She giggled. "A lover who scorned him?" She paused, her black brows knit, her thin, sensuous lips compressed. "Was she pretty, was he handsome? Did they marry? And oh, yes, we want to know if there are more lovely poems."

Lake laughed, remembering her jubilant youth, and how she had once had a passion for fine poetry and prose, a love instilled in her by her grandmother. "Oh, girls, there is so much poetry in the wide world, mmm," she hummed, reflecting upon this situation, and then told them many stories about famous poets, first of Burns, then of the poems of Byron and Shelley and Keats, and their individual tragedies. The girls cried at this sorrowful news, just as if these fine young men had recently died; many more stories she related to them, of Dickinson, and Browning, and Plath, as they washed clothes in the foamy river, about poets in ancient times and poets now living, and the historic times these architects of sound and rhythm and pattern lived in.

After the laundry was done, Lake reflected on how much she knew about such things, and she thought of her college days, and why she had forgotten such wonderful learning.

On the road back to their path, Lupe said the most curious thing. "O Lake, when we first heard the poem—by Mr. Burns?—yes, by Roberto Burns!—well, we thought," she continued, playing with her long, thick hair, "Antonio had written it about you."

"You are so beautiful," Consuelo said, in earnest.

"The envy of the women of the village," Grezelda added.

She was stunned into breathlessness, having long forsaken her once-cherished beauty for a sickly guise of sallow cheeks and a gaunt physique. "Beauty, I?" she managed to ponder, and even though she heard their honest words, she was listening to a new dialogue within her, and seeing a vision of newly carved and delicate pink flesh. "Oh, no," she chastised herself, "they are being kind. I am like old woman to them." And she was not yet thirty years old.

Even though she had decided to look directly into a mirror to behold her emaciated face after her marriage, she had slowly slipped back into self-pity, and so had trained herself to concentrate to look at certain sections of her face—the right, doughy side, then the left, doughy side, then the sunken, bony cheeks, the scaly, rough forehead, the frizzled, stringy, thinning, brown hair; on occasion, by accident, she had acquired a full frontal view of her sunken mask and atrophied body, and had retched in horror at the smoldering human wreckage, just as if she had witnessed a downed plane with dead bodies strewn all about it. But that was long ago.

Later that day, she sat before the wooden desk, staring at the closed case in which resided her vanity mirror; but, alas, she could not open its box of unknown faces, and she shoved it aside.

Tony walked by, back from the fields; he kissed her, holding her close. "Good crop today, sweetheart."

She smiled, but it soon drained from her by force of her anxiety. "Am I beautiful?"

He set her out from himself, looking intensely at her, for mixed in her words were fragments of black, burning powder shot, and he could still smell the incendiary smoke from their ferocious might. He felt, no, he wore her pain, and breathed in her agony as he stared into her imploring eyes. He had always told her she was beautiful, many, many times, and she had always acknowledged it, but he had waited and hoped for her to ask this question for months. "Yes," he said, as if he was saying it for the first time to her or to anyone. "Yes, my love, you are so beautiful, as beautiful as a woman can hope to be."

Tears were ready to flow from her eyes as she embraced him again. "O Tony, Tony," she sobbed, "it's been so long; I thought it would never happen again, that I never deserved to have it happen…"

And what of her miserable mistress, Disease, her constant companion? Yes, it had fled, as its ungracious host earned the right, by virtue of living this natural life, to chase it out, it now having taking up residency in the sunbaked, hard land.

"I'm healed," she whispered, joyous. "I'm alive."

He had known for months, and had waited anxiously for her to feel it, to say it, to understand it as he had once understood his own rejuvenation. For the last three months, she had not had any symptoms of her illness, but she had not dared to speak of it to anyone. She now realized that the nausea she had felt at the wedding was an anomaly.

She fell upon her knees, and Tony fell with her.

"I don't deserve it, I don't," her voice was trembling with rapture and fear; "I was such a horrible creature."

He kissed her warm tears, and said nothing, but held her next to his warm body, caressing her soft, bare, brown shoulders; he rocked her back and forth, faithfully listening to her contrition, faithfully listening to her torment, being there for her, understanding her, honoring her.

In her deepest moods and reverie, she often chose seclusion, and right now, she wanted to be alone with her thoughts.

There was a place, out in the verdant forest, a special, isolated encircling of Cypress and Dogwood trees that secluded its center from view, which Lake sometimes visited, walking barefoot, a practice that she often did, which exhilarated her; she resided there now, sitting under a particularly old and handsome Cypress tree, her head resting on its sturdy, corrugated, crooked brown trunk as she thought of the eternal struggle the mind and physical body wage between the hemisphere of pain and bliss.

She wiped away a flurry of pious tears. "Without pain, I am still lost; O, how I thought this should never come, nor that I deserved such luxury of flesh," she whispered, and fell forward, laying her head upon the moist, cool green grass. "O grandmother, you saved me from the corrupt world, but I could not save you." She reflected upon the person she had once been, and marveled at her once-vacuous heart and selfish soul. "I lived to serve myself; how can a person know who they are and what they are supposed to be in life, or even what life is, if they live in such moral depravity?" She spat largely, as if she were vomiting out her ignoble past.

"I must remember who I was," she decided, after a long reverie, and then walked home while the bashful stars began to reappear in the darkening sky. She spoke very little to her husband, but informed him that she would continue her journeys to her private sanctuary after her labors.

"And Tony, three of the girls are interested in learning…"

He embraced her, picking her up. "Darling," he cried.

She smiled, cautiously. "A little bit at first for them," she smiled; "slow and steady wins the race, remember?"

The little brown adobe schoolhouse took three refugees from ignorance that Spring, three young women who wanted to know more about life than hard labor and washing clothes by hand and cooking from scratch and incessantly working on tasks that they knew many people around the world simply did not engage in and, subsequently, stopped them from engaging in activities they desired; yes, they loved their country and their land and their families and their culture and their relatives and friends, but now they wanted knowledge, and they would not be denied.

Lake and Tony, fluent now in Spanish, schooled the young ladies after the chores of the day were done, but mostly, it was Lake the girls sought out for advice.

"Tell us about life in America," Grezelda asked one day as she sipped from a large cup of warm atole.

"Yes, Maestra, tell us all about your beaux!" Lupe giggled.

"And how you kept them waiting in torment for a single kiss," Consuelo said, radiant and sparkling, from the clear amber complexion of her face to her strong, agile, bare, brown feet.

"Girls," Lake responded, feigning a frown as she put down her instructor's book on reading, "for shame!" but she smiled at the thought of her once-unmatched dominance over the flaming society of the male species. "Well, it is true, while in my prime, I was the belle of the ball." But they had no understanding of this, and so she narrated with precision and passion the adventurous life of a charming ingénue who lived in the netherworld of the good graces of fabulous wealth; yet, this personal account of such stories were like the fairy tales of princes and princesses the girls had heard as children.

Consuelo stared at her. "But you sit before us, now; here, with us, a princess."

Lake laughed, looking at them. "You are princesses," and then she thought, "Yes, they are the true princesses of the world…" And when she thought of her life as a youth, it paled in comparison to these extraordinary beauties, for they were modest, and of good character, loving, kind and unselfish. "Yes," she decided, "here is woman, real woman, as they should be, as they were meant to be."

"But you do not seek that life again?" Lupe asked, starry eyed.

"It sounds so exciting, like being in Mexico City all of the time; bright lights and music and dancing!" Grezelda cried.

"No," Lake answered, solemn now, knowing she could not adequately explain it to them.

She still had not looked at herself full in the face.

It was a bright, sunlit Spring day of warm breezes and fresh aromas pouring over the land, and she was lying in her special idyllic pasture, looking up at the bright azure fire in the white-cumulus cloudy sky, listening to the wildlife sing its special song, thinking of who she was, and what she must do.

"I must see them again, to see them again, to see myself with such people," she whispered, staring at the deep, penetrating patch of icy blue sky. "Grandmother, you will be proud of me, I will not fall in with them; O, Grandmother, you loved me so much that you did this terrible thing for me…" She sought not to weep. "But you left me before you could see the person you knew I could be, now; O, Grandmother, you believed in me, and I love you, still, I will always love you…"

Of course, she had heard every word and detail and intention the night Matthew Gershon and Tony had met. She had bridled all of it, letting it swirl inside her raging mind like a tempest in a teapot. "But you will be proud of me for what I am about to do, Grandmother," she proclaimed, sober now, her face grave with resolution. "I will do what I must, and only then will I know I am truly alive." She carefully observed a magnificent Golden Eagle sailing high above. "I will go back to them, and O, Grandmother and Lisbeth, you will be so proud of me."

That night, she told her husband she was going back to the ranks of the blue-blood elite.

The Need To Know

"I have saved up enough money to make the trip to New York," she said to him, her face engulfed in light shadows as they sat in the small adobe home. "I have to do this; I have to know in light of who I am…"

He said nothing, with an expression of great repose upon his face.

She cursed him. "Don't be silent when I need you, Anthony." But this sharp jab at him only served to seal any beginning cracks in his stone artifice. She pleaded, "One thing doesn't go your own way and you fold," and then watched him get up and walk outside.

He would not talk to her for two days, and he disappeared after his daily labors and chores, returning to his secluded haven in the undulating hills.

One the third day, he returned late at night, standing in front of her in their room; he wanted to support her and listen to her and console her anxious mind, but as he stood there, he felt that this position would weaken him in his own eyes, in her wifely eyes, and in the eyes of the village. "Go," he finally said to her. Her cold countenance heaped abuse upon his burning scalp. "Go, go and live with your own kind; it's what you wanted from the beginning." He didn't mean it, but he was hurt, and he now meant to hurt her.

"How dare you," she cried, standing up, "how dare you imply that you are intimate with my private thoughts." She smiled bitterly. "And if I want to go, I will; I don't need your permission—machismo." And she spat hugely upon the dirt floor.

He went about doing his food chores, ignoring her completely.

She remained quiet for a duration of time that she decided was adequate for his anger to wane. They ate in silence, wanting to speak, but deadening themselves to doing so.

True Love, as it is known by True Lovers, is not merely a fleeting emotion, a soaring feeling, but an intricate part of the human psyche as much as joy and happiness; to end its existence in one's heart takes a skilled assailant schooled in the ancient art of unrestrained enmity, and in the lost art of self-isolation, thus cutting off nourishment to the starving, pleading cells of poor, abandoned Love; and once this resilient, seemingly immortal Love dies, the host feels a cold emptiness, for he has lost an emotion required by all human beings who wish to know what it means to be truly alive.

He felt his love for her dissolving, and he grieved, and sought to console her, but his burning pride bribed his mind to disobey his heart, and so, he did not speak to her before she left for New York City.

She left three days later, and at her departure, he would neither speak nor communicate to anyone around him; and yet, he did not forgo his daily labors in the fields and his respon-sibilities in the village.

He would sit in front of her small vanity mirror, and stare at the ugly form he perceived. "Alone again," he whispered to himself, condemning himself, persecuting himself, "alone forever, as I always knew I would be."

She had boarded the airliner with the best intentions to heap all her natural and unnatural scorn upon the gala event awaiting her; nay, in fact, she had crafted a steely resolve to attend the stellar gathering to remember only how amoral and avaricious she had been, and how amoral and avaricious were the attendants.

When the jet approached the distant twinkling lights of the magnificent skyscrapers, she felt as if she had taken a magical flight to the hills of Mount Olympus.

"Proud starry mother and father gaze, from the internal recesses of black space, upon their luminous siblings below," says the poet of a city that streams with incandescent splen-dor, "admonishing that thou can strive for perfection, but thou shall find only subjugation."

Man adorns himself with pieces of Beauty, in hopes that a sliver of Nature will make him greater than himself.

When she stepped out into the crisp, electric air, which hovered like a laceration around the airport, she felt the tingling appetite of yesterday bulging in her liberated blood vessels; every breath seemed to slough off the old scars that had grown vast and deep to cover up her old, sullied self; yea, her old self had died long ago and her new virgin self had been born of trial and woe, but now this second skin was dying, turning sallow and thin, like a dewy red rose picked in the peak of cool morning and left to die in the hot sun.

She did not want to think of it, but it came, as easily as water rolling off an alligator's scales, the breathless acknowledgment of returning to her rich girl's favorite playground. Yes, she chastised herself mightily for such palpable heresy, shaking her head to rid her mind of such thoughts. "I am only here," she reminded herself, as she gazed in wonder at the cascade of enchanting dancing lights, "to be sure." Nevertheless, a grotesque fever had already begun, like a long-dormant flower activated by the rare, desert rain and sun, spreading throughout her every limb and senses.

She sat in the cab, trembling with excitement, her memory liberated by the passageways and skyscrapers and bright lights, and the hustle and bustle of diverse life, and the endless choices for adventure and intrigue; she felt as if she were re-entering her birth womb, as the yellow bullet slid effortlessly into the very hot breath of the beast, the very heart of fantasy, the place known as the City of Dreams.

The world she had experienced through the developed, wistful eyes of a peasant girl was now put into purgatory in light of this new world, and just as two primary colors form a third, so too did the comingling of these two singular ideas.

She stepped out of the cab in front of the Hotel Ritz-Carlton in Central Park; people were hurriedly moving up and down the sidewalk, cars were flooding the streets, shops were busy with customers; she felt as if she stood at the mound of a sacred temple, wherein lived the goddesses of Beauty, of Fertility, and Love; of Birth, of Life, and Vitality; of Pleasure, of Joy, and Soul. "But I am not here for such things," she admonished herself, stepping into the elevator, and once inside her room, she quickly dressed in attire more appropriate to the fashion and conventions of this city.

Men, men, everywhere, and plenty of virility to drink; men, with their savage, shameless, thirsty stares, bored into her emerging soul and lit her slumbering fires of sensual desire;

she commanded the walkways as she once had, she central-
ized the attention of handsome men as they walked by her
and past her and turned round to give further testimony to
her voluptuous figure; for she was, without doubt, the most
ravishingly beautiful creature these male flesh monsters had
seen in what seemed an eternity. Men, the romantic, lustful
fools, fall in love with every unique Beauty they see, thinking that she is more beautiful than any other creature as long
as they are pursuing her; but once she is conquered, she loses
her luster, and he goes adventuring after the next short skirt.
But that night, they, these poor, pathetic male hunters, were
forced to admit to their burning desires that this green-eyed
damsel was far more intoxicating in her loveliness than any
single female they were presently courting.

Lake Seville was now the earth goddess, having sprung
from the rich, living soil and being adorned in the rarest finer-
ies of Nature. She was an authentic specimen of robust natural
comeliness in a landscape of women who relied on artifice to
create an illusion of beauty.

The women of this city and every other city operated on the
same eternal instructions, to wit: to appear more attractive to
the opposite gender, they highlighted their physical differences
to men. The women here had become masters at this sleight of
hand, creating serene beauty where before only dullness existed;
women who had destroyed their natural good looks by poking
and picking and scraping and tweezing it from an early age
now had nondescript faces that had to be transformed daily
into multicolored masks of pure symmetry—women with soft,
flabby bodies who stuffed themselves into expansive, expensive and exquisitely fashionable clothes to create the idea of a
curvaceous, tight physique, and who doused themselves with
fragrant perfumes to excite the senses of their dumb prey; these

women were city-built, city-tested, city-refined, but untested against strong women of the land who had fabulous, hard bodies hewn from real labor, good nutrition, and hard, unceasing exercise; yes, the illusion created by city women could not long endure if they stood next to a true earth woman, for their true identity would be exposed and their pale image would burst and be engulfed in a darksome pitch.

Lake Seville, in her short, white, cotton Spring dress and brown leather sandals, walked down Broadway like a woman borne from the glorious past when females wore scintillating, raw, unblemished flesh that had been soaked in the vital rays of the nourishing sun, her long, thick, curly, lustrous hair swaying down her lean back; men stood stoned to infatuation as they beheld her, their minds feeble, their faces struck dumb, for they beheld the soul sister of Aphrodite and Venus.

As she walked past the female wildlife on this crowded main street, it seemed as if she inhaled all of their illusory, straining beauty, and turned loose their true identity for all to see, that of a chalky, flabby, weak, pale sack of inflated, about-to-expire goods.

Lake wore no makeup, her luminous hues and tones coming from an inner, natural purity derived from earth, wind and sky—unlike her sister city folk, who painted on a dirty canvas with a dirty brush in a dirty place to create an unfinished symphony doomed to mediocrity.

Whither she gracefully glided, she brought a testament of a rich and vital nature, found and embraced: hers; and hitherto she exposed a languid and buried nature: theirs; whither she swayed luxuriously, she commanded the luminescent rays of light to fall upon her, as if the ethereal nymphs of golden sunbeams danced around her and kissed her luscious skin and gave her an iridescent and boundless glow; and those women who were wrapped in the smear and gob of paint and polyester and perfume, they felt their puny shine dull and die; whither she went, she was adorned in a chromatic, combustible Technicolor, while other women fell into a vat of polluted, worm-eaten, muted colors; and whither she walked boldly and proudly and fully in every dimension high and low and long and deep and wide, women around her dissolved into a bloodless, lusterless, indistinguishable blob, a vapor, a specter to be taken up by the least inconsequential wind.

She was a fertile, honey-scented, rainbow-soaked flower bursting with throbbing seduction, and they, these shrinking women, were ugly, scrawny weeds, with wilting yellow leaves and rotting, shallow roots.

She was Truth; they, a lie; her Beauty, immortal; their looks, ephemeral; she, a consuming fire; they, a smoking ash.

She subdued women by her transcendent Beauty.

As it was, she was moving her strong and slender bronzed-skinned figure in a naturally luxurious gait toward a nightclub, wherein the richest and handsomest of human beings congregated to inspect each other's genetic superiority, and to wage storytelling of their most recent debauchery.

Lake Seville, late of the Mexican states, walked into the musical theater, and so astonishing was her appearance, that all eyes swept to her elegant form. She could feel the adoration of the men, the red-hot jealousy of the women, and she was pleased. She was beginning to forget why she had come to this fabled city.

She had not meant to come to this flesh palace, but her feet, the old memories in her splendid, strong feet, had laid an irrevocable course to her former pleasure zones. Her new heart was strangely silent.

"I am home again," she thought, feeling the loud, pulsing beat of the metallic music against her luxuriously soft skin, but she also felt the delicate harmonies penetrate into her cells, reviving them, energizing them, remarking them. "Remember," the mother music seemed to be shouting, "remember your blessed history of wine, song and dance! Live, girl, live as you deserve to live!"

And where was her old mistress, Disease? Long ago dead, dead, dead long since, dead and buried, but it had left fragments of stingers in her that cunningly raged against this unfettered joy.

She partied till dawn, and she never once thought of her faraway, ancient, tranquil life in the village; but then once, indeed, when she exited into a powdery, orange-colored blazing sky, she did remember something about the rising of the sun and what it had meant to her, and her mind traced this hallowed history to Mexico; but she frowned and laughed, and when she began to walk down the busy streets with the shops opening their doors and the people scurrying about, and the savory, baked smell of civilization came to her, it all went away.

Entropy

The Summer sun boiled the inhabitants of Village de Francisco and peeled them like soft yams.

Tony woke up the morning following her departure, and lay on the white cot, still as a corpse. Time flowed in gentle streams around him, and he took no heed.

"Up, friend," a husky voice came beckoning through the humble home, "get up, you lazy bones!" A large, dark-haired, swarthy-skinned head lent itself past the sacred barrier of the door entrance. "Tony, eh? Are you home, good friend?"

It was Juan, one of the elders of the Village, who, along with Teresa, had been the educators up here and had encouraged the people to send their children to the schoolhouse.

"Yes," Tony replied, his head still lying in his clasped hands and folded arms that rested behind his head.

Juan entered, taking off his hat. "Are you sick, Tony?" But upon inspecting his friend, his quizzical, wrinkled face relaxed. "Oh, I see," and he took a chair and sat before him. "Sick at heart, my good friend," he said, somberly, "it is sickness for the body." Tony said nothing, as was the custom of his esoteric, male race. "But you know," Juan continued, his forehead creased now by a frown, "at least you can work hard and forget for a time," and he held up his thumb and index finger close together to express a small gap, "if even for a little time. But, you know, a sick body cannot forget; like Nina, who has the cancer; and Francisco, who has paralysis from the stroke, and little, precious Louisa, who lost her tiny hand in the crop machine." He stood up, not accusing yet accusing, his voice gentle to the emotional pain of his friend, but hostile to the essence of the pain in relation to the cruel world. "Ricardo says you are 'cuckold,'" and he made play with his two index fingers as horns sprouting out from his dark forehead, "but I told him, you are just married to a stubborn woman." He stared at the staid face of his supine friend. "And Ricardo tells me any man married to a stubborn woman is a woman." He threw up his hands. "What does he know, eh? He beats his woman like she is a yellow, three-legged dog; so do not pay him any mind, Tony, you just lie in bed and think about things. You are a thinker, Tony, you must do what you do best to figure all of this out. I just tell you these things because people talk;

the women know they run the house but they know the man is macho and he likes to make the big decisions. This is Mexico." He hunched his shoulders. "It is all appearance, you know." He carved a cursory smile onto his face—a smile that was a hot vapor in the wind—and then put on his big, yellow straw hat and began to walk away.

"Do you think I care about what others think, Juan?"

Juan turned round and immediately removed his sombrero and stood inside the doorway again. "No," he stated, simply, "in this case, you are a man, indeed, not to listen to gossip." He smiled and turned to leave once more.

"Juan, do you think I am lazy if I don't work today?"

Juan frowned. "You are not feeling well; it is up to you, Antonio."

Tony looked at him. "But Louisa works every day despite the loss of her hand, and she has every right to be depressed."

"I suppose so," he answered, rubbing his black-stubbled chin.

They were silent for a short spell. "Juan…"

"Yes."

Tony rose from his soft bed. "You would make a very good psychologist."

He smiled outwardly, hiding a deeper, knowing smile.

It was the second day of her absence from the village, and the vast majority of the men cast disapproving glances at Tony as he worked alongside them in the yellow cornfields; these were men he labored next to, ate with, spoke with, laughed with, whose celebrations of their family, relatives and friends he attended, whom he relied on, were now his village, his family, his friends, but now he had stepped onto the smoldering ember of that intractable notion, machismo, and the boiling blood of the men could not be appeased by the silence of the defendant.

He stepped out into the hot sun, dressed in his white cotton clothes, and he could feel the sweltering heat burst onto his cool skin; he headed off toward the dusty fields to join the men and women in their efforts to harvest the valuable corn crops.

Tony assumed his position as cutter of the yellow stalks, working diligently, silently, dedicated to precision work, not yielding to the temptation to look at his fellow laborers, their heavy stares clinging to his skin like dew on a peach in the early morning birth of dawn.

The chastisement of the villagers lay like a circle of red flaming fire around him, choking his ability to see and hear the people as he had known them. "I am from without," he thought, glancing about at the hard stares of the men, "and I may never be from within again." It was burning hot, steaming hot, sweat pouring off his hot body, and yet he could feel their red-hot coal-like stares burning their hard brand on his face.

The girls of the village quit coming to the little brown schoolhouse. He had no visitors, save Juan, whose wife had died of cancer only a while ago; Juan no longer cared about the random direction of the tribe's convictions and acquittals.

The next day, for the celebration of the birth of a child, Tony was not invited; the day after that arrived, and red, inflamed human resentment strode past his house, each villager leaving a small trail of angst behind them; their anger toward him built up like a barrier, brick by brick, encircling him from them. Many days had transpired and she was still gone, and he had ostensibly done nothing to punish or bring her back. Even some of the old women thought she should be whipped with a black leather belt for her transgressions; the young girls were not so certain, but said nothing, in deference to their elders and the ever-present image of the thick, black leather belt.

Another day dragged its omnipresent time clock into the boiling red sun, but a slowed, arduous, painful ticking of seconds dug its sharp heels into the soft brown soil, entrapping the players of the village in a tightly confined space where they all breathed the same volatile air.

In the morning, Tony lay like a prisoner on his sweat-soaked white cot. "She isn't coming back, and I can't stay here." He felt the fool for having come here and believing that life could be different elsewhere. "I cannot outrun myself." He would leave for the States the next day.

The next day, Tony, with no fanfare, departed from the village. Rain had begun to fall. It was the close of a sultry and long Summer and the abrupt beginning of a cold and long Autumn.

Epiphany

She frowned, her face soured on the idea she had just summoned forth. She cursed. "Did I really wash clothes in the river?" She laughed as she danced, thinking such archaic thoughts inside her bubbly head. New York had scrubbed its abrasive bristles against her tender memories and bloodied them onto a fabric of finest silk and finely spun gold, and there those old days would be embalmed, buried under a new pyramid of joy and riches and music and civilization.

"I will live again," she laughed, thinking of the money her grandmother had left her. "I will be Lake Seville, who I was meant to be, not who I became because of my illness; I did what I had to do when I was ill, but that was yesterday," she thought, and sang and hummed to the rhythmic beat of the loud band in the noisy nightclub, "and yesterday is gone."

"Tony is gone, too," she reasoned, sitting down to drain her shot glass of wine, "it's been too long. Good Tony," she smiled in reflection; "he was good for me when I was in my altered state, but that is over—but you seek your level wherever and whoever you are, no matter the circumstances, and he was what I needed for the moment; but that is over and things like that don't have to be forever, no reason at all." She began to grow agitated at this reverie, for she began to feel a pull of emotion toward what he had with her and what they had gone through together; but she banished these memories. "Oh, he'll understand, he's a sweetheart; he knew it would never last, he used to say so all the time."

Somewhere, there was a faint echo of thunder seeking to break through a great barrier, a faint voice she recognized, a voice pleading for recognition, a voice persistent and unyielding. "Come back," it chorused, as it again and again broke against the high stone walls of the citadel she had recently erected around her heart, but she would have none of it, and she suppressed its melancholy song with her own merry tune.

She decided to visit the old shops and restaurants and places she had known so well and would soon know again. She became joyously lost for days, simply inhaling and touching and seeing the intricate fabric of her magical old environs.

"The gala event is tonight," she sang, in her hotel room once more; "it will complete my miraculous resurrection," and then she left to go and rent her attire for the evening.

She stood before the mirror, wearing the rented full-length silken white gown and long white gloves and imitation pearl earrings and diamond necklace, but she was still not looking at herself full in the face. "Not yet," she smiled, "not now, not here." The moment she waited for to unfurl the full force of her natural beauty must be at the grandest event of the year, a celebration she had grown up attending, an event as common to her as bowling night to a commoner. It was at this sterling festival of mingling celebrities that she would regain her rightful place in a society she felt she had helped create. "I have just been away," she whispered, tilting her head as she surveyed the length of the dress and how it wrapped so sensuously around her elegant figure.

The Pennsylvania Society has its annual weekend gathering not, as one would suppose, in Pennsylvania, but in New York City, the highlight of this event where politicians, businessmen, lobbyists, and celebrities, being a black-tie affair on a Saturday at the Waldorf Astoria Hotel; and Lake arrived there without an official invitation, black limousine or ostentatious wealth; she lifted her divine body out of the yellow taxi and slowly walked up the milky-white-colored marble steps, breathless with anticipation at the reception she would receive. Surely, they will exalt at my physical return, she thought, stepping onto the last step and looking at the security guards who stood in front of the giant white double doors.

It was as if she had stepped onto the very same spot of the silvery flowing stream once more. She was astride a prevailing calm as she neared the entrance. "Why, I'm home, Grandmother."

The granite-faced monoliths with the visible earpieces intercepted her locomotion with their giant's hands. "Identification," one of them grunted, his dark eyes aflame with the promise of intransigence.

She had thought that somehow through the miraculous process of osmosis the guards at the palace doors would know her identity and step aside to allow the fairy princess in to make her triumphant entrance. But instead she was adrift, a listing ship on a stormy sea, unable to sink or swim.

"Lake," a voice rang out from inside the fabled ballroom, "is it really you?"

She peered inside, and smiled broadly when she recognized an old acquaintance of her family.

"Oh, Jemison," the elderly woman said to one of the guards, placing her wrinkled, bejeweled hand upon the black coat sleeve of the hulking beef-eater, "this is Lady Camille Seville's granddaughter, Lake," and when she put out the other wrinkled hand to take the slender, toned arm of Lake, the real magic commenced.

People had told Lake there was no magic in the world, only joy and health and love when you were young and then pain and suffering and sorrow when you grew older, and she had believed all of it, until now; this was true magic, she knew, magic given to those who wake up in privilege and fall to ruin but then rise again to the highest echelon of human society. "This is what I deserve after so much suffering," she thought, gliding on the finely polished surface that was like smooth, fine glass, as she spied the characters of her once and future fairy tale world. Here she was in the germ of power, and yet she could not fade the image of herself standing in her bare feet, squishing her toes into the soft, cool dirt and pebbles and feeling so alive, and smiling and laughing at the children playing with simple toys and experiencing the simple joys of life, and the image of herself sitting among the soft green grasses in her quiet spot and being as happy as she ever was, and all of it without great wealth or power or busy ideas; and she heard herself, from thousands of miles away and a lifetime ago, say with a voice born from wisdom that was gained from truly living, "But I was happy."

She was escorted, arm in arm, by Dame Whittingham, who herself was worth more than the combined wealth of all the peasants who lived in the entire Mexican state where Lake had lived. "Will they remember me?" Lake thought, but then she thought of Tony, and she felt sorrow grip her heart. She smiled larger, and banished his image. "From another life," echoed in a sad refrain deep inside her, "long ago, and far away…"

Delightful music serenaded her mind into a pleasanter place, the perfumed air excited her senses, the healthy conversation of educated people intoxicated her, moving her closer to imploring the upper class of society to restore her superior standings. "I deserve my rebirth," she pondered, nearly now into the nucleus of the maelstrom of power.

"O, everyone," Dame Whittingham proclaimed, through the broken filters of her smoke-filled, sooty lungs, "look who has come back to us."

Euphoria flushed pink thrills over her silken skin as Lake acknowledged this happy moment of embrace by her own kind. People of great importance crowded around her, their faces lit by an unavoidable curiosity and a smile created by proximity; greetings from old acquaintances and eager new ones abounded as she held hands and talked and laughed, and every moment she flowed without remonstration into their insular orbit, her freshly new skin of life created in Mexico peeled away.

She expected the interest in her reappearance to fade quickly, a sparkling snowflake falling on a hot sidewalk; but it did not, for it was stoked by the interloping reporters, who began to construct speculations to fuel their digging questioning.

The imperious reporters were shooting absurd questions and the people around her were whipping her for personal anecdotes and the whole crowd of guests was being led into a desperate frenzy to know this very moment the esoteric circumstances of her disappearance.

She soon found herself on the hardwood stage in front of a microphone that the singer of the band relinquished to her; her heart fluttered, her stomach ached, her face burned rapture-crimson. The richest and most powerful people in New York were here and they were looking up at her, their penetrating stares putting the lost pieces of the Lake Seville puzzle back together again, and she was intoxicated with ecstasy.

"Word has it that you were in Mexico," one reporter asked from the center of the circulating fury. The electric buzz hummed in the hushed audience as they looked to center stage.

"Why, yes," she said, her mind still lost in the fervor.

"How did you get your health back?" another asked.

"Are you a rich heiress again?"

Ripe laughter erupted, seeded along with rich applause, producing much delicious fruit as approval of her welcome home.

Her gracious smile embraced them all. "Thank you, I am well, but that is a story…"

"Will you write a book about it all, Heiress Seville?" a guest shouted.

She raised her eyebrows in wonder. "Well, maybe…"

"What was it like living with peasants?"

"Yes, what was it like being with peasants who still live in the Stone Age? Were you doing research on a cure for your condition?"

Some of the curious had already turned and continued on with their former conversations. The smiles of her interrogators, of the audience, seemed too familiar. She cursed her old self for seeing duplicity in every motive of the rich and powerful.

"Are you glad you're back with your own kind?"

She then heard an importunate voice searing into her mind, "You need to be with your own kind," and she knew he had once said this, long, long ago.

She tried to smile, but a red-hot tingling sweat erupted on her skin, and she only seemed to frown. "Well, maybe later," she whispered in a barely audible voice, and turned and walked off the stage; and by the time she returned to her place, the population of the party had resumed their former positions on the well-scrubbed floor and their former conversations that came from their well-scrubbed teeth.

A few of the reporters approached her.

"Miss Seville, you're news—miraculous recovery from an illness while in the company of peasants," one female reporter began.

"I like the angle—peasant medicine cures heiress, where modern medicine fails," another added.

"And say," one of the reporters said, "is that a wedding ring on your finger? Married to one of those peasants, eh? A real love story!"

"Oh, those Mexican people," a young beauty said, who was standing next to them, "haven't they closed the borders yet? Don't you just think we have enough of them for slave labor as it is?"

"Well," a young man began, with a smear of arrogance across his handsome face, "I think of the old days—why, Congress abolished bringing slaves into America in 1808, didn't it? And didn't the South have enough of those darling black mommies and daddies to supply more baby slaves?" The white faces sprayed white laughter.

A young beauty said, "See, universities are good for more than just drinking and partying; not much more, but just enough." They laughed again.

Each particle of unrestrained laughter, each chord of musical humor, every bobbing head dissembled the woman Lake so desperately wanted to become. "Tony," she heard herself saying.

Unrepentant and cruel, racist jokes from the depths of a shallow tumor of callous disregard for human life flowed like the black milk from the rot of a decaying tree; ethnic jokes that were boiled from the sweat of taskmasters of days past, when upon a whim or fancy they unhitched their anger onto innocent servants and slaves, flowed from the members of this tight circle of socialites and their human pets, the local reporters.

The alluring young woman gestured toward Lake. "You really didn't eat corn and beans and all that, did you?" she asked, incredulous, as she held her crystal glass of sparkling pink champagne.

A magnificent specimen of physical genetic perfection stepped up to the crowd, her stunningly beautiful face glorifying the haughtiness that is the vital life-force upon which her kind subsisted. "How could you," she said, unabashedly to Lake, "lower yourself to live with such filthy people? They aren't like you, they don't think like us; why, their very presence in this country has weakened us socially and economically. They are a veritable pestilence on earth."

"Well, Miss Seville," a male reporter said, smiling in glee, "do you defend illegals in our country?"

She wanted to believe that these people were just an aberration, that other groups here were more enlightened and noble, that if she just moved about she would hear profound dialogue on the great issues in society and their boasting acts of munificence; she then threaded her way through the clumps of animated faces with gaping mouths that spewed malicious gossip in the same manner princes and princesses weaved and bobbed after coronations, and she heard their scorching verbiage, where they hung and crucified the common man to his lowly station in life; where they praised the CEO's and condemned the worker's woes; where they evinced supreme contempt for workers' rights and supreme adulation for the right of the Corporate State to grow without restraint. She became sicker and sicker at heart, but then she remembered and she remembered quickly and too easily the conversations those around her had when she was growing up, and the words and meaning were the same. "In every generation," she pondered, "there are vile people doing vile things; O, Grandmother, you were so right." She thought of firing taunting curses that would put a fire in the soft, flabby bellies of her unwitting assailants, but she also thought of the ancient proverb, "pearls before swine," and so reached over and dislodged her two pink pearl earrings and clasped them in her tight fists as she stared with a stabbing stare at the crowd, and then moved on.

"Very good, good, very, very good," Dame Whittingham said to Lake, after the angry young woman had approached her and told her how she felt, "your grandmother would have been so proud."

Lake could only smile now while her eyes welled up with pride and regret.

Dame Whittingham placed her tired old arm around her, walking her toward the exit doors. "You don't belong to us anymore, Lake, darling," she said, emphatically, and pulled her back to face her. "You belong to the very least of the world, and they are better than we could ever hope to be," and she motioned about the ritzy hall. "We are, all of us, prisoners here; some of us willingly, others unaware." She smiled as she looked at the glittering bodies, and her face grew solemn. "They suck the blood out of the rest of the world to finance their precious games," she said, sorrowfully, and then she turned back to face Lake, "but you know now, and that makes you completely free." She saw the bewildered look on the handsome face before her. "Your grandmother and I used to have long talks about how much she hated the mire she lived in, but she also knew that in order to confound and confuse the powerbroker, you have to live in their polluted waters." She walked Lake again toward the exit. "She wanted you to be free of this, all of it." She began to weep. "I don't know how she did it, but you are free," and she embraced her. "O Lake, before she died, she told her most intimate friends not to help you until you were as you are now; we didn't understand what she meant, but I understand now. O, how I longed to tell you, but you disappeared for so long, and then I found you, and told Matthew, who was also looking for you, where you were."

Lake closed her eyes, and as she did so, she felt her old, new self begin to emerge again. "Tony," she murmured.

Dame Whittingham, holding Lake's hands, spoke again with love and devotion. "I don't why you came back, but go back, my darling child, go back and reclaim the paradise you found." She embraced her once more. "Go now, go back to the real world, where real people, the ones we need to exist, whom we tried to bury with our unquenchable quest for power and mammon, and forget about what you used to be, and who we are, and truly live," she whispered passionately, and then she held her out from her, thinking of a lost era and a lost friend. "O, Lake, your grandmother would have been so very proud of you."

They embraced once more, and a tearful and grateful Lake turned and walked swiftly through the opening doors and for a brief intermission she stopped and closed her eyes and felt a slow purging pour throughout her body, and her body became numb as her mind was anointed with a sprinkling of virtue. Her feelings left her naked, for she now knew the Truth, that the people in the simple Village de Francisco were the true nobility of the world, and that the people she had once admired and stood behind in the palace of delights were the real peasants. "Power," she reasoned, her countenance tingling with revelation, "and money do not elevate one nor make one successful; it is deeds, it is heart, it is mind," but she was weeping again, "it is motive, it is love…love," and she began to walk quickly down the Cinderella steps. "O Tony, Tony, Tony, how much I love you and miss you; darling, I will be home soon…"

She bolted along the remaining walkway and into the waiting carriage that would, alas, not turn into a pumpkin at midnight, where she was soon dropped her off at her hotel and then fled down the hallway to her room; and once there she tore off her gown, even as she was making a reservation for a flight to Mexico.

She vomited like a font of hot steam in a bubbling hot stream, depositing the bitter brew into the hotel sink. She stood back and looked at an old, gruesome friend, knowing she had brought this upon herself; but she knew why it had been resurrected. "How could I have suffered to let him be subjected to one last affair with this immoral sickness?" she cried, slowly wiping her mouth free of the vile smell. She knew she was not physically sick, but she could not celebrate it. "Can an alcoholic rejoice about drinking only once after quitting?" She slammed shut the bathroom door. "How did this happen? Did I go mad? How can I be so sure of something and then realize how foolish I was?" and she tore at her lovely brown hair, screaming and shouting, and finally, standing in front of the mirror on the wall, still not looking at herself fully, she said, her face contorted by pain, "Now, I cannot look at myself," and she looked away, in shame. "O Grandmother, you were right and I was wrong; why couldn't I see that? Why do I have to live out my failures?" She dropped to her knees, holding herself fast, sobbing, "I was living the life of a princess, with my prince, in the land of a real fairy tale." So great was her anguish that she could not speak, so great was her torment when she thought she might lose him forever, and she moaned and groaned and rocked back and forth for a long time. "O God, I had it all, I had it all and now I might lose it all; why, God, why do I have to throw away the things I love, only to grab onto something I will hate…"

Rain was falling upon the city as she got into the cab and was taken to the airport. She sat in the brown leather seat and looked up to hear the broadcaster speak of flooding in certain parts of Mexico. She heard nothing more but the tolling of the bell that announced her complicity in betraying her brethren and her husband and her physical regeneration. She screamed in a silent rage and ran to the phones.

"No more promises," she whispered, frantically, as she dialed the numbers, "only living…" She closed tight her wet eyes. "Be there, be there, be there…"

Rain Rain

Tony had walked ten miles and ridden with farmers the last five to the house of Eduardo, his rancor increasing with every step taken, and with every step imagined, he pondered a life squandered, a life ending, a life beginning; but he also thought of his old self, and he felt great shame. "I have been blinded by health," he said to himself, walking the last mile along the dirt road. He gazed up at the darkening gray skies, heard the loud reports of thunder, and beheld the vein-like structure of white lightning firing up in the dark clouds. "Health," he continued, watching the rain fall gently, "became my new mistress; how could I forget how long and how much I suffered? Have I learned nothing? Have I forgotten all of my vows, that if I ever was to regain health, that I would be grateful for the smallest gains?" He spied the modest home of Eduardo, which was set back discreetly from the road. "I found love once; I can find it again."

Eduardo was not at home, but soon, he came driving up in his blue sedan; he would ask no questions as he exited the car, for he had long ago learned that no questions were necessary, or even profitable, from him in such circumstances. "Hello, Tony," he said, plainly, and then waved his unannounced guest into his home.

"I am going back to the States," Tony stated, adamantly. "It didn't work out here…"

"Fine," Eduardo responded, pouring the two men hot chamomile tea, "make yourself at home."

Tony had not expected a total lack of curiosity from Eduardo. He found himself unable to follow any particular discourse, and thus, standing next to the white-tiled kitchen counter, he pondered his fate.

The men brooded in their silence, Eduardo going about his business, checking phone messages, Tony standing next to the window, looking out at the pouring rain.

"Do you mean soon?" Eduardo said, casually, sipping his hot tea with indifference.

"Yes."

"Well," he said, taking a large gulp, "that will take some doing," and he gestured toward the window, "the rain, you know; we expect some problems."

It was a conversation camouflaged, two men speaking from behind giant boulders, boys wearing masks and throwing single-packet verbal grenades that exploded in the air and trickled down on the recipient in a plume of purple smoke.

Tony was thinking around himself, ahead and behind and past himself, but he could not put himself where he needed to be: in the future. "Do I really want to go? Will she come back? It's been four days; it isn't like she can't pick up a phone," but he dismissed this current parade of wandering thoughts with a grimace and shake of his head.

"It could take a few days before I can get you out; the heavy rain is here, and roads and bridges might be out."

"What about the village?"

Eduardo shook his head, frowning, complete with furrowed brows. "That isn't your concern anymore, now is it?"

The rain was coming in huge torrents. The men looked out the window.

"It's just rain," Tony said, disturbed; "it rains here all the time."

Eduardo walked softly on the hardwood floors to the wall map. "These areas," he began, pointing to red pins stuck in various areas about his mother country, "have had heavy deforestation damage, either by locals, companies or foreign corporations." He shrugged his shoulders. "It doesn't matter; the wound to Nature is the same—deep." He walked back to the counter and resumed sipping his simmering cup of tea. "Mexico is a vast natural resource largely ignored by the greed of the world, until now; oil, natural gas, minerals, cheap labor…" He smiled, not of joy, but of sadness. "Mexico, a nation of peasants tucked under the ripe nipple upon which the mightiest nation on earth suckles, its two brown hands stretched out, thirsty still." He drained the cup, poured another, also rich with sweet amber-colored honeycomb, then walked to the window, staring out at the cold rain. "Ours is a rich history of a noble people plagued by debauchery and corruption." His words were as hard and cold as the rain. "Why didn't we flourish like the Europeans and the North Americans? Can you imagine if we had repulsed the first Spanish Conquistadors? Did you know that early on, the British tried to defeat the Spanish in the Americas—maybe things might have been different; if our civilization had grown unchecked, would we too have found Democracy early on? Did we need the gabacho to bring gunpowder and disease to destroy us, to cow us?" The timbre of his voice was like a steel hammer banging on a wall of thick glass. "O my Lord in the great merciful Heavens, how the Mexican has been abused by aliens, how he must beg and scrape for food, cross polluted rivers, face death, live in the dark for fear of capture; O, poor, humble peasant, thou art noble here, peon there; imprisoned here, free there, but not free," his voice trailed down, its volume crushed by despair. He now turned his attention to his guest. "Tell me, why do we have to leave our own land to look for jobs? Why? When will it all end, when will our people not risk death crossing the border?" He no longer spoke to anyone alive, but to the past and the future. "When will we not swim across polluted rivers, pay coyotes to cram us into hot vans like we are dumb mules, climb barbed-wire fences, pay blackmail money to stay there…" His voice strained and cracked under the weight of the oppression he felt. "We should put up walls to keep our own in until we come up with a solution." There was a faint perception of his head shaking back and forth. "No, no," he whispered as he turned to face his guest. "Then we would not have such wonderfully humble folk such as thee to come down and help the poor peon learn how to wipe his nose like a good American. America," he frowned, "you just have to make the whole world in your own image, don't you?"

When one has his head in the mouth of a roaring lion, does one speak impudence?

"But that doesn't affect you anymore, does it? You are running away, back to the land of wealth and opportunity." A scowl built by the pain of nearly two hundred years of failure widened like a bloody fissure across his dark face. "Most come because of a guilty conscience, others to impose their decadent lifestyle upon the grateful peasant." His chagrin became engulfed by a sinister shadow. "As if," he growled a laugh, "as if we need his civilized stamp upon us to understand the proper way of living…"

The howling wind was blowing cold rain against the thin glass of the window, creating an intermittent moan that ached and throbbed. Eduardo seemed to stare past the storm into an ethereal dimension into which the unleashed enmity of man flowed like boiling lava. "Americans think the whole world should live like them; isn't this the mark of the true imperialist, where outside your sphere of influence everyone else is a barbarian? Are you any different from the ancient Japanese or Chinese? My grandmother," he expelled a sad sigh, "she came to America at a time when the Mexican was seen as a bridge between Man and monkey, when he was deloused with white DDT powder as if he were a smelly pack of rats; ah, yes, but you needed those rats to do your laundry and clean your houses and work your lawns, and lift your rocks and bricks and build your walls, which still stand today…" He shook his head. "She would say to us, her little mijos—she would say to us, 'Grandchildren, when we were standing there with that sticky powder all over our bodies, it was the only time I felt white—when I was poisoned.'"

But like a candle lit in a room with little oxygen to feed it, it quickly dies. Tony had returned nothing, for he knew there was nothing he could say to alter the character of the bitter man before him, a truth he knew better than most; and so, he merely turned and walked out of the door, but then stopped, and turned around. His words were daggers sharpened by the promises of the past. "You once said that giving up is easy to do in this land; well, it looks like you have," and then turned and headed back to the village.

He was walking alongside the muddy road, staring down at the green grasses that grew in the fields, not knowing why he was returning. "I can't go back," he reasoned, "but I do need my things; but how can I go back? It is true they do not know why I left." He looked up at the steely gray clouds and the heavy torrents of rain. "Right now they are drinking atole; O, but I can't think in this ridiculous weather, it beats my head into a delirium." One idea would assume shape in his mind, but it would be ripped asunder by the tiny, liquid bombs piercing his skin. "I can only think of the selfish rain."

Little tributaries soon formed along the dirt road, washing away into the puddles and streams in the fields as the rain increased. His long, cotton white pants and shirt were soaked, his yellow leather work boots soggy, his body buried in wet; his downcast face led his downcast body as he plodded along. "It is my own fault; I ran away from strife, and in such things I am my old self; so I go back and retrieve my personal belongs, and I come back down the hill despite the rain; it will all be over soon; the rain will not last forever, and tomorrow, I will be home, safe, back among the faithless fold, and soon I will forget about the cold rain." He shook his head as the hard rain pounded upon him. "Tomorrow, rain, I will not think of you or fear you; that is the sentiment in civilized nations, at least those not living in the bottom lands." He heaped abuse upon the wet terrain around him with a grimace. "Awful, just terrible," he waxed bitterness, like a sculptor who makes a clay statue in the rain, "what can be done in this backward land? I must not lie to myself, this is a dead country, a frozen revolution; a hundred years from now it will be the same—why throw good money after bad?" He continued to plod, soaked, cold, irritable, occasionally looking up the road. "Was I mad?" The cool embers of defeats from long ago were summoned to awaken from their dead slumber. "These people—these primitive people, they live like savages, really—they are best left alone; peasants, all of them, just peons." He felt a twinge of hurt, of regret stabbing his heart when he thought of his village, of the people who had been kind to him; but it did not enlarge his enmity of the entire indigenous population if he did not apply the full force of his contempt for all of them right now. "No, they're all peons." It felt better to denounce them as "peons" because, to him, this spiteful word led their image into a deeper valley of ignorance. He felt himself become ensconced inside a hard shell of intolerance. "What a waste, what a fool I was," he lamented. "One year in this wasteland, and what about me, my retirement, my needs? My wife…" But he could not speak of her. "…And these people betray me, and over what? They deserve to rot in their ignorance." He felt bolder as he spoke aloud. He spat upon the muddy road. "In a day, a mere day, I will be back in civilization, where the rain just means rain, and you are safely tucked inside your warm, cozy, modern house, and drinking hot tea…"

He was cold, yet his wrath toward his peasant captors burned brightly inside of him. He cursed them all, all who had abandoned him. The rain increased its wrath.

It was pouring so hard he could barely see the outline of the small hills around him. He cursed the loud rain beating upon his yellow sombrero; he cursed the icy wind, the puddled road, the fact of his aloneness. There was an eerie stillness caused by the rain, as if Nature itself had paused in its living. "The whole world sleeps, and yet I walk," he thought, "because I walk between two worlds."

His skin felt hard and frozen. "In a day, I will be forever gone from this place," he whispered, looking up at the dense configuration of clouds that were now a solid, sooty black, "and you can rain on some other poor fool." He desperately wanted someone to come by in a gloriously modern automobile and offer assistance, but so desperately wanted to continue to hate this land that he really wanted to get back to the village by himself, knowing this deed would cripple his dying affection for these people. "I don't need them," he cried, feeling the bullet drops of rain smash into his face. "I don't need anyone; I didn't need anyone when I was ill, no one came to my rescue then," and he beat his chest, "and I don't need anyone now!" He cursed the whole wide world.

No one did come by. His bitterness increased with every step as he fumed and brooded over his wasted life, and when he neared the village, he was far removed from the man he had been only hours before.

When he entered the path leading to his adobe home, he was glad no one had helped him along the road. "By tomorrow," he kept saying to himself, "I will be free." He paused by the deserted crop fields, walked by the wells, and soon, he saw the small, humble homes. "I could just go back inside my house and forget about all of it; maybe she will return, maybe…" He shook his head. "Don't be weak," he whispered, "life begins tomorrow in California, U.S. of A."

He was on the main road now, and was inside the village, and stood before his home, and stepped in, expecting to find her, but found nothing; he stood there for the longest time, imagining what it was like when they were together; he heard a car pull up to the road, and in a moment, he stepped back outside, looking at an empty yellow car; he then walked down the road and around the corner to where the schoolhouse dwelled, to see what he could see, but seeing no people about, he walked back and peered into the small dwelling where he and his wife had taught. The three young women who were their first students were inside, teaching two younger children, and when they saw him, they waved their hands excitedly at him, and sent the two children out to greet him. He waved back, and looking to his right, shock soaked his face ashen white. The two children hugged him.

But then he looked up and saw what he did not want to see, for the enormous hillside the schoolhouse was built into had just shed its outermost layer of skin in the way of mud, tons of it flowing straight down upon the small structure.

It is in this moment, this in-between moment, between life and death, when some are certain to live, and others are certain to die, that the human character is united with a higher or lower moral philosophy. This was no time for him to think but only to act, and to act swiftly and decisively; thus, after pushing the children away, he ran, but toward the schoolhouse, seeing the innocent, exuberant faces of his students, scream-ing to them to come out; and when he was completely inside, all tucked safely inside the bosom of the adobe structure, the avalanche of wet, sticky, heavy mud broke from the hill. A woman on the outside screamed.

The little brown schoolhouse had been swallowed whole.

Homecoming

S he could not sleep on the plane, for sleep is for the contented soul. She sat wide-eyed, staring at the electrical storms shooting across the black horizon. She felt unbalanced, her soul tilted at the universe, the universe mocking her as it provided a mosaic she had unwound and wound in her own corrupt image. "I am so lost, so utterly lost," her soul confessed, "I don't know what I am supposed to do or who I am or why I am; O, it was so simple being rich and beautiful, because once you are rich and beautiful, society expects you to just be rich and beautiful, all day and all night." She then loosed tainted images that were held intact by the centrifugal force of her memories; she let loose all of the colored, thin frames of her sinful past onto her virgin, pink, forming conscience, so she might eject her old self into the crystal cathedral of icy space.

"I was a sterling, beautiful butterfly who crowded miserably back into her dried, old chrysalis, and now," she felt herself wanting to weep, but she chewed her weakness into ribbons of strength, "I don't know who I need to be, because," she frowned, looking outside at the wispy clouds, "because I have no great experience in it, having only lived it just recently." She punched the beige seat. "How can one not know the right thing to do? O, Grandmother, you knew, didn't you, but you couldn't forgo what you had already become, and therefore you did what you knew was wrong; but why? Yet, with me, mmm," she hummed, closing her eyes, "with me, you saved me." She meditated upon this truth for a time. "But no one saved you; shouldn't there be someone to save sinners like you? Isn't there someone who is supposed to be there for us, no matter how far we have sunk into the mire? There is so much suffering in the world; O God, why do you allow it?" And then she thought of her illness, and her face fell into her hands. "It was even easier to be ill," she thought, shaking her head, "because all I expected of myself, all anyone expected of me, was to get well; there were no expectations beyond that; O, this world, this accursed world, it can be so beautiful, if you just start in the right direction…"

The landing in the Mexican airport was smooth in the hard rain. Lake heard about the dreadful flooding near her village, and she hung her head in shame; she made two phone calls, rented a car and sped off for the Village de Francisco. The wet asphalt roads leading out of the womb of civilization slowly faded away, giving way to muddy streams of hard dirt and soft dirt and lopsided, shifting roads; some roads were blocked off, while others were strewn with abandoned cars; bridges were still intact, but straining under the harassing tide of water that violently ran under their metal bellies; and despite it all, she navigated her way successfully to the village even as this rainstorm was at its zenith.

When she drove into the village, nothing seemed to have changed. She smiled. "Female intuition," she laughed. "Tony would have loved that." When she had spoken his name back in the Grand City, it had caused her to see that world in a different light, and when she said his name here, it sounded so right and familiar, like the tolling chimes of birds in Spring, like the soft timbre in the call of the warm yellow sun to the verdant foliage to awake from their Winter slumber; it was a name invoking a pilgrimage of her heart to remember what was precious in life, to embrace someone who completed her, understood her, honored her and protected her and was, above all things, loyal to her. Without him, there was no real life, just existence, the daily maintenance of the fragile body, while the fragile mind and heart and soul withered like pink roses planted in a cave that was littered with tiny holes in its rocky crown to let in peeps of precious sunlight.

She removed herself hesitantly from the yellow sedan, for she felt the boughs of tension building from every adobe house, built from the disapproving eyes of the people, now falling upon her head. "I am back, so get used to it," she whispered, glancing up and down the wide, dark path that ran between the houses. She walked to her home and stood at its entrance, not certain of what lay beyond the white wooden doors. She nearly knocked, but sidestepped the impulse, and decided to walk up to several homes to see if the young women of the schoolhouse were home; and she knocked on their doors, and she went into their homes, but the girls were not there, and the adults would not tell her much; and so, she walked back to her home and went inside. She felt nauseated when it appeared as if the place had not been lived in for days. "He's left, he's left me," she moaned, grabbing her face on either side and pulling her hands up through her wet hair. "You can't go home again; I was a fool," she cried, and she broke an object that was easily breakable, and regained the cool air outside, shame and regret prancing about her flushed face. She didn't know what to do or where to go, so she just started walking toward the schoolhouse. "Maybe someone will know something…"

But it was at this precise moment when she beheld him walking up to the little brown building. She stood, awed and numb, staring at him as he first looked into the building and waved at its occupants, looked over to her, and then she watched as the children embraced him. It was then that she noticed the rapidly collapsing hill of mud above the school-house, whereas his eyes, following her lead, found the same portent of doom; and then, without words or hesitation, after pushing the children to safety, he ran into the small building as the hillside covered it.

And it was then that she screamed a scream that originated deep from within the vast wilderness of her grieving soul.

Unmerciful

When the people of the village heard Lake expel such a horrible shriek of terror from her slender body, they rushed out of their homes, their eyes instinctively following her wild run down the road toward the schoolhouse; and when the people stood before the muddy monolith, they were humbled, for they knew they were in the presence of some physical force greater than themselves.

It was tons of loose, wet soil and debris, rock and root and tree, sitting atop the small building like a good mother hen atop her lone, precious egg; it was fifty feet deep of this potent brown slime, and thirty feet wide down its gooey, sloping sides. The villagers stood in mass resignation and capitulation against this skyscraper of Nature, stunned into capitulation, retardation, willing submissiveness; to them, this was their tragic history, the sad history of Mexico, peasants battling supernatural forces above and beyond their feeble control, frightened and bowed before an enigmatic and all-powerful presence.

Lake was furiously digging at the base of the skirt of this mud mountain while the two children who had come out of the schoolhouse told their elders who was inside, and how Tony had rescued them and then ran to the girls before the collapse of the hill.

All of the villagers took to the weighty task, using any kind of spade, hoe, stick, cup or bowl, or any instrument sufficient to scoop up and away the mushy brew of runny soil and rock and shrubs and twig and streams of water, water, everywhere, incessant water pouring down upon them from the thundering, sooty skies. The mud dressed them in its personal sticky suit, spitting little brown dirt balls into their faces, onto their hair, clogging the cold pores of their icy skin. The villagers dug in a manic fury, neither speaking nor looking at each other.

The mountain exhaled its might in copious mud tears, just as any wounded creature might weep against its antagonists. The diggers gained an inch, and lost a foot, but they did not acknowledge it; they gained a foot, and lost a yard, but did not acknowledge it, so determined were they to scalp the fat, lazy hill of mud until it bled out the life within; so, with every chop and dig and scoop and push and pull, the people plowed their will into the enemy, thinking freedom from without to their loved ones within.

The villagers dug as if a single organism, dedicated to the sole task of diligently uncovering the muddy peels of this mud heap. Twelve hours hence, and the squatting behemoth had shed a tiny fraction of its girth, but the villagers waged war like veteran soldiers. The silent battle slowly crept into a darkness that spilled in streaks and billows over the land; the rain was unceasing: sometimes there was drizzle, sometimes thundershowers, but always a relentless presence of rain. Lights were set up at the base of the dig. Every hour or so, villagers would lend their ear to the base of the hill to listen for sounds of life.

During the night, blessed hope came from the Village de Zapata. "Hola." Maria's blissful voice illuminated the night. Large smiles and hearty handshakes welcomed the helpers, who had also brought fresh, warm, nourishing food; and thus, the villagers of Francisco ate and rested, but not speaking of the living tomb within as their neighbors dug; yet there was one who ate but did not, would not, could not rest, digging all the faster with her long, square-ended metal shovel, digging just like a steam locomotion that gains muscle and speed as black coal is fed into its fiery red belly. Her mind and heart and soul had but one vision, born from a single purpose, and that was to free the inhabitants therein, and by doing so, in a fashion not understood by her, she might dig herself out, too; the more she dug, the stronger she became, the lighter she felt, the easier her breathing. Her heavy burden within was becoming lighter with every heavy molecule removed from the barrier without.

The combined efforts of the villagers produced minor yet obvious scars to the mud colossus.

Eduardo rolled up in his blue sedan in the morning. "The roads are becoming flooded, and bridges are out," he said, walking up to the digging crew, and once apprised of the situation, he too began to dig.

The cold, light rain became hard, pounding heavy raindrops, digging into the mudslide. The day wore on, and the diggers dug on.

Night came and a dense fog of blackness enveloped them; many of the diggers, exhausted, now rested, ate, and slept. The normal whimpering of Lake's physical body to slow down and rest only induced harder work in her; she was machine-like in her piston-driven movements as she removed the watery soil to the sides and behind her, while she looked at no one, spoke to no one, acknowledging only the enemy before her.

In the third hour of the a.m., a low rumbling spread throughout the digger's camp. Lake felt the mud at her feet thicken, oozing against her pant legs, forcing her back as she cried to the others to awaken. She surveyed the new shedding of the hill's skin with a flashlight, but she saw little of the true scope of the damage; when morning came, all was revealed.

It was still raining when darkness pulled back its sky veil to evince a cold, black-gray dawn. The villagers gasped as they realized the magnitude of the mud mountain, for it was now nearly twice its size in its girth, and half more its size in length. The diggers stood, motionless, a feeling of smallness and insignificance crushing their will to win. Their bodies fell as if they had been violently stomped into the soaked earth. Some of the women cried, some of the men cursed, but Lake simply pulled up her dirty shovel and thrust it back into the base of the grinning monster. And then she raised her head skyward and closed her eyes, and whispered, "Would that my tears reach those beneath me, and touch my love, and let them know we have not forgotten them, nor have quit the task."

Hope had been extinguished for those villagers who were laboring to free their loved ones, but their resolute faith in the miraculous compelled them to dig, although the digging was now more methodical, as if, with every shovelful, they were anticipating more hillside eruptions.

The rain came down with such force that the landscape around the diggers became shrouded in a streaming blur, and the diggers paused to gaze in awe at the might of this storm. A huge pile of soil sloughed off the hillside and onto the mountain of mud. The diggers stared in abject silence. The voices of reason told them to surrender to the almighty will of providence. They felt like tiny ants trying to dissemble an august mountain in a small stretch of time, and no matter how much they sought to keep sober of mind and optimistic about this righteous endeavor, they knew that failure had arrived; still, as they knew those trapped in the small schoolhouse were probably alive, they had to dig. No one dared voice the treasonous image of pessimism, but its vicious seeds had been planted in their hearts and minds, and their actions bespoke them. They dug slower, and with dull, rhythmic, coerced movements; everything now was simply for effect, and still they would put their ear to the base of the hill to listen for the faint echoes of hope.

The third day came and the mountain of mud looked remarkably intact and whole. Imperceptible leaks of slimy debris had rolled down the hillside like dirty tears of glee that mocked its human fleas—sometimes it was a slice of mud, or a bolt of soil, a chunk of rock and twig and leaf, and all of it plugging the minute holes dug by the diggers.

On the fourth day, the diggers were weary, and wanting to rest and eat more often; much discussion went into the problem of work not done, money lost, chores not finished, opportunities gone; by the fifth day, the rain had abated, the sun appeared briefly, and the watery hill of mud was stickier and more manageable, but three of the workers had already gone back to their homes. On the sixth day, the sun was hot, no relief from the government was in sight, and the hill of mud still grinned its malicious grin of triumph, and only the relatives of those trapped inside remained, as did Eduardo and Maria and Juan.

Lake was layered in mud, her clothes stiff with hardened dirt, her face smeared with mud, mud massaged into her beautiful hair and yellow straw hat, mud stains on her beige pants, mud on the sleeves of her white shirt; she labored in intense silence, steadfast and true in the quest to remove every particle of debris in her way. Now, she stood halfway up the monolith, for its gelatinous goo had somewhat hardened, baked by the scorching sun, and there she dug directly atop the submerged schoolhouse.

Dusk bled down the sides of the red horizon; the rarefied air sizzled with musty scents; the life of the surrounding hills and forests sang its song of reanimation, and the remaining relatives of those still inside the mud tomb, utterly exhausted, turned to leave for good.

Lake looked down upon them, dropped to her knees, and put the left side of her face to the gritty mush. "I hear their heartbeats, still," she cried, and bounded up, staring at her audience below.

"We're through, Lake," the father of Consuelo said. "She could not survive for such a time; she would want us to go back to our work, to live."

"And you know this," she cried, aghast, "you know the thoughts of your children who lie buried below? You're going back to live? This is living, this," she shouted, gesturing about, "fighting for the life of those whom you love; that is living, not going back to the cruel yoke of toil and pain you've been harnessed to your whole life; that is forever—this is now, you have to give up everything for the chance of now…"

"We're going home; we have much work to do," the father of Grezelda said.

"Six days is long enough," said the father of Lupe. "When do we stop, eh? The government does not come; you do not know this land, you do not know floods and earthquakes here; we have all been in places at such times, and there are no survivors this long." He looked away to the fields. "We have much work to do, for the living…" He stood with the other families, as if awaiting her blessing for them to abandon her.

One of the mothers, silently weeping, waved her hands in misery. "We have to go, when do we stop? Life is cruel! God takes those whom He chooses!"

"And where is your faith?" Lake cried, her countenance aflame with passion. "God is everywhere for you, but when you need a miracle…"

"Where was God when little Juan died of cancer?" one of the mothers said, her body bent over in agony from the digging. "Where was He when Carlos was killed by bandits, and when little Maria died of tuberculosis?" She looked up, grimacing into the darkening sky. "God takes those whom He wishes; we work, and we die; it is the way of life." She wept. "My child is gone; life is cruel to us." She shook her head. "And who are you to tell us about our lives and when we should walk away, you who have lived the good life and have never known such suffering." She walked away as if towed along in the awful wake of her husband's dust.

"Life is cruel," Lake shouted, "but I thought your faith in God comforted you," and she gazed at the burial ground beneath her feet. "My faith lies beneath me," she said, her face whispering pain; "maybe I will find faith in death." She looked back to the slowly fading images that disappeared up the dirt road. "And maybe I will find faith with every shovelful of earth," she whispered, and she thrust her heavy shovel into the squishy mud. And she stood proud and erect, shouting at the fleeing people, "But I do know what I will find, I will find those whom I love," and her head lay, as if crumpled by grief, to one side. "Is it not the duty of the living to seek after the comforts of the dying and to bury our cherished dead? What else can I do," she cried, "what else can I do to show God my loyalty to Love and Honor?" She gazed up into the formless swirl of fog and gloom.

"What do you want of me, why is this happening?" she shouted in a plaintive cry of absolute abandonment and loneliness. But she thought of her life and his life and where she might have been and how it all might have been different if she had not become ill. "O God, it is all me, it's just me, no one to blame but me; it's all of us, no excuses for any of us; we make excuses but in the end, we all know better. I dug my path with my pride but it doesn't have to be, anymore." And she buried her head in her hands. "I don't want this, anymore; I want peace, God, show me peace, lead my soul to rest." And she lay there for a few minutes, thinking of what she had and what she wanted, and then she rose up.

She commenced digging again, her arms shaking from ache, her body aching from exhaustion; but she did manage to turn her head and address her sole companions on this quest. "Thank you," she said, full of pathos, and continued to dig. Eduardo and Maria and Juan nodded their heads and smiled.

Revelation

She wanted to believe he was still alive, but she could not hide her strict pragmatist upbringing from her intrusive heart; she was an educated woman, and knew that a human being could not last more than three or four days without water, and even if they had food and water, she knew they had little air. She heard herself whisper inside her heart that he was dead, but she would not acknowledge it, and instead her dialogue followed a logical course to include God.

When she wanted to physically disintegrate and lean on her arms in blessed rest, she called on God; when she wanted to crumple to the heap of sticky mud and weep like a lost child, she called on God; when she mused upon life or death for those buried beneath her or her ideas for her own salvation from the wreckage of sin and pride, she called upon God. She gazed up at the frozen white points of starlight in the midnight sky, and she exhaled deeply. "You always win," she smiled, "in the end; we huff and puff and shout and curse, but in the end, we can't know, because we are merely human…"

During the night, footsteps of shamed creatures scurrying along in their shamed dress approached the battle hill of mud; and lo, it was the villagers, returning to the war general they had capitulated to; Lake, in her utter exhaustion, condemned them for the luxurious rest they had incurred while she had strained with every shovelful of obstinate soil, and she was not ashamed.

Morning gloom came on the wings of fog and rain. Lake cursed the rain, cursed it for its inherent simplicity, for its apparent innocence and necessity; fog wrapped around her legs, splashed the hill and crept over its girth like a creeping snake.

At noon hour, she felt a slimy ooze trickle against her high yellow boots, and though she understood its origin, she desperately fought to assign its nature to other insignificant roles. "It is a small mudslide," she reasoned, panicked, "just a tiny…" but her words were eclipsed as she looked up and saw a wide river of mud dripping down the slope of her mud hill battle. The slide had been small, but enough to fill up much more of the wounds of the hill from the past few days.

Thus shrouded in her chainmail of smoky fog, she collapsed onto the sloping hill, felled by the weight of anguish. "O God," she screamed into the slush, "what do you want of me?" And she listened to the fading clamor of her once-vapid and immoral existence, and she groaned from the deepest and truest and most loving part of her being, "What else do you want of me? Have you not punished me enough? I know what I was and that person is dead, long gone and dead," and she could feel her inner human-inspired peace collapse as she looked down at the impassable way, and she began to sob, and then raised her eyes to the high vault of Heaven, "O God, you sent him to me so I might yet be saved—he is my way back, he has given me life, the very breath I breathe, the very water I drink, the very food I eat; did you bring me back from the dead to die like this, to show me life and then to destroy me when my salvation rests below me? You are not that cruel; I cannot lose him now, now that I know, that I really know who he is to me, and how much I need him; he is me, and I him—I lie below with him: we live below together; he dies, I die; he lives, I live; he has always been me, and I him—and it was You who brought us together, You, O Lord, who showed us who we were and why we belonged with each other and must be as one," and she looked out into the slowly drifting chilly fog, her tears of piety streaming down her florid cheeks. "You know I cannot do this alone; I only know that without Your help, I die," and she buried her head in her hands; "we all die." Those things visible only to the heart lay like a beckoning vision before her, and she felt herself sink into the funeral mire. "O God," she whispered, passionately, "save me, save me from myself, save me from the world, save me, save me, save me," she said over and over and again and again inside of her dying self. And she lay, sideways, immersed in the mud, listening to the constant digging of those at the base of the monster. She closed her eyes tight and prayed for salvation; and lo, she could feel her old flesh slough off, as an old filthy rag is discarded for new, and she could feel a new creature forming within her, noble and good, thus burying that which was conceived in the corruptible temple of Man's mind and heart and soul; and after some time, she felt her fleshly burden lighten, her spirit increase, her strength renew, and arose to resume her digging. The dense, wet fog began to clear.

Hours passed, and the progress of the diggers was without merit, but their commitment to last until they completed the task was now unshakable. Thus, they dug and dug and did not whine when rain pelted them and brought more mudslides; they did not threaten rebellion when the mud pile seemed to grow bigger, nor were they tempted to quit even though no sound of life had ever come through the mound. This would be their monument to be dissembled in sorrow and grief, and then life would go on, as it had and would and must; this was their life, good and bad and pain and loss and birth and marriage and death and destruction, but they knew they must never surrender to the trials of the land, or they too would perish.

More hours passed, and they all dug in a controlled, steady manner, and then… And then, there came from far away a distant whirring sound, easily distinguishable from the digging and soft patter of falling rain, for it was the fast purring of mechanical parts chopping the air. Lake halted her digging, her face stung by hope. "Is it yet true?" she thought, and as the clear sound of helicopter blades clipping the air neared, she began to shout and wildly move her arms about. "Here, here," she shouted, and she nearly flew down the hill. Everyone was looking into the far crimson dawn horizon, now.

Lake jumped to the muddy ground, looking up excitedly at the nearing heavy-lift Mi-26 helicopter that carried the giant caterpillar bulldozer beneath its steel belly; after the bulldozer was liberated from its steel cables, the helicopter set down not too far from the dig site, and out hopped Matthew Gershon, who met Lake as she ran and leaped into his arms. The rain had stopped.

"I just got your message," he said, holding her as a father does his own child. She explained to him what had recently occurred, and with the greatest haste possible, he directed the driver to begin deconstructing the soon-to-be-extinct warrior hill of mud.

The diggers watched in a kind of wide-eyed wonder as the huge tractor gouged enormous chunks of the mud pile and deposited it so easily and so simply onto the ground. The rectangular, steel-plated scooper picked up the mush and placed it on either side of the quickly disintegrating hill of slop, tears of mud streaming down the steel-plated sides. Men with echo detectors scanned the mound for the precise dimensions of the housing structure; soon, they signaled to the driver that a few more feet would reveal the schoolhouse.

It was a strange sight for those who had battled the mud hill for so long, to see it so easily and quickly taken apart; there was a sense of relief, but also the feeling of being deprived of a final and private victory.

There, a gentle scalpel was used on the next scoop, and a small portion of the white roof was revealed; the diggers gasped with anticipation; there, to relieve pressure on the fragile structure, mud was scooped from the rooftop; there, to the front, a gentle precision carving away of the clinging wall of mud commenced until slowly it revealed the picture that had always been in the mind of the diggers: the yellow wooden door of the schoolhouse as it was adorned by a fresh burst of dazzling golden sunlight.

Lake stood motionless, her arms wrapped around herself, while the other diggers held each other's hands in the choking silence. No one moved, nor spoke, nor gestured; all was quiescent as the deeds to be done manifested themselves in the minds of the people there.

The parents of the three girls rushed in.

Time stopped, breath too, for those on the outside awaiting word, their bodies shaking for fear of the unknown, their minds blurred with feelings of joy and sorrow as they stared at the mud-smeared, opened wooden portal and listened to the cries therein.

And then the impossible became possible and every miracle they had ever wanted came true, when Consuelo, weeping, came out impossibly alive, holding fast to her weeping parents; and then Lupe, weeping, came out with her weeping parents; and then out too came Grezelda, weeping, walking arm in arm with her weeping parents through the magic portal, and all of the girls with their parents stood together, crying and hugging and praying and giving thanks to God above. But then came an unmercifully long interval of empty space at the site of the small opening, where no movement occurred, where no expected person came out, and Lake still stood, her hands on each side of her muddied head, her body trembling, her lips quivering, her face bleeding hope and fear. She could neither move nor speak, tears of piety pooling inside her emerald eyes, and she was ready to live, ready to die, ready to scream horror, praying to shout praise.

And then, yes—and then, in the shadowy mist of the magical portal, there slowly emerged the figure of a man, and he stood, more alive than he had ever been. Lake let go the last remaining vestiges of arrogance and its natural residues and became fully human, weeping like a baby at its christened birth.

She rushed upon him and leaped into his waiting arms and she hugged and kissed him and loved him and adored him, saying, "Tony, Tony, O Tony, I love you so much; I never gave up, I never stopped believing," and she said these wonderful things again and again and so many times, yet each time was it new and fresh and spoken with ardent affection and love.

He kissed her and adored her as they twirled around, as he hugged her, he said, "O Lake, Lake, I love you, I love you so much, I have waited so long for you, I have always loved you…"

The outer rigid, jaundiced covering of their eyes that had for so long filtered all information to their hearts finally dissolved and rained gently down into the mud below.

New Beginnings

There was natural rejoicing in the Village de Francisco for many days thereafter, and the people never seemed to tire of hearing the marvelous story concerning the provisions the girls had stocked in the schoolhouse immediately before the long ordeal had begun.

Everyone, the next day, was sitting around the big campfire on the hill behind the village, happy to hear the story once again about the stocking of supplies in the schoolhouse. The geological engineers were given the first storytelling because it was the manners of the village to allow this; well, the engineers did not waste any time marveling at the great effort the people had put in to rescue their loved ones, and praising their heroic stance against the mud beast; and then they spoke of the importance of keeping weight off the schoolhouse or risking collapse of the structure, and that the digging had assuaged the risk; but still, in the end, though they praised the Heavens above that they were wrong, they insisted that the building should have collapsed under the great weight of the mud hill. And soon enough they were finished, even with the stories of helping other villages, and everyone was pleased, and then turned their attention to the girls, who were anxiously awaiting their turn at story time.

"Well, you see, Grezelda had remembered that Antonio and Lake had talked about earthquake drills in America, and she wanted to prepare—"

"For an earthquake or a mudslide," Grezelda interjected.

"Hey," Consuelo, said, arms raised, "who is telling the story this time? I thought so, Grizzy," she said, smiling. "Anyway, so, we, I mean, Lupe and Grezelda and I, carried much water and food…"

"You thought it was too much, don't you remember?" Lupe laughed.

"Girl," Consuelo protested.

"But you did, Consuelo, you complained with every trip."

Everyone laughed because they could laugh now, and they especially celebrated the simplest achievements, eyeing their girls with awe and wonder.

"Well, anyway," Consuelo continued, "we finished, and we were in there, teaching Jose and Araceli, and when we saw Antonio, we sent them out to give him a great big hug…"

Now there was the natural pause in the retelling of the story, as there always had been, and always would be, for here was the crucial moment where the Hero was born and where he would live forever in the minds and hearts of the listeners for generations to come; yes, the tale would change, as twice-told tales often do, but the honor and loyalty of the heroes would be intact, for otherwise, the story would become only a story told and soon forgotten; it was because of what he did, freeing the children and then preparing to sacrifice himself for the young women; and it was what Lake did, unyielding in her determination to free those trapped below; and it was what the villagers did, despite, in the beginning, their weak faith—for they did come back—it was this magnificent human element that compelled the story to be told right.

The pause celebrated, Consuelo finished the beautiful tale, including the astounding part about the shaft of air that was found in the floor of the schoolhouse, air that flowed from an unknown deep cave that originated from behind the hill. Lake and Tony sat together, hand in hand, her head upon his sturdy shoulder, listening to the story, listening to the precious heartbeat of each other, thinking of Love. Eduardo was there, as were the men who had come to help, and Maria and Matt Gershon were all there.

The next day, the villagers cleared the schoolhouse of remaining mud, and the hill was secured and deemed safe by U.S. geological engineers.

When all was said and done, there was a grand celebration, and there were warm tacos and taquitos and cool beer, mariachi music and kisses and dancing and colorful dresses and more dancing and laughing and the pure spirit of peace and tranquility; but soon, those who had come to help from distant lands had to go, yet they departed with promises of loyalty from the villagers.

Eduardo stood with Tony, watching the helicopter fading into the billowy clouds and blue sky dome; the men still had not spoken since last they talked in Eduardo's house, but this is the way of men, the way of stone silence to clear the cluttered path of bad memories. It was Eduardo who put out his hand, and it was Tony who clasped it firmly, but it was both men who embraced each other. "We are God's poem," Eduardo said; "we just need to see the Author."

Tony smiled. "I want to believe that," he said, as his dutiful wife, who had remained at a proper distance, now joined them and hugged Eduardo, and then held the hand of her husband as they waved at Eduardo as he drove away down the dry, cracked mud road.

"You will soon," Eduardo shouted, his hand out the window and waving goodbye, and then he and his blue sedan vanished down the road.

Lake frowned. "Should I ask?"

"You will eventually," he laughed.

They walked arm in arm down the road. The storm had passed, and everywhere there was life bursting in vibrant hues—of ripe green and plumes red and fiery orange in the petals of the flowers and sizzling blue in the great sky, and melodic sounds of black birds singing high and red-breasted birds singing low; the cycle of seasons had begun anew, so life began again, too.

"So, you're not so light a sleeper, after all," he began.

"Hmm," she answered, feeling the warm breezes pour light kisses upon her smooth countenance.

They walked, hand in hand, onto the winding trials; yellow-leaved Creosote Bushes sat along the path, green Yuccas and Junipers that grew in great clusters, where above them Red-tailed Hawks and Merlin Falcons soared; the air was lathered with a musty, lusty scent of renewal.

"I was not going to let you die knowing there was a way to rescue you," she said, finally, once they were deep into the woods. She stopped and looked at him. "Darling, you must understand that it isn't my money, it's God's money." She smiled, gazing at his frown. "You think I converted at a time of crisis, a temporal conversion of circumstance and opportunity."

"Would you respect me if I simply nodded?"

"No," she said, and they continued their peaceful trek. "We must never disguise our true emotions. Do you really think I can be hurt by the honest opinions of my husband, whom I love more than my own life?"

They kissed passionately.

They spoke on the subject of God and faith, religion and superstition, myths and ancient beliefs held by modern man.

"I shall lead by example," she decided later that night as she lay next to him in their humble adobe home.

It was a Saturday morning, as Tony and Lake were teaching the twelve children in the temporary schoolhouse, the old one having been demolished for the purpose of safety, when one of the elders came into the place.

"Maestra Lake, Maestro Tony," Teresa, one of the most respected women of the village, said, "could we see you out on the hill after lessons?"

"Of course," Lake said, standing at the chalkboard. "Consuelo, can you take over?" Consuelo smiled first at Teresa, then nodded to Lake. "We'll come now."

"Oh, I don't want to interrupt," Teresa protested, mildly.

"Don't worry, Teresa," Tony said, "we're nearly finished." He and Lake joined Teresa outside, while Consuelo, Lupe and Grezelda, and the children, rushed excitedly to the windows and doors to watch them.

"Miss Consuelo," one of the young girls asked, "do they know?"

"No," Consuelo returned, smiling largely, "we Mexicans are a quiet people, not given to gossip at all." All of them laughed.

There was a sloping hill covered with plush green grass and purple and yellow flowers that lay right above the village, and there stood nearly everyone from the village; the last of the people to come were Teresa, Tony and Lake, and the three young women and children of the school, who came up surreptitiously from another route; as it was, the villagers applauded as Tony and Lake ascended the hill.

"Antonio and Lake Siciliani," Teresa began, wearing her yellow and red dress, "we, the people of the Village de Francisco, wish to show our appreciation for all you have done for us." Cheers erupted from the people assembled behind her. "We know that both of you have given up many of the comforts of the States to come here; we know that you never had a real honeymoon; so," and then she said in English, "we have decided to say 'muchas gracias' in our own way," and she motioned them to her. "Thank you," she said, again in English, handing them a white envelope.

Lake was smiling and biting her lip as she opened the envelope, and then she produced two tickets.

"Two trains tickets to Mazatlán," Teresa said, "and hotel reservations for three days." The villagers cheered.

Lake wept. Tony embraced Teresa and began to shake hands, while Lake hugged everyone there; everyone was happy because everyone felt as if they were living to help not only themselves honestly, but honestly helping their own family and their neighbors; it was a genuine sense of community the people felt, an emotional structure erected by an innate human desire to be part of something bigger than themselves; thus, in all of their cruel lives, from the moment of their births in this hard land, to the slow, painful walk to the cold grave, they wished to boast that they had done something good, of their own free will, for another, and this had just been one more reaffirming event that gave them over to hope and the will to endeavor against all trials and tribulations.

Presently, the Sicilianis were waving at Eduardo through the window of the train at the station as the locomotion pulled out toward its destination.

When Eduardo drove them back to the village, some four days later, they saw, to their great astonishment, a much grander schoolhouse, replete with red and blue and white ribbons about its freshly built structure. The people, in their festive clothing, laughed and cheered.

"Look, Maestro," Grezelda said, holding both of their hands as she hurried them to the new structure, and then waving her hands about, smiling, "and it's not near any hill."

Oh, how the villagers laughed, then!

Tony and Lake inspected the large schoolhouse, and declared it to be the most wondrous building they had ever seen.

The festivities commenced, and there was dancing, the men dressed in their black leather boots and finest blue jeans and white cotton, long-sleeved shirts and black bow ties; and the women, in their multicolored green and white and red dresses, some with their thick black hair put up in tight buns and others with long black hair flowing down their bare brown shoulders, and the children dressed in their Sunday best, all of them celebrating the exciting changes in their lives. There was cold beer and hot tacos and spicy salsa, and a flood of small, sugary treats. But this was a celebration of more than just new beginnings and gratitude for lives won; it was for lessons learned and lives lived for a purpose. And even though they were mere human beings, their foibles accentuated in this unyielding land, their emotions exploited too often by suffering and loss, this time, they had done the right thing, the thing they knew in their hearts and minds was the right thing to do, by not capitulating during the dig; and so they celebrated this goodness, they cultivated it and breathed Love on it; in a world of injustice and pain, it was an act that was pure and noble, and by such luminous deeds in the light of such hardships and suffering, they were better able to see their path in Life as a Community of One Culture and One Nation.

At emerging twilight, as the music died like embers in a cold hearth, and the people cleaned up from the celebration, Tony and Lake stood upon the hill of bright flowers, holding each other close as they watched the people below.

"Eduardo said he drove by the stand the other day, where the man gave you the herbal tea our first day here," Tony said, not yet looking at her, "and he saw a curious thing: the man had a small, bright red building instead of the shack he once had." Now, he looked at her, and saw her furtive smile. He knew her mind, and he felt her gentle feminine pulse upon his heart. "So," he continued, feigning ignorance as he gazed upon the village, "where do you think the new town should be built?"

She turned to him, smiling largely, and embraced him, putting her beauteous face to rest on his strong shoulders. "I wish my grandmother and Lisbeth were here to see me, now."

"They would be so proud of you, Lake Seville."

She looked up at him. "Lake Siciliani," she whispered, and kissed him, and then looking into his eyes, realized that he was the only mirror she ever needed to know that she was beautiful; that there were no stories of princes or princesses, no fairy tales, knights in shining armor come to save the damsel in distress, but life, real life, and in such a life, by loving and honoring each other, and respecting and caring for each other, and being loyal and kind to each other, he had become her Prince Charming, her bold and chivalrous knight, her faithful husband; and she, his beautiful princess, his grateful damsel, his faithful wife; and then she placed her long, golden-brown-haired head once more upon his strong and broad shoulders as she gazed at the small village below. "You know we can't do too much at once; we don't want track homes, U.S. of A."

"No."

"Water lines, electricity, and sewers first, after our geological engineers assess the water availability, I think; and oh, that car of Eduardo's—it has to go." He hummed in agreement. "We'll work on it."

"Yes, darling."

"Hmm," she hummed. "Darling, you know I don't want to coerce you to learn about my Faith."

"No, of course not," he said, gently teasing her.

"We will have discussions, sometime? You will study world religions with me and then my Christian Faith, to see the Truth?"

He hugged her. "We'll work on it," he said, and he smiled. She smiled, too; and then, right there, atop a high hill of yellow budding daisies and blue cornflowers and vibrantly red roses, they began to dance, waltzing elegantly and proudly and unabashedly in front of the whole wide world.

And so, as it was, they had what we all have.

They had Love.

-Finis-